EMPEROR'S : BLADE

Other Books
By
William Hatfield

LGBT Fiction
TNT Series
Menu for Murder
Blown Choices
Bare Soles
Cheating Deaths
Deadly Views

Science Fiction
Fists of Earth Series
Captive Audience
Duel Roles
Tough Crowd

Pawns of the Blade Series
Emperer's Blade

Short Story Collections
Key Notes

EMPEROR'S: BLADE

William Hatfield
Published by William Hatfield

ISBN-13: 979-8-5870-2860-9

This book is a work of fiction.

The characters, incidents, and dialogue are drawn from the author's quirky imagination and are not to be construed as real. Any resemblance to actual events or persons, living, dead or undead, human or alien, is entirely coincidental.

Cover Design and Illustration by Jim Harrison/MetaVisual
Interior Design and Layout by Symes Design

Author's Note

Emperor's Blade is the first of possibly five or six volumes in my historical science fiction trilogy, Pawns of the Blade.

Sigh, yes, I know the definition of the word trilogy.

I had a very clear plan when I started writing this book. As with all battle plans, it didn't really survive first contact with the enemy.

Or in this case, the actual outlining and writing process.

There are three stages in my story of the development of the Scoloti, what the Scythians of the ancient Greek era called themselves. I thought I could cover each stage in one book. Stage one worked well, and one book covered it quite nicely.

The second and third stages, on the other hand...

We'll see.

I majored in History, specializing in the ancient Middle East at the undergraduate level, and the Scythians always intrigued me. They held their own with any and all empires, invading hordes, and were instrumental in the destruction of the Assyrian Empire, among many other accomplishments. They were the origin of the Amazon mythos, and possibly the best archers in history.

Then they just sorted of faded into obscurity.

I'd about forgotten about them until a visit to the dentist office, and some time well spent in the waiting room, reading a story in the National Geographic about the Scythians. By the time I left with my new filling, my mind was whirling with ideas about how to explain their fate.

See? Going to the dentist is always a good idea.

Dedication

As always, I can't thank my Beta Readers enough for their assistance in the editing and motivational roles. But I will try, as always.

Thank you, A.J. Wilcox, Dena Bovee, Bruce Goll, Karen Johnstone Voiles, Rae Williams, and Sharon Weisenborn. Keep pushing me.

Thank you Beverly Symes, of Symes Designs for all your assistance and attention to detail in the file adaption process.

I have had a talented friend provide me with brilliant covers to my Key West series, TNT, since its conception. Jim Harrison, of MetaVisual, has done the cover art and illustration for the first five books, and the pending sixth book in the series, Related Matters.

When I told him I had a new science fiction series started, and described it to him, he took some notes, asked me some questions that seemed to show he was thinking much deeper about this than I was. Less than forty-eight hours later, he presented me with the first draft of this cover.

It's great to have brilliant friends. Thank you, Jim.

And as always, thanks to my wonderful wife, Karen, for her patience with my writing obsession.

Prologue

Now, on a planet, far from everything, except the star it circles.

Lady Telepileya gazed across the amphitheater, seeing many familiar faces from her previous classes. She saw older students, now Speakers in their own right, and even a sprinkling of the cadre of peers she'd trained with, so many harvests ago. These old friends hung to the back, allowing the younger, excited, new students to crowd to the front, even though the acoustics of the room allowed her voice to easily carry to every corner.

Those in the front were mostly attending their first telling as a student Speaker. A few second-year students were sprinkled among them, and she would draw upon them as the morning progressed. After lunch, they would go to another class, with one of the other teachers, to continue learning the story of the people.

She was tall and lean, and although she'd experienced almost eighty harvests, her age didn't affect her ability to remember every word she'd learned when she was one of these young novices. She was dressed for comfort, in a long-sleeved red tunic, loose brown trousers, and tan felt shoes. Her long, dark hair, liberally sprinkled with strands of grey and even white, was wrapped into two long braids, both reaching beneath her buttocks. The braids were ornate and complicated, but she always did them herself, laughing to others that she wasn't quite ready to be waited upon.

The students were all dressed as she was, except their clothes and shoes were all light grey, and the first year students, having only seen six harvests, wore several layers, so they would not chill in the cool, early autumn air. She found that she didn't really notice the cold as much as when she was a young maiden.

She cleared her throat quietly, and the room immediately became absolutely silent. She smiled as she let her eyes slowly sweep the room, searching the eyes of the students carefully, looking for that extra spark, or the clear lack of one.

Her duties were to teach the new students the early history of the people, how they came to be who and what they were now. One aspect of that was weeding out those unsuitable for the memorization of major portions of the history of the People, the Scoloti. A proficient Speaker for the people had to have a keen memory, as well as understand more than just the words. They also needed a voice capable of telling that which needed to be told, to remind the people.

The Scoloti, as great as they were, were not alone, and certainly not the most pwerful people in this vast, mostly empty, yet terribly crowded, universe.

"Speaker Telepileya?"

She smiled down at a tiny female first year student.

"Yes, Apprentice Korga? Do you have a question?"

The little girl smiled timidly at her, nervous at the attention, yet proud of the honorific, even if she hadn't really earned anything yet.

"How did we come to be here, where we live now?"

"That is what you are here to learn, young apprentice," she said kindly, but allowing her tone to show the needlessness of the question.

Another first year apprentice, this one a boy named Gortami, spoke up.

"Were you alive when the people were taken from our home near the Marshes of Maeotae?"

The older students tittered and eagerly awaited her response.

She stared at the young boy, and watched him wilt under her withering glare. She let him sweat for a few more moments, then relented.

"You are all here to learn the story of how three powerful tribes came together at a harvest gathering, with great plans for the Scoloti, and more. You are also here to see if you have what it takes to become a Speaker for the people." She let her eyes sweep around the room, ignoring the amused looks on her contemporaries in the back. "You will hear, and learn to tell, the story of how we were betrayed, and attacked in a cowardly manner, and all the events, both glorious and sad, that transpired to bring us to this wondrous world we live on today."

Speaker Telepileya sighed. She'd done so many of these classes, for so many years, and always found that starting the process anew seemed to become a greater task every year. She also noticed it seemed harder to get past that first step, every year.

Perhaps it is time to turn this duty over to the next generation, she thought.

But, as she had for so many decades before, she reached within and drew the strength to push forward. Her voice rang clear throughout the room.

"This is the story of the Scoloti, and of three great tribes that came together early, to the harvest Gathering, twenty-three hundred and fifty-seven years ago."

She watched the room as she spoke, and knew all ears in the room, even those of her fellow Speakers, was attentive to her every word and inflection. En masse, they all seemed to lean slightly forward, as if to both hear and see better.

"Their leaders, their kings, had a plan to consolidate all the tribes, from the Paralatae to the lowly Dahae, into one mighty..."

Chapter One

Aboard the Hshtahni Battle Cruiser Clonoschk, more than twenty-three hundred years ago.

Commander Azimoth stood to the right of Lord Bakhtochk, looking over the shoulders of his four bridge crewmen, each manning his or her own station. They all had multiple screens showing everything from the engineering deck of the Hshstahni Cruiser Clonoschk, to the ship's defensive stations, to various views of the planet below.

Lord Bakhtochk, as senior Hshtahni on board, was logged in as captain, but his role in the actual functions of the ship was ceremonial, and usually limited to the overall picture, not the mundane operations of the ship itself. The lord was only in his eighth century of life, and had ambitions far beyond his years.

He was old enough to have lost his wings, yet young enough to remember having them, and Azimoth concealed his smile as he saw his lord's eyes stray to the fourth station, which was committed to watching the antics of his three brood, via a low altitude satellite they'd dropped into orbit, along with a horde of others, as they made their approach to the planet.

The three siblings, all barely into their second century, were winging over an enormous wall that seemed to run for hundreds, if not thousands of glinks, along mountain ridges, rugged terrain, and desert. They were terrorizing the local inhabitants, and clearly enjoying themselves.

The youngest, male Char Lakhmoshk, wore a torch harness, and was scorching wherever he saw the primitives gathering in numbers, to try to form a defense. His older brother, Char Pohkclaushkclt, and sister, Charna

Piquihkh, ignored his antics, and winged along the winding wall, examining it as they flew high above.

Commander Azimoth discreetly looked to see how his lord was reacting to the mix of behavior. From the indulgent look on his face, he was seeing exactly what he expected to. It was difficult to accurately interpret the expressions and body language of the large warm-blooded reptile, but Azimoth had been part of his retinue since soon after his own commission. He could usually read his lord well, and what he currently was reading was envy.

He saw his lord sense eyes upon him, and yawned in an exaggerated manner, showing the multiple rows of powerful, and very sharp teeth, filling his mouth. Azimoth kept his expression masked, probably not fooling his lord any more than he himself was fooled.

Azimoth was of average height and build for a male Mba, tall, rangy, well-toned muscles, if not in a bulky, heavy-gravity race sort of way. But his entire body could have fit into the maw of his lord, although it might have taken folding him to be able to close his mouth. So when his lord yawned, it was a daunting sight. But Azimoth knew his value to his lord, and knew he was appreciated, so never let the typical Hshtahni methods of intimidation affect him. He thought his lord was amused by his lack of fear, and conviction of his value, and recognized it didn't affect his complete loyalty and ability to anticipate and assist his lord.

Lord Bakhtochk looked at the scene below them, watching the denizens mill around their impressive pyramids. The complex directly below them looked old, almost certainly more than twenty centuries. They'd seen a new one being constructed in the distance, and had been surprised to see that all the construction appeared to be with manual laborers, using clever methods and sound theories. It seemed at odds with the primitive nature of the planet's inhabitants.

Lord Bakhtochhk spoke in a low rumbling voice, and Azimoth turned to give him his full attention.

"Begin preparations to depart. We shall store all information and data on this system, this planet in particular, in a separate, secure set of files." His lord turned his head to stare at him directly. "Once we are en route, tell your crew this trip is to be kept classified. Any mention of this world whatsoever, will result in the entire crew being executed, as well as all living family members, whether on this ship or not."

His lord raised one eyebrow significantly.

"This would include yourself, and yours."

Commander Azimoth bowed his head and nodded.

"Understood, my Lord." Azimoth risked looking up at him.

"May I ask what you intend, so that I might help prepare?"

Lord Bakhtochk exhaled heavily.

"I intend to acquire a population transport ship. We will return here and capture a sizable number of the local primitives, as well as their livestock and grains, and anything else that seems pertinent. We will put them into stasis, and take them to a secure location for testing, and hopefully, training."

His lord stared at him, and Azimoth lowered his head in acquiescence.

"We shall keep the very existence of this star system, this planet in particular, shrouded in secrecy. We will not even allow the existence of these primates to be known until we have thoroughly examined them, and know their full value."

"This is sound reasoning, my Lord," Azimoth agreed, fully meaning his words.

"When we return to home base, your crew and my offspring will be kept in total isolation while I make arrangements to acquire the population transport ship. You will be the only exception to the quarantine of the crew." He sighed again heavily. "I expect this will not be well-received by my children, so you and I will have to make haste quite extraordinary to our usual methods."

"I understand, my Lord," Azimoth said, not sure he kept the amusement from his voice and facial expressions. He was sure he'd failed a moment later.

Lord Bakhtochk stared at him, leaning forward slightly.

"Do you have offspring, Commander Azimoth?"

"I do," he admitted, wondering if he'd just committed self-genocide for his family.

"Then you will appreciate how hard it can be to control their impetuous nature," his lord said, and returned his attention to the screens showing all three of them now spraying crowds of bipeds with flames. He wagged his massive head from side to side, and snorted, causing most of the Mbi on the bridge to flinch.

"Retrieve your crew from the surface, and let us go convince my heirs to quit playing with their food."

Azimoth could have almost sworn he heard humor in his lord's voice, but Hshtahni were rumored to not have a sense of humor. He suspected there was much not known about the Hshtahni, and that was by their own intent. He told his communication officer to recall the foraging party, even as his lord continued to speak.

"I will spend the return voyage impressing upon my children the need for discretion, and their temporary exile from home. The stakes are high, but I would be a fool to expect them to easily submit to my will on this issue."

"You are no fool, my Lord," Azimoth responded, and wondered if he'd been too presumptuous.

Lord Bakhtochk snorted.

"I would like to think not, but when it comes to my children, I am not so sure." He wagged his head.

"Carry on, Commander."

Tribal homelands of the Scoloti tribe, the Auchatae, 323 B.C.

The young man, barely more than a boy, gave ground to the older opponent. The boy was dressed in thick, felt trousers, several layers of thick woolen and felt tunics, and tried to block the sword strikes with his round, wooden shield. He clearly knew he needed to counter to slow the attack, but the constant barrage of blows came too fast to do anything other than block and give ground.

The other man had a full, black beard, long coarse hair pulled back into a single, thick ponytail, and was merciless. He swung his long double-edged sword overhand, causing the youth to block the blow with his own shield.

The older man quickly continued the attack, striking hard with his own shield, causing the smaller boy to stagger, almost fall, before side-stepping and giving yet more ground.

King Gelon stood on a low-sloped hill, watching the action below. Scyles, his only remaining son, was practicing his swordsmanship with Swordmaster Targitai. Gelon could remember being trained by Targitai, as well as the swordmaster's own father, Teutar, before him. The lessons were brutal, but necessary.

Scyles was clever, and very quick to pick up instructions, and Targitai was a brilliant, if somewhat mercilous, instructor. His son's skills were substantial. The problem was he simply didn't have the body mass or musculature to hold his ground with the sword.

Gelon sighed, remembering how different his two older sons had been. Ciscus, the oldest, had his father's build and strength, as did his second son, Gnur. By the time they were Scyles' current age, they could hold their own with anyone in battle. He had groomed Ciscus to replace him, when he fell in battle, or died of natural causes.

Scyles, on the other hand, was much leaner, built more like his mother than Gelon.

His dreams for his kingdom surviving his death had been dashed six years ago, at Olbia. General Zopyrion, one of the Macedonian King Alexander's primary generals and advisors, had made the mistake of trying to march into the heartland of the Scoloti. The Scoloti had dealt them a devastating defeat, and the general was killed in battle near Olbia. He had seen Zopyrion fall himself.

Unfortunately, he had also seen Gnur fall, surrounded by the enemy. Ciscus had fought his way to his brother's side, only to find he was too late. Then, he too fell, under a volley of enemy arrows.

Scyles hadn't gone into the battle, only being ten years of age at the time. He was Gelon's only hope of having a son replace him as king upon his passing. His wife, Queen Myrina, had told him she wished to try and bear him more sons, but she was long after the best time for giving birth, and the midwives feared she would not survive another childbirth.

Despite the warnings, they kept trying to conceive, but without success.

Ah well, he thought. At least it was a pleasurable task, even if there were no results.

He hid a smile at the thought, as he sensed the object of his lustful thoughts approach from behind. She came up on his shield side, knowing him too well to risk surprising him on his sword arm side.

His wife put a hand on his left arm, giving him a slight rub, then leaving it there as she came close, inside his shield. Without taking his eyes off his son, he leaned over enough to give her a kiss on top of her head.

"How does Scyles perform today, husband?" she asked in the low, sultry tone he could listen to for hours.

"He lacks the strength to hold his ground," Gelon said, hiding the disappointment in his voice. "In a battle, he will be beaten down by most fighters. I fear, when Targitai or myself no longer live, he will be challenged, and almost certainly killed."

"He's very fast, and you know how intelligent he is," Myrina said fondly. "He will think of ways to avoid letting himself be put in an unwinnable situation. And Targitai says he's already the best archer in the tribe."

"He is that," Gelon admitted. "He may even be the best in all the tribes. But he won't be defending his kingship with arrows alone."

"You need to be patient, husband," she chided him gently. "He is still barely more than a child. He still grows into his body."

Gelon shook his head, but didn't respond.

As they watched, Targitai stopped the swordplay, and Scyles mounted his pony. He began a series of riding maneuvers, shooting at targets. As they watched, he made every shot he took, and his speed was impressive.

His wife laughed.

"I believe Targitai saw us up here watching, and has him shooting to show off his best talents," she said.

"It's to save the boy embarrassment, but it won't save his life," Gelon retorted, and she frowned up at him.

"His archery skills are superior, and will keep fresh kills in the cooking pot, as well as kill his enemies long before they are in sword's range."

Gelon sighed and decided to change the subject. They both loved Scyles without reserve, but their ideas of how to protect him and preserve his place in the tribe differed greatly.

"We leave for the fall Gathering soon, as you well know. The harvesting is almost finished, and we will be leaving before the bulk of the tribe," he reminded her. "We play a dangerous game this trip, and members of the other tribes will exploit any weaknesses they perceive."

Myrina looked at him with trepidation.

"Are you sure of our course in this matter?" she asked, her frown of concentration increasing. "Meeting secretively with King Orik and King Agathyrsus will not be received well by the other tribes. Our three tribes comprise a large portion of the people, but hardly an overwhelming force."

"You will recall that meeting with King Orik serves another purpose, besides deciding the leadership of the people," Gelon reminded her, and they both looked down at their son, now practicing with his sling. He had to admit, Scyles had remarkable skills with the sling, and his accuracy was already legendary with the people. "Princess Arga is now fifteen, and she and Scyles have known each other since they were very young."

"Queen Opis informed me last year that she began her monthly bleeding several years ago, and I worry that King Agathyrsus will insist that Scyles marry Ifito, and Arga wed her twin, Kavas. They are a year older than Scyles, and he is eager to bind the tribes together through marriage," Myrina said, her tone very serious.

"Tied in marriage through their kin," Gelon agreed grimly. "I do not care for the way those twins spend so much time together, and I fear they would try and dominate both marriages."

"I also believe Scyles and Arga have come to recognize the need for their union, and have accepted that future together," Myrina said, a smile replacing her somber expression. "I think they both wish this to happen, maybe even sooner rather than later."

"If I have my way, it will happen this gathering," Gelon said grimly. "If we put it off much longer, Agathyrsus will become a problem."

They looked at each other, and Gelon wondered if his expression was as troubled as hers.

"There is much Orik and I need to discuss before Agathyrsus arrives," Gelon said. "That is why he and I agreed to reach the gathering point at the marshes six days before the gathering is planned, and told Agathyrsus it would be four days."

He gave his wife a crooked grin.

"Of course, we will arrive seven days early, to pick out the best site, with the strongest defensive position."

"Of course," Myrina said, and looked thoughtful. "We will have twelve hundred in our party as agreed. The fighters you chose, which are our best, and their families, as well as livestock, grains and belongings. The rest of our tribe will arrive with the rest of the harvest on the appointed day."

She rubbed her cheek unconsciously, and Gelon smiled. She didn't even know she did that when she was deep in thought, but he found it very endearing.

"Do you think Orik and Agathyrsus will both adhere to the size limits for their parties?"

"I think Orik will, but Agathyrsus?" Gelon shrugged fatalistically. "Our numbers should be enough to give him pause, but who knows?"

As one, they both turned to watch Scyles retrieving his arrows. After a moment, Gelon turned back to his wife.

"We meet, supposedly, to try to choose a new great king to replace old Atheas. He has been dead for nigh on fifteen years, and no one has managed to assert enough control and influence to replace him. Until we do so, our people will be weaker, and more susceptible to outside dangers."

"Do you hope to become the great king?" Myrina asked, looking worried.

Gelon shook his head.

"No, I would rather Orik assume the title. The Paralatae tribe is larger than ours, and Orik has many friends, including myself." Gelon put his arm around her shoulders and steered her back towards the camp. "I would rather be his strongest supporter, and not be the obvious target of assassins, either for myself or Scyles. If something happens to Orik, his very young son will need a mentor and protector, until he is old enough to assume his position."

"And you would be that mentor?" Myrina asked, nudging him with her shoulder as she smiled.

"I, or Scyles, with the help and strong right arm of Targitai," Gelon admitted. "He will be the son-in-law, and husband to Orik and Queen Opis's beloved daughter."

Myrina laughed out loud.

"You are always thinking, my husband," she teased him.

Gelon looked at her intently, and smiled.

"Can you tell what I am thinking now?" he asked, and she laughed dismissively.

"You are a man," she pointed out. "If you are awake, I know what you are always thinking of."

They both increased their pace back to the camp.

And to their tent.

Chapter Two

Commander Azimoth ended the transmission and stared at the blank screen thoughtfully. He brought up the data for the armed population transport freighter he had just purchased for Lord Bakhtochk, and quickly reviewed it.

It was called the Muschwain, and appeared to be exactly what they needed. It currently had ten thousand stasis pods, although there was probably space for five times that many. They could store either medium or large bipeds or quadrupeds. All the stasis pods could be converted to handle either, so they wouldn't have to worry about trying to match the proportions perfectly.

They would meet the sellers, the Adazi, in a secluded star system that was uninhabited. The sun was an old red giant star, expanding as it neared its death. The process was slow enough, stable for a dying star, and easy to monitor, so there was little danger. The fact that it clearly was releasing gases as it expanded, eating everything it came in contact with, including the few planets in orbit, made it an unattractive and potentially dangerous place to be. So they shouldn't have any accidental encounters with anyone other than the Adazi.

Azimoth knew the Adazi couldn't be trusted, and were a very deceitful race, if somewhat stupid. They had agreed to each side only coming in a single ship, but he wouldn't put it past them to try and betray the deal. They had to know a Hshtahni cruiser would be more than a match for any single ship they sent, so he was planning to be extra vigilant upon approach.

They were also providing six hundred menial workers with the ship, from a race called the Meyores. They could operate simple machinery, such as antigrav sleds, for transporting the unconscious bipeds and their livestock, and whatever else was deemed necessary, but not much more. They did know how to operate the stasis pods.

He sent all relevant files to his lord's computer, and decided he would need to make a report in person. He snorted air through his snout, and left the secure room, knowing his lord was with his offspring in the large lounge next to the bridge.

Lord Bakhtochk was watching the large door as he entered, and not for the first time, Azimoth wondered how his lord always seemed to know he was approaching. He noticed the three young Hshtahni were also watching him. He studiously ignored them, trying to not even glance their way.

Young Hshtahni were notoriously high-strung, and easy to bring to anger. If they interpreted one look at them as a challenge, his family would be receiving word of his death soon after.

"Lord Bakhtochk, I have finished settling the details of our purchase of the Muschwain, and set up the meeting at the system you chose."

The younger male Hshtahni, Char Lakhmoshk, snorted and looked at his siblings, then Azimoth.

"And what is a Muschwain? It sounds like a bowel movement to me," he said in a voice just below a roar. He looked at his siblings for their reaction, and was rewarded with two very bored-looking Hshtahni.

"The Muschwain is an armed population transport freighter, or generation ship, as the Adazi call it," Azimoth said in a careful, even tone. He focused on his lord, who seemed amused at his plight. "I think we should expect them to renege on the deal at the delivery site."

"How many extra ships do you expect them to have lying in wait?" His lord didn't seem particularly interested, but Azimoth wasn't fooled. He hadn't gotten to his ranking by being careless.

"They are supposed to only bring one, but most Adazi ships travel in increments of six," Azimoth said, and lifted his shoulders in resignation. "I think we should expect the other five to be very strategically placed."

"Can the Clonoschk defeat six Adazi ships in open battle?" Lord Bakhtochk asked the question almost as if uninterested in the answer, and

Azimoth knew he needed to word his reply very carefully.

"If the freighter's weapons are disabled, it will be a difficult battle, but we should be able to handle them," Azimoth said, and wondered if he was being too confident. "If I have a crew on that freighter with live weapons, it shouldn't be a problem."

"What if you're wrong, Mba?" Char Lakhmoshk asked, giving his head a serious shake that ran down his thick neck and caused his shoulders to flex, and wings to partially unfurl.

"Then we all die, My Lord," Azimoth said in the same even voice, wondering if he had a death wish.

All three young Hshtahni stared at him in startled silence for a moment, then burst into their frightening version of laughter. Char Pohkclaushkclt, the oldest male, turned to his sire and roared.

"I like this tiny Mba, Father. He has courage and is clever, for a non-Hshtahni." He also loosened his wings just enough to allow them to give a flap that blew air across the lounge. "Now I see why you don't just eat him."

"Indeed," Lord Bakhtochk said in a voice laced with irony. He eyed his progeny fondly, and finally turned back to Azimoth, raising a heavy eyebrow, as if surprised to see him still standing there. "I have often wondered what the reason was." He snorted, and spoke as he turned away again.

"Get us under way, Commander Azimoth."

"My Lord," Azimoth said, and left the room with relief.

Tribal homelands of the Scoloti tribe, the Auchatae.

Targitai looked up on the hill, but saw no sign of King Gelon, or the queen. Good, he thought, smiling crookedly to himself. Better they not see the methods he was teaching their son.

Scyles presented so many contradictions, Targitai had initially been baffled on how to make him the warrior he needed to be. Learning the traditional sword style of his people wasn't a total waste of time, because, if nothing else, he would need to know what to defend against.

But if young Scyles was going to live long enough to assume his father's crown, he was going to have to find a different style of attack. Targitai had thought about the tactics he and other masters taught women to compensate for their weaker bodies, and discarded most of them. First, it was something that would get Scyles ridiculed by his peers, and second, they weren't really good methods to try to win fights.

Targitai doubted he'd ever trained anyone as intelligent and quick to understand, as young Scyles. He learned each technique, and practiced until he perfected it. But that didn't increase his upper body strength, or do anything to enable him to withstand an assault by a skilled warrior half again his size.

His archer skills were the best in the tribe, as well as his ability to use the sling. His accuracy was astounding and, despite his limited arm strength, it was as if he'd figured out how to get every bit of leverage in each shot, with power far beyond what anyone would expect.

His work with the spear was average. Although accurate, his range was somewhat limited. On the other hand, he was very good with knives and the axe. His throwing ability with both were as accurate as his sling or bow. If he was able to close on an enemy, he was deadly, especially with knives.

Targitai realized he'd been standing motionless for a while, and Scyles was looking at him quizzically.

"Swordmaster, is there a problem?" the young boy asked with real concern in his voice.

Targitai snorted and shook his head.

"The problem is," he started, making up his mind. "Trying to keep you alive in a fight, boy."

"I would like that," Scyles admitted, a slight smile coming to his face.

Targitai kept his own smile hidden. When King Gelon told him some years ago it was time for him to help his son become an able warrior, he'd had his doubts. The boy was smart, and skilled, but was too nice to be a great warrior. In a battle, you had to be ready and able to kill an opponent, to show no mercy. He always showed kindness and a true empathy for others, and that worried the swordmaster.

Targitai had been afraid that Scyles didn't have the killing edge. Or the mental strength to know you might take damage in battle, but had to have the toughness to ignore the pain. He'd discovered that although

Scyles wasn't as physically strong as most boys his age, he had a mental toughness, and a physical toughness as well, which could make him very dangerous.

In theory.

Targitai eyed the lad and sighed, not for the first time.

"Boy, today we are going to work on some more things that you don't need to be telling your parents about," he began, and stopped when Scyles grinned.

"What is so funny?" he demanded.

"I've seen you fight at the gathering several times, at least once when the drunk facing you was trying to kill you," Scyles reminded him. "You didn't use any fighting style you teach, and it was less about skill and technique, and more about how to do maximum damage to parts of the body."

"Anything I've shown you of that sort is not for casual practice fighting," Targitai started, and Scyles nodded in understanding. "You don't want to cripple your tribemates, or anyone else you wish to have as a friend or ally. You can learn these moves, and we'll walk through them, faster each time, until I think you have it. Then we will put that move away, and not revisit it until you need it in battle, or in a fight over a maiden."

Scyles blushed, and Targitai resisted the urge to laugh at him. He knew the woman Scyles had gained his manhood with, and she'd told him what a sweet and considerate lover he'd been, even with his inevitable shyness and embarrassment. She'd also told him that for a boy, he had a lot of vigor, certainly more than an old man of his years.

Targitai thought the queen had chosen Scyles' first sexual partner well. He shook his head in confusion. How had he gotten his mind wrapped up in that? He turned his attention back to Scyles.

"Okay, boy, we're going to do more fighting with no weapons," he said, and leaned over enough to slap Scyles on his left knee. "You may not know it, but this breaks very easily…"

Tribal homelands of the Scoloti tribe, the Paralatae.

Arga drew back on her bowstring and let the arrow fly. It nestled into the target, flush against one of her previous shots. That made four arrows in a row, all clustered in the check area.

Not bad for a girl with only fifteen harvests, she decided. Now if she could only translate this accuracy to when she was riding a galloping pony. Riding, she was missing the entire target more often than hitting it, and when she did, it wasn't necessarily a killing shot. Although the one shot last time, the one that was so low on the torso, would have certainly hurt an enemy. Especially if it was a man, she thought, smirking.

"So, you're proud of your shooting now."

Arga started, knowing Ariapithes, her father's Swordmaster, would not let this opportunity to keep her humble pass. His next words proved her correct.

"Perhaps another bout on horseback would be in order," he suggested. She knew it wasn't merely a suggestion, and sighed, going to retrieve her arrows.

She didn't know why she had such difficulty learning to shoot while riding. Last year, at the harvest gathering, she had watched Prince Scyles of the Auchatae tribe put every single arrow into a tight ring, no larger than her balled fist. It didn't matter if he was standing, kneeling, running even, or riding. He even took several shots leaning forward to shoot from under the neck and head of his pony, and some lying back on the haunches of the fully galloping horse.

If Scyles can make all those shots, I should be able to get more than a random shot from a lazily galloping pony into the kill zone.

Thinking about the young man she'd known as long as she could remember, she found herself blushing. She knew full well what their parents intended, in regard to their futures.

It would be together, as a married couple.

When they were very young, they played, hunted, fished, and even learned rudimentary swordplay in the same company, their two mentors watching indulgently from a distance. Neither of them had the slightest idea their futures were already tied together in the heads of their parents.

Despite her being a girl, Scyles had always treated her as an equal in the practices, as well as everything else they did together. Which made sense, to a certain extent. Even though she was a year younger, she'd been as big as he before seeing her first ten harvests.

16

It was only last year that they began to understand the plans their parents had for them, and how intertwined their lives were expected to become.

Arga knew her future marriage was supposed to be an advantageous arrangement, and love wasn't to be considered a major factor in the plans. That would come later, she was assured by her mother. The marriage, and resulting children, were the important goals she needed to focus on, she was told.

She'd rebelled at the entire idea. She'd been cool to Scyles, even though she knew the plan wasn't of his making. She found herself keeping a watchful eye for other possible choices among the men in her own tribe.

After all, she had no desire to be uprooted and separated from her tribe and family, hauled off to live with strangers, and a man she barely knew.

In fact, just this summer, Skulis had caught her eye. He was a hulking young man, two years her elder. She had been discreet, and not let him know he was in competition with Scyles, for her attention and, quite possibly, her body. She suspected he'd sensed something, however, because he regularly found reasons to cross paths with her, to show up for archery practice at the same time as she, and many other coincidental contacts.

Arga was touched by his constant attempts to gain her attention, and more than a little tempted to encourage him. But then she would think about her parents hopes, and a vision of comely and intelligent Scyles, would come to her mind. She would remember when they were very young, and would roll around on the ground, trying the new wrestling moves they'd just learned, on each other.

The picture of them doing that now came to her unbidden, and she felt her face heat up even more. And it must have been a visible heat, because Ariapithes snorted, and put his hands on his hips.

"It would appear your mind is on other things, Princess," he said in a dour voice. "This will be enough for today. If you see your little brother, send him to find me. At least, he is of an age to fully focus on the task of destroying his enemies."

Arga nodded, not meeting his eyes, grabbed her various weapons, and headed back to their tent. She knew her little brother, Serlotta, had snuck off with his bow and arrows, looking for hare. He had only seen seven harvests, but was already a handful. Finding him would be a pleasant alternative to helping pack for the fast-approaching trip to the gathering. They were leaving in two days, and there was still much to do.

Searching for Serlotta would give her time to consider options that would dictate her future.

She knew both families favored their immediate union, felt resentful of the decision being taken out of her hands, and so was favoring Skulis. But there was another factor that gave her pause to doing anything that might damage her parent's efforts.

King Agathyrsus and Queen Latoreia of the Caitiari tribe had lobbied hard for the sake of their seventeen-year old twins, Kavas and Ifito.

They proposed that, since their twins, Scyles, and herself were the only royal children of marrying age in the three tribes, it only made good sense that she marry Kavas, and Scyles take Ifito as his wife. Both were very attractive, and of course, Kavas was first in line for the kingship of the Caitiari. He was also known as a very competent fighter, ruthless and brilliant.

Arga knew Kavas would be considered a more favorable match, and the Caitiari was the largest, after hers, of the many tribes of the Scoloti. It would be foolish to not at least consider him as her future husband and father of her children.

She also knew it would be foolish not to recognize that he favored no woman above his own twin sister, Ifito. The rumors of the two of them relieving each other of virgin status were lurid, and their incestuous behavior still ongoing.

Arga sighed, and decided encouraging Skulis was her best immediate step. She would not be pushed into a liaison that would last her entire life. It would be her decision to make, no matter how foolish it was.

There, she thought. That wasn't so hard to decide. But she noticed it was much harder than she'd expected to expel the vision of Scyles, smiling at her as he handed her a fishing pole last year.

Sighing, she went to find her little brother.

Chapter Three

Commander Azimoth watched the Adazi shuttle return to its ship. He glanced over at one of his crew and she shook her head, her ears flapping with the motion.

"No sign of any other ships yet, Commander," she said, her eyes never leaving her displays.

"Keep watching," he said, knowing full well his words were unnecessary. But he was nervous, and felt the need to stay on top of things. He glanced at a screen showing Fizrald, on the bridge of the Muschwain. "Have you got the sheathes and weapons functional yet, First Officer Fizrald?"

"The sheathes are ready to activate. I did a quick test, and they're now functional," she said, and glanced over her shoulder, out of the range of the view screen. "All weapons are re-programmed to full strength, and ready to fire. The search parties have located two groups of Adazi, concealed in the holds, and based on where they are, we think we'll find the third shortly."

Azimoth nodded without speaking. The Adazi were predictable, and he and Lord Bakhtochk had agreed they would try these tactics. What they wouldn't expect were two young and feisty Hshtahni, in addition to the extra eighty Mba warriors that had slipped on board while the new crew were inspecting the weapons and sheathes.

The Adazi had manually pre-set the weapons to a safe setting used for training purposes, hoping it wouldn't be noticed. And they'd jury-rigged the sheathes to look active, and show a visible barrier, but one that wouldn't stop anything from passing through it.

Meanwhile, the cruiser was fully powered up, and all shields and weapons were ready to activate. Azimoth watched the shuttle reach the Adazi warship, and the hold open to receive it.

"Fire," he said quietly, and powerful beams tore through both the shuttle and the open hatch behind it. "Approach the enemy on the pre-programmed spiral course, and keep scanning for the rest of them. First Officer Fizrald, when you find the third group, attack immediately. Take no prisoners," he said with no inflection in his voice.

By the time he turned around to address his lord, the Adazi ship exploded, and the shuttle with it. As he gave a quick summary of his report, he heard his first officer declare they'd found the third group of Adazi, and were engaging.

Azimoth gave the order for both ships to head out of the system on the pre-arranged route, but one of his crewmen barked out a warning.

Ahead of them, five ships separated from their hiding spots and came into formation. He quickly scanned what data they had on the ships and felt cautious optimism.

"Muschwain, form up behind us to our starboard, as planned. Use whatever you can bring to bear to cover our rear. All weapons pods, prepare to engage."

"Commander Azimoth, do we have the speed to outdistance them?" Lord Bakhtochk spoke quietly, and he knew why. No Hshtahni would ever admit he would willfully avoid a battle with an enemy, but the stakes of this venture were high, and he would accept the ignominy of fleeing if it would save the mission.

"Clonoschk has the speed and stealth capability to avoid them and leave, but the generation ship has neither," Azimoth admitted grudgingly.

"Then we fight," Lord Bakhtochk said, and he could hear the satisfaction in his lord's voice. "Commence."

Azimoth glanced at the readouts on the five approaching ships. Their routes were close enough to his estimations that he decided his original tactics would suffice for the first run. He'd taken the initiative of charging forward to engage with the enemy rather than allowing them the time to fall into an attack formation that would maximize their capabilities.

"Hold your position in relation to us, Muschwain," he warned, and then the firing commenced.

Twenty-three microns later, all five enemy ships were destroyed, and Azimoth took stock of the damage they'd received.

Muschwain had received very little fire, and had managed to avoid taking damage. Clearly the Adazi hadn't wanted to destroy a valuable ship, not to mention their warriors secreted on board.

The Clonoschk had not been so lucky. Although two of the Adazi ships were destroyed in the first wave, the other three were able to cause some damage. Some of the Hshtahni cruiser's shields had buckled and there was some structural damage to the hull, as well as some compartments.

But all their weapon systems were still active, and in the second wave, two more ships were destroyed, and the fifth took heavy damage. It had tried to flee out of the system, but Azimoth had been merciless, and run them down, killing everyone on board with massive disruptor beam shots.

Disruptor beams caused living cells to immediately stiffen and die. A person hit in a limb would still be alive, but the flesh where they were hit was now necrotic, and unless the limb was immediately removed, it would spread, killing the victim in hours or less.

His final step had been to destroy the lifeless ship with one well-placed antimatter missile.

Azimoth looked at a screen detailing the casualties and damage to his ship, and sighed.

"Lord Bakhtochk, I recommend we move your flag to the Muschwain, leaving enough crew aboard the Clonoschhk to run the ship and man the weapons. We have a large contingent of Meyores on the generation ship, and we need to familiarize ourselves with the function of the stasis equipment, as well as thoroughly search the entire ship for any remnants of the Adazi troopers." He debated internally for a moment, then pushed forward. "Transferring you and your progeny will free up the Clonoschk to fight with abandon, should we come in contact with any hostile forces."

"Char Pohkclasushkclt will remain aboard this ship, nominally in command, but I and my two youngest will transfer to the other ship."

Azimoth felt his lord's eyes bore into him as he spoke quietly.

"It will be his first command, and is his right."

"Yes, My Lord," Azimoth nodded, his mind racing down lists of things they needed to do to make this transfer. "I will start the process."

"Commander," the Hshtahni spoke even more softly.

"Yes, My Lord?" Azimoth wondered what bombshell was about to be dropped on him.

"You and your crew performed adequately." He straightened up to his full standing height and looked at his oldest child. "Well enough, apparently, since we did not die this day."

Commander Azimoth left the bridge to the sound of both Hshtahni laughing heartily.

The steppes of Mkhnach, north of the present day Sea of Azov

Scyles urged Earth Runner to walk a little faster to bring him up next to his father.

"I think I recognize landmarks from last year, and we're very close to the Anerez Reka," he said, hoping to impress his father.

"We have been on the steppes of Mkhnach for the last two days," King Gelon said in a mild tone. "I hope you noticed that before just now."

"I knew from the terrain, but the steppes look alike, and it's hard to pick out landmarks we only see once a year," Scyles said, hearing the defensiveness in his voice and wincing.

"If you live and rule on the steppes, every detail must become a memory, every campsite with solid defensive features must become your second home." Gelon gestured ahead. "The hills ahead are easy to recognize. We will camp to the east of that lower swelling hill, giving the Paralatae the area from that hill to the Anerez Reka. The Caitiari will make their camp to our east."

"Why do you give the Paralatae the best strategic position?" Scyles asked doubtfully. "They have the river for protection on one flank, our tribe on the other. We have competing tribes on either side of us."

"Very good, Scyles." His father smiled broadly at him. "But this also reduces the opportunity for the other two tribes to conspire against us, since they either have to cross our camp, or go north, clear of our position, to reach the other tribe's camp."

"And we will have hidden sentries, watching that area very closely," Scyles finished, grinning in triumph.

"The ships of merchants from the south are also used to docking right where we'll be," his father reminded him. "So when they arrive, we will be well positioned to get the first sales of grain and livestock, thereby securing the best prices."

Scyles felt his father's eyes upon him and glanced over at him curiously.

"Son, this is perhaps the most important gathering either of us will ever attend. There is much at stake." His father now sounded much more like his king than his father. "King Atheas has been dead for fifteen years, and the tribes have still not agreed to his replacement. He left no living sons, and for the people to survive, we must settle on one choice."

"Do you wish to be the great king of the People, Father?" Scyles asked with misgivings. If his father was the great king, it would be his own duty to someday replace him, if he could hold the position.

"No, I wish to grow old with your mother, desperately trying to give you more little brothers and sisters until I am old and feeble, and your mother says enough," his father said, laughing. "Being the great king is not the way to achieve that. No, I favor King Orik. He has the respect of most of the tribes, the largest tribe, and many will support him. He would make a good king of the People. And I would make a valuable ally for him and his family."

Scyles felt his father's eyes on him again, but he knew where the conversation was about to go, and wasn't convinced he agreed with the future his parents had planned for him.

"And this is where you become so important," his father said firmly. "We arrive four days before the three tribes are supposed to meet. This gives us the chance to choose our own camp, and when the Paralatae arrive, help them quickly fortify theirs. It also gives us the chance to tie the two tribes together," he said, and Scyles winced.

"Scyles, you and Arga played together when you were too young to walk, or even ride. You've spent time together every gathering since, and it is time for you to marry. Your union will give Orik the support he will need, and if he falls, myself, or you, if I have fallen, will become regent for the young prince, Serlotta, until he is old enough to rule on his own."

"I don't know that Arga will wish to become my wife, Father," Scyles said with misgivings. "I had hoped to find a maiden and fall in love with her, as you and Mother did. You didn't have to marry for advantage, or be told you had to."

"Your mother and I were thrown together by circumstances, and if I hadn't married her, she would have probably been sold to a household. Her tribe was decimated, and her family gone or dead."

Scyles wondered at the tone in his father's voice and turned to him.

"So you weren't in love when you wed?" he asked, confused. Both his father and his mother had often commented on how they knew they were destined for each other the moment they met.

"We were," his father admitted. "But my parents wanted me to marry someone for advantage, and there was none in making her my wife. But I resisted their choices, and fought for the right to marry her. In the end, even my father agreed I had made the right choice."

"I want to have that thrill of meeting a woman, knowing she's the one I would choose, rescue her if necessary, fight off other suitors, and make her my wife." Scyles could hear the stubborn tone in his own voice, and knew he sounded petulant, but he wanted his father to understand him.

"How do you know all that isn't destined to happen between you and Arga?" his father asked gently. "She is a very impressive girl, and will be a beautiful woman and a strong wife. But you may have to fend off Prince Kavas to make her your wife. His father has very strong wishes for his twins and both of you. This is a power play to tie the three tribes together as family. And I fear he will use it to try and eventually combine the three tribes under his leadership."

"You wouldn't let him though, would you?" Scyles asked, shocked at the idea of his tribe being assimilated into another. And that one in particular. "You are a stronger warrior than King Agathyrsus, and I am sure you would beat him in battle, if necessary. And I can beat Kavas, if it comes to that."

His father looked at him with surprise on his face. Scyles knew most of his tribe thought him weak because he wasn't as big as his brothers had been. But the swordmaster had been working with him for as long as he could remember, and at some point had started teaching him unconventional techniques. His training had accelerated the last few years, and things he'd learned before suddenly fit with the new training.

"Well, your confidence is refreshing, if somewhat surprising," his father admitted, smiling. "Son, if you refuse to marry Arga, I will not force you. But I ask that you consider her without rejecting her just because it is our wish. Given my choice, we would wed you the day after the Paralatae arrive. By the time the Caitiari arrive you would have already consummated the marriage, and it would be settled."

"No pressure," Scyles muttered under his breath, and his father heard him and guffawed. He blushed, and thought about Arga, and how much he'd enjoyed her company until the previous gathering. He said as much to his father, who smiled indulgently.

"Scyles, I just told you about our wish for the two of you to marry, and you didn't like being forced into anything, or that you wouldn't have a choice." He leaned over and slapped Scyles on the shoulder. "When do you think her parents told her the same thing?"

Scyles felt his eyes widen as he realized his father was right. Her parents had most assuredly told her their plans last year, making her resent him as much as he now resented her. He revisited the events of the previous year, and how, despite their getting along well the first few days, by the end of the second week of the gathering, when the tribes broke camp and returned to their current territories, he and Arga had barely been able to speak to each other without fighting. He suddenly realized they had much more in common than he'd ever thought.

"Oh," he said, and his father guffawed again.

They both turned as they heard the sound of galloping. It was Targitai, and his expression was grim as he reined in his horse.

"Scouts have discovered signs of a band of horsemen to the west. From the tracks, they believe it to be a raiding party of between twenty and thirty Dacians or Getae." Targitai raised his shoulders expressively. "There aren't enough of them to actually threaten us, but they could steal a few hundred of our finest horses if we don't track them down."

"Are we sure there's only one band?" Scyles asked, and his father nodded his approval.

"We're checking," Targitai admitted. "But so far, the only tracks we've found have been the one group to the west."

"Get enough mounted men together to deal with them," Gelon said. "Gather them near that ravine, and pass the word to the outriders to bring the herds in closer."

Scyles already had his swords and Gorytos on, and began to rummage through the roll of his belongings strapped behind his saddle, for his armored jerkin.

"Oh no you don't," his father said firmly. "You and I do not go out of camp into a fighting situation at the same time. We can't risk both of us getting killed."

"You're the king, you should stay here, then," Scyles began stubbornly, and his father turned to stare at him. Scyles hadn't been the recipient of that look in a couple years, and he'd forgotten how intimidating it was. Even so, he tried to argue. "How will I ever get any experience if you keep me safe in camp every time something like this happens?"

"Your time will come," his father said shortly. "In the meantime, you'll do as you're told. You are not riding with us."

Scyles glared at his father, saw Targitai grinning and transferred his angry expression to him. Targitai wasn't cowed in the least, but he had a speculative look on his face as they both turned their horses away and rode to the west side of the caravan of riders, horse-pulled carts, some loaded with provisions, some tiny huts mounted on wooden wheels.

Scyles sat on his horse, fuming. He tucked the jerkin back into his roll, and directed his mount at an angle so he wasn't directly following his father and the swordmaster. When he got close to the outriders, he paused and looked up and down the thick band of his tribe, and the terrain outside the sentries.

Although most of the land around them was grasslands, there were many dense groups of trees. Good places to mount an ambush from, he decided. He saw at least four islands of forest that would make good staging areas to fire arrows from concealment, then attack swiftly if the Auchatae lost discipline and broke ranks.

He knew any group of men escorting his father would be well-trained and not flustered by a few volleys of arrows, but all it would take would be both his father and Targitai getting wounded or killed to cause disarray and confusion to the party.

Scyles saw a modest sloping hill ahead, with decent cover in the form of trees and some rock formations. He made his horse trot briskly down the edge of the tribe, nodding or greeting the sentries. They probably thought he was just showboating, showing he was paying attention, trying to make up for not being in the attack party.

When he reached the edge of the hill, he dismounted, flipped his lead rope over a low branch of a tree, and quickly made his way to the western edge of the knoll. He was now well outside the sentry line of the tribe, but he hadn't followed his father, so technically, he wasn't exactly disobeying orders. His logic sounded very weak, even to him, but it was all he had.

Scyles pulled his bow out of his gorytos and quickly strung it. He grabbed a handful of arrows and stuck them into the dirt in front of him. He looked around the side of a large ledge of rock, so as to not have his head silhouetted on the horizon. His father and Targitai rode into view, pairs of outriders either going into the wooded patches, or at least riding up the edge, checking for any horse sign.

One pair neared a very dense clump of trees, surrounded by thinner thatches of saplings and small pines. One of the men leaned forward, and there was an immediate volley of arrows fired at them. One of them flew off his horse, the other sagged forward, both receiving at least two arrows that easily pierced their layered mail jerkins.

The volley was followed with another, this time aimed at the main party. Scyles noticed his father block an arrow with his shield, and Targitai do the same, but he didn't watch to see if they were hit.

Scyles began firing into the woods as fast as he could, aiming at places that looked like good hiding spots or that arrows had come from in the first two volleys. He was firing two or three arrows per shot, trying to appear to be a party of archers, not just one.

He heard shouts and cries of pain, and hoped it was the raiders, and not his father's party. He kept the pace of his firing going, and hoped he didn't run out of arrows too quickly. His father's men were also firing into the forest now, and suddenly a group of riders broke out of the woods, riding away from the ambushed Auchatae.

Scyles quickly drew one arrow back and let it fly. He didn't wait to see where it landed before he fired at a second rider, then a third. By that time, Targitai was leading a charge of riders after them, all of them firing themselves. He saw he'd hit all three of his targets, but only one had been knocked off his horse by the arrow's impact. The other two sagged in their saddles, and were quickly run down and killed by his tribesmen.

As suddenly as the ambush started, the battle ended. All the raiders were down, either dead, or quickly being finished off by Targitai's men. He saw his father look up at the hill, his eyes searching for the source of support. Scyles ducked back from the edge of the rock, and trotted back to his horse.

By the time he retrieved his horse, and rode around the rocky hill, the raiders' bodies had been dragged into a large pile, and all the heads removed. A couple men were using a thorny tree for a makeshift display of the heads. Others were retrieving arrows.

Scyles nodded to his father as he rode by, and found as many of the shafts he'd fired into the woods as he could. A few were damaged by hitting trees or rocks, and he handed those to the men trying to fit all the heads on the one tree. They nodded their thanks and stuck the arrows in the ground, and jammed the heads down on the nocks.

One of the men handed him an armful of his arrows, and nodded his approval.

"Most of these were sticking in dead men, young prince," he said and grinned, showing his teeth. "Were these your first kills in battle?"

"They were," Scyles admitted, surprised he didn't feel more pride. He thanked the man, and decided there was no point in putting off dealing with his father any longer. He pulled out a soft piece of horse-hide, cleaning the arrows enough to put them back into his gorytos, as he let his horse pick his way over to where his father was doing the same.

"Your king told you to stay with the main body of the tribe," his father said in a voice that Scyles recognized as the one he used to hide his anger. That was when he was the most dangerous, Scyles knew.

"You told me I was not riding with you," Scyles corrected him, careful not to sound too cocky or belligerent. "You said we couldn't ride together. We didn't. I was ahead of you, checking out that rocky line of hills, when the shooting started."

Scyles watched his father's face as he considered his words. The anger was still there, but he was doing his best to hide a grudging admiration of his tactics.

"You shouldn't have been outside the perimeter alone," he started, and Scyles cocked his head at him.

"You want me to get someone else in trouble?" Scyles shook his head. "I am responsible for my own actions, and will not drag anyone else into this."

"If they'd figured out where you were, they could have volleyed your position, or even charged you."

"I had the high ground, and you had half again the number of men they did," Scyles pointed out. "The moment we began searching for them, their only option was to flee. And they took too long realizing that to do anything but die."

His father glared at him.

"Do you know what your mother would do to me if you'd gotten hurt today?"

Scyles winced, but stood his ground.

"Father, I know I am your last son, but I have to gain experience." He rubbed some blood off a shaft, and examined it to see if it was clean enough. He decided it was.

"Father, I am sorry I went against your wishes, but I did not go against your orders," he said, and held his breath, wondering if he'd gone too far.

His father watched him put the arrow into his gorytos, and begin to wipe down another.

"How many of your arrows had blood on them?" he asked quietly.

Scyles glanced at the handful left to clean, and shrugged.

"Nine, I think, maybe ten," he said, keeping the pride out of his voice. "But some of them were in the same person, I think."

"That was an impressive volley you gave them," his father said, and finally smiled. "I heard the men retrieving the arrows talking about it."

Scyles felt pride at his father's words, but was also embarrassed. He didn't like showing off or bragging. He just wanted people to know he could take care of himself, and hold his own in battle. He was also feeling oddly sad about being the cause of death, even indirectly, of so many men that were basically following their leader's orders. But those kind of thoughts were signs of weakness, he knew, and pushed them away.

"They were blind shots, except for the last three," he pointed out. "More luck than skill."

"Perhaps," his father said quietly, then gave him a thin smile, and winked, after making sure no one was watching too close. "But you have drawn your first blood in battle. Now go tell your mother we're both fine."

His demeanor changed completely.

"Next time you don't do as you're told, it'll be the flat of my sword you're feeling," he suddenly shouted, and leaned forward at Scyles, menacing. "Now get out of my sight!"

"Yes, Father," Scyles said, and hung his head as he turned his horse, and urged it forward. He doubted they were fooling anyone, but it was good to remind the men that he didn't expect, or get, special treatment, just because his father was king.

Scyles wished Princess Arga had seen that battle, and blinked in surprise. He wondered where that errant thought had come from. He was sure she could care less about him, and was probably dreading that she would be seeing him soon, if last year was any sign.

The steppes of Mkhnach, north of the present day Sea of Azov

Arga rode alongside her mother. They were about a horse-length behind her father. She could feel her mother stealing looks at her from time to time. Arga knew what was on her mind, and abruptly, she came to a decision.

"Mother, I do not wish to wed Prince Scyles," she began, suddenly very nervous. She hurried to continue. "I am not ready to be packaged off to another tribe, married to someone I do not love, expected to share his bed, and bear his children. Anyway, you need me here. Serlotta is a handful, and there are certainly very good choices in the young men of our own tribe."

"All you say is true, Arga," her mother said, and she saw her father's shoulders suddenly bunch up. They clearly weren't in full agreement on this subject. "But you have bled monthly for three years, and are a woman in all ways that matter. It is time for you to choose your future."

"What if I do not yet wish to tie myself to a man for the rest of my life?" Arga said, and winced at the snippiness in her voice. "I'm sorry, Mother, but what we speak of is forever."

"Unfortunately, there are those that will use your reticence as a reason to pursue their own objectives all the more strongly," her mother said, and then stopped, a slight blush coming to her face. "Is it the fact that we speak of a commitment to a man that is the issue? Does your heart lean more towards women?"

"No, Mother, that is not it," Arga said quickly, feeling color come to her own face. "No, definitely not that."

"Hmm," the older woman said, looking at her curiously. "Did you never wonder, or experiment with another girl?"

"I did get curious, while watching some of the warrior women's relationships with each other," she admitted, and her face continued to heat up. "Lampedo and I were both curious, so we decided to see how it felt to kiss and embrace each other."

They rode in silence for a few minutes, and she watched her father's head begin to turn three distinct times, then stiffen and stay facing forward. Arga glanced at her mother, who was observing the same thing, a knowing smile on her face. She felt her daughter's eyes on her and turned to face Arga, winking.

"And how was it? Did you feel passion?" They exchanged grins. "How long did you experiment with each other?"

"Oh, we still do," Arga said, and they both stifled their laughter as his shoulders bunched up. "We kissed and fondled, and realized we could satisfy each other far better than any man, and without risking either of us becoming with child. We have been lovers for over two years now. If she hadn't given in and married Savlius, and gotten pregnant almost immediately, we would have become warrior women and reveled in our lust for each other."

Her mother's shoulders shook, she was laughing so hard, and her father finally turned around to look at them.

"You aren't as funny as you think," he said dryly, and eyed his wife with a show of annoyance that lost out to an indulgent smile. "If memory serves, I know a woman that dabbled for some time, trying to decide her preference."

"Aren't you happy at my decision, husband?" her mother said, and they both grinned at each other. Then he turned back to facing forward, but his words stayed with them.

"Remember, although the Auchatae will be understanding, if somewhat disappointed, there might be another tribal leader that is far more insistent, and we will see him in only a few days."

Arga and her mother stared at his back, and exchanged concerned looks. Finally, her mother spoke.

"Arga, I will defend your decision, whatever it may be." Her eyes danced. "Even if it is to become a Warrior Woman and forgo children."

"Lampedo and I thought kissing and some fondling was pleasant, but it wasn't what we were looking for, or preferred. We only tried the one time," Arga admitted, smiling as her father's shoulders slumped in relief.

"That is your choice, daughter," her mother said, and Arga could tell there was more coming. She wasn't wrong.

"I know you've noticed at least one boy in our tribe, maybe more. I know you would be happy to postpone having to deal with any of this for another year or so." Her mother's voice was earnest now, and Arga listened carefully, wanting to get her mother's entire message.

"Tomorrow, we will join the Auchatae at the gathering site. People will expect you and Scyles to spend some time together. You will be seated next to each other at the feast tomorrow night, I am sure. No one would be surprised if the two of you slipped away to take a walk and discuss things."

"I wonder what those things could possibly be," Arga said dryly.

"I wonder," her mother agreed, smiling. "But I ask one boon of you. I understand you do not wish anyone to be pushed upon you, and I support your feelings on this. But just because some of us think Scyles would be the best choice for your husband, you shouldn't react by automatically eliminating him from your choices. He may be the one, he may not be. But get to know him better, without committing to anything. I suspect he has a lot of the same thoughts about you being chosen for him, so you might find you have that cause in common."

She nudged her horse closer and reached over to put her hand on Arga's arm.

"Spend some time the next several days, giving both him and yourself a chance to make your decisions for the right reasons. That is all I ask."

Arga found herself nodding, in spite of her conviction Scyles was most certainly not the best choice for her. But her mother's logic made sense, and she would be a fool to automatically discard him. Her father was also right. In a few days, King Agathyrsus and Queen Latoreia would be pushing their son, Kavas, on her, with much more determination. And she knew that faced with him being forced upon her, she would join the Warrior Women first.

They rode in silence for a while, and Arga thought about her mother and father, and how their marriage must have come to be. She finally asked the question she probably should have asked several years ago.

"Mother, when you and Father married, was it because of love, and your choice, or was it arranged as a union for strategic purposes?" she asked, and had another thought. "Or were they just trying to get you out of the yurt? How old were you when you wed?"

"I was sixteen, a year older than you," her mother admitted, and looked at her father as he turned around to look at them. He had an amused expression on his face. "Mind the trail, old king," she said, and he laughed. "The women of the family are having an important conversation, and men aren't needed at the moment."

He laughed and faced forward again, his eyes searching for landmarks ahead of them, Arga knew.

"And no, it wasn't love," she admitted. "My parents wanted me to marry a prince in another tribe, to cement friendly relations, and I did not wish to do so. When I was fifteen, I joined the Warrior Women of my tribe, and swore off men."

"You what?" Arga was aghast. She'd never heard this story. "You preferred women to men?"

"I still do," her mother said archly, and stared at the back of her husband fondly. "It's not something you can change in yourself. It simply is. Although I enjoyed the company of both sexes, I definitely preferred women to men. But, after we were wed, your father showed me respect, and we talked and talked. I discovered that, although I preferred women to men, I didn't prefer them to one man in particular."

"Smart decision," her father called out over his shoulder without turning around.

"Shut up, old goat," her mother called out, and Arga could only stare, first at her, then her father, in confusion. "I am thinking Serlotta needs a little brother, but don't know if you'll have the strength to help with that, exhausting as this journey is."

Arga blushed and started looking around, wondering where else she could be at this moment. Despite the fact that she was looking at her fellow tribesmen, the vision she saw was of a young man, not that much bigger than herself, riding a horse and shooting arrows faster than she could follow. Her vision slowed his horse and turned to face her, smiling.

She shook her head, clearing it. What her parents requested made good sense, and she would give Scyles a chance to impress her. But she didn't give him much chance of success. Her eyes found Skulis, riding his horse off to the left, well out of hearing range, she was happy to see. As if he could feel her gaze, he turned to look at her, smiling when he caught her watching him. She hurriedly turned her attention to the trail ahead.

She doubted Scyles could compete with such impressive competition. But she would give him his chance. Better to know early on, and eliminate him from the choices.

Chapter Four

On the northern fringe of the Maeotae Marshes

King Gelon wiped sweat from his brow, and tested the stake he'd sunk in the ground. He decided they could finish staking down the main tent without his assistance. The center post looked solid, as did the other supporting posts. He nodded at his wife and she gestured with her head towards the approaching horseman.

He joined Targitai as the horseman arrived. The rider jumped down, and the horse stood patiently until the rider spoke to it. None of them bothered watching as it trotted off. It would join the others at the feed and buckets of water being hauled up from the spring by the younger boys and girls.

Gelon noticed his son helping haul the water, and wondered about that. Scyles had a yoke with a full bucket at each end, but instead of resting it upon his shoulders, he was carrying it slightly elevated, which meant the weight was being held by his arms and shoulders. As he watched, Scyles curled his forearms, and he suddenly knew what his son was doing.

Scyles is trying to increase his strength in his upper torso, he marveled. Carrying water was already an exhausting job, and he was intentionally making it harder. He realized Targitai was watching him watch his son, and looked at him questioningly.

"Did you suggest this to him?" he asked, and his swordmaster shook his head.

"No, and I never would," he said, shaking his head in disapproval. "He's the king's son and doesn't need to be doing menial chores."

"Like digging post holes?" Gelon asked quietly, and Targitai winced.

"No, you are the king, and if you choose to take part in the hard labor, you show your humility and sense of appreciation for the hard work your people do every day. People love you for that, and brag that you don't think you're better than them. He is the son, the prince, and needs to be establishing himself as a future ruler."

Gelon just looked at him, and the other man sighed and shook his head.

"With you, they understand. But do you think they understand his reasons? Or will they think you assigned this task because you don't trust him with more important things? Or as a punishment of some sort."

"We're setting up camp, and dealing with the results of a long, forced march," Gelon said. "There is no task too menial for myself, my family, or you, for that matter, to do to show our appreciation to our people."

"Very few kings of the people think that way," Targitai pointed out, and Gelon smiled at him.

"And is that such a bad thing?"

"Some people will say it makes you look weak," Targitai said, and winced as he anticipated the response.

Gelon smiled crookedly and flexed his left bicep. It was impressive, and it was his weaker arm. And they both knew it.

Targitai accepted defeat with good grace.

"I bow to your wisdom, my king," he said, and bowed slightly.

As one, they turned to the young rider, who had been listening to this entire exchange. They looked at him and he fidgeted, nervous under their scrutiny. Finally, Targitai slapped him on the shoulder, almost knocking him over.

"You have a message for us, boy?" Gelon asked gently.

He looked startled, then embarrassed.

"Yes, Sire. Outriders report a body of horsemen and carts moving south, about a day's travel behind us. It looks to be the Paralatae, and is about the same sized group as ours."

"Any sign of the Caitiari?" Targitai asked brusquely.

"None, Swordmaster," he answered. "The Paralatae have sent some riders ahead, scouts, and they will be close within the next several hours."

Gelon nodded, and dismissed the rider, who fled in relief. He turned to Targitai again.

"And so it begins," he said dryly. "You think they will press forward today?"

"No, they will probably camp where we did, leaving them a very short day of travel tomorrow." Targitai grinned at him. "I think you'd better start planning on hosting a feast tomorrow night."

Gelon grinned mirthlessly. Myrina was already well into that process, and he didn't need to worry about it, other than to make sure security for the camp and the feast was adequate. And that was Targitai's job.

"Ensure we have sufficient guards posted tomorrow night during the feast, and a good number of sentries concealed around the perimeter of the camp." They exchanged looks, and Gelon sighed. "Tell those that draw duty tomorrow night will not be needed the nights of the next two feasts. We will have plenty of those over the next several weeks."

"Will one of them involve a wedding?" Targitai asked, and Gelon shrugged.

"I hope so," he admitted. "And I hope it is very soon, before the Caitiari arrive."

"You know what he wants," Targitai said, glancing around to make sure no one was within earshot. "He will be furious."

"King Orik and I are of one mind on this, and we've developed a good friendship over the years. We will stand together against him, if need be."

"I thought this early arrival was to cement plans to dictate King Atheas' successor," Targitai said, fingering the handle of his short blade.

"I still have hopes," Gelon said, and then admitted. "But I will be satisfied with getting these two married, her in our camp, this gathering over and done with, and our tribe back on our grazing grounds, preparing for the winter."

"I, as well," Targitai admitted. "Scyles is confident he could beat Kavas in a challenge, but I don't know that he's ready."

"Speaking of which, I saw him sparring with some of the others, using two swords instead of one and his shield," Gelon said tersely. "Would you please explain?"

"It was his idea," Targitai admitted. "And to a point, it is good to practice. Once a battle commences, shields get broken, or lost. Knowing another way to fight is in his best interests."

"As long as he doesn't think that is a choice made before the fight begins," Gelon said, and knew he sounded ominous. Anyone but Targitai would be looking to flee right about now, but the swordmaster just shrugged.

"I don't think so, but the boy has a point," Targitai said, and hurried to continue. "I have watched him experiment with sword patterns of defense and attack, and to someone who had never seen such a style before, it would be quite daunting."

"But against an experienced fighter, it is a good way to get killed," Gelon muttered, watching his son carry yet another load of water up to the large troughs and skins they were filling. Scyles put the two buckets down, and spun the heavy stick as he walked over to the pile of empties. Gelon raised his eyebrows at how fast he was spinning it, and with complete control.

"I think perhaps I should have attended more of his training sessions under your tuteledge, old friend," he muttered and Targitai laughed.

"Your son has different skill sets than you or I," he returned. "I think you are going to be surprised the first time you see him in battle. He thinks, always."

"A good fighter, one that's still alive, has to have instincts and habits built by knowing the moves so well, he doesn't have to think about them," Gelon said, frowning.

"That is true in almost all cases," Targitai agreed, not elaborating. He saw something in the distance he apparently didn't like, and called out to several men hauling the cart with the flooring carpets for the main tent. He hurried over, leaving Gelon with his response still on his lips.

"Faker," he muttered after the swordmaster, and turned back to watch his son talking to his mother. He nodded his head.

"That's where he gets it from. Certainly not from me."

The steppes of Mkhnach, north of the present day Sea of Azov

King Orik watched his travelling camp take shape. His tribe had been making this sort of trek for so many generations, the work was well-defined as far as who did what. And since it was a camp for only one night, more emphasis was placed on getting the basics set up, and depending on heavy rotations of guards through the night, rather than making defenses, as they would do if planning on staying for any length of time.

Tomorrow's camp would be that sort. He wished his out-riders would return with news of the site of the gathering. He suspected the Auchatae would be a step ahead of him, but prayed to the gods that the Caitiari weren't.

Orik trusted King Gelon, and felt they had a natural kinship and alliance, if for no other reason than counteracting the aggressive ambitions of King Agathyrsus. He hoped he and Gelon could meet and resolve certain issues before the Caitiari arrived.

One issue in particular, couldn't seem to be removed from his thoughts. Even as he had that thought, she rode up.

"Papa, the scouts return," she called out, jumping off her horse in a most warrior-like manner. He nodded his approval, a begrudging smile coming to his lips.

Gods, she was the spitting image of her mother at that age.

"Unless they're right behind you, we'll be waiting for them for a while," he told her gently. "Calm down. Remember, you're a princess."

Arga sniffed and fed her horse a handful of feed, stroking his neck as he ate.

"One more part to my body hanging between my legs, and I'd be the future king, and able to do anything I want, with your blessing," she retorted, and he winced at her earthy humor.

The two men staying in his immediate area both laughed, and he fixed a steely stare at them. They both immediately sobered up, and one of them took Arga's horse from her, nodding to his princess.

"Leave us," Orik said, on impulse. "My daughter will guard my back while you find your suppers. We will wait here for the riders."

They both nodded, and shot looks of gratitude at Arga. One of them seemed to extend the look longer than was natural, and it didn't go unnoticed by Orik.

Skulis, are you thinking to try and woo my daughter, Orik wondered idly. It made sense. He was only two years older than she, and already a warrior with the reputation of being very willing to initiate a fight. And apparently, he was very proficient.

Of course he is, Orik thought, shaking his head at his own stupidity. Ariapithes, his Swordmaster, wouldn't have assigned him to his current duties if he weren't.

He cleared his throat, and Arga's attention came back to him, her cheeks showing a little more color than usual. He hid the urge to sigh. That would complicate things, if she was truly interested in the young man.

"Papa, what do you think the scouts found?"

"We will know soon enough," he said, and unrolled the parchment map he carried. She came to look over his arm at the map. It showed the area of the gathering, with the Anerez Reka feeding the Maeotae Marshes. He wondered which spot Gelon had taken. He knew what his choice would be, under these circumstances. Well, maybe there were two good choices, for different reasons.

"The riders are almost here, Papa," she said, pointing to two horseman approaching at a gallop. As they passed the sentries, someone threw an apple at one of them. He caught it with one hand, took a bite, and flipped it to the other horseman, who deftly snagged it.

Orik grinned, not hiding his envy at their youthful joy with their duties. They slowed as they came up the hill. Then they were right in front of him, suddenly in no hurry as they leisurely dismounted.

He snorted.

"My foot and your asses might meet soon," he said, and one of them immediately sped up his pace and stood before him, giving a slight bow of the head.

Orik unrolled the map and, crouching, laid it flat on the ground.

"Who is there already, and where is their camp?"

"It is the Auchatae, and they are here," the scout said, and pointed to an area east of the river, but not flush to it.

Orik frowned and looked at his man. Auric had been scouting for years, and was very familiar, both with the map and the terrain. There was no question of his being right. But it was an interesting choice Gelon had made.

"Any sign of the Caitiari?"

Auric shook his head. Orik told them both to go get some supper. Their faces showed their gratitude, as they grabbed the reins of their horses and hurried away.

Orik looked at Arga.

"Did you see where he pointed?"

She nodded, and leaned against him to look closer at the map.

"Where will you choose for our camp?" she asked, her eyes looking at every detail of the map. It was very old, and was usually kept safely wrapped in a carrying case. He watched her reach forward, but not try to touch the old parchment. She ran a finger down the river, and then across the shore bordering the marsh.

"Where would you?" he asked and smiled as watched her furl her eyebrows in concentration.

Finally, she pointed at the land between the Auchatae and the river.

"Here."

"Why?" Orik asked, proud of her, but careful to conceal his approval.

"We would have the river to the west, the Maeotae Marsh to the south, and an ally to the east," she said slowly. "We would fortify our northern boundary, and have watchers on the river and at the marsh, but it appears to be the most defensible place to be."

"Why do you think the Auchatae chose their site, and didn't take your choice instead?"

Arga shook her head.

"I don't know," she admitted. "There must be a factor I don't see. Their choice leaves them two vulnerable borders, to the north and to the east."

"What about the western approach?" Orik asked.

"They have us there, and we would defend the border and warn them," Arga said slowly, and looked at him, obviously expecting a trick.

"And why would we do that?" Orik asked quietly.

She looked startled, then nervous.

"We are allies. You and King Gelon have been friends almost since you were my age. Our tribes have ties…" She stopped as she realized the potential weakness of her logic.

"We might have ties," Orik agreed solemnly. "We might not, after we have met."

Arga exhaled in exasperation.

"You think I should agree to marriage," she said in a flat voice. "Despite the conversation on the trail, you think we need this marriage to secure the tribe."

"I am not saying that," Orik corrected her. "I am saying every action has consequences and results. It could be that a marriage between our tribes would cement a long kinship between us that would translate to having a partner in any conflict."

41

"My marrying Scyles might initiate an offensive against us because then I could not marry Kavas," she shot back, and Orik concealed his pride at her quick mind.

"And so, you have learned the first lesson of this discussion," Orik said in an approving tone.

"What is the second lesson?" Arga was quick to follow up.

"You haven't learned that one yet," Orik said in a mild tone, and she shot him a suspicious look. He smiled at her, and wished he could protect her forever from these kinds of worries and concerns. But better she learn while she could still take advantage of her knowledge. "What other reason could King Gelon have for choosing his current position?"

Arga frowned at the map, and her finger moved back over the sketches on the parchment. She followed the shoreline of the marshes to the east, and looked up at him.

"Would King Agathyrsus set camp to the east of the Auchatae?" she asked, outlining the area she meant.

"I would expect so," Orik admitted. "His only other viable choice would be across the river from us, but unless he brought boats in numbers, that would put him at a logistical disadvantage. It would make no sense, unless he intended before he even arrived to attack whoever is in our position."

"Too risky with the rest of the tribes arriving soon after him," Arga mused out loud. "Unless he somehow managed to secure a total victory, he would almost certainly be attacked when the remainder of our two tribes, and the rest of the people arrived."

She shook her head, and stared up at him.

"Why did King Gelon choose that spot?"

Orik nodded his agreement with her capitulation. He pointed at the map.

"Assume we're right about placements. Ourselves on the river bank, Gelon in the middle, the Caitiari on the east side of them. If King Agathyrsus wished to have a secret meeting with me, how would he do it?"

Arga started to point at the northern borders of the projected encampments, and paused, considering. She shook her head, slowly let her hand hang over the map as she moved it south until it was over the marshes.

"Unless he used the dead of night, he can't," she finally said. "And even in the dark, there is a better than fair chance King Gelon's sentries would spy them trying to sneak past to our camp."

"So, although he doesn't control all communications, nothing happens without his knowledge," Orik said, and watched the light come into her eyes. "You control communications, you control the situation. It is quite an advantage."

"So he doesn't trust us?" Arga asked, frowning. He knew what she was thinking. Gelon was a good man, and truth be told, a good friend of his. But sometimes, conditions changed, or became uncertain.

"That might depend on a number of factors," he said, knowing what her reaction would be.

"So, it comes back to Scyles and me," she almost snarled. "This almost makes me wish to become a warrior woman, just to spite everyone."

"Spoken like the daughter of the woman I love," he said, and she looked at him in surprise. "You know, when we married, she became my partner, in every way. In love, as the mother of my children, in managing our family and wealth, and in planning, both short term and long, the safety and future of our tribe."

"Why did she stop?" Arga asked slowly. "Was it because she bore us? Did being a mother change all that?"

"Who said she ever stopped?" Gelon asked, and grinned at her. "As impressive as I am between the hides, sometimes we just talk, you know. And while you're busy confusing poor Skulis, we have many opportunities to talk on the trail."

Arga blushed, and Orik smiled, although he didn't find much to be cheerful about at the moment.

As much as he and Opis wanted her to be happy, and make her own choices, they both very much hoped she would find merit in the idea of marrying Scyles.

The security and survival of the tribe might depend on it.

Chapter Five

On the northern fringe of the Maeotae Marshes

Gelon watched King Orik and his family separate from the body of his tribe. Most of them were streaming towards the slight swelling hills that would become the site of their camp. He wasn't surprised to see Orik's Swordmaster, Ariapithes, riding parallel to his king, off to his right a few horse lengths. Queen Opis, Princess Arga, and little Prince Serlotta rode behind him.

He smiled as he noticed their armed riders loosely fanned in an arch behind the royal family, staying well out of easy hearing range, yet close enough to be able to provide arrow cover. He was amused that their escort was exactly the same size as Targitai had in position behind his own family.

He rode forward to meet Orik, bringing his horse next to the other king, so they could share a hearty handshake, and then embrace, still on horseback.

Targitai and Ariapithes met in much the same manner, off to the left. He knew that both men, even as they greeted each other with sincere pleasure and respect, were watching the other's men, the surrounding terrain, and even the horizon, looking for any conceivable threat.

The two queens and the children met in the open space between the two kings and their two protectors. Myrina and Opis were as close friends as could be for two women that only saw each other several weeks every year. They hugged, still on horseback, and then gestured for the three children to come forward.

"Good to see you again, old friend," Orik said quietly, and Gelon nodded.

"It looks like you had no surprises during your journey," he said, and Orik nodded in relief.

"Aye. I half expected to see the flags of the Caitiari flying when we approached," he admitted. "Although the original schedule should have him arriving in two days, it would not surprise me to have our scouts telling of sightings before this day ends. We saw you had some unwanted guests. Coveting your herds, I assume?"

"Yes, about twenty Dacians," Gelon admitted. "Scyles made his first kills in battle when they tried to ambush my party."

"Kills?" Orik asked softly, and Gelon didn't pretend to not understand.

"Yes, kills, at least six, possibly as many as nine." Gelon made no attempt to hide his pride. "He was on a ridge above their hiding place, and his volleys of arrows looked like that of a raiding party."

"I've seen him shoot," Orik said, nodding. "He's the best archer I've ever seen."

Gelon looked at him in surprise. He thought for a moment.

"You saw the Sarmatian in the Great King's retinue," he pointed out, expecting his friend to qualify his praise upon remembering that.

"Yes, I did," Orik said simply.

They sat on their horses quietly for a moment, both of them remembering both battles they'd won, and a few they'd lost. Gelon shook his head, ridding himself of the memories of the past, if only for the moment.

"We don't have much time, and many things to talk about and decide," Gelon said grimly. "You know Agathyrsus will advance himself as the logical and best choice to replace Atheas as the Great King. I will support your claim, and stand with you against any challengers."

"Thank you, my friend," Orik said, looking surprised, and perhaps a little touched at Gelon's words. "Your support will be critical. To be truthful, if any number of other kings laid claim instead of him, I would be sorely tempted to stay out of it completely. I don't think we will see another great king live to see ninety harvests."

"I understand, and don't envy the road ahead of you," Gelon admitted, and slapped his friend on the shoulder as they moved a little away from the women and children. "But I will be there at your side, on that you can depend."

"One could not ask for a better friend and ally," Orik said, and his expression soured a little. "I fear I have less progress on another front to report than I would have liked."

Gelon laughed and resisted the urge to look back at the children.

"I am encountering resistance that I suspect is very similar," he admitted, and they looked at each other with concern. "I am not so sure they don't find each other pleasant enough, or that there aren't already feelings between them. But..."

"But neither your son nor my daughter like being told they have to do something," Orik finished for him. "Especially something of this magnitude."

"Aye," Gelon agreed glumly. "If we had more time, and arranged to meet a few times over the winter, I think they would naturally move towards not only accepting their union, but craving it."

"Are you saying your son is craving my virginal daughter?" Orik said, pushing his face closer to Gelon's.

"He is my son," Gelon said pointedly. "Of course he is craving your daughter."

They both roared with laughter, and together, turned to look at their families.

The two women had knowing looks on their faces, and the boy looked as curious as he should. But the looks on Arga and Scyles' faces sobered both of them. They clearly knew they were the topic of discussion, and neither looked thrilled at being talked about, or being pushed in any direction, even one they might want.

They turned away, and snuck glances at each other guiltily. Then their senses of humor won out, and they grinned again.

"So, is your son a virgin as well?" Orik asked, staring at Gelon.

"Of course not," Gelon scoffed. "We made sure he got some experience under seasoned guidance."

"Well, good. I would hate to think my only daughter would lose her maidenhood to someone that didn't even know which parts fit where, and how to use them properly," Orik stated, and they both chuckled for a moment, then the humor dried up. "I would see them wedded, either tonight, or tomorrow latest. What if they refuse?"

"Then King Agathyrsus will be mounting pressure for them to marry the twins," Gelon said in a morose voice. "And he will not accept their refusing."

"He will not be forcing my daughter to do anything," Orik said flatly.

"Or my Scyles," Gelon agreed. "But if they are single, or even betrothed, he will not accept that without a fight. And it is in none of our best interests to be fighting each other. You and I know this. He knows it as well. But his ego will make him try and force the issue." He sighed. "I'm not so sure that, even if they were wedded, and bedded, he wouldn't try and renounce that and force the issue."

"Then we will indeed have a fight on our hands," Orik said grimly.

"Aye," Gelon agreed. "Myrina thinks the two of them having a picnic this afternoon, with minimal supervision, might help their willingness to progress."

"You don't think that's too obvious?" Orik asked doubtfully. "I think they will see right through it."

"Of course they will," Gelon agreed. "Both of them are smarter than you or I, but I'm sure you've been honest with her, as we have with Scyles, so our suggesting this would be in character, and almost to be expected. I think they will consider it as a weak attempt to convince them. Let them spend time together. It will either prove we're right, or show we're sadly mistaken. Either way, we have nothing to lose by trying."

"Agreed." Orik said, and gave Gelon a slap on the shoulder. "This is definitely Myrina's idea. You and I don't have the cleverness to see that this is actually quite devious."

Grinning like fools, they turned back towards their families.

Scyles passed the sentries from his tribe guarding the old trail that passed between near where their camp was, and the Paralatae's. He didn't slow as he approached King Orik's sentries, passing them with a nod.

He let his horse walk, leading another for Princess Arga. He had two guards and both had asked to lead the horse for him, but he'd refused. He'd also reminded them that they were to practice their best spying skills, because if he saw anyone other than the princess while they were out riding, he would shoot without warning.

He knew they were both sure he would never actually shoot at one of his own guards, but they also knew that if he did, he would hit his target. They took his point to heart. He and Arga would have their privacy from prying ears.

He wound through the scrub trees and bushes, gradually picking up the pace until his horse trotted smartly as he rode into the Paralatae camp. No one challenged him until he approached the main yurt. Then two guards stepped forward while two others stayed back at a distance, bows in hand, watching him closely.

"What do you want, young prince?" one of the guards said as he reached for the bridle of Scyles' horse. The stallion's head reared back and his teeth bared. The guard smiled approvingly, taking his hand away.

"I wish to see Princess Arga," he said formally. "She is expecting me."

"What makes you so sure she wants to ride with you, boy?" King Orik said sternly as he came out the main entrance of the sprawling tent.

"I'm not sure at all," Scyles answered truthfully, grinning at the king. "But if she does, I have a horse for her, and a lunch packed."

Arga appeared behind her father and laid a hand on his arm.

"Quit teasing him in front of your men, Papa," she said dryly. "They will all take him lightly, and he will have to fight to prove his worth."

"Princess Arga," Scyles said, and his voice was suddenly rougher, and he had an over-whelming urge to cough. He slid off his horse, and led hers forward a couple steps. "May I offer you this horse to ride? Her name is Scarlet Sky."

"An old, tame mare, I assume," she said, scratching the red filly between her eyes. The horse shook her head in warning. Arga's eyes lit up. "Perhaps not so tame or old after all," she admitted.

"I've ridden with you before," Scyles reminded her. "I know your skills on a horse."

She nodded her appreciation to him, and quickly mounted, even as he started to offer a hand. He bit his lip, and leaped back on Earth Runner as she turned the filly and began to trot out of the encampment.

"Have her back by mid-afternoon," King Orik said sternly. "Her mother will want her to prepare properly for the feast this eve."

"Yes, Sire," Scyles said, and pulled his horse around and gave him his head. He immediately sped up to pursue the filly. By the time they cleared the outer perimeter of the camp, he'd come up next to her, and she looked over at him mischievously.

"You picked well," she admitted. "I like this filly. She has a mind of her own."

"She reminds me of someone I know," Scyles said, and she shot a surprised look at him.

"You're remarkably cheerful," she observed. "As if you thought you'd just acquired something of great value."

Scyles winced, and glanced around. His men were well off the trail, and following his orders. Hers were riding behind them, not crowding them, but not giving them much of a sense of freedom either.

"Princess Arga, I would like to discuss the situation we find ourselves in," he began, wincing at how formal and stuffy he sounded. "I think you'll find our thoughts are more similar than you might expect."

"Call me Arga out here," she said curtly, not looking at him. "Formalities are for formal events. Scyles," she added, after a moment's delay.

"I will, Arga," he said, and was surprised at the pleasure he felt saying her name. Reluctantly, he returned to his prepared speech. "We need to be able to talk without feeling someone's eyes and ears over our shoulders. Could you tell your guards that we wish to have at least the illusion of having an afternoon to ourselves, and that if I see anyone other than you, I will put an arrow in them?"

She snorted and grinned at him.

"You wouldn't dare actually shoot them," she said, but he could tell she was intrigued.

He said nothing, but pulled his bow out of his gorytos, and effortlessly strung it. He lay it across his lap and stared at her. She laughed and shook her head, but pulled her horse to a halt, and turned to face back at the two men following them.

"We wish to enjoy this afternoon without you sniffing our horse's backsides. Fall back and become more discreet." She glanced at him and then continued. "If Prince Scyles sees you again this afternoon he will put an arrow in you. We are going to that hill to have lunch and talk. You will be able to see us from a distance, and guard my safety and honor quite adequately."

The two men looked at each other, nonplused, and one of them shook his head.

"Princess, you know we can't leave you unattended. And the prince would never shoot one of your men. More importantly, one of King Orik's men."

The other man snorted. "And it's not like we would let him actually hit us."

Scyles said nothing, but pulled an arrow out of the gorytos, pulled back on his bow and let an arrow fly before any of them could respond. She ducked her head, although the arrow didn't come anywhere near her. He'd shot off to their left, eastward towards his own tribe's grounds.

All four of them watched the arrow arch high into the air, and as it began to descend, the second man made a comment in a loud voice.

"I think he missed us," he said, and they both laughed, even as their eyes followed the flight of the arrow.

A rabbit suddenly jumped up and took one hop before the arrow skewered it, pinning it to the ground. Scyles had anticipated its path of fleeing perfectly.

"Allow me to offer you lunch," Scyles said in a dry voice. "If I see the smoke of your cooking fire, I will not shoot. But if I can see the flames, one of you will need a healer tonight."

Without saying a word, both he and Arga urged their mounts forward, and slightly increased their pace. Scyles watched as Arga tried to secretively look back and see what the two men were doing. He saw the expression on her face and kept his grin from appearing.

"Well?" he asked.

"They went to get the rabbit," she admitted. She looked over at him, her face unreadable. "That was a very good shot."

"Thank you," he said, and slowed his horse a little as they approached the hill.

He wanted to tell her something but had no idea how to say it. He decided to just start talking and hoped the words would be the right ones.

"Arga, we have known each other since we were old enough to ride. We've both known this day might come."

She didn't answer, and he pushed forward, wondering when it had gotten so hot. He wiped his forehead and continued.

"I think we are of like mind in regards to our being strongly encouraged to marry each other, and immediately." He stole a glance at her, and saw she was listening with interest. "I consider you my friend, and know you will make a wonderful wife, partner, mother and queen, someday. And if this was a year or two from now, and we'd been exploring the idea together, I think you would make me a very happy man to marry me."

"Are you saying you do not wish to marry me at this point?" Arga asked, and he couldn't tell from her tone, what she was thinking.

"Arga, at this point, I do not wish to marry anyone," he blurted out before he could try to temper his words. "You are a very impressive young woman, and I think it would be easy for you to steal my heart. But I have things I am trying to accomplish to become the best warrior, prince, and someday, husband, father, and even king, I can be. Marrying you now would probably be the smartest thing for us to do, but I do not like being told I must do anything, even if it is my father and mother telling me."

"I know," Arga exclaimed. "I have always liked you, but I do not wish to marry, and be taken away from my tribe to live with strangers. I do not like the idea that I am expected to marry you as early as tonight, or maybe tomorrow, and be pregnant with my first child before we've even returned to your tribal lands."

"So, in this issue, we are of the same mind?" Scyles asked, amazed at how well this had gone. If they both stood together, they could surely withstand the pressure their parents would apply.

"We are," Arga said, marvel in her voice. She grinned at him. "Let's enjoy this day. You got me out of having to help set up camp, and I got you away from…?" She looked at him questioningly.

"Three or four hours of my father's swordmaster torturing me and calling it training," Scyles said, and they both laughed. They looked at each other and she got that same mischievous expression on her face.

She urged her filly forward suddenly, and her words carried back to him.

"Race you to the top!"

Arga didn't remember when she had enjoyed an afternoon as much as she had this one. The moment Scyles told her he wasn't ready to marry, she felt the weight come off her shoulders, and felt confident that between the two of them, they would be able to talk their parents into allowing them to put off marriage, whether it was between them or someone else.

Last year, she had blamed him for the situation their parents had put them in, and she'd been cold, and even mean-spirited to him, but he didn't seem to hold a grudge.

They shared an enjoyable meal that Queen Myrina had packed for them. He'd started a fire, up near the summit of the hill, by the large old tree they both remembered so well. He'd skewered bite-sized pieces of lamb and roasted them over the flames.

"We need to slow down, or we won't have an appetite for the feast tonight," she pointed out, and he nodded, even as he took another bite of the meat. She laughed, and they sat in companionable silence together, looking out towards the marsh to the south. She knew there was a sea beyond it, but she'd never seen it, and said as much.

"Father took me down through the marsh to the sea's shore, and there were merchant ships, from faraway lands," Scyles said, his eyes looking distant to her. "The men on the ships spoke many languages, mostly ones I've never heard before."

"I don't remember you doing that," she said, thinking back.

"You weren't really talking to me for much of last year's gathering," Scyles said, reminding her. "It was one of the last days. By the time we got back, your tribe was packing to leave early the next morning."

"I was so mean to you," Arga said, feeling guilty.

Scyles shrugged.

"You were angry, and had a right to be so," he said. "It looked like we would have no choice, and you were very, very angry."

"That didn't give me the right to take it out on you," she said, and impulsively put a hand on his arm. "I'm surprised you're even speaking to me this year. You had as much right to be angry as I."

"You've always shown your feelings more than me," Scyles said dryly. "And I was angry. Very angry, but not at you."

"How do you control your anger? I would have taken my head off, were I you," Arga said, and giggled at the image that came to mind. Her pulling her head off and walking around with it under an arm.

"I was angry more at the circumstances than at any one person in particular. I could never be angry with you, and being mad at my parents is not very useful." Scyles winced, as if recalling painful memories.

"Why couldn't you be mad at me?" Arga asked. "I was the one being mean to you, and you didn't deserve it."

"Even so," Scyles said, and smiled, a little wistfully. "Just because I do not wish to marry anyone now, doesn't mean I would never want to marry you."

She didn't know how to respond to that, so said nothing.

They walked around the perimeter of the hilltop, looking first over at Scyles' camp, and the sight of the very top of the royal yurt jutting up just above the scrub treetops, then the marsh to the south. Arga said she thought she could just barely see the sea. Scyles didn't argue, but she could tell he doubted it.

They looked to the west, and he pointed out where her family yurt jutted up above everything near it, near the top of the hill that ran down to the river. Then they looked to the north and Scyles snorted.

He walked over to his horse and she blanched as he pulled his bow out, along with two arrows.

"You're not really going to shoot them, are you?"

He grinned at her, and she breathed a sigh of relief. She searched the land below them, and thought she saw what might have been one of them. Or, it could be a bush.

"When you see them later, tell them I could see them both," he said, and stared north as he drew one arrow back, let it fly, and almost before it had taken to the air, took the second shot. She followed their paths, and they each struck a different tree trunk dead center, about a horse length apart.

A distant shout echoed up to them, and she laughed out loud.

"You are mean," she said, not meaning it at all.

"Thank you," he said seriously. "A Scoloti prince must be ruthless, and ready at all times to make an enemy soil his trousers."

She watched him glance to the southwest and saw disappointment appear on his face. She didn't have to look to know what he saw.

"The sun will be leaving us soon," Arga said, feeling the same disappointment. She would see him very soon at the feast, but this day was one she would keep fresh in her mind as a treasure. "You had better return me before my Papa sends his swordmaster to retrieve me."

Impulsively, she leaned in close and kissed his cheek, very softly.

"Thank you for today," she said, and they both turned to their horses, and the too quick ride back to her yurt.

Chapter Six

Commander Azimoth looked at the flight plan and sighed. Lord Bakhtochk had made it clear that time was not a factor in this portion of the trip back to the primitive planet, but he thought this path was bordering on lunacy and complete paranoia.

They had left the star system with the destroyed Adazi ships on a path away from familiar space, then made four distinct changes in direction, gradually making their way closer to their goal.

His lord had made it clear that he didn't want anyone to be able to track them from their own space, and extrapolate their origin or their destination. And he expected the return trip to be every bit as cryptic to anyone seeing them.

Space was huge and infinite. One or two deviations would have been more than adequate. Instead, they would do no less than six course changes before reaching the star system containing the planet with the primitives.

Azimoth did a swift calculation and decided the remainder of the journey would be no more than one day, and breathed his relief.

He'd transferred most of his crew and all the Hshtahni to the generation ship, with the exception of the oldest male child. He was ostensibly in command of the cruiser, but Azimoth's first officer was doing the actual duties of running the operations of the ship.

Azimoth was eager to get to their target planet. He'd had far too much free time during the voyage, although, as a result, he was very familiar with all the features of the generation ship. This included the wide array of subsidiary equipment that had come with the ship, convincing him all the more that the Adazi had never intended for them to keep the ship.

He looked at his console again and clung to the thought that there was only one more day before their arrival.

On the northern fringe of the Maeotae Marshes

Orik pushed his bowl away and vowed to eat no more. King Gelon and his queen, Myrina, had outdone themselves, throwing this "impromptu" feast together. He watched several Auchatae wrestling in the open space in front of the family tables, and the rest of the tribe members attending. They were good, but no better than any number of men from his own tribe.

He casually leaned forward enough to see how his daughter and young Scyles fared. He thought they looked as if they were getting along well enough, and that they seemed to enjoy each other's company. Please, gods, let them decide that a life together wasn't some form of punishment or requirement that doomed them to an eternity of misery.

Orik felt eyes behind him and turned to see Gelon watching both him and the couple, the same concerns clear on his face.

"What do you think?" his friend asked, and he didn't pretend to not understand.

"They seem to like each other well enough," Orik said, and then qualified his comment. "Assuming they aren't acting, simply for our sake, and secretly loathe each other."

Gelon grinned and slapped him on the back.

"I don't know about your daughter, and she is a woman, after all," he whispered at a volume that carried farther than Orik thought it should. "But my son isn't that good an actor. If he doesn't like something, or someone, he can have the best blank, unreadable expression I've ever seen, but he can't pretend to like someone, or enjoy himself, if he doesn't feel it."

"If you're going to make snooty remarks about women in general, you should try and keep your whispers below the level of shouting," Myrina said, taking a sip from her cup. Next to her, Opis grinned and took a bigger sip of her own, and they tapped their drinks together. Myrina looked at Gelon and grinned at him as she finished her words. "Dear husband."

"I will keep that in mind, dear wife," Gelon came right back at her, his own grin undiminished.

The original seating had the two kings next to each other, with their queens flanking them. Serotta sat next to his mother, and then it was Arga, with Scyles seated next to her. Ariapithes and Targitai bracketed the royal families, each sitting at the end of their tribe's royal families.

It hadn't taken long for the seating to shift. Opis had been the first, rising to shoo Targitai away, sending him down the table to sit next to Ariapithes. They ended up moving over to sit next to Orik, with Serlotta on Targitai's left, followed by Arga, then Scyles.

"So," Opis said, taking another sip, smaller this time. "The rumors of Scyles' archer skills appear to be based on the truth."

Orik grinned with her, and noticed that while both Ariapithes and Targitai seemed to know what she was talking about, Gelon and Myrina didn't. They looked at each other curiously, then at Opis.

"Was my son showing off?" Gelon asked, and shook his head. "He is very good. I'll give him that."

Opis snickered and looked at Orik, silently urging him to be the one to tell the story. He obliged, giving a quick accounting of the young prince's determination to have a quiet afternoon without intrusions.

"When I asked Arga's guards about it, one of them said he was glad the rabbit wasn't that big. If he'd eaten more, he would surely have shat his trousers when the arrow embedded in the tree he was leaning against," Orik managed to get out before lapsing back into laughter. They all joined in, although Targitai raised his hand, an uncharacteristic broad smile on his face.

"The two men assigned to guard the young prince felt very slighted that although he supplied your guards with lunch, he didn't provide the same for them."

They all had a good laugh at that, and their attentions moved to the young man sitting at the left end of the long table. He felt their eyes upon him, and of course, not being deaf or unconscious, knew exactly what they were laughing about.

He shrugged.

"I assumed my mother packed them a nice lunch, knowing they would have nothing to do all day."

"I would assume they could catch their own lunches," Myrina responded primly. "There were two of them, and they did have their own bows."

Everyone laughed, and the conversations broke into smaller groups again. Orik watched as Scyles and Arga began talking again, their voices low enough to be unheard, with heads tilted slightly closer to make it easier. He felt Gelon nudge him, and nudged him back.

The two kings turned to look at each other.

"Boys, no wrestling at the supper table," Myrina said, and Opis giggled. All three of them looked at her and she blushed.

"This fermented mare's milk feels stronger than usual," she admitted, taking another sip.

"So, you're right," Gelon said, moving right back to where the conversation had been earlier. "They seem to be getting along well enough. Do you think they're coming to terms with the need for this marriage?"

Orik felt more than saw both women wince, and resisted the urge to do the same. If there was one thing he was sure of, the two could hear every word being said. Any important conversation needed to move away from this table, and preferably, out of this room completely.

Scyles's next words proved the truth of his thoughts.

"Mother, Father, King Orik, Queen Opis, may I say something?" he started, and Arga immediately interrupted him.

"All of you, I will be saying something," she said, and her voice was very intense. Scyles looked at her in surprise, and prudently nodded for her to continue.

"Scyles and I enjoy each other's company, very much," she started, and held up a hand when she saw their expressions begin to change to happy ones. "But, we have talked, and find we agree on several important points."

"Right," Scyles said, flinched, and gestured for her to continue when she changed her attention from their parents to him. Her fiery eyes didn't seem to daunt him, but he was obviously wise beyond his years, because he kept silent.

"As I was saying, we like each other, but neither of us are willing to marry, or even commit to marriage, at this point." She stared at them for a moment, as if daring for them to interrupt, then continued. "Over the next year, we believe that if we could find opportunities to visit each other's tribes, and each other, we might find ourselves willing to consider a union to further cement the undeniable bond between our two tribes."

She leaned forward to look over the table at the two wrestlers, one a Paralatae, the other an Auchatae, currently trying to choke each other into submission. Orik heard his wife suppress a laugh, and kept his expression blank.

"This doesn't just apply to our relationship. I do not wish to speak for Scyles, but I am not interested in any other men, or unions, either within our tribe or without. I will not accept any offers or demands for my submitting to marriage to anyone at this time. If anyone tries to push me too hard on this, I will join the Warrior Women, disavow my position in my family, and swear off men forever."

There was a long silence, and finally Opis cleared her throat. She looked around at the rest of them, then back at her daughter.

"Very good, daughter. I don't think there is any confusion among us regarding your intentions and desires. The Warrior Women would be fortunate to count you among their ranks."

She leaned forward a bit more, to see Scyles easier.

"And you, young Scyles? Do you feel the same way?"

Scyles bit his lip, looked at Arga, and a small smile stole his lips as he stood.

"I do not intend to join the Warrior Women," he began, and everyone at the table started laughing, as if appreciating the lightening of the mood via humor. "But as far as our feelings for each other, unwillingness to marry at this time, and wanting the opportunity to spend more time over the next year, getting to know her and her tribe better, I agree completely."

"Give us the time to properly get to know each other, and in time, you might well find all your goals met," Scyles said, and sat back down.

"Let us hope we have the luxury of that time," Gelon said brusquely, and Orik found himself nodding. "But neither of you will get any pressure from the queen or myself," he vowed.

Orik looked back and forth, up and down the table, fighting the urge to start an argument about this. But he knew that would be a mistake.

"Orik, grumpy old bear," his wife spoke quietly, but her voice carried the length of the table. "Tell your daughter what she wishes to hear. You know her well enough to know that when she feels this strongly about something, she will do as she says, if only in spite. Don't consign her to a life with the Warrior Women. She doesn't even like girls."

There was a moment of shocked silence, and then Myrina laughed out loud. The men all began to look at the platters of food, as if seeing them for the first time.

Except for Orik. He knew his wife was correct. He knew what he had to say. That didn't mean he had to like it.

He watched one of Gelon's men approach Targitai hesitantly. He didn't know what was being discussed, but was sharp enough to know there was conflict involved. He finally looked down the table to Arga, his only daughter.

"Daughter, we shall honor your request. Any further discussion on these topics will be at your prompting."

"Thank you, Papa," Arga said, and flashed him the smile that always made him happy to have a daughter. In particular, this daughter.

Targitai cleared his throat, and looked at both kings. Ariapithes was already on his feet. They both moved behind the table to stand next to their respective kings.

"Sire, scouts from both our tribes have sighted riders from the Caitiari. And there is more." Ariapithes looked over at Gelon, who was hearing the same message from Targitai.

King Gelon stood, looked at Orik, and motioned at the exit with his head. Then he turned back to the queens.

"Ladies, duty calls us away for a few minutes. Please carry on in our absence."

They both nodded, and he could feel their eyes as he followed Gelon out of the yurt. When they were well away from the yurt, Gelon turned to him.

"My scouts say the main party of Caitiari are camped where we did the night before arriving."

"As did we," Orik admitted. "It's a good site."

"It is," Gelon agreed, but something in his tone made Orik look at him closer. "Especially, if your party is half again as large as both of ours combined."

"Half again as…" Orik turned to look at Ariapithes, who shrugged.

"We are still awaiting our own scouts from that area," he admitted.

"My scouts counted over thirty-five hundred in the Caitiari camp, based on horses, carts, and camping sites being set up," Targitai said somberly. "We will be fortifying our eastern boundary throughout the night, and have our own sentries well out from our camps, to keep theirs at a distance, if possible."

"He's a day early," Gelon observed sourly.

"Of course, and we're that and more," Orik reminded him, and Gelon looked at him wryly.

Orik grinned and shook his head. "Sorry. I don't mean to make excuses for them. The gods know we have enough going wrong right now."

"Such as our eldest children," Gelon said, shaking his own head in dismay. "They were looking so comfortable, and the stories about this afternoon looked like there were great portents for this marriage."

"This marriage that isn't happening," Orik pointed out dourly.

"Perhaps," Gelon said, and something in his tone made Orik look at his face closer. "Do you think your daughter would sneak out of the camp tonight if he asks her to?"

"If they aren't interested in pursuing each other, why would they meet?" Orik asked, and immediately felt like a fool. He felt his face darken with the idea of why Scyles might be trying to lure her away from the camp.

Gelon laughed.

"You and I would both likely have but one reason, and that wouldn't necessarily be the worst thing that could happen tonight," he said, and Orik nodded, thinking. "After your first impulse to throttle him and beat him within an inch of his life, what would your reaction be?"

"Arga becoming pregnant with his child wouldn't necessarily be a bad thing, in the long run," Orik mused. "Of course the women would wail, and scream at them, and there would be comments..."

"And our children would be married so fast they'd still be sweaty from the acts that got her that way," Gelon finished his thoughts.

"Acts?" Orik had to ask, although talking about Gelon's son causing his daughter to be with child shouldn't be a topic to be discussed so bluntly, and with humor.

Gelon looked at him.

"At their age, did you ever stop after one time?" he asked pointedly.

Orik tried to frown at him, and failed, ending up grinning and having to make an effort to not laugh out loud.

"Most importantly, the end result is our children married, and successors being conceived," he said, and Gelon nodded in triumph.

Belatedly, both he and Gelon realized that they had an audience. As one, they turned to look at Targitai and Ariapithes, standing nearby, listening and looking amused.

"Why are you still here?" Gelon asked, blustering to try and intimidate them. He failed utterly. "Shouldn't you be out protecting us, or something?" he finally asked, physically conceding his failure.

Both men nodded and began to turn away, but Orik stopped them.

"Wait, wait," he said, thinking furiously, wondering how to word it so it wouldn't sound like how he meant it, and having no idea how to do so. Gods take it, he thought viciously.

"Have you anticipated that Scyles might come to our camp to take Arga out...for a walk?" he finished lamely, and all four of them had to smile wryly at his choice of words.

"We have men that will be in position, and we will both be there as well, monitoring the situation, making sure nothing goes wrong," Targitai said confidently.

"You will stop him from succeeding?" Orik asked, wondering if that was such a good idea.

"No, no," Ariapithes corrected him, grinning broadly. "We will make sure no outsiders wander into our camps and interfere, or try to spirit them away. As far as their succeeding in having a private moment together, we request your guidance," he finished.

Gelon looked at Orik and sighed.

"I don't remember this being so difficult with my first two sons at this point in their lives," he admitted, and Orik shrugged.

"This is my first one, and I'm certainly not prepared for all this..." Words failed him, and he gave up, turning back to the two other men. "Protect our children, and don't make it easy for them, but give them every opportunity to give in to their natural desires."

"I bet neither of us will ever say that again," Gelon predicted, and Orik laughed and slapped him on the shoulder.

"I'm not even admitting I said it now."

"Perhaps I should go with them," Scyles said uncertainly, watching their fathers leave the yurt, with Ariapithes and Targitai close behind. "If they're worried, the Caitiari may be posing an actual threat, not just trying to manipulate successions through marriage."

Arga shook her head, and waved an arm at the yurt full of people from both tribes.

"If they do pose a physical threat, these people will be reacting shortly," she said, and glanced at their mothers. "They would not leave the queens, or ourselves, for that matter, sitting around drinking."

"Good thinking," Scyles admitted, looking at her. "I think you scared them earlier."

"Good," Arga said, smiling at the memory. "That wasn't necessarily my intention, but I wish them to allow us to set our own pace." She glanced over at him, not quite meeting his eyes. "Did you mean what you said?"

"I did," Scyles said firmly. "Under no circumstances will I join the Warrior Women," he said with a straight face, and she gave him a hard slap on his arm. They were both startled by how loud the slap sounded, and Arga felt her face begin to redden.

"You know what I meant," she said, and Scyles rubbed his arm ruefully, giving her an accusatory look.

"I did," Scyles said slowly. "I would like time together before we make such an enormous commitment, but if circumstances forced us, there is no one I would rather have at my side for the rest of my life."

Arga stiffened. That didn't sound much like a man who didn't want to get married. She didn't speak immediately. Instead, she ran his words through her head again. Were all his actions just an attempt to passively help their marriage come to pass? She hoped not. If he was playing a role to get close to her, it would be disappointing indeed.

"You sound more like someone eager to marry me than to wait a year or two and see if we're right for each other," she said slowly, not totally sure what she wanted to hear him say at this point.

"I like roast lamb, and curried vegetables," Scyles said slowly, and Arga blinked in confusion. Was he comparing her to supper? He saw her expression and hurried to continue. "If I decided this morning when I woke, that I wanted roasted lamb and curried vegetables, and knew that if the day went right, I would have it for supper. That doesn't mean I want that meal for breakfast, and in the mid-morning, or even for lunch. It means if I rise, do my work, do the things necessary throughout the day, my reward that night could be lamb and vegetables. But if I don't do the right things, such as butchering the lamb, making sure I have vegetables, and the curry marinade, doing everything I should, I might have cold mutton and a turnip for dinner. Or, worse, go without."

"You're comparing marrying me to cooking supper," she said, shaking her head in dumb wonder.

"That may not be the best example," Scyles began and stopped as she turned to stare at him. "Okay, it is not a good example. But my point is, I do not wish to marry now. If circumstances forced us to change our minds, I would not find you to be a repulsive choice."

"Oh, so you don't find me too repulsive," Arga said, and wondered that she was enjoying teasing him so much. "I suppose that is a step up from being supper."

Scyles sighed, and looked around the room.

"They are going to end this shortly, and we need to talk, without worrying about listening ears," he said, and looked at her. "Are you tired?"

"Not at all," she admitted, and realized it was true. "I couldn't sleep if I tried, probably for hours yet. And we do need to talk. I do not wish to leave this at trying to decide if I'm supper or not completely repulsive."

Scyles laughed, and smiled at her sheepishly.

"I am sorry," he said, looking around the room. "I find myself continuously watching people, trying to keep our conversation between just us, and I can not talk to you intelligently under these conditions. You require all my attention, and it is what you deserve. I will escort you back to your yurt when this finishes, and then sneak back into your camp to get you. Can you find a way to change into older clothes, and get out of your yurt without getting caught?"

"Why do you wish me in older clothes?" Arga asked suspiciously, looking down at what she was wearing.

She had a long open-fronted skirt, a very dark blue, that looked elegant, yet gave her freedom of movement, with a burgundy kurta heavily embroidered with gold thread and plaques sewn into the fabric, with a wide black belt liberally adorned with small, round, golden metal plates and a wide beaten gold circular buckle. Her long-sleeved tunic was also dark blue.

She wore a traditional Scoloti calathos, a cone-shaped hat with a broad band of fur around the brow. It also had numerous gold platelets adorning the basket-shaped cone. She wore her best boots, a golden tan with darker bands crusted with dark platelets, and heavily embroidered with black thread.

These were her finest clothes, and she thought she looked very attractive. Although that wasn't her intention, she thought with a glimmer of self-doubt.

She looked at him suspiciously. He looked very nice in what was probably his best clothing. Brown felt trousers with liberal gold embroidery, matching loose-necked tunic, and a black kurta, again heavily embroidered in gold threads and patches. His dark brown boots looked very comfortable, and she suspected he'd gone for comfort over his best looking boots.

Something she should have done, she decided, flexing her feet, eager to free them from these boots that were still stiff with newness.

"Nothing is wrong with your clothing. You look beautiful," he said. "And dangerous, very daunting," he hurried to say, as if sensing she would not be trivialized. "But if we're going to be sneaking around in the dark, do you really wish to wear your best feast clothes?"

"What about you?" she asked, although she saw the sense in his words, and suspected she knew what he was about to say. He didn't disappoint her.

"I have a change of clothing with my horse, along with my bow and other things," he assured her. "After I return you and your mother to your yurt, I will go back into our tribal camp area, change, and come for you on foot. Wear something dark, if you can," he said, almost as an afterthought.

"Where are you taking me?" she asked, smiling in spite of herself. "And do you really think you can sneak into our camp, undetected, and make off with the enormously popular and beloved princess?"

Scyles smiled at her and didn't answer.

Chapter Seven

Scyles finished tightening his boots, stood upright and considered. He wore black trousers and tunic, and a dark brown kurta. He'd decided against wearing a hat because it would stick up too high, and he would be prone to knocking it off. Instead, he wore a leather headband, with his dark hair pulled back and tied into a long ponytail.

He considered what weapons he should take, and decided his usual knives had to be part of his wardrobe, as well as the long narrow axe tucked into his dark-brown belt. Of course, he had his sling around his neck, looking all the world like a boring necklace with a leather pouch as a pendant.

He eyed his swords and gorytos wistfully. Traipsing around the woods and hills without them would make him feel vulnerable, but wearing them would almost certainly spoil the mood, as well as make it more difficult for him to be as silent as the little mouse in the field.

He led Earth Runner across the hard, rocky ground, carefully brushing the ground behind him with a small branch. Scyles tied him with a loose knot in the middle of a clump of bushes. The knot would come loose if his horse tried it, but unless he was gone for a very long time, or something happened to frighten it, the stallion would stay where he was, and probably sleep standing.

Scyles started making his way westward, picking hard surfaces where he left no tracks, loosely towards Arga's family yurt. He exhaled in frustration and went back for his swords and gorytos. He didn't feel comfortable being responsible for Arga's safety without his weapons, and would feel naked without them.

Anyway, if he were in hostile territory, with enemies all around, he would have to move quietly, with all his weapons. Making it easier for himself for convenience was a dish he did not relish.

Fifteen minutes later, he found her, crouching behind a cart, watching the direction she assumed he would come from. He silently made his way close behind her, and stopped, debating how to let her know he was there without startling her. Covering her mouth with a hand seemed a great way to lose a finger or two.

Finally, he reached down and picked up a tiny pebble and tossed it so it struck her shoulder. She turned, saw him in the starlight, nodded, and made her way across the small stretch of open ground to him.

He led her out of the camp the way he came in, stopping her several times. They crouched behind what little cover there was, both times, waiting while a guard walked by once, and while a man made his way to the fenced latrine area. They quickly left him to his needs and made their way out of the camp.

Scyles put a finger over his mouth and she nodded. They made their way through bushes and shallow gullies, winding a crooked path until he could see the hill ahead.

Arga saw it about the same time, and looked at him. He understood what she wanted to know, and whispered that as long as they were quiet, they were okay. There were no sentries anywhere near them at the moment.

"Is that the same hill as this afternoon?" Arga asked, looking at it with a doubtful expression on her face.

"No, this is the taller one closer to the river," Scyles said, and elaborated. "I figure they won't expect us to go farther into your territory. Most of them seem to be farther to the west and north of us."

"Most of them?" Arga looked at him in surprise. "Are they already out looking for us? For me?"

Scyles grinned at her and led her around a couple boulders to a small path he knew was there from last year, and they made their way up toward the crest of the hill. A group of three trees were clumped near the southern edge of the small flat area on the top.

"There are a lot of sentries, including a good number of scouts, on both sides of the boundary between our two tribes, men and women from both tribes," Scyles said. "I think they anticipated that we would wish to spend more time together tonight."

"Should I return to my camp, so you do not get into trouble?" Arga asked, sounding disappointed. "I suppose they do not wish us coordinating our rebellion against their marriage plans."

"I think you removed that from their immediate concerns with your speech tonight at the feast," Scyles said dryly. "No, they already know you're not in the camp, so there is nothing you can do to change that. I believe they are more concerned that we might be behaving in a way not totally suitable for an unmarried young prince and princess in the dark woods without supervision."

"Oh," Arga said, and didn't say more.

Scyles risked a look at her as he pulled a piece of wood close to a good-sized boulder and offered it to her as a seat. She sat down, still looking deep in thought, and he sat on the ground next to her, crossing his legs, and leaning back against the boulder.

She sat on the log for a while, then moved over to sit next to him, leaning on the boulder, their shoulders not quite touching.

They looked up at the stars, enjoying the beauty of the sky and the silence and comfort of the hill's asylum, watching the nearly full moon begin to peek over the horizon.

"So, did you bring me here to seduce me?" she finally asked, speaking slowly, clearly taking great care with her words.

"We've been here some time, and I've made no move," Scyles pointed out. "If I did, I'm not doing a very good job of it."

"Oh, I don't know," Arga said, and took his hand in hers. "You could have done much worse. I find this very comfortable."

"But if I did seduce you, I would be betraying your trust, and taking away your ability to choose when and with whom, you will mate," Scyles pointed out. "I could never betray your trust in such a way."

Arga said nothing, and they sat quietly for a while.

"You are very different from any of the young men or boys in my tribe," Arga began, then shrugged. "Or any other tribe, for that matter. You speak differently, you act differently, your ideas and thoughts are…unusual."

"My parents wanted me to have a more complete understanding of the world outside the People," Scyles said, and frowned. That didn't really say what he meant. He tried again.

"They brought a Grecian teacher to instruct me in ideas and events happening beyond our view," Scyles began, and smiled. "Two different times and teachers."

"What happened to the first one?" she asked curiously.

"He was very good at first, demanding, but he knew ideas, and philosophies being explored beyond our borders, by the Grecians, the Mitsri, the Persians. He called himself a philosopher."

"What does that mean?" Arga asked, and he could hear the genuine interest in her voice.

"As far as my first instructor goes, it meant defiler of little boys," Scyles said grimly. "I had seen ten gatherings at that point, and resisted. He slapped me and I stabbed him in the thigh." He smiled, without humor. "He was bleeding very much when my father came and found me standing over him, with my knife in hand."

"What did King Gelon do?" Arga asked, sitting sideways, watching him in fascination.

"He found out what Eugenius wanted me to do, which was put his male part in my mouth, and forced him to find out what it was like to have it in his own mouth," Scyles said, feeling his face twist into a caricature of its usual pleasant expression.

"He was big enough for that to be possible?" Arga asked, shocked, but looking intrigued.

"It is very possible, if you remove it first," Scyles said, and Arga laughed out loud, and looked around guiltily at the sound she'd made. "He didn't survive the experience, although my father said it was my cut that killed him. He bled quite freely from the wound."

"Good," Arga said, and he started at the vehemence in her voice.

"That was my first kill," Scyles said, and she nodded and sat back. She looked over again, curiously.

"And the second teacher? Did he learn from the mistakes of the first?"

"Yes," Scyles said, and laughed. "Mother and Father made very sure he knew exactly what happened to Eugenius, and why. He was my teacher for three years."

"What happened to him?" Arga asked, and he could tell she expected the worse.

"The agreement had been for three years, and ended. He missed his people and home, and wished to return to Athens." Scyles closed his eyes and easily pictured the old man. "I have often prayed to the gods he made it home safely."

"But you don't know for sure?" she asked softly, and he shook his head. "I shall pray for him, too. What was his name?"

"Theophilus," Scyles said, and felt pain at the loss of his childhood friend.

Arga nodded, and leaned back, facing forward again. They both sat quietly for a while until she finally spoke.

"The Caitiari are a threat to both tribes, and our being stubborn is putting our people in danger, isn't it?" she asked, her voice impossible for him to read.

"Our parents think so," Scyles admitted. "Our kings think so. But still, we have a right to choose our destiny."

"Do we? Do we really?" Arga sounded agonized. "We are royal born, and are expected to perform our duties, both to family and our tribes. And, for that matter, to our kings as well. Are we being selfish?"

She turned to look at him, leaning slightly against him.

"What about your parents? Was it arranged?"

"No, my mother was from a tribe that was decimated by hordes of northern invaders. She came into our family as my father's wife with almost nothing in the way of a dowry, or anything, other than the clothes on her back." Scyles smiled and stared at the stars, remembering his parents telling him this story. "My father was immediately smitten with her. He was forbidden to see her again, and told he would marry a maiden from an obscure tribe in the eastern steppes."

He laughed.

"He married her, and consummated the marriage immediately," he said. "My oldest brother was conceived that night."

"If my parents were clever, they would forbid us from seeing each other," she said, and they both laughed. "We'd marry, just to spite them."

"Only if we were in love," Scyles qualified, and she turned her head to stare at him. He looked down at her and shrugged. "I will only marry for love. If it falls in line with duty, all the better."

"We might find ourselves forced to marry sooner than we wish, to protect both tribes," Arga pointed out.

"We might," Scyles agreed, then winced and held his breath. He had unwittingly talked himself into a corner, and knew she was clever enough to see it.

"Hmm," she said, and her head leaned against his shoulder. Their hands were close, resting loosely on their respective legs. Slowly, Scyles started to reach out for hers, and found her hand already doing the same thing.

They clasped hands and sat without speaking. Scyles wished he knew what she was thinking, but she didn't seem inclined to talk at the moment. He decided he could wait her out. It wasn't like sitting here, holding her hand with her head on his shoulder was any kind of hardship.

They heard someone grunt and start swearing on the other hill, and Scyles began to laugh. Arga shifted her head upward so she could see his face.

"What did you do?" she asked, and he grinned down at her, liking her smile very much at that moment.

"While we were on the other hill this afternoon, I might have tied a bush around so if someone inspected our lunch site in the dark, they might release the tie, causing the bush to swing around and slap them, hard," he admitted, and she giggled. Then she lowered her head back against his shoulder and sighed.

"So, was it poor choice in wording, or did you confess to loving me a few minutes ago?" she asked, and Scyles winced. He really didn't want to get this wrong, but he couldn't lie to her either. He would not lie to her.

"Arga, I think we will marry, at some point." He took a deep breath and continued before he lost his nerve. "If you so chose, I would marry you tomorrow, gladly. But if you choose to spend a year or two deciding, I accept that as your right and a reasonable decision. I will wait for you."

She didn't say anything for a moment, then looked up at him again, a sly look on her face.

"You did not answer my question," she pointed out and squeezed his hand.

"No, I didn't," he admitted. He took a deep breath and took the plunge.

"I am in love with you, dear Arga." Scyles felt light-headed with the joy and fear of uttering those words. "I didn't even know it until today, but I am. And I'm not even sure at what point it happened or when I realized it. But I do."

She didn't say anything, and he felt depressed. He knew he'd just doomed any chance of ever having her become his wife, and he didn't know what else he could have done.

"This doesn't really change anything," he said, hearing the lunacy of his own words, but rushing ahead anyway. "It is still your decision, and whatever you decide does not change my feelings for you. I know it feels like I betrayed your trust, and…"

He stopped as she put her fingers across his lips.

"Stop speaking," she said, and he did. Her hand moved from his lips to his cheek, and she cupped it tenderly. "Whether we marry tomorrow, or a year from tomorrow, it will be to each other. Our lives and fates are as firmly intertwined as this embroidery," she said, fingering the threads on her kurta. "I find myself, despite my best intentions, in love with you as well."

They stared into each other's eyes, and their faces began to move closer, and he saw her close her eyes in anticipation.

Then he heard the sound of a small rock, rolling on the hill below them. Grimacing, he placed a finger on her lips, causing her eyes to pop open in surprise. He grinned at her sheepishly, and pointed down the hill with his head.

She nodded and they rose to a crouch and she followed him as he led her down the front face of the hill, moving slowly, making sure of their footing. When they reached the bottom of the hill, he started to steer her around towards her camp, but she pulled him to a halt.

"Just in case they catch us," she said quietly, and they kissed.

Then they were creeping, moving from bush to bush, until they were in the scrub trees and able to speed up the pace.

Scyles was in some sort of heaven or Valhalla, or perhaps on Mount Olympus. The taste of her lips clung to his, and he had to deliberately put the memory away, so he did not accidentally reveal their position, while daydreaming of many more kisses with her.

He liked that she easily kept pace with him, trotting briskly. It was a good solid pace for crossing miles in good time.

She felt his eyes upon her and blushed as she looked at him. She looked ahead and saw what looked like men with torches between them and the camp.

"Can you really get me back to camp, and get away without being caught or seen?" she asked, and he could hear the doubt in her voice.

He smiled at her as they ran.

Targitai wouldn't easily admit it, but Scyles had managed to impress him. They'd found his horse, and thought he might come back to it with the princess, but he hadn't. In fact, he'd left it as a lure to tie up men. He was sure of it. Wherever he and the girl had gone, they'd walked.

Which made more sense if you were trying to remain unseen. Especially if there were two of you. Plus, the entire area of the two camps wasn't so large it couldn't easily be walked fairly quickly.

So, Scyles rode away from the camp, passed the sentries on the border, found a hiding spot for the horse, changed clothes, probably into dark, older clothing he could writhe around on the ground in, and went back to Princess Arga's camp.

She somehow managed to sneak out of the yurt, and had probably also changed into older clothing. He couldn't see her running around in the dark, wearing the beautiful outfit she'd worn at the feast. They either designated a meeting point, or he happened upon her, and then he spirited her out of the camp, and went to...

And that was where things got confusing. They had no idea where the two went.

Or what they did, when they got there, he thought, trying to feel grim, but having a hard time resisting laughing.

Targitai decided he would confer with Ariapithes, and see if they'd had better luck. He whistled the sound of the thrush, and heard an immediate response to the west. He walked up to the sentries on the border between the two tribes, nodded and passed them without a word.

Within two minutes he met up with King Orik's swordmaster. They glared at each other for a moment, and burst into laughter.

"So, old enemy, where are they?" he asked, and Ariapithes shrugged.

"We found where he came up behind her, inside the camp, and followed their tracks out and south until we hit the rocky terrain leading to the hills."

"Which one did you decide to search first?" Targitai asked, and Ariapithes made a face and grunted.

"I decided to give the boy a chance and have my young protégé decide how to lead the search. He chose the same hill they lunched upon."

Targitai shook his head. "I would bet three good horses Scyles took them up the taller hill tonight," he said, and Ariapithes nodded sagely.

"I expected the same, and we are right," he admitted, and then told about the snare the boy had set on the first hill.

They both had a good laugh at that.

"That man will have a red face for a few days, both from embarrassment and from the impact of the branches slapping him," Ariapithes said, smiling. "It is a good lesson for him. A real enemy and he would be dead now."

"So, were you able to catch him on the other hill?" Targitai asked, and wasn't surprised when Ariapithes shook his head.

"I believe he heard the trap go off, and they went down the south face," he said, and stepped closer to Targitai and lowered his voice. "I found where the two of them sat, very close, very close, for some time. But no sign of, oh, active movement on the ground, rolling, or stretching, or..."

"I understand your words," Targitai said, holding up his hands in submission. "So, my boy retained his honor, and didn't remove hers."

"Something I am both surprised and happy to see," Ariapithes admitted. He cleared his throat. "From where they came down the hill, swinging west around it and then due north would have gotten them to the camp fairly quickly, if with a slightly greater chance of being discovered. But he took her east, around the south side of the smaller hill, and then swung north, very close to the border between us."

Targitai grimaced.

"Did he somehow convince her to return to his yurt?" Targitai asked, wincing. Taking the girl's maidenhood on a romantic hilltop under the stars was one thing. Taking her back to his hides, would almost certainly result in their getting discovered, and the sense of outrage at displaying her dishonor would be tremendous.

"No," Ariapithes said, and laughed at the expression he saw on Targitai's face. "He did a large circle and brought her back to our camp, almost the same way he took her out." He shrugged. "No one was watching for them from that direction."

"So she's back in her yurt?"

"I would assume so, and will know shortly," Ariapithes said and a rueful expression came to his face. "The idea of both having to ask the king or queen if their daughter is where she belongs, and explain how this stripling managed to befuddle my best men and yours for hours, does not appeal to me."

"I don't imagine," Targitai said, trying to keep a straight face, and failing completely. He started laughing, and after a moment, his friend of many years joined in.

They walked past their guards on the border and it only took a few minutes to reach the grove of scrub trees where the horse was concealed.

"Show yourselves," Targitai said, and four men came out of nowhere. He nodded, approving their dedication on a task that was, in truth, merely an exercise in executing a manhunt.

He and Ariapithes walked into the grove, expecting to see Scyles' horse. It was gone.

The two men looked at each other for a moment, and Targitai held up his hand in warning.

"Guards, here, now." He kept any annoyance out of his voice. It really wasn't that hard, since the entire evening had degenerated into some sort of farce.

The four men approached, and looked around for the horse, blanching when they realized it was gone.

"May I safely assume one or more of you assisted Prince Scyles, or did he manage to pass all four of you, collect his horse, and somehow get past all of you, for a second time, with the horse in hand?"

The four men looked at each other, and the leader of the group sighed and bowed his head. "No one helped the prince, Swordmaster," he said. "It is all my…"

"Enough," Targitai kept his voice neutral. After all, they did fail. "Return to the camp, get yourselves something to eat, and get some rest. Tomorrow we have far more serious challenges facing us."

They fled without a word.

He looked at his old friend, and they both laughed, and shook their heads. Finally, Ariapithes looked at him, a smile on his face.

"As mortified as I am, I am glad Princess Arga has found her future husband, and that it is Scyles. He is a very impressive young man."

Targitai looked skeptically at his friend.

"Do you think so?" he asked doubtfully. "Your princess seemed to close that door firmly this evening at the feast."

"Tomorrow, watch the way they are aware of each other, the way they look at each other, how often they somehow manage to touch," Ariapithes said, looking a little envious. "They are in love, whether they know it or not. I do not see it taking until next gathering for them to marry."

"How did you become so wise in the way of women?" Targitai asked, grinning.

"I have found true love four times, and can see the signs in their face and voice," Ariapithes said confidently.

"You've only ever had one wife," Targitai said, confused. He knew his old friend's wife well, and knew she adored him, and he, her.

"Yes, but she left me three times," Ariapithes pointed out. He looked thoughtful. "It gets harder to convince her to fall in love with me each time. Perhaps it is time to settle down," he mused, and Targitai had to laugh.

He embraced his friend, and slapped his shoulder as they parted.

"You go back and take the ridicule from your king, and I go to report to mine."

Targitai grinned at Ariapithes.

"I think I have the easier task. I have to tell my king how impressive his son is."

Orik lay on his back, Opis tucked under his arm. They were under the soft felt covers, even though there was little chill in the air. The covers were pulled just above their waists. They were both nude, in the act of recovering from an enthusiastic bout of love-making, and still sweating profusely.

"I wonder if we should be embarrassed that our passions were sparked by watching our daughter and her future husband play their little game," Opis said drowsily, almost asleep.

Orik opened his mouth to say something rude, but heard the hide over the entrance rustle as it was opened. His mouth snapped shut and he waited.

Hours earlier, Opis had said they should set a trap to awaken them when their daughter tried to sneak back in. He'd put some dancer cymbals in her bedding, so when she tried to shift the covers to get in, they would ring.

He could barely sense movement beyond the hanging wall between their bedding and Arga's. Then he heard a single ring, clear and loud, and Arga, muttering under her breath.

"Goodnight, Arga," Opis said, definitely awake now. He could see the laughter in her eyes. "I hope you and Scyles had a fun evening. You'll have to tell us all about it when we break our fast."

She put a hand over her mouth, and Orik could see she was having trouble keeping from laughing out loud. Her body shook a little as she did so, and Orik gasped as she incidentally vibrated against some sensitive parts of his body.

She immediately sensed his reaction and looked over at him, her expression changing from humorous to something more akin to lust. She reached down to verify at least one part of him was fully awake, and smiled at her discovery.

Without much resistance, he gave in to her lustful intentions.

Arga lifted the doorway cover just enough to allow her to slip inside, and quietly made her way to the partitioned area with her sleeping robes and felt covers. She quickly removed her clothes and pulled a full gown of felt over her head.

She smoothed the cloth out, silently enjoying the feel of her hands running over parts of her body, and pictured Scyles as the one using his hands to such good purpose.

Resisting her urges tonight had been far harder than she would have believed. She was pretty sure that if the searchers hadn't gotten so close, she would have surrendered her maidenhood on that hilltop.

She was mildly surprised and amused that the thought didn't disturb her.

She laid down and began to pull the covers over to let her slip beneath them and sensed something sitting on the covers just a moment too late to prevent a single tone from ringing out, clear as the night sky.

"Couldn't the gods have helped me out just this one time," she muttered, and heard a stirring in the next partitioned area where her parents slept.

"Good night, Arga. I hope you and Scyles had a fun evening. You'll have to tell us all about it over breakfast."

Not in this lifetime, she vowed silently. She set the cymbals away from her covers and pulled them up to her chin. The vision of Scyles came to her unbidden, and she didn't try to dispel it, either.

Then she heard a rustling from her parent's bedding, and a low laugh, and groaned.

Really, she thought. After the passionate night she didn't quite have, they were now going to torment her with their own lovemaking, and she would have to listen to it?

She pulled an extra blanket to her and tried to block her ears, wrapping it about her head, her arms holding it firmly in place.

For a moment, she thought it was working, but then she could hear the hoarse sound of their heavy breathing, and her mother made a whimpering sound of pleasure.

I have terrible, mean, sadistic, cruel parents, she thought as she closed her eyes in resignation.

Chapter Eight

Scyles purposefully came into the camp from the south, thinking he might be able to enter without anyone recognizing him. Not that it really mattered at this point. He was back at the camp, Arga was safe in hers, and they had done nothing wrong. But he'd started something and wanted to finish it successfully.

He'd walked Earth Runner after sneaking him away from the four guards. There was no way he could disguise the sound of a running horse, so why try? He decided to walk the stallion the rest of the way.

There were a couple men riding in the south gate, and he edged up close behind them and no one said a word to him. He separated from them soon after they were inside, and made his way to where his family's herd was being grazed. There was a boy a couple years younger than he, feeding and watering horses as they were returned, and Scyles turned his over to him without saying a word.

The boy didn't even look up, and Scyles was sure he didn't know who'd brought the horse in.

Scyles walked without hurrying back to their yurt next to the main dining tent the feast had been at. He was debating trying to sneak in, but didn't particularly wish to get killed by his father mistaking him for an intruder, so he walked right up to the front entrance. Fooling his tribesmen, and Arga's as well, was one thing. Trying to fool his father was another entirely.

He was surprised to not see a guard. Even though the camp was secure, the king's tent always had at least two guards on duty, one at the front, the other at the back. Scyles went around the side of the yurt, and saw something on the ground, tucked up against the tent wall.

It was the bodies of the two guards. Both had their throats slit.

Scyles opened his mouth to cry out an alarm and then snapped it shut again. The killer might be very close, perhaps even inside their yurt this very moment. He had his gorytos with his bow and arrows, but wasn't going to let shafts fly in a confined area anywhere near his mother. Instead, he pulled his necklace off, slipped the little string of hide loose, and it was now his sling. There was already a round stone, carefully picked days ago, in the pouch. He pulled out his short sword with his left hand, careful not to make a sound as it slid out of its sheath.

He began to swing the sling, even as he found the seam where the large strips of cloth were tied together. He took a deep breath and slashed down the seam with all his might.

Cutting the ties released tension and the two sides sagged, opening a large enough gap for him to leap into the yurt. Just outside his parents curtained off sleeping area, a dark figure crouched, holding what appeared to be a knife in his or her right hand.

The killer whirled, and flipped the knife to reverse it. Scyles had interrupted him just as he was about to creep to his parents' bedside. Now he was spinning, faster than Scyles would have believed possible, his arm already coming forward.

Scyles didn't hesitate.

He let the rock that had been in the pouch fly, as hard as he could, and it flew true. It careened off the cheekbone of the man, and his knife flew wide, yet close enough Scyles felt the wind of its passing.

The man was wearing traditional Scoloti clothing, loose trousers, tunic, and kurta, all in black, but what was not traditional was the hood over his head, and the swath of black cloth covering his entire face, save his eyes.

The stone bounced off the cheekbone and tore into his nose, and the man staggered. Even so, he still managed to draw both his swords.

Scyles didn't hesitate and leaped forward, slashing across the two blades before the man got set. As he did so, he also swung the sling, empty now, across the other's face, striking his nose almost as effectively as a whip.

The man swore in pain, and Scyles' sword slapped both the other's blades aside, causing the man to lose his grip on his long sword, but in the process, Scyles also lost his own blade. He drew both his knives from his thigh sheathes, and when the man tried to counterattack, managed to parry his short sword with both knives, locking them together.

Scyles was face to face with him, perhaps his forearm's length apart, for a moment, and they glared at each other. Then Scyles slashed out with his left hand, and the sharp edge of his knife pierced the other's kurta as if it were butter. He managed to lock his other blade with the assassin's, and stabbed with his left hand, burying the knife in the intruder's side.

The man faltered, and Scyles flung himself forward, knocking the man backwards into his parent's sleeping quarters. The man, even while injured, was stronger than Scyles, and shoved him off, and started to roll to his feet.

Scyles let his second knife fly, and the man raised his left hand with the sword to block it, but missed, and the knife went right through the back of his hand. The man roared in pain and rage, and tried to take his sword into his right hand, but Scyles' father slammed the flat of his axe on the side of his head, and the man slumped to the carpets, dazed.

His father's face was a picture of fury as he kicked the man in the side, then pulled him up enough to strike a mighty blow to his head, knocking him unconscious.

Scyles and his father stared at each other over the body of the enemy, and he was awed to watch his father slowly regain control. He was totally naked, and his long, thick black hair was unbraided, and hung over his shoulders, almost to his waist.

"Are you injured?" he asked thickly, and Scyles mutely shook his head. His father looked closer at the unconscious man, and saw his face, then the two knife handles sticking out of him, and he nodded, smiling grimly.

His mother was arranging a blanket to cover her own nakedness, and she looked at the man on the carpet with horror. Her attention shifted to Scyles, and her eyes flitted from limb to limb, looking for injuries. Her relief was palpable when she finally met his eyes. Then her expression turned to anger.

His father pulled a robe on, and felt Scyles watching him. He grinned crookedly and glanced at Scyles' mother.

"We thought you might like a little brother or sister," he said, and winced when she backhanded him on the arm. She was in no mood to make jokes, or listen to them, Scyles saw.

Targitai rushed into the yurt, drawn bow in hand, his eyes searching for an enemy. More men followed him, and at his gesture, gripped the man and lifted him to his feet.

"Where are the guards?" Scyles' father said thickly, and Targitai shook his head that he didn't know.

"They're both dead, on the south side of the yurt, next to where I came in," Scyles said, his voice sounding shaky to him. He stepped forward and took his knives back, wiping the blood off as well as he could on the front of the assassin's kurta. Then he did the same with his short sword.

The men stared at him, and he wondered why. Targitai turned to one and gestured with his head. The man went out the hole Scyles had made coming in.

Scyles found his sling, and opened his pouch and began looking at the stones, trying to find the most perfectly round one. He decided one would do, and put it in the sling's pouch and made it into a necklace again, tucking it under his tunic.

"You didn't draw your long sword?" his father asked, his fury almost under control now.

"To cut the seam, I felt the short sword would allow me a stronger swing, since I had to use my left hand," Scyles said. "I wanted to be able to let the stone fly the moment I saw whoever was inside."

"You didn't draw it after losing the short sword?" his father pressed him, and he knew what he was thinking.

"We were at close quarters, and I felt having both knives would give me an advantage," Scyles said, and shrugged. "I was busy, and didn't have time to think about it."

His father and Targitai exchanged looks that Scyles couldn't read, and he wondered if they thought he'd made a bad decision. He really hadn't had time. Everything had happened on instinct from the moment he first swung the short sword.

"See what you can find out from him," his father said to Targitai, who nodded.

"He is a guild assassin, probably from Persia, and I will almost certainly not be able to get him to reveal who hired him," Targitai said, and his father nodded.

"I think we know who hired him," his mother said, her shaking voice showing her fury was still in full force. "That bastard, King Agathyrsus, has gone too far this time."

"Proving that will be difficult," Targitai said, and looked at his king. "A challenge would be risky."

"You don't think your king can defeat him?" Scyles' mother asked in a deceptively quiet voice, and the swordmaster winced. Scyles didn't blame him. He knew that tone.

"I'm sure he can, or he can have me do it." Targitai grinned without mirth. "I know I can. But so does he. No, he will never accept a direct challenge."

Everyone stood still, looking at each other for a long moment, and then, as if on cue, they all looked at Scyles. He flinched in alarm.

"What?" he asked, nervously shifting from foot to foot.

None of them responded immediately. As he watched them, their moods gradually lightened.

"How was your evening, young prince?" Targitai asked in a neutral tone, and all three adults laughed when Scyles flinched. The swordmaster looked at his parents with amusement. "I was coming to see if you were still awake, and wanted my report on how I spent my night."

"Anything you would like to tell us, son?" his father asked, and Scyles snorted.

"No," he answered honestly. "But I am tired and think I will try to get some sleep after I repair the outer wall I damaged."

"Leave it," his father said firmly. "We will take care of it in the morning."

"I can do it…" Scyles began, and stopped as his mother raised her hand.

"Scyles, you know we have horses that can sew better than you," she said, her anger finally abated. "Are you sure there isn't anything you'd like to tell us about how you spent your evening?"

"Very sure," Scyles said with feeling, and went to his sleeping quarters.

Scyles lay under his bedsheets, thinking about the evening. He tried to clear his mind and fall asleep, but the vision of Arga sitting next to him, her head on his shoulder, their holding hands, would not go away.

He finally gave up after several hours of tossing and turning. Rising, he put his breechcloth on and went to the water trough, and rinsed himself. He then rubbed oils into his skin, rubbing hard to loosen muscles tight from tension. Then he went back to his sleeping quarters and dressed, choosing to dress for comfort. He would change when the Caitiari began to arrive. He'd hoped to get a good night's sleep, so he would be at his sharpest when dealing with King Agathyrsus, but freshened would have to do.

Perhaps the gods had a plan, and required him to be dull-witted for it to succeed, he thought dourly. Oddly enough, the idea cheered him.

He went to the main yurt to see if there was any food laid out yet. He was mildly surprised at the number of his tribesmen that were clumped together at several of the long, low tables, eating out of bowls. He saw a group of the warrior women at their own table, their stares stopping any men considering sitting near them. A few older women brought fresh bowls of food out, probably cold leftovers from the feast last night.

He sat on the carpets at one of the tables with a cluster of men sitting at the other end. He chose a spot not so removed to imply any disdain to join them, but just distant enough to make conversation difficult.

An old woman brought him a bowl with a good-sized hunk of bread, and some cold meat, as well as a mug of mare's milk. Scyles looked at the mug and raised an eyebrow, and she shook her head, smiling at him.

"No, Prince Scyles, it is not fermented. It only left the mare a few minutes ago," she said, and winked at him. "This could be a very big day for you, and you'll need all your wits about you." She leaned over and whispered. "You've got all the men in a lather about the chase you led them on last night."

"Chase?" Scyles asked in an innocent tone. "I escorted the princess back to her tents and then returned here." He shrugged. "I did stop and admire the clear night skies and the beauty of the gods a little more than usual, but it was a quiet eve."

She laughed as she straightened.

"I hope you're more convincing with the men that that, young prince."

He watched her stroll briskly to the back of the tent, and wondered if she was exaggerating. That thought didn't last long.

The men at the end of the table allowed him to take a few bites, and drink some milk, then, as one, moved down to sit around him.

Lik slumped down across the table from him. He was two years older than Scyles, and leaned forward on the table with a look of anticipation.

"Scyles, the yurts are abuzz about you this morning, and last night, truth be told," he said, and nudged the man next to him. "Rumor is, you had an exciting evening, both playing with the sentries of both tribes, and the Princess Arga as well."

"I don't know what you mean, Lik, but I would be very careful saying anyone was doing anything with the princess. She has a father with a temper, and Ariapithes has a kill list longer than all your parts, laid end to end." Scyles tried to deflect attention to the other. "And that includes that tiny little one that disappoints so many women."

The other men at the table laughed dutifully, but their focus didn't change, and Scyles sighed inside. He didn't care to lie to his tribesmen, but his actions of the night before were not open to discussion, at least not by him.

Before anyone had a chance to say anything, a group of about eight men entered the tent, wearing kurtas showing them to be Paralatae. They looked around the yurt, as if wondering if anyone would complain, and then picked out an empty table and began removing their sword scabbards and gorytos.

Scyles didn't pay them close attention, once he saw that there were no royal family members among them. He almost didn't notice one, a tall, heavily muscled, young man perhaps a year or two older than himself, recognize him. But the man, in the action of lowering his gorytos to join his swords at his feet, froze, and his face immediately flushed with anger.

He dropped his things, and began to circle around the tables, making his way directly to Scyles. His fellow Paralatae saw who he was fixated on, and looked at each other with poorly concealed glee. Scyles noticed several of his own tribesmen begin to rise to their feet, but they were too slow.

The man sped up his pace, and Scyles cursed, and rolled away from the table to his feet, just in time to meet the man's rush.

"You foul the name and reputation of the princess, and think you will steal her away from us!" he shouted and threw himself at Scyles, swinging wildly with his left hand.

Scyles didn't quite get to his feet before the man's first blow struck his head a glancing blow. He spun away, taking the force of the blow indirectly, rolling over to come to his hands and knees. It was a hard blow, and stung him mightily, but not a solid contact, and didn't do any damage. He rose off his knees to a position on all fours, and charged straight into the larger man, using his legs to drive the man back, off his feet.

They both landed, with the other man on the bottom, and Scyles heard the air come out of his lungs with a loud gasp. He kept driving forward, rolling the man, keeping him off balance, until he was able to end up on his back, the man laying across the top of him, facing up.

Scyles had his right arm, under the other's same, with his right hand gripping the back of the man's neck. This forced the man's right arm to stick straight up, unable to move. Scyles had his left arm around the front of the man's neck, holding his own right tricep, cutting his breathing off. His left leg pinioned the left arm of his attacker, making his options very limited.

The man tried to buck him off, but he held on, steadily increasing the force on the man's throat.

"I do not wish to kill you," he whispered in the man's ear. "Troubling times are coming, and I would have you as an ally, a friend."

The man snarled, and didn't stop trying to tear himself loose. Scyles increased the pressure all around, and the man gasped. He was already getting low on air, and his strength was beginning to wane.

"I know you admire your princess, and can understand why. But you must know, our marriage is inevitable," Scyles said quietly, trying to keep the men circling them from hearing clearly.

"No!" the man tried to roar, but it came out more as a groan.

"I love her, and will treat her with respect, as she deserves. She also loves me. Nothing happened last night between us." Scyles hesitated, and gambled. "We will be married, possibly as soon as this eve. You can not change that. But it will be a good union, and we both already love each other. She will make a great queen of the Auchatae. We would have your friendship, both of us."

The man said nothing, and still struggled, but was on the verge of passing out. Scyles was listening closely, not wanting to accidentally kill the young man. His anger was based on a misperception, and genuine feelings for his princess. Arga had mentioned him last night. This reaction wasn't totally his fault, and he didn't deserve death.

"Yield," he whispered. "There is no dishonor in this. We would welcome your friendship and support. Please yield."

He stopped struggling, as if startled to hear the plea in Scyles' voice. They both lay immobile for a moment, then he deliberately slapped the carpet with his left hand. It wasn't a very loud or strong slap, but Scyles felt it and immediately loosened his grip on the man's neck.

He pushed him over to their left, and rolled to the right, coming to his feet facing his adversary. He waited to see if the capitulation was real, or just a ploy to get loose.

The man lay on his back for a moment, then clumsily rolled over to rise to his hands and knees. He stayed there, trying to bring his breathing back to normal. He finally raised his head and stared at Scyles, who stood above him.

Scyles gave him a moment, then offered his hand. The man looked at it, and nodded almost imperceptibly, and took it. Scyles helped him to his feet, not releasing his hand.

"I would be your friend." Scyles paused, not knowing what to call him.

"Skulis," he said finally. "My name is Skulis."

He finally straightened to his full height and felt his neck with his free hand. He turned it back and forth, and looked at Scyles ruefully.

"My name is Skulis, and that was a masterful hold," he said, and looked around at the circle of men of both tribes standing around them, waiting to see what happened next. He nodded and turned back to Scyles. "Friend."

Scyles smiled in relief, and clasped his shoulder, and saw Skulis wince. Before he could say anything, the flaps of the entrance flew wide open, and Ariapithes and Targitai strode in purposefully, looking around, both immediately fixating on the two of them. Behind them came the two kings, and Scyles saw Skulis wince.

The circle of tribesmen faded back, giving their leaders room to approach the two fighters.

"We heard reports of a brawl," Ariapithes said, looking around at the other tribesmen, all of whom seemed to remember they had somewhere else to be, and disbursed back to their morning bowls. He turned back to his man.

"And the reports pointed to you as the instigator, Skulis," he said, and the younger man wilted.

Before he could speak, Scyles slapped his hands together, and laughed, although it didn't sound in the least bit authentic to him. Or to the four older men, judging by their expressions.

"I told my good friend Skulis of a wrestling move Targitai recently taught me, and said I could take him down with it, anytime, anywhere," Scyles said, hoping the gods would forgive his lie. "To be fair, I didn't expect him to immediately take my challenge, but it was a good match. You would have enjoyed it."

Targitai took a step forward and stared at him.

"You're teaching men from other tribes my personal techniques of battle?" he said ominously.

Scyles blanched and his mind raced.

"Only one of our friends, the Paralatae, and only my best friend, Skulis," Scyles stammered. "Our tribes are very close, soon to be even closer, and I trust this friend with a secret or two. He is discreet and an ally," Scyles finished lamely.

"Did it work?" His father asked in a mild voice.

"Did it...oh, the wrestling move," Scyles stuttered, startled by his father entering the conversation.

"It worked only too well," Skulis spoke up, covering for him. "He took me down so fast, and put me in a chokehold I couldn't break, I would say it worked well. King Gelon," he finished awkwardly.

"Hmm," said King Orik, glancing at Scyles' father, then back at Skulis. "Did you learn the move? Could he perform it on you again?"

"I learned much, and no, he couldn't use that trick on me again," Skulis said, and glanced at Scyles, a glint of humor in his eyes. "Although, I suspect that isn't the only trick he knows."

The two kings looked at them, then at each other. Without speaking, they went to the royal table they'd sat at last night. Targitai slapped Scyles on the shoulder hard enough, it nearly knocked him down, and followed them.

Ariapithes, the Swordmaster of King Orik, looked at him closely as he passed.

"We will have a conversation sometime soon," he said, and a crooked grin came to his face. "I would like to hear more about your 'tricks' last night."

Without waiting for a response, he followed Targitai.

Scyles and Skulis looked at each other, relief on both their faces. Skulis glanced at the swordmaster, then at him, and cocked his head questioningly.

"I have no idea what he's talking about," Scyles said, and they sat down next to each other at the table. The older woman from earlier brought them both tankards of mare's milk, and Scyles noticed it was fermented.

He decided he'd earned it, and picked them both up, handing one to Skulis.

"Friend," he said, and extended his drink.

"Friend," Skulis answered and they tapped their drinks to each other and drank deeply.

One of the scouts trotted into the yurt, and immediately went to stand before the two kings, speaking in low tones. They looked at each other gravely, and Scyles' father looked at Targitai.

The Swordmaster turned and faced the room.

"The lead elements of the Caitiari have arrived, and the main body is not far behind. It appears to be much bigger than was originally agreed upon.

Scyles and Skulis looked at each other, then at the tankards of fermented milk in their hands. Scyles sighed, and they both set them down.

Chapter Nine

On the Hshtahni Generations Ship Muschwain

Azimoth stood in front of the view screens, looking at an image of the planet below. It was attractive, with large land masses surrounded by more water than Azimoth had ever seen. His home planet was arid, and water was precious. The home planets of the Hshtahni were mostly land masses with modest waterways and small bodies of water interspersed between vast ranges of mountains and desolate terrain.

This planet was practically inundated with the precious commodity. Even the high sodium content of the largest bodies was no problem. Removing sodium from water was common and necessary on most planets.

He sighed and turned to his first officer.

"Release the drones." He enlarged the picture on the screen until only a portion of the planet was visible. He pointed to where the large river flowed past the pyramid constructs into the large interior sea. Then his fingers moved up to the north side of the sea, and waved over a swath of territory.

"We shall look in a colder environment. See if you can find some group, perhaps in migration, close to ten thousand units, including the larger livestock." Azimoth felt his lord enter the bridge and settle into his large cradle area.

"Tell me your logic on where you search, and why?" his Lord spoke, the rumbling causing one of his Mba officers to flinch.

Azimoth turned and strode over to another screen that he and Lord Bakhtochk could look at together.

"My Lord, I feel the bipeds in the cooler regions will be more adaptable, with more potential than the ones in the arid region. The bipeds near the pyramids are mostly slaves, and their health is probably suspect. I also believe they might have a lower ceiling in capabilities, due to their mistreatment." Azimoth kept the fear out of his voice, as best as he could. "There are many tribes to the north, and many migrate seasonally. This means they come into contact with other tribes, and therefore, might have more experience with adapting and fighting. We can eliminate the aggressive genes, or reduce them to what we decide, but taking tame parnecka and trying to turn them into Tryr is much more difficult, if not impossible."

"Are those your only reasons?" his lord asked him in a deceptively mild tone.

"No, My Lord. If they are migrating, they will have all their belongings and everything we need to keep them alive while we evaluate them. Livestock, grown food, personal belongings such as blankets, extra clothes, their tools." Azimoth took a deep breath. "All this will not only help us feed and keep them initially, it will also help us evaluate their capabilities."

There was no immediate response from his lord, and Azimoth wondered if that was significant. The silence dragged on, and the drones began to reach an altitude to scan and search for potential targets.

"I notice you use drones provided with this ship, rather than our own, which are more sophisticated," his lord said. Azimoth breathed out in relief. This was something he was confident about.

"Yes, My Lord. Although they are inferior to those of the Clonoschk, they are adequate to the task. This way, when we've decided on our target, we can be recalling the drones while the Clonoschk stuns the populace. Then, the cruiser can go to a higher orbit and watch for other ships while we send the shuttles down and secure the cargo."

"Hmm." His lord looked at the screen for a few moments, and nodded his massive head. "Very good, Commander. I approve your decisions. Keep me informed."

Lord Bakhtochk turned and made his way off the bridge, and Azimoth exhaled in relief.

"Brilliant, Commander Azimoth," his second officer said, and he nodded his thanks. They were both from the same litter, and had supported each other as needed in their climb through the levels of rank.

"Bring us down to the lowest secure altitude, prepare the shuttles and those miserable creatures that will do the loading. Make sure each shuttle has adequate Mba Warriors on board."

"Yes, Commander."

Azimoth went and sat in his command seat, his knees suddenly weak. He wished he could howl, but it would be bad for morale.

On the northern fringe of the Maeotae Marshes

Gelon rode with Targitai at his side, and four of his best men behind him. Scyles had wanted to come, but Gelon had refused. Both of them, with limited resources and defenses, out at the border of their camp, might well prove to be irresistible to King Agathyrsus. He saw King Orik and Ariapithes approaching from his left, along with four men of his own.

He and Orik had agreed to put two-man sentry posts around the perimeter of their respective camp areas. He saw Orik had the young man, what was his name again, that Scyles had "wrestled" with, earlier in the morning. He looked little worse for the wear, and Gelon was glad.

The main body of the Caitiari tribe was visible in the distance. He could also see single riders interspersed around the plains, and one larger group of horsemen directly approaching them.

As he suspected, King Agathyrsus and his bodyguard, Koloksai, and perhaps a dozen warriors made up the group, and sped up their approach. Gelon turned to see where Orik was, and was relieved to see him pulling up.

"Safety in numbers, eh?" Orik said, and looked at the group fast approaching. "Perhaps a few more numbers in our party might have been good."

"Too late to do anything now," Gelon muttered, and Orik nodded.

They arranged themselves side by side, with Targitai and Ariapithes bracketing them. Their men were fanned out on either side, all with strung bows on their laps, arrows already nocked.

King Agathyrsus rode up and reined his horse to a halt. He looked at them dourly. His eyes looked past to see the markers defining their respective camp areas.

"You're early," he said in a gruff voice.

"So are you," Gelon told him good-naturedly. "No damage done. This gives us more time for talks before the rest of the tribes arrive."

"You both seem to be taking up a lot of ground," Agathyrsus said, and pointed to the border between Gelon and Orik's tribes. "Were you to shift, we could fit between you nicely."

"This is only a portion of my tribe," Gelon said easily, but there was iron in his voice. "We need this much space. We occupy the same amount as we always have, year after year."

"As do we," Orik agreed. "There is plenty of room, as there always is every year, bordering on the marshes. There are fresh water streams and springs spread liberally through the area."

"Yes, there is plenty of room on the other side of my area," Gelon said easily. "Or, you could take the area across the river."

"Neither are what I wish," Agathyrsus said, his tone growing surlier.

Neither Gelon nor Orik said anything. They simply stared at Agathyrsus, waiting him out. He finally turned to one of his men, and pointed at the open space beyond Gelon's camp. The man nodded, whirled his horse around, and raced back to the body of the tribe.

"Your counting seems to need some work," Gelon said mildly, sitting up straight to stare at the Caitiari tribe. "You brought a bit more than twelve hundred total. Looks about three times as much."

"We heard rumors of raiding tribes on the trails, and I did not wish to endanger my family," Agathyrsus said, on the defensive for the first time. "It matters not. We are all allies here. Hopefully, by the time the rest of the tribes begin to arrive, we will have made a decision regarding the successor to King Atheas, as well as several agreements of a more personal nature."

"We shall see," Orik said, and Gelon sighed, knowing what he had to do, but not wanting to.

"I would like you and your family to join us at my yurt today for lunch," Gelon said, trying not to grit his teeth.

"Will King Orik and his family also be in attendance?" Agathyrsus asked, his tone guarded.

"Of course," Gelon said, and glanced at Orik, who nodded his agreement. "After all, we are all friends here, almost family, in some ways."

Orik suddenly rubbed his nose hard, and Gelon wondered if he was trying to keep from laughing.

"Damned itchy nose," Orik said, and looked at Agathyrsus with a wry smile. "Please plan on dining at my yurt this evening. You can host us tomorrow, Agathyrsus."

"Of course," the king of the Caitiari said in a tone that bordered on sarcasm. "You would honor me with your presences. Now, I must go and direct the layout of our camp, since it isn't in the spot we'd intended."

"We'll ride with you," Orik said, smiling broadly, and Gelon hid his own smile behind his hand.

King Agathyrsus grunted, and they made their way eastward, down the border of Gelon's camp.

Half an hour later, Gelon and his party rode into the camp, and he went right on to his yurt. No one was there, and he walked to the great yurt next to them. Myrina was directing the men moving more low tables into the main room, and adding a table to the royal platform.

Gelon looked around, and his wife saw him and put her hands on her hips.

"What?" she asked indignantly. "You don't think I saw this coming? Don't worry mighty lord of the lunches, we'll be ready, and it will be tasty."

She smiled at him, and he couldn't help but smile back.

"It'll be fit for a king," she promised, and her smile broadened. "Or three."

Arga was only half listening to her mother go on about their hosting a feast tonight for the heads of the three tribes. Her mother had already pressed her for details about last night. Her father made several comments before he left with some of his men, for the Auchatae camp. She noticed that Skulis was one of them, and wondered if she should say something to him, to stop any ideas he had about the two of them.

But, she decided, there was always time for that later.

She heard horses approaching, and looked out the front of the family yurt to see her father and his riders returning. Several of the men gathered the reins for all the horses as everyone dismounted, and took them off to feed and water.

Her father walked up to her and looked at her critically.

"You may wish to change into something more impressive soon," he said. "King Gelon and Queen Myrina host us and the Caitiari royal family for lunch today, and of course, we host them tonight for supper."

"I knew about tonight, but neither Mother nor myself knew about lunch," Arga began, and her father stopped her with a raised hand.

"No way you could know, sweet Spring Blossom," he admitted, calling her by his favorite nickname. She had been very young when he began calling her that, and didn't do so as often, but she liked it when he did. "A lot has happened since young Scyles spirited you back into the camp late last night." He considered for a moment. "I guess very early morning would be more accurate."

"What has happened, Papa?" she asked, moving the conversation away from her and Scyles' antics the night before. Or so she thought.

"After dropping you off, nearly at our camp's entrance," he started, and frowned at her impish expression. He sighed visibly and muttered under his breath. "Or right at our yurt flap."

He continued with his original comment. "Your young prince returned home and interrupted a Persian assassin, about to kill King Gelon."

Arga gasped. "What happened, is he injured, or worse?" she asked, fear striking her rigid, unable to even move.

"No, King Gelon is fine," Papa said, and Arga looked at him in confusion. He grinned at her reaction, and then relented. "Another moment or two, and he might have had his throat slashed from ear to ear, but Scyles found the dead guards, came in fighting, and actually wounded and disabled the assassin." Her father stared at her, musing out loud. "Not many can make such a claim. And it was close. But Scyles took him down, wounding him badly."

He saw her expression and laughed.

"No, Scyles suffered no injuries," he admitted. "Which is good, since when we arrived, the first thing young Skulis did, was attack Scyles to defend your honor, which, according to you, needs no defending." He eyed her closely as he said the last bit.

Arga ignored that. She couldn't believe Skulis attacked Scyles. What was he thinking? Oh, she thought belatedly. Those little glances of mine, coupled with all the speculation about whether Scyles took my maidenhood, gave him plenty of reason to think Scyles deserved his wrath.

"What happened?" she asked in a faint voice.

"Skulis came into the common yurt, and when he saw Scyles, took right off after him," her father said, and laid a hand on her shoulder. "Now, neither of the boys would give us the straight story. They both defended each other, and claimed to be the best of friends. But Gelon was able to get the full story out of several of his people."

"And?" she asked, wondering if she could spirit herself away and flee back to the main part of the tribe, days behind them on the trail. Anything to relieve her of her mortification.

"Skulis got a punch in, then it became a wrestling match and Scyles took Skulis down and put him in a choke hold," Papa admitted, shaking his head. "Skulis is so stubborn, I would have thought Scyles would have to choke him unconscious, but apparently, he convinced Skulis of his honorable intentions to eventually marry you, and that you both wanted him as a friend. That you would need his friendship, and asked him to yield."

"Skulis would never yield, while he was alive or conscious," Arga said with conviction. "He's far too egotistical and stubborn."

"I would have thought the same," her father said mildly. "But he did. And then they were tight as thieves, breaking their fast together."

"Is that all that happened?" Arga said, her voice sounding distant to her.

"I would think that to be enough," her father said dryly.

"Now, go tell your mother I wish to wear the blue kurta, with the gold and red lacings, this afternoon," he said, gently pushing her towards the main yurt. "And that we will have more guests than originally planned on, for supper, tonight."

"Yes, Papa," she said, and made her way to the other yurt, feeling more than a little dazed.

Arga picked at the food in her bowl. It was very tasty, but she had no appetite. The yurt was packed with the upper echelon of all three tribes, and, in her opinion, the royal table was far too long. She was seated near the far right end, with only her little brother Serlotta, and Scyles, sitting farther away from the center, at least at this end. Ifito and Kavas sat at the far end of the table, which suited Arga.

Her mother sat to her left, and Arga could almost feel her mother trying to shield her from even the view of the Caitiari. But King Agathyrsus was making no bones about his intentions.

Before they'd even been seated, he'd tried to rearrange the seating to allow his twin children to sit next to her and Scyles. Queen Myrina had firmly said there would be time for the children to reacquaint over the next several days, but that for now, this seating fit the occasion.

And that was that, when you were in the Auchatae common yurt. Scyles' father might be the king, but his kingdom didn't extend to the meals. King Gelon had made no bones about it when Agathyrsus tried to press the matter.

King Gelon and Queen Myrina sat in the middle, with King Agathyrsus and Queen Latoreia to his left, and Arga's parents to her right. The children occupied what Scyles humorlessly called the 'Nether regions' of the line of tables.

She was seated just far enough away to not be able to hear the conversations between the parents clearly, but every now and then she would catch a phrase, or word or two. King Agathyrsus was pressing for everyone to agree to his children marrying her and Scyles.

"This solution makes the most sense," he said loudly, standing with his cup of mare's milk in hand. "We can agree that tying our tribes together by marriage is the best solution. And the only combination that truly binds all three tribes is for my Kavas to take Arga as his wife, and for Scyles to take Ifito as his."

"Technically, that only ties your tribe to each of ours, but gives no direct bond between the Auchatae and the Paralatae," King Gelon pointed out, his voice carrying well as the conversation died around the room. "And I think the children themselves have something to say regarding choosing who they will spend the rest of their lives with."

"They will do as they are told," King Agathyrsus said in a biting tone. "It is not the place for children to tell their parents what will be. It has always been this way."

"Not always," Arga's father said in a mild tone. "Some of us at this table fought to make their own choices." He glanced over Queen Myrina at King Gelon, an amused, if somewhat strained expression on his face. "And time has proven those decisions to be sound ones."

King Gelon nodded his appreciation, and turned to the king of the Caitiari.

"I will not force my son into a marriage he does not wish, and I believe King Orik and Queen Opis's daughter has made it quite clear she will not consider such an option at this time." He grinned, despite the seriousness of the conversation. "I believe I recall the words 'I will join the Warrior Women and swear off men for life', or something of the sort. Let the children decide for themselves."

"My children are in favor of this decision, and Kavas wishes to marry Arga immediately." He didn't even look at his children or his wife. "We could have the ceremony when the tribes arrive and are settled in place. It would be a favorable portent to the successful results of our decisions to be made at the gathering this year."

"Such as choosing the new Great King?" King Gelon asked in a deceptively quiet voice, and Arga's eyes widened as she recognized he was growing weary enough with this discussion to consider a faster, more permanent resolution to all these matters.

"Isn't that why we came here early?" King Agathyrsus asked in an imperious voice. "And we will begin discussions on that, perhaps this very eve. But right now, we can begin bringing our tribes closer together, through advantageous marriages."

"My daughter will..." her mother began, in a furious voice that made Arga freeze. She hadn't heard her speak in that tone since, well, in a long time.

"What my wife is saying," Papa interrupted her, staring her in the eyes intently. She looked ready to argue, then desisted.

Arga saw him squeeze her hand reassuringly, and turn his attention back to the other king.

"My daughter expressed herself very clearly, just yesterday, and she will not be marrying anyone at this point. And I will support her decision. This matter is closed."

"Nothing is closed until I say so," King Agathyrsus shouted, and everyone at the table froze. Without looking, Arga knew all three of the master fighters standing behind their respective kings, had shifted on their feet. In front of them, she saw men from all three tribes begin to look around the room, and eye their weapons, stacked by tribe, near the entrance.

Of course, no Scoloti warrior was ever totally unarmed. Even she had a dagger concealed in her kurta, and another smaller one in a boot.

Without knowing she'd done it, she was standing, and her voice surprised her as she spoke in a loud voice. There wasn't a hint of a tremor in her voice, even though she was terrified at what she was about to do.

"I have something to say," she said loudly, and both her parents began to shake their heads violently. She suspected they thought she would play the peacemaker, out of fear of them getting hurt or killed. Or maybe they thought something else, but it didn't matter.

Arga was going to speak, and her words were going to count.

"Papa is correct," she began, and she had the attention of everyone in the room. "Yesterday, I said I would not submit to being forced to marry anyone." She let her gaze slide across the room, ending up looking at the royal Caitiari family far to her left. "I meant it at the time, and I mean it now. If I am forced into a marriage not of my choosing, you should begin preparations for burying my husband, because the first night he sleeps, will be his last. His family will wake with the vision of him with his man parts in his mouth, held closed by my dagger plunged through his chin and mouth, the tip buried in his brains."

Everyone sat back, shocked at such a visual declaration by a girl barely having achieved womanhood. Even King Agathyrsus looked speechless, if only for the moment.

Arga hurried to continue before she got interrupted. She had the full attention of the room and couldn't let that pass.

"Last night, I met with Prince Scyles, and we walked under the night god's lights, and had the opportunity to talk without interruptions. We discovered we were in love with each other."

She felt rather than saw Queen Myrina lean forward to look past her at her son. She could see the tension in her papa's shoulders and neck, but his eyes never left King Agathyrsus.

"He proposed to me, and I accepted. We will marry as soon as our parents make the arrangements. I expect this to be either tonight or tomorrow." Arga looked down to the end of the table at Prince Kavas. He looked angry, yet oddly relieved. For that matter, so did his sister.

"Prince Kavas, you are an impressive prince of the Scoloti, and any woman would be honored to have you as their husband. I am sure you will be an excellent one." She smiled at him to ease her next words. "But it won't be to me. My heart is spoken for. I wish you well, and know you will find the perfect woman for you."

She looked down at her parents next to her.

"Papa, Mama, I beg your forgiveness at the suddenness of this, but I will be wedding Scyles, and ask for your approval." She looked beyond them at King Gelon and Queen Myrina. "I would also ask your forgiveness in not giving you warning that we felt this way, but it kind of just... happened," she finished, feeling her courage and strength flee her. She looked around, wondering what to do. Belatedly, she realized who she should have looked at much sooner. But she was afraid to even glance that way.

Scyles solved that problem. He stood, sliding Serlotta's bowl and cup in front of the chair he'd just risen from.

"Sorry, little brother," he muttered, probably thinking his voice wouldn't carry. But many people seated closest to the table, as well as most of the royalty at the table, heard him clearly, and there was a tittering of humor.

Serlotta shifted over a seat without saying anything, and Scyles looked at Arga finally, standing next to her. She looked back at him, hoping she didn't look as terrified as she felt.

"Arga, I wish to make my proposal formal, in front of witnesses," Scyles said, and she saw the glint of humor in his eyes. "In front of our families and the people of our tribes, I tell you it is my wish that we wed, as soon as it can be arranged, and that I love you, and will protect, honor, and provide for you, with all my resources, for the rest of my life, and beyond. I wish you for my wife, my lover, my partner."

Some people gasped at that. They all believed that after death, there were more journeys, and most couples expected to travel them with their mates, but it was rarely asserted in a proposal.

King Agathyrsus opened his mouth to protest, but Scyles was too quick for him.

"Will you marry me, Arga of the Paralatae?"

"I will, Scyles of the Auchatae," Arga said, startled to find she suddenly felt shy. She raised her eyes to meet his. "I love you, and will bear you strong sons and beautiful daughters, and be your partner in everything, until death and beyond."

"I witness this proposal and approve it, in the name of the myself, King Orik, her mother, Queen Opis, and the Paralatae tribe," roared her papa, surging to his feet, raising his cup.

"And I add to his witness of this proposal, and approve it, in the name of myself, King Gelon, his mother, Queen Myrina, and the Auchatae tribe," King Gelon bellowed, rising to stand next to Papa. They knocked their cups against each other's and drank deeply.

Scyles handed her the tankard she'd been drinking out of, and raised his own. The drinks tapped lightly against each other, and they sipped cautiously, their eyes meeting over the tankards. They lowered them, and Scyles leaned forward and gave her a light kiss on the lips.

Then their fathers were hugging them, trading them back and forth several times.

King Gelon looked down on her and beamed.

"You've made four parents very proud and happy," he declared. "I welcome you to the family."

"Thank you," she said, not quite sure what to call him. Then Queen Myrina was hugging her, basically repeating her husband's words.

She was feeling dazed by all the emotions, and reactions of everyone around her. But as she hugged her own mother, Arga looked over her shoulder to see King Agathyrsus and Queen Latoreia talking to each other angrily. Their children seemed bemused, and not all that upset by the uproar. But Arga saw the queen realize she was looking at them, and the glare she gave Arga would have killed a weaker woman.

I have gained a husband and second family, as well as enemies that would celebrate my death, she decided. But that was a matter for another time. She turned around to find her future husband. Hugging him a few more times right now would surely make her feel better.

In that, at least, she was correct.

Chapter Ten

Aboard the Hstahni Generation Ship Muschwain

Commander Azimoth looked at the screen and read the reports. Several possibilities had been found. After reading about the choices, he decided that one had more merit than the others. He was about to contact Lord Bakhtochk, but the wall between the bridge and his bridge lounge opened, and his lord entered, and settled on his lounge, even as he observed the data on one of the screens.

"You have made a choice," he rumbled. "Tell me the particulars, and your rationale."

"Yes, my Lord," Azimoth said, walking hurriedly to the display of screens by the ledge. "We found a site, with a fairly large group of bipeds, with an accompanying herd of their livestock." He looked at his pawheld screen. "There are slightly more than six thousand bipeds, with approximately thirty-three hundred quadrupeds of one species. They seem to serve multiple purposes, including transportation, both by riding and pulling carts, as well as a food supply. And then there are a little more than six hundred of another, smaller quadruped, primarily a food supply, and several hundred of a third quadruped, which we haven't yet discovered the purpose of."

Azimoth checked something. "As well as a food supply, the first two also provide material for clothing, as well as other items of functional purpose."

He looked at the synopsis analysis. "If the bipeds don't work out, we may find the larger quadrupeds to be a more valuable find, as they serve many purposes."

"Where are they?" Lord Bakhtochk asked idly, and Azimoth pointed out the location on one of the screens.

"It appears to be the end point for an annual gathering of tribes, or other sociological groupings." Azimoth checked the area nearby. "There are no other natives in close proximity, so I believe we could harvest the entire grouping, storing almost all of them in stasis, keeping some bipeds awake to study. We could also keep a few of the quadrupeds to feed them, and thereby not deplete our own food stores."

"How big an area are they spread over?" Lord Bakhtochk asked, and Azimoth thought for a moment.

"It's about equal to the manicured portion of your estate on Hshtahni Prime," he said, and his lord nodded his massive head.

"Very good," he agreed. "Make your final preparations."

"Yes, my Lord," Azimoth said, and turned to his men, sighing in relief. He looked at Second Officer Zoun, and nodded.

"Prepare to recall drones."

On the northern fringe of the Maeotae Marshes

Scyles sat in a daze, his bowl of meat, vegetables, and grain ignored. Arga sat next to him, her food bowl as untouched as his. They both responded when spoken to, but mostly, they just sat, holding hands, pretending to listen to family and friends, saying a few words when it looked necessary, occasionally taking a sip of their fermented mare's milk.

Arga took a sip, looked inside the tankard in surprise and showed Scyles that it was empty. He opened his mouth to call for more, but she stopped him by squeezing his hand and placing her other hand on his arm.

He looked at her in surprise.

"I do not think I should drink any more of this until tonight," she said, her voice a little rough. "I wish to keep my wits about me."

Scyles showed her his own half-full tankard, and nodded his head in agreement. And then he smiled as she took it from him, drank a healthy swig, and placed the tankard back near his hand.

"You could have warned me," he said, gently chiding her. "I was so surprised I just stood there, when I could have been next to you, supporting you, and defending our decision."

"Our decision?" she asked, and he looked at her. Her tone sounded uncertain, full of self-doubts.

"Our decision," he said firmly. "I told you last night, I knew we would marry someday, when you signaled you were ready." He nudged her with his shoulder. "Some signal."

She giggled, and nudged him back. "I thought you did a very good job of adapting, and I think you spoke up at the perfect moment."

"Thank you, my love," Scyles said, and became very aware of how close their faces were to each other. He leaned forward and kissed her softly on her lips. She smiled at him, reached up to put her hand behind his neck and pulled him back to her for a slightly longer kiss.

They separated, but didn't sit back. Scyles felt he was lost in her eyes, and knew he could gaze into them for the rest of his life.

Most of the people around them yelled, making lewd suggestions, thumping on the tables with their tankards.

Arga blushed and he knew she was hearing some of the suggestions of how they should spend tonight, and the details of exactly how to do what. He felt like blushing a little himself as he heard some of what was being said.

"Hey, we're not married yet, so keep your suggestions appropriate," Scyles yelled out at a group of men his age that he supposed were his friends. He'd never really had true friends, so perhaps they didn't qualify as such. But they were clearly feeling like they were good enough friends to have fun at his expense.

He saw Skulis cuff one of his own tribesmen in the back of the head at one of his gross suggestions, and thought his new friend was about to start a brawl, but the man took one look at who'd cuffed him, and said something, grinning weakly as he raised his mug.

Skulis laughed and patted the man on the shoulder, and moved on. His eyes came to look at Scyles and Arga, and his mouth tightened in pain, momentarily, but then it was gone, and he was smiling broadly, raising his glass to them.

Scyles picked up his tankard and held it up as well. They both drank deeply, their eyes locked. When Scyles lowered his drink, Arga took it out of his hand and finished it.

Skulis must have thought he looked surprised, because he laughed, nodded, and kept walking around the room.

"You won him over," Arga breathed, sounding puzzled. "How? You just defeated him in battle."

"I showed him the respect he deserves," Scyles said quietly, and felt her eyes upon him.

"I think you will make a very good husband, father, and someday, king," she said shyly and wrapped her arms around his waist, resting her head on his shoulder again.

Scyles looked nervously over at King Orik and Queen Opis, who just happened to be watching them at that point. They both looked very solemn, and he felt his heart leap into his throat. He was about to stir Arga, and get her to sit up straight, and show a little more decorum, but both her parents picked that moment to start laughing.

King Orik looked at their drinks and raised his eyes questioningly. Scyles firmly shook his head no. He looked down at Arga, and saw her eyes were closed. Her mother saw that about the same time, and smiled and made some comment to the king that Scyles couldn't hear in the noise of the crowd.

"Maybe we should get her home soon, let her rest so she'll be ready for whatever tonight brings," Queen Opis said, looking at Scyles slyly.

"Will the wedding be tonight?" Scyles asked, his mouth suddenly very dry.

"Is there a reason to wait?" she asked, and obviously enjoyed his discomfort.

"No, no, not at all," Scyles said, trying to think about what he needed to do to prepare for suddenly having a wife. "I need to speak to my parents about, uh, well..."

"Where you will bed her?" Queen Opis teased him.

"I assumed you would take her to one of your hills, and consummate your marriage there, under the lights of the gods," King Orik said innocently. "That appears to have worked well for you last night."

"We did nothing last night," Scyles spoke firmly, not wanting her reputation to suffer. "We talked, held hands, and kissed one time, at the bottom of the south face of the hill."

"And that is all you did?" Queen Opis asked, pushing him to continue.

"I kissed her again, near her yurt, but it was quick, because someone was approaching," Scyles stammered.

"I thought you proposed last night," King Orik said, looking at him thoughtfully. "Surely such a moment warranted more than just a kiss."

"You will have to ask her about that," Scyles said desperately. "I am not a man that tells the secrets of the woman he loves."

The king and queen looked at each other, and seemed to like that answer. As one, they turned back to him.

Scyles looked down at Arga for support, but her eyes were closed, and could he hear her...snoring?

"I suppose we should get her back to our camp," the queen said, grinning at her unconscious daughter. She looked at Scyles slyly again, and he winced inside. "If you and Arga aren't sure of where you should fulfill your marital duties, you could both sleep in her sleeping robes in our yurt. It's right next to ours."

"Uh, I'll let Arga decide what she feels is best, but I do not think that will be her choice," Scyles said, trying to sound firm. He wondered if maybe sleeping out under the lights of the gods wasn't the best idea, after all.

Arga chose that moment to awaken. She looked around, a little dazed, and then looked up at Scyles face, hovering over her. She smiled at him and straightened up, and groaned and held her head.

Scyles could hear her parents laughing at her, but ignored them.

"Arga, let's stand up and make our way out of here," Scyles said, and stood to help her. "I'm going to take you back to your yurt, so you can sleep, and refresh yourself for tonight. Can you ride?"

She looked at him indignantly.

"Of course I can ride," she said, frowning as she felt her head wonderingly. "Did I drink that much?"

"It's an important occasion," Scyles said, holding her against him as he turned her towards the step down to the carpeted floor. "We marry tonight, so you need your rest."

"Okay," Arga said agreeably, and let him lead her off the rising. Then she looked at him. "Where will we sleep tonight?"

"Well, your mother kindly volunteered our staying in your sleeping quarters tonight," Scyles began, and she vehemently shook her head. A moment later she was holding it with both hands, moaning.

"No, not there," she finally said. "Unless you want your in-laws to hear every single sound we make, no."

"I'm glad we agree on that one," Scyles admitted. "I'll ask my parents if we have an unused tent we can borrow..."

"Or we could sleep on the hill where we spoke last night, under the lights of the gods," she said, sounding thoughtful.

"We would have to make sure no one knew," Scyles said, and she nodded, more cautiously this time. "Otherwise half of both tribes will be trying to intrude on our evening."

"Hmm," she said, and opened her mouth to say something, but stopped as they both heard the sound of screaming and shouting from outside.

Scyles had his swords and gorytos already strapped on, and was carrying hers. He handed them to her, and helped push people out of the way so they could get out the main entrance.

Scyles looked around, expecting to see armed men attacking, but there was no sign of intruders.

He saw several men pointing up in the air behind him, and turned to look, pulling Arga around with him.

They both gasped as they saw a large cart of some sort, floating in the sky far ahead of them, and very high. It slowly drifted forward, and as they watched people farthest away from the common yurt begin to fall to the ground, along with the horses they were riding, and even several sheep that were being led towards them.

The line of fallen tribespeople grew closer, and appeared to be directly beneath the flying cart.

Scyles swore and whirled, grabbing one of the shields left by men eating in the common yurt. People were collapsing only a short distance away, and the cart kept approaching. He yelled his defiance, pulling Arga behind him, and down to the ground, raising the shield to cover them as completely as possible.

He took a moment to look at her terrified face, and was furious. They weren't even married yet, and he'd already failed her.

"Be brave, Arga," he said to her, and his voice seemed to pull her away from her terror. "Whatever it is, we face it together," he managed to say.

Then there was nothing.

Aboard the Hshtahni Generation Ship Muschwain

Azimoth gingerly stepped out of the shuttle, onto the planet's surface. He hadn't been on a planet in quite some time, and it felt good. He wished he could shed his uniform and run free for a while. He knew there was wildlife on this world, and it had been solar cycles since he'd hunted.

Sighing, he walked down what he supposed passed for a street, between two large tents, looking at the variety of colors of the biped's clothing. He knew there were three distinct camps, and suspected they were competing tribes.

These people lived in primitive conditions. He would call it squalid, at best. One of his squad leaders, Officer Gauzor, met him at the junction of two of the muddy lanes acting as roadways for foot and quadruped traffic.

"Report," Azimoth said brusquely.

"We've started packing everything at the two outlying camps," Gauzor said. "We've found a surprising number of paired bipedal units, in some sort of sentry duty, around the perimeters of each camp."

"Send some drones with heat-seeking capabilities to look for any teams we missed," Azimoth said. "And measure the distance between the teams you did find, see what their schematic theme is, and extrapolate where any more might be hidden."

"Yes, Commander," Gauzor said. He looked around them. "There are quite a few of these creatures. I think we will fill all the stasis pods and still have primitives to deal with."

"That's acceptable," Azimoth said. "We'll want specimens to examine and dissect, as well as their leadership, to question."

He pointed at the tallest tent.

"I believe that is the epicenter of the commanding primitives. Start at the extremities and put all specimens in stasis, working your way to this site. When we run out of pods, whatever is left will be our specimen sampling."

"Yes, Commander," Gauzor said, and turned away, giving instructions to his sub-leaders already at work at the other two camps.

Azimoth walked to the entrance of the large tent, and knelt by the head of one of the large quadrupeds. It was an impressive-looking creature, and he idly wondered how fast it could run. It wore a harness that looked like it came off quite easily, and he reminded Gauzor to have the minions remove all harnesses and clothing from the creatures going into stasis.

He also reminded him to store anything that looked like weapons separately, so they could be secured beyond the reach of any of the bipeds that were kept awake.

Azimoth looked at the people that had spilled out of the tent as the cruiser approached. He saw that the bipeds had not reacted in a uniform manner, which was surprising. He would have thought the sight of the cruiser would have either frightened them into immobilization, or caused them to flee blindly.

The cruiser had to be unlike anything they'd ever seen before, so that would be the expected response. But he saw some men with the stringed weapons in their hands, and had observed several try to fire at the cruiser, even though it was much too high for their shafts to reach.

A few others had their edged weapons drawn, as if they could physically battle the stun force beams.

Just outside the entrance, he saw where what looked like a male and female had been together as they faced the oncoming cruiser. The male had drawn the female behind him, and tried to cover them both with a crude shield made of the product of some of the larger plant life.

It had been a futile effort, of course. But Azimoth had to admire the determination and defiance the act had displayed.

Azimoth realized that Lord Bakhtochk was correct. This planet really did have a multitude of treasures and resources. If he was able to shape the raw potential of the denizens of this planet, it would provide much wealth and power.

Azimoth sighed, wondering glumly if he would see any of either. It seemed unlikely.

Chapter Eleven

Aboard the World Ship Kchoatkhakh, in the common space of the Hechktar and Trixmae

Zechkreeshrrprhkq exhaled heavily, causing the clay around him to bubble. Next to him, his nephew and protégé, Achkptrrshkqk, did the same. They both lounged in the clay pen, enjoying the cool sensation, and feeling the moisturizing effect on their durable hides.

The clay was deep, covering them up above their shoulders, hiding their six legs splayed out wide, as well as their two forearms, each with six digits, two of them opposable thumbs. They both had their chins resting on hover plates, allowing the multitude of long, fine tendrils under their chins to remain above the clay.

Zechkrreeshrrprhkq didn't have to look at his nephew to know his large, round eyes were wide open, if somewhat unfocused at the moment. He was young, not even aged a thousand cycles yet, and still had so much to learn. But, even at this young age, Achkptrrshkqk was showing signs of mastering skills and abilities that should have taken him many more centuries to develop. He knew, by the time his nephew doubled his age, he would be a formidable and very capable Hechktar indeed. Zechkrreeshrrprhkq had been charged with guiding his training, and overseeing his growth into an adult.

His nephew's eyes came into focus, and he looked up at the screen displays on the wall. His tendrils writhed in a concerted effort to coordinate their functions. His nephew's eyes shifted to him, and the interest showed clearly.

"Do you feel it, Uncle?"

Zechkrreeshrrprhkq wondered what he meant, then felt his own eyes widen. Even as he interpreted the data and focused on one screen in particular, he marveled that his nephew had actually sensed the phenomenon before he did.

As one, they felt the disturbance in space. A small tunnel in space opened, and a ship emerged. It barely cleared the mouth of the tunnel before the gate shrank and disappeared.

The ship was not streamlined and looked more like a collection of cubes than a vessel capable of space travel. But since it never entered a planet's gravity well or atmosphere, streamlining didn't matter.

It was the Trixmae ship Turcrishe, and Zechkrreeshrrprhkq realized it was at least partially disabled. Or perhaps drained of energy was a more appropriate description, he decided.

"Turcrishe, do you require assistance?"

The response was sluggish, and not well-formed, which was cause for alarm. The Trixmae were a powerful race, and although it was theoretically possible to destroy anything and anyone, there were no recorded cases of a Trixmae ship ever being severely damaged, much less terminated.

"Uncle, what has caused this?"

"One moment, Nephew.'

Zechkrreeshrrprhkq caused tractor beams to stabilize the Trixmae ship and draw it towards the Kchoatkhakh. The moment the ship was being drawn to a dock on his ship, a flood of data poured from the Trixmae aboard the Turcrishe, and both Hechktar immediately stood upright, letting the heavy jet of water wash the clay off their bodies.

By the time they were both out of the clay pen, rinsed, and liberally coated with special lotions to moisturize their hides, the Turcrishe was docked.

He could tell there was no attempt being made to enter his ship, and upon receiving a quick summary of what had occurred, both he and his nephew stepped on their personal hover lounges. As they made their way to the bridge, he evaluated the situation.

"Do not worry. Rest and recover your strength. I know the drain and burden of your temporal travels. You are secured to my ship, and I will take us where we need to go, to deal with this situation."

Zechkreeshrrprhkq caused a tunnel of his own to open, much bigger to accommodate his world ship, and without hesitation, entered. He watched space fold in upon itself and checked with the Trixmae.

"We shall arrive in the vicinity soon, and will examine all the facts, and come to a decision. Rest and recover. We share duty in this cause."

Zechkreeshrrprhkq grunted heartily and allowed his body to reduce inner pressure. His nephew did the same, and they settled down on their lounges. The Trixmae brought unfortunate news, but it would be a good lesson for his nephew's training.

"Nephew, allow me to clarify the situation…"

Aboard the Hshtahni Generation Ship Muschwain

Azimoth watched the steady parade of anti-grav rafts make their way from the dock area to the giant cargo holds dedicated to storing and maintaining the stasis pods. These rafts were modified to hold stasis pods on a platform that could be unloaded directly into the cradles that would secure them.

He estimated the Meyores had moved about two thirds of the livestock and bipeds that would be kept in stasis into place already. Everything seemed to be going very smoothly, which gave him misgivings.

He contacted Third Officer Hazin and told him to dedicate at least one shuttle to transporting the bipeds that were sprawled around the large tent that appeared to be their headquarters. They looked very hardy, and he was concerned that they would begin to gain consciousness before they were locked into one of the empty storage holds.

Azimoth knew they could stun the primitives again, but wasn't sure what effect that would have on them. He didn't wish to needlessly kill any of them. They appeared to be a valuable commodity, and it wasn't in his nature to waste resources.

He saw Razel, one of the Mba security guards, directing a group of the Meyores to pile all the clothing taken off the primitives stored in stasis into a nearby storage hold. He walked down the wide concourse hallway to inspect how things were going.

Azimoth was pleased to see that the Meyores didn't seem to be having any trouble attaching the rafts of stasis pods to the cradles, insuring they wouldn't lose power, killing the contents.

Razel saw him and his snout wrinkled in disgust.

"I think we should have left their clothing, if you can call it that, planet-side," he said, and shuddered. "I don't think they ever clean them, and I have never smelled anything so disgusting."

"I think you'll find that when you have the Meyores go through all the clothes, you will find hidden weapons and other artifacts we may wish to study," Azimoth said, and pointed to the hatchway to where the bipeds not put into stasis would be contained. "We will also need to search the ones we kept out of stasis, for the same things," he said. "In fact, we should search those first, before they begin to wake."

"Do you wish the garments stripped off them first?" Razel asked, looking a little nauseous at the thought of having to do it himself. "We will almost certainly need to clean them and put them in some sort of standard garb."

"No," Azimoth decided. "The fact they wear garments may only be for comfort from the elements, but it could also be because of some sort of religious taboo. We do not wish them immobilized and irrational due to some moral violation. That would make it very difficult to accurately test them and learn their capabilities."

Azimoth started to turn away, then turned back, remembering something.

"Do not forget to tag the ones not put into stasis with translators," he said. "Once they awaken, they will begin to speak to each other. It shouldn't take the ship's computers long to analyze their language and be able to translate so we can issue them commands."

"What about their hygiene facilities?" Razel asked, his lips curling away from his teeth in disgust.

"They seem similar enough in size and proportion to the Meyores that we can probably use the same equipment. And from what we could see at their camp, their interior organs produce the same results, and they are used to having common areas for defecation and urination." Azimoth looked at his paw-held terminal, and nodded in confirmation. "It appears we will have approximately one hundred and sixty of them conscious, so allow enough units for that number. Put some sort of visual barrier in the middle, so if they have modesty issues between the sexes, it will accommodate them."

Azimoth checked his paw-held again, and nodded his approval. It appeared that the Meyores were almost done transferring the natives destined for stasis, and were loading the remaining primitives, as well as several of each of their animals, to be butchered for food, as needed.

The Meyores still had to bring the various carts, tents, and other belongings up to the Muschwain, but that wouldn't take long.

"Make sure all potential weapons are stored in a separate secure hold," Azimoth said, and Razel nodded. "I don't feel like killing some of these primitives, just to show them they are no longer free, and that resistance will accomplish nothing."

Azimoth sighed, and decided he'd better give his lord an update. Everything was going very smoothly, and normally this would make him a very happy Mba.

But there was something about these primitives that made him nervous, and he would be glad when they were fully loaded and well on their way back to their base planet.

Almost every one of these primitives had some sort of weapon, and Azimoth had certainly seen enough proof during their last visit to this world that they were very prone to violence.

It would be good to get rid of these creatures on Tolokh, and for him to be back on the bridge of his cruiser.

Aboard the World Ship Kchoatkhakh, in the common space of the Hechktar and Trixmae

Zechkreeshrrprhkq watched the large, totally self-contained, clear-walled tank slide into the conference room. It was large enough that both he and his nephew, and two or three more Hechktar could have comfortably fit inside.

Of course, since the Hechktar couldn't breathe methane, it would have meant their deaths, but the tank was already full, in any case. The Trixmae writhed inside, the countless thick slithering tentacles, looking like nothing so much as hundreds, or even thousands, of eels, constantly jockeying for position, or acquiring sensory gratification through their movements.

Zechkreeshrrprhkq had once asked which it was, or if there was another explanation. He had gotten a very cryptic message he interpreted as meaning it was none of his business, which had induced one of his bellowing laughs.

Neither he nor his nephew, or the Trixmae, for that matter, were laughing this day. This was a day of grave concern, and there were limited choices for resolution.

The Trixmae would need more time for a full recovery. His ship had provided the tunnel for both of their ships to travel to a point between the planet they had been cultivating for as many millennia as he'd lived, and the naturally formed powerful tunnels that appeared to be near the projected path of the Hshtahni ships.

As powerful as the Hechktar and the Trixmae were, creating their own tunnel to force other ships into, was beyond their abilities. Certainly, they could destroy the cruiser, but destroying the generation ship would mean the deaths of thousands of Humans. And they'd spent so long gently guiding them as a species; that thought was repugnant.

It might be possible to disable the generation ship without destroying it, but seizing it would almost certainly result in its destruction. The Hshtahni would rather fight to the death than submit, and if they were defeated, they would take the ship with them into the void of annihilation.

That only left one choice.

There were two tunnel gates, close to each other, relatively near the path the Hshtahni would take to disguise their last stop, as well as their destination. Zechkreeshrrprhkq knew they could cause both Hshtahni ships to veer slightly off course, causing them to come within range of the tunnel gates. Opening one of the gates while applying pressure to force them into its range would be difficult, but well within their capabilities, especially once the Trixmae returned to full strength.

One of the tunnels led to a star system that was well isolated from any known space-faring races, and another one of their "projects". He would rather not send them there, because culling the Hshtahni off that planet would be difficult. They were a very capable race, and although not in the same power range as the Hechktar or Trixmae, they would not be easy to deal with on a planet's surface.

There was also a real possibility that the Hshtahni were already dealing with tunnel manipulation. There were many tunnel gates surrounding that planet, going to different systems spread throughout the galaxy.

No, he didn't favor that idea, and was glad to find that the Trixmae agreed with his logic.

That left the other tunnel. It led to the outer borders of the Egelv Empire, and although very distant, and unknown space to the Hshtahni, they would eventually be able to calculate how to return to their own space. It wouldn't be a fast trip, but was certainly doable.

Which also was not ideal.

But it would give him and the Trixmae time to come up with a plan on how to recover the Humans. It wasn't as if this was the first time they'd had to intervene in an attempt by a Hshtahni ship to take a Human sampling, or to expose their existence to the unfriendly universe around them. Fortunately, in the previous attempts, they had become aware of the Hshtahni incursion early enough in the process to block any actual removal of Humans from the planet.

This time it would be harder, more complicated. But the fact they were dropping the Hshtahni so far from their own known space, the trip home by traditional space flight would take several solar cycles, once they figured out where they were. Isolated from any source of assistance for the Hshtahni meant removing the Humans from their clutches should be possible.

Which, at this point, appeared to be the best they could ask for.

So be it, he decided.

Chapter Twelve

Aboard the Hshtahni Generation Ship Muschwain

Gelon felt his forehead throbbing and opened his eyes cautiously. He was looking at the back of Targitai's kurta, and wondered why they were laying on the ground. Then he realized that it wasn't ground. It was some sort of smooth surface, very hard, and uncomfortable.

His swordmaster stirred, and Gelon tried to roll away from him to climb to his feet. His way was blocked, and he awkwardly shifted around in the space he was in. It was his wife behind him, and he saw her eyes pop open, then close again as she grimaced. Gelon pushed himself to his hands and knees, looking around as he did.

He saw Scyles standing several horse lengths away, in the process of helping Princess Arga to her feet. They both looked like they were suffering the same headaches he was, and from the look of it, Myrina as well. The princess came to her feet, and moved under Scyles' protective arm as they both surveyed the confusion around them.

Gelon saw they were in some sort of giant building or tent. The fact that the ceiling was high, but not arching, made him assume it was a building of some sort. Or perhaps a giant cave.

But the ground, or floor, more likely, as well as the four walls and even the ceiling, were all perfectly flat. And the walls and ceiling looked as hard and unyielding as the unknown surface of the floor.

Scyles saw him, even as he felt Myrina grab his kurta to help her pull herself to her feet. His arm instinctively swept around her, pulling her around so Scyles could see her, and that she was not injured.

The area they were in was very full of people. In fact, he noted, the same people that had been in the yurt. At a distance, he saw the guards that had been posted around the outside of the yurt, as well as the women that had been serving the banquet lunch, and some other people he suspected had been near the yurt when the giant flying cart had arrived.

Targitai edged close enough to speak to him in a quiet voice.

"Sire, I don't know where we've been taken, or how they managed to subdue everyone." Targitai looked grim. "But whoever is responsible for this took our weapons away. All my weapons, including my knives, are missing."

Scyles made his way through the milling crowd of confused tribesmen to Gelon's side, Arga firmly planted under his left arm.

"I still have my sling and pouch," he said in a low tone, his eyes constantly moving about the room, looking for clues or understanding. "And I have a small knife in my boot."

Arga started, and felt her leg, then began to bend over. Scyles pulled her back upright.

"We don't know if our captors are watching us or not," he pointed out, both to her and to the rest of them. "Any weapons we do have, let's keep them out of sight for the moment, until we have a good opportunity to use them."

"Sound thinking, Scyles," Targitai complimented him. He looked at Gelon. "I will have several of my men discreetly ask around the room, so we may get some sort of idea of what we have to work with."

Gelon nodded, turned back to his son and clasped both him and Arga on the shoulders.

"Good thinking, Son. And I'm glad to see you have the good habit of always carrying claws to defend yourself with, Arga," he said, smiling at his future daughter-in-law. "One in a sheath on your thigh, and another in one of your boots?"

"Yes, King Gelon," Arga answered, looking shy at addressing him, clearly not sure what to call him now.

"You are about to become family, Princess, so, it is Father Gelon and Mother Myrina, Father and Mother, or whatever you feel most comfortable with." His smile to her was genuine. He felt his wife edge closer.

"What it is not, is King Gelon or Queen Myrina, or Sire, or anything of that sort," Myrina said, and pulled her away from her son so she could give her a hug. "Welcome to our family."

Arga blushed, but returned the hug wholeheartedly, Gelon was happy to see. Scyles could not have found a better choice than this girl. And it would bring their two families much closer together. That thought made him wonder, and he began to look around.

"If you're looking for Papa and Mama, they're over there," Arga said quietly, pulling her kurta straight after the two women released from the hug, but not going back to clinging to Scyles. Gelon liked the fact that she considered herself more than capable of defending herself, and not needing Scyles to constantly be watching over her.

Gelon followed her gesture and saw King Orik and Queen Opis, arm in arm, watching them. He nodded, and began to make his way across the short space between them.

"Should I be glad to see you here or not?" Orik asked him, grimacing. "And do you have any idea where 'here' is?"

"No idea at all," Gelon admitted, and looked at him critically. "Your weapons are gone?"

"Yes, but they missed the three knives my wife always wears," Orik admitted, looking around the room coldly. "And anyone that was able to find at least one of them would warrant death at my hands."

"I am more than capable of dealing with that myself, husband," Opis said, slapping him on the arm.

"Keep them out of sight for the moment, if you would, Queen Opis," Gelon said tightly. "We don't know if our captors are watching, or listening, for that matter."

"So we decided, as well," Orik admitted. He started to continue, but a familiar voice began calling out stridently.

"Where are my children? Kavas! Ifito!" King Agathyrsus was striding around nearby, calling out, his eyes searching frantically. "Can anyone see the royal twins? Where are they?"

"We have not," Gelon called out to him, and turned to Myrina. "Targitai and I are going to help look for them, and assess who we do have. I also wish to see if there is a way out of this room."

"Go," Myrina nodded to him. "I will stay with Scyles and Arga. We will join her parents, and Serlotta."

Arga made her way over to hug them. Gelon watched them look back at him, and then turn to make their way over to the other family.

Gelon smiled at Targitai grimly. They both looked around the room, at the crowd milling about, aimlessly wandering with no purpose or plan.

"Get your best man with numbers," Gelon said, sighing. "Counting this meandering herd is too hard for two old warriors as ourselves."

Targitai nodded glumly.

"All shuttles have returned to the ship, Sir," Second Officer Zoun said, and Azimoth nodded his head, absentmindedly. His eyes flicked from screen to screen, watching the shuttles being emptied of the last of the tents, carts, any loose objects that were related to the primitives. Everything would be stockpiled in a large storage hold, to be sorted out and analyzed at their leisure.

He was also watching the mostly conscious primitives not in stasis, making notes as he searched for signs of who the leaders were. Three of them were obvious, and he finally decided that they were the only ones. His people had already reported that there seemed to be three distinct camps, and each had their own special color-coding of shields, banners, and in some cases, clothing.

"As soon as everything necessary is secured, return us to Tolokh, in mirror course changes to our trip here," he told Zoun, and made the cameras zoom in on some of the primitives.

"Isn't dehydration a side effect of being stunned with some species?" he asked, seeing some of the older ones being lowered to the deck, looking rough, and not in good shape.

"Yes," came the response, and he nodded.

"Commander Azimoth, what progress has been made on being able to communicate with the primitives?" Lord Bakhtochk asked, and his two children made impatient sounds. He knew the two younger Hshtahni wanted to get a firsthand look, and perhaps a taste, of the newly discovered species.

"The computer says it is correctly interpreting seventy-three percent of all verbal communications, and the number is increasing. Rudimentary conversation should be possible now, and will only get better, the more they speak," Azimoth said, and turned away from the screens to look at his lord.

"Have you identified the leaders?" Lord Bakhtochk asked him, watching him closely.

"I believe so," he admitted. "There appears to be three distinct tribes, and they all have variations in their speech, dress, regalia, and each had their own camp. "It appears that they have a heredity-based monarchy, in patriarchy form. I have identified the three kings."

"Kings," his lord mused. "How grandiose and arrogant of them. They have barely crawled out of the mud, and they think ruling is their right."

"Yes, My Lord," he said, not knowing anything else to say.

"Bring them to me. Have your crew put some of them to work, bringing water and food supplies to them. Keep control of them."

"Yes, My Lord," Azimoth said, and hurried off the bridge.

By the time he got to the storage room holding the primitives, he had eight of his troopers, armed with energy handguns set on stun, and twenty of the Meyores. They arrived at the hatch, and he watched his sergeant organize their entrance.

He looked at Azimoth, nodded, and he and his troops rose on the balls of their feet, and the hatch opened.

Scyles stood listening to his father and King Orik talk. They had been discussing tactics to attempt to escape, but decided they didn't know enough about their captors to accomplish anything, at the moment. They'd done a quick headcount by tribe, and found that King Gelon had the most tribe members with fifty-three males of fighting age, twenty-nine women, fourteen of whom were capable fighters. There were also fourteen children too young to fight.

King Orik and Queen Opis had twenty-one men, nine women, all capable of fighting, according to Opis. They only had one child, Serlotta. Of course, he was too young to be in battle, and if there was conflict, he would be with Queen Myrina, and she would watch over him.

King Agathyrsus had brought twenty-four warriors, eighteen male, and six female, and his family. The two children weren't in the room, and no one quite knew what that meant. His wife was no fighter, and she would join Scyles' mother, along with Serlotta, if fighting broke out.

There were enough knives to give about a third of the warriors a blade, but they were being kept out of sight for the moment. Scyles' father and Orik had agreed that keeping their existence secret was more important than any tactical advantage they would give at the moment.

Agathyrsus' men didn't have any of the blades, since their women were reluctant to give up their own blades. The only other women in their party, the queen and daughter, weren't in the habit of carrying a hidden weapon.

He had argued that enough knives for his men should immediately be handed over, but Gelon and Orik had refused, saying their actions might be seen. There would be time for that later.

Scyles stood next to Arga, and wanted to hold her so badly, but she'd told him she wasn't helpless and although she wanted to hold him as well, it was more important to show readiness than give in to romantic urges.

He'd reluctantly agreed. His mother made a point of congratulating him for coming to terms with the fact that women were almost always right, and he'd made the right decision to not try to stifle her.

Scyles was still thinking about that conversation, running it over and over in his head. He was beginning to come to the conclusion she was probably right.

Orik looked at him and smiled grimly.

"If we're destined to be sleeping in this room, everyone together, we should hasten to get you two married," he said, glancing at his daughter with determination. "If you're going to be sleeping next to him, you're going to be wedded to him, and that's the end of the matter."

"Yes, Papa," she said meekly, bowing her head, but glancing at him with a smirk on her face.

Anything further they were going to say was interrupted as an opening appeared in one of the walls, as part of the wall slid out of sight, apparently into the wall next to it.

Everyone turned to the sudden opening in both dread and anticipation, wondering what would come through.

Scyles watched two strange-looking creatures enter the room, holding something about the size of a horse's hoof, pointing it towards the people, but not at anyone in particular. They saw that no one was making any aggressive moves, and spread out. Four more joined them, also carrying something in their hands.

Or paws, Scyles thought in awe.

King Agathyrsus stepped to the fore of his group and stared at them.

"They're wolves, or dogs," he said, his tone dripping with contempt. "Dogs walking on their back two legs, and wearing clothes."

They do look like dogs walking upright, Scyles marveled to himself. They wore some sort of harness that covers their private parts, and held what he assumed were more weapons, nothing on their feet, or paws. Their heads were shaped like a hound, with a long muzzle, and a very full mouth of canine teeth. Their ears were long and upright. Scyles couldn't tell if they were in that position permanently, or just at certain times.

Scyles watched another of the creatures enter the room, standing just behind his men, or canines, or whatever they would be considered. This one looked around the room casually, and his attention finally came to rest upon the kings.

This one is their leader, Scyles decided.

He moved slightly to stand between their captors and Arga, partially blocking their view of her. He cursed to himself as he saw the leader notice his movement and focus on him for a moment, then his eyes continued to shift, observing the people. Scyles wondered what he was thinking.

His eyes stopped when they returned to the kings. He looked at them closely, and seemed to nod to himself.

"My name is Commander Azimoth. You have been taken from your home world to work in the service of the Hshtahni Dominion. Any attempts to resist or escape will be met with extreme measures."

Scyles gaped. He could hear the doglike creature speaking in what had to be his own language, but a voice in his ear, or in his head, spoke in the language of the People. Around him, he could see others in all three tribes shaking their heads in confusion, tilting their heads, trying to understand.

"Your new master, Lord Bakhtochk, summons you to meet him." The dog man, as Scyles thought of him, pointed at his father, then King Orik, and finally, King Agathyrsus.

"You three are kings of your tribes, am I correct?" He didn't wait for an answer. "You will come with me." His eyes wandered over to Scyles, and he suddenly felt a chill go up his spine. "You, and the female behind you that you tried to shield when we stunned you on the planet's surface, and you, and you, come with us as well. You will go with this warrior," he said, pointing at one of the dog men.

The other two chosen were his mother and an older woman that had been one of the women serving at the lunch feast.

His father's face darkened, and he tore his eyes away from Scyles' mother's and was about to argue, when Scyles stepped to his side.

"I will take care of Mother, Sir," he said, and stared his father in the eyes. "This is not the moment for this. I will guard her with my life. Go, find out what we're up against," he said in as low a tone as he could.

His father stared at him as he slowly got control back, and finally nodded, and grasped his shoulder with a huge hand.

"Be wise and careful, Scyles," he said, and his voice was hoarse with emotion.

Targitai stepped forward, as did both of the other swordmasters.

"My king goes nowhere without me at his side," he said, and tried to follow them out the wide door.

The leader of the dog men nodded, and one of his warriors raised the object in his paw and did something. Scyles wasn't quite sure what, but his father's swordmaster fell to the floor immediately.

"Come," their leader said, and turned and walked out of the room. His dog men pointed their weapons at them, and Scyles forced himself to walk forward, following the three kings, and leading the women.

The dog men directed his father and the other two kings to the left, down a large passageway with walls, floor and ceiling of the same materials as their prison. The leader and four of his dog men walked with them, watching them closely. When Scyles started following, one of their captors said something that sounded like no in his ear, and pushed him in the other direction.

The four remaining dog men led them to an intersection of the large passageways, and made them turn right again. They were accompanied by twenty smaller short-haired grey creatures that looked like nothing so much as large rats, walking on their hind quarters. He noticed that some appeared to be female, with extra teats, but they all wore simple loincloths.

The passageway ahead was long and he could see other groups of the grey creatures, leading what looked like rafts that floated in the air. They finally were made to stop at a hatch and one of the dog men did something on the right side of the door, and it opened.

Scyles took one last look down the passageway at the other group, and saw that the rafts were piled high with what looked like swords, shields, bows, and other weapons of war. He made a mental note of which hatch they were taking them into, and tried not to look too interested as he followed the lead dog man.

It was a huge room, as big or bigger than the one they were being held in, and it had a wide variety of things from their camps. He saw one corner walled off with several horses and sheep penned inside. There were also bags of grain, and many other foodstuffs, piled in no particular order, along with cooking pots, bedding rugs, and kegs, some full, some empty.

His mother pushed past him and looked around. She saw the horses and told the other woman to go see if any of them could be milked. One of the guards walked with her.

She looked at Scyles, frustration filling her face.

"We need water, or milk. Some of our people are suffering and need liquids to drink. But not fermented milk, so these kegs are useless at the moment," she said pointing at four of them. "But some of these are empty, so if we can find water, we can fill them."

Scyles nodded and looked at one of the dog men.

"Are there any streams nearby? We need water for drinking, washing food, and more," he said, and watched two of the dog men look at each other and make odd sounds that he finally realized was their version of laughter.

"No streams," one of them finally said, and walked to the wall, and pushed a flat spot that stuck out from the wall with a strange-looking device below it. Water came out of the device, and he released the spot and it stopped. "Show these Meyores what to do, and what needs to be carried back to where you are being held."

"Uh," Scyles said, looking around, intimidated by the thought of figuring out priorities and what needed doing.

"Does the place you keep us have these water holes?" his mother asked the dog man, and he nodded. "Good. Then we can take the cups back and people can serve themselves. We'll take some kegs to fill and put around the room."

Scyles watched his mother begin telling the strange grey creatures what needed to be gathered together, and had Arga helping her in a matter of moments. After a minute, she turned to stare at him.

"You may be a prince, but you can help out here. First, I want you to…"

Scyles obeyed and began directing some of the strange rat creatures to roll the bedding rugs up, and pile on one of the empty rafts. But even as he followed his mother's directions, and began sorting some of the foodstuffs out, his mind kept coming back to the room down the passageway.

The one full of their weapons.

Gelon followed the dog man guard, between Orik and Agathyrsus. He was uncomfortably aware of the others behind them, walking with their weapons in their hands, or paws, or whatever the appropriate name for them were.

His mind felt as though it was sloughing through thick, waist-deep, mud. And although the leader of the enemy, and he could think of them in no other way, had said Targitai would recover, that he was only unconscious, he worried for his old friend.

And where were they taking Myrina and the children?

Gelon knew he needed to quit thinking of Scyles as a child. He had more than proven himself last night. Although he hadn't struck the decisive blow to the assassin, he'd fought him equally up to that point. Gelon knew, only too well, how dangerous and deadly these Persian assassins were. Their guild was renowned for their unbelievably high success rate in fulfilling their contracts. The assassin had given up nothing about who hired him, but his accent gave away his home.

He saw a large door ahead, and wondered what they were walking into.

"Be very careful, fellow kings," he warned in a low voice. "Who knows what lurks behind that door."

"I want answers, and I want them now," Agathyrsus said angrily. "Where are my children? For that matter, where are the rest of our tribes?"

Gelon shot a quick glance at Orik, and caught his eyes. Orik saw him and nodded in agreement.

The large door slid to the side, and they entered another large chamber. There were so many amazing things inside, he didn't know where to look first.

The walls were covered with pictures. But these pictures moved, as if alive. Or as if the subjects painted on them in such fine detail, were alive.

There were tables of sorts in various places around the room, all of them with more of these dog men. They all had more of the pictures, some of them showing the same thing as the larger ones on the walls.

But the object that captured all three of their attentions were the three large creatures lounging on a platform that floated above the floor. It was probably about the same size as the interior of his common yurt, and that was good, because those three creatures filled it completely.

They looked like some sort of lizard, but huge, with thick hides that looked more like a castle wall than any sort of flesh. Their skins were scaly, but the scales were thick, and looked very hard, and unbreakable.

The largest of the three was almost twice the size of either of the others, and his head was massive, as big as many of the carts in which the people hauled their belongings. He yawned and Gelon felt both men on either side of him flinch at the sight. The creature had either double or triple rows of large teeth that filled the mouth completely. He, and Gelon was only assuming it was a he, had a tail that stretched out far behind him. He had four legs that looked very muscular and powerful, and as covered with thick scales as the rest of him. He had four thick toes with long, deadly-looking nails that more resembled talons.

He also had two arms that looked like miniature versions of his legs in every way, except smaller, and in addition to the four fingers was a thick thumb, all having the same talons as his paws.

The other two monsters on the raft, and he could think of them as nothing else, were much smaller versions, but otherwise similar, with one dramatic exception.

They both had very functional looking wings. The hide looked tough, but not as heavily armored in appearance as the bigger one. Gelon decided it would be possible to damage those wings with their weapons.

The biggest one was a dark grey, with streaks of black and lighter grey interlaced. One of the smaller ones was a bright red, the other, a deep, dark blue. He wondered if the big one was perhaps much older, maybe even the parent, of the two smaller ones.

Or were they different breeds entirely? They were clearly from the same origin, but perhaps one tribe had wings, one did not.

"I have heard of beasts such as these," Orik said in a low voice. "To the east, the land of the Zhou has many stories and pieces of art depicting creatures similar to these. And the Medes that lived in Persia, long before the Persians, passed down tales of horrors inflicted on entire cities."

"They called them dragons," Gelon muttered, almost inaudibly.

"Right," Orik said, sounding vaguely irked that Gelon knew that.

The three kings were brought to a halt before the large grey one, and Gelon decided he was probably the leader of their captors.

"I am told that the three of you are the leaders of your various tribes," the largest dragon stated, his voice rumbling in such low tones, it felt more like a distant storm grumbling. "Identify yourselves."

"I am King Agathyrsus, king of the Caitiari tribe of the People," Agathyrsus said, and continued. "I demand to know why we have been taken prisoner. And where the rest of our tribe members are. In particular, I have two children that were with me when we were attacked. I demand to know where they are."

Gelon mentally shook his head at the man's arrogant attitude and tone. It was clear that whatever these creatures were, they were formidable, and had resources and weapons that were beyond anything he'd seen in his lifetime. If Agathyrsus wasn't careful, the Caitiari would be selecting another king soon.

"I am King Gelon, of the Auchatae tribe of the People," he said, and left it at that.

The large reptile's head cocked to the side in an unconscious gesture that was disturbingly similar to their own mannerisms. He leaned forward a little, and sniffed in Gelon's direction. After a moment, he did the same with Agathyrsus, and finally, Orik.

"Interesting," he said, and looked at Orik.

"I am King Orik, of the Paralatae tribe of the People," he said, and copied Gelon's tactic by saying no more.

"You say, your tribes are of the People," the creature said, his gaze shifted between them in a very casual manner. "What people do you speak of?"

"The Scoloti," Gelon answered, wishing to slow Agathyrsus's apparent death wish down. "We are a mighty race, with many tribes such as our own, and have defeated many other empires, and races in battle."

"Do the Scoloti have a single king that rules over all of these tribes?"

Gelon hesitated, sensing a trap, but Agathyrsus charged forward with his words.

"That was the purpose of our three tribes meeting at the gathering before the arrival of the rest of the tribes, to decide which of us would become the Great King of the Scoloti." Agathyrsus gathered himself up, and Gelon decided he was trying to look formidable, but the circumstances made that near impossible. "I have one of the largest tribes, and would have been the chosen Great King," he finished, and both Gelon and Orik turned to look at him for a moment.

"That remains to be seen," Gelon said in a deliberately casual voice. "There is a very good chance he would not have been chosen. King Orik's tribe is the largest, and he does have many allies amongst the other tribes."

"Such as yourself," the giant lizard stated, and watched all their reactions.

"Such as myself," Gelon agreed.

"Well, those will be memories you can all cherish as time passes, but that situation no longer exists."

The dragon lifted his head, and looked down at them, opening his mouth as if to yawn, showing his rows of deadly sharp and pointed teeth.

"I am Lord Bakhtochk, of the Hshtahni Dominion, and you are now my personal property." He stood up on all four feet so his massive head towered over them. Off to the left, the two winged creatures did the same. One of them batted his wings several times, and the wind generated made all three kings sway in the stench-filled air.

"You are no longer on your planet, but aboard our generation ship, the Muschwain," he stated. "So escape is not an option. Any attempt to resist or rebel will be met with fatal consequences. We are taking you to one of our planets to evaluate your species, and see if you have any value."

The large grey head turned to the leader of the dog men, and stared at him. He took the hint and his men turned the three of them around, and out the door, which slid shut behind them.

"What about my children?" Agathyrsus demanded, and the dog man shrugged his shoulders.

Gelon and Orik walked together as they watched Agathyrsus rant and rail against the dog man, with absolutely no results. Neither of them said anything for a while, until Orik finally turned to Gelon.

"You spoke well in there, Gelon," he said, almost sounding envious. "Perhaps you should be the great king."

"No, you have the better demeanor, and the people like and respect you," Gelon said quietly, trying to not let Agathyrsus hear them. But he was too busy arguing at the dog man to notice anything they were saying. "I and everyone in my tribe will support you fully."

"It may be a moot point, now," Orik said wryly, waving a hand around him. He turned to Gelon and shook his head in confusion. "That will be what it will be. But there is one thing I would like to know very much."

"What is that, my friend?" Gelon asked curiously, and Orik stared at him, looking perplexed.

"What in Hades' name is a planet?"

Chapter Thirteen

Aboard Egelv Destroyer Mountain Edge, just outside Egelv Empire claimed space.

"Mountain Edge, your meandering paranoia has led us far beyond our borders. It is time to turn back towards Egelv space."

Captain Rost Fott grinned at First Officer Van Dono, and then looked hopefully at Second Officer Rel Steen, who was on duty on the long-range detection station.

"Anything? Anything at all?" he asked, and both Egelv officers smiled at his wistful tone. They looked at each other, then back at him and shook their heads in mock dismay.

"Everything looks exactly as it did last time we were in this area, Captain," his second officer said apologetically. "I think we're going to have to obey the orders of our illustrious leader, Commodore Mit Obet, and return to our own space. All suspected unknown anomalies have been identified as being exactly what they seem."

"Our tour is near its zenith, Captain," Van Dono said. "I believe we need to regroup with the rest of the squadron, and make our way back into the quadrant we're supposed to be in, so we can be relieved, and return home to Egelv Prime."

"How boring is that?" Rost Fott muttered to himself, but both men heard him.

"How boring will it be to go home in time to attend my own union to my lovely near-mate?" Rel Steen asked, the question clearly hypothetical. "Attending the ceremony in person, and being on time will do wonders for the odds of the union being lasting and fruitful."

"Ah yes, the lovely Lema Azon," Van Dono teased. "I suspect if you have any actual leave coming, every effort will be made to be fruitful."

All three men laughed. Rel Steen's near-mate was not only stunning in appearance, but very intelligent, as well as charming. She also shared his love of living life to its fullest, and taking challenges in stride.

Rost Fott was a little jealous. In truth, he'd had several relationships that had appeared to be good choices towards a long-term commitment, but none of them had ever worked out.

"Mountain Edge, please respond." Mit Obet's voice sounded a little testy, and Rost Fott decided it was time to give in, and allow him and his ship to be drawn back into the fold. "Captain Rost Fott, I know you can hear me. We are going to be hard-pressed to return to our quadrant before the Fifth Squadron arrives to relieve us. Raging River and Comet's Tail are returning to our proper positions, and you need to do the same. Respond now."

"Commodore Mit Obet, we hear you, and are heading towards your position." Rost Fott nodded to Van Dono, and Mountain Edge did a tight, sweeping turn, and began to accelerate to catch the other two ships. "Set your courses, and we will catch up within the hour."

"About time, Captain," Mit Obit said sharply, and then lightened his tone. "Let's get relieved on schedule, and head home. We can synchronize all three ships and have a squadron feast on the way back."

"Sounds good," Rost Fott said, and realized it did sound enjoyable.

"You will not believe this, Captain," Rel Steen said slowly. "There is some sort of anomaly forming in front of us. It's just outside Egelv space."

"What kind of anomaly?" Rost Fott asked, somewhat skeptical that his second officer wasn't having fun with him.

"I don't know," he admitted. "I've never seen these kind of readings before, and the energy levels are off the charts."

Rost Fott stood looking over Rel Steen's shoulder, seeing what he saw, and hesitated. There was no hope Mit Obet would believe him. But there it was. And it was the kind of thing they would always investigate. Unknown power surges in remote space, near nothing of any consequence, warranted a closer look.

Rost Fott sighed and keyed his transmitter.

"Raging River, Commodore Mit Obet, I know how this is going to sound, but we're getting readings of an extremely powerful anomaly just outside Egelv space in quadrant XW-8420." Rost Fott winced, and nervously ran his long brown fingers through his straight white hair. It was a nervous habit he'd had as a child, and thought it long defeated.

"Mountain Edge, what kind of keldor dung is this you're trying to feed me?" Mit Obet sounded very annoyed, and Rost Fott couldn't blame him.

"Commodore, these are legitimate readings." Rost Fott hesitated. "It resembles theoretical black hole energy flows we learned about in academy. Gravity fields are fluctuating, and shifting in random patterns."

"Captain Rost Fott, you're in deep space, far from any star system or other factor that could influence or create gravity fields." His voice was dripping with disdain. "You can't be registering fluctuating gravity fields."

"Commodore, I assure you, we are," Rost Fott said, and was startled as First Officer Van Dono spoke up.

"Commodore Mit Obet, this is Mountain Edge First Officer Van Dono, and I wish to affirm my captain's sighting. We are getting gravity surges that would endanger the ship if we were half the distance from the area that we currently are."

Rost Fott glared at Van Dono, but his first officer didn't meet his eyes.

"Well then, I recommend you do not decrease your proximity by fifty percent," the commodore said in a dry voice, resonating doubt. "Rost Fott, be truthful to me. Is this report a real phenomenon?"

"It is," Rost Fott said simply.

The commodore sighed.

"Fine. Mountain Edge, we are doing a sweeping turn and will be in your vicinity within half an hour." He hesitated, then continued forcefully. "This had better be real, gentlemen. If this is more mischief, I will write up every officer on your ship."

"Awaiting your arrival," Rost Fott said in a wooden voice. He turned back to look at the screen of the space in front of them, and read the columns of figures that rolled down the screen next to the picture.

"Record all data and displays connected to the phenomenon," he said, nodding to Rel Steen. He still couldn't stand to look at his first officer. "I pray to Gar, it doesn't fade away before they arrive."

"To Gar," both of his senior officers said in unison, and Rost Fott heard the rest of his bridge crew echo them.

He stared at the screen and waited.

Aboard the World Ship Kchoatkhakh, in unclaimed space near two tunnel singularities.

Zechkreeshrrprhkq comfortably rested his massive head on the mobile control station in the cradle especially designed to fit him. His fine tendrils were moving at a frenzied speed across the controls, even as he concentrated on controlling the power involved in such a major action.

He felt the Trixmae stir in the holding tank, and felt relief. Soon, he would have a boost in power, which was important. The actions they were taking required so much energy that could expand out of control, or leak into other fields and cause countless disasters.

Once started, the operation they were attempting had to be controlled until completed. If allowed to grow out of control, or to flow into the wrong places, it had the power to literally turn them and their ships inside out, causing instant annihilation.

The Hshtahni ships were beginning to shift closer to the expected location of the tunnel entrance. They were only now realizing they had a problem, and that something was drawing them off their course settings.

So far, he was causing the gravity fluctuations to draw the Hshtahni ships closer, at which point the Trixmae would open the tunnel, drawing them in. Zechkreeshrrprhkq had some ideas on how to retrieve the thousands of Humans, and this tactic would give them the time to do so.

"Open the tunnel. It is time." Zechkreeshrrprhkq felt exhaustion setting in. The power necessary to perform this task was vast, and he was fast wearing down. Then he felt Achkptrrshkqk add his strength to the effort, and the tension and strange sensation known as pain eased off enough for him to control all the energies.

The Trixmae and two Hechktar watched as the two ships were pulled into the tunnel. Then they were gone, and it closed behind them.

Zechkreeshrrprhkq sighed in relief and sagged loosely on the raft, his chin still resting on the controls. Behind him he felt his nephew slowly slide down to lay, exhausted, in the mud, only his eyes and snout showing.

The Trixmae, also showing signs of exhaustion, began to communicate at a rapid pace.

He felt dismay at the news.

There were ships at the far end of the tunnel. There hadn't been when this operation had started, but sometime between then and now, they had shown up, and would be there when the Hshtahni emerged.

There was nothing to do at the moment. Not until his and the Trixmae's strength was regenerated, at least to a certain extent.

The realization that they might have just committed over six thousand Humans to their deaths came to him in a rush of sorrow and self-incrimination.

"Uncle?"

He sighed, and without turning, reassured his nephew.

"We will investigate. But first we must recover. Abide, Nephew. We will right our mistake."

But in his mind and multiple hearts, he knew it wouldn't be that simple.

Aboard the Hshtahni Generation Ship Muschwain

Azimoth was restless. He was the commander of this ship, and he should be on the bridge. He had people that could take care of questioning these primitives, and guiding them on the procedures they were to follow on the voyage back to Tolokh.

He received word from his security chief that all the Meyores were now secured in the vast loading dock. All hatches had been locked, and there was nothing else of any import in the dock.

Azimoth didn't agree with jettisoning six hundred more or less healthy workers, even of limited capabilities, to save on the cost of feeding and caring for them. Surely their value offset the cost of feeding them for the duration of the trip home.

But his lord had been firm, and there was no arguing with a Hshtahni. They couldn't be allowed to live, since they would not only witness, but help in the acquisition of these new bipeds. They would almost certainly talk about it, unless they were disposed of.

"Open the outer hatches," he said in a tight voice, and forced himself to watch on his handheld. The bodies of the Meyores shot out of the dock as if solid projectiles on target on an enemy ship. He purposefully didn't allow the display to show from too close. The sight of so many bodies decompressing at once was depressing, no matter what race they were.

And messy, he thought dourly. After this interview and assessment session, he would have his guards take some of the people, as they called themselves, to the dock and have them clean up any mess not disposed of by the harsh cold exposure to space.

The picture of the tiny bodies shooting away from the ship was replaced by a screen showing their course, and that they were deviating from it. He ordered the course correction necessary, and the ship began to swing back on course, only to be pulled back off.

He noticed the Clonoschk appeared to be having the same problem.

"Finish this up, then report to personnel," he told the guard directing the inspection of the primitives. "I'll be on the bridge."

He didn't know what could be causing them to be pulled off course, but he didn't like it.

And he was very sure he knew four Hshtahni that would like it even less.

Gelon watched the dog man that seemed to have the highest rank hurry out of the room, and his men begin to speed up their recording of the names of the people, and their tribal affiliation.

After a short time, the one in charge got a message on the little box he carried, and called to his dog men. They left abruptly, saying they would be back later to complete the inventory.

"They seem to be in quite a hurry," Scyles said, looking at him thoughtfully. "Did you feel that a few minutes ago?"

"What?" Gelon asked curiously.

"I don't know," Scyles admitted. "It was very subtle, but it almost felt as if the room moved a little bit."

"How could that be?" Gelon asked skeptically, and his son shrugged.

"How can they have a cart that flies?" he asked, with a resigned expression on his face. "But I am sure I felt a very slight jerk, or roll, or something."

Arga had walked over to them as they spoke and she looked at Scyles in surprise.

"I felt that. A few minutes ago?" she asked, and he nodded.

They both looked at Gelon, and he shrugged.

"I felt nothing, but perhaps I was distracted."

Gelon looked around the room and had a premonition.

Something, something big, was about to happen. He didn't know what, but something in the situation had changed. And there was something he wanted to do before the world went insane yet another time.

He looked over at Myrina, and saw her talking with Orik and Opis.

Perfect, he thought. It was as if she sensed his gaze, because she turned and looked at him, and smiled as she saw him watching her. He nodded at the other king and queen and wagged his head for them to come over.

The three of them came over and looked at him curiously. He grinned mirthlessly at them.

"Something is about to change. I don't know what, or what will cause it, but there is something I want done before everything goes to Hades again."

Both women smiled, and as if planned, all four parents turned and looked at Scyles and Arga, standing nearby, holding hands and talking quietly. They felt eyes upon and them and looked over. Both flinched at the sudden attention.

"Guilty conscience?" Myrina asked, and all four adults laughed at their expressions.

"What is it?" Scyles asked, suspiciously.

Arga got a knowing look on her face and smiled, sneaking a quick look at his face, suddenly looking shy.

"Son, when we get the chance, your sling will be our only weapon with more reach than a man's arm. Soon, you must be constantly aware and ready for action," Gelon said, looking very serious, then relented. "But before that, we need to resolve your and Arga's status."

"Our status?" he asked, and looked wary.

Arga laughed softly and hugged him.

"We're getting married. Now."

"We are?" Scyles looked at her, and then his mother in panic. She smiled at him, stepped forward, and kissed his cheek.

"You are," she said, glancing over at Arga with humor on her face. "They're very brave until you finally corner them. Then you have to coax them off their horse."

"I'll remember that," Arga said gravely, and looked at her mother, startled, as she gave a sniff.

Orik gave his daughter a hug, then swept Scyles into a huge embrace.

"You're a good boy, and will make a great man and king," he said and pulled Scyles close. "But hurt my daughter and I'll snuff you like a candle, boy."

Scyles nodded, not speaking.

Gelon looked around the room and shouted out.

"My son Scyles, and Princess Arga will marry today. In fact, they will marry right now!" Gelon looked at Targitai, who, as always, was nearby, and watching over him carefully.

"Targitai, find two men and thrash anyone that tries to protest this marriage."

His old friend grinned fiercely. "My pleasure, Sire."

He glared at the people gathering around them.

"You heard the king," he called out. "No one will be dragging this out. No one," he repeated, looking at King Agathyrsus, who stood with his wife and some of their men nearby.

Gelon and Orik looked at each other and grasped each other's arms in a kinsman handshake.

"Let's get this marriage going so they can get to consummating!"

Scyles and Arga both blushed as the crowd roared their approval.

Scyles and Arga lay beneath the blanket, she firmly planted in the crook of his shoulder, his arm around her, pressing her naked body to his.

They both looked at the makeshift walls of bedding giving them the illusion of privacy. They could hear members of both tribes beyond, loudly discussing in lurid detail, what they imagined was happening right now, and Arga looked up into his face, blushing furiously. Then she started laughing.

"Is my face as red as yours, m'lord?" she asked demurely.

"Let that be the last time you ever call me m'lord," Scyles said, stalling.

"We are equal in every way, just as our parents are. You are my love, and I would be yours."

"You are," she said, kissing his chest, running her fingers through his thin chest hair. "My love."

They kissed, and a few whoops on the other side of the hangings confirmed they had no actual privacy, but there was nothing to be done about that, so they ignored it.

Her head came back to rest against his shoulder, and he squeezed her with his arm. Scyles didn't know what couples talked about between bouts of love-making, but had to admit, the intimacy was almost as pleasurable as the actual sex. A thought came to him.

"You didn't bleed much," he said, not worried about it. Just curious.

"Every girl I know breaks herself within a year or two of monthly bleeding," she said in a casual voice. "Mother says it's all the time spent riding horses that causes it. I was still a virgin."

"I know. You told me the other night," Scyles said, and gave a start. She giggled.

"That was last night," she said, and they both laughed. The movement caused them to rub together in certain places, and their attentions came right back to each other.

"I am so happy we didn't stand firm on our plan to wait a year," Scyles said, and froze. What if...?

"Are you happy about that?" he asked hesitantly. "I know you wanted to wait, and with good reason. And I would have waited." He held his breath as she didn't answer immediately.

"Despite our intentions, I am very happy," he said slowly, fearing what she was going to say. "What are you thinking?" he finally asked desperately.

"I am thinking that even as sure as I was, I was also wrong," she admitted. "Don't get used to it. When we quarrel, remember, I will generally be right, and you will always be wrong."

Scyles laughed again, and she joined in. Arga rolled over so she was partially draped over him, and he raised his head to kiss her softly on the lips.

"I am very happy," she admitted. "I am glad we married, and that we are doing exactly what we're doing right now."

Voices outside their little haven rose in volume, and lewd suggestions were being shouted out.

"Even like this," she admitted, looking around as if to catch someone peeking between the hanging cloths. "Speaking of which," she said, her hands wandering not at all aimlessly, under the covers. "How long before we can do certain things again?"

Scyles gasped as her hands found what they were searching for.

His passion was his answer as he pulled her tight against him.

The room lurched and they rolled over, Scyles protecting her with his body as he looked around, wondering what was happening.

"This is not a convenient time to have to go to battle," he gasped, feeling the weight and pressure in his groin.

Arga laughed and grabbed him by the sides of his head, giving him a fierce kiss.

"Whatever we do, we do together, my love," she said, and Scyles kissed her back, every bit as aggressively.

They stared at each other, lying tangled in the covers, limbs and parts exposed, sounds of the people preparing for battle all around them.

"We will finish this later," Scyles promised, and rolled off her. They both began searching for their clothes so hastily tossed aside.

"No, dear Scyles," she said, slapping his bare butt. She grinned at him, with more than a hint of a very undignified leer.

"We will continue this later," she corrected, and they both laughed as they dressed as quickly as possible.

Chapter Fourteen

Aboard the Hechktar Worldship Kchoatkhakh, near the two tunnel singularities

Zechkreeshrrprhkq turned to Achkptrrshkqk in sorrow.

"Our valued ally, the Trixmae, just informed me that the Hshtahni generation ship jettisoned over six hundred living Meyores into space after they cleared orbit with the Humans. Six hundred and four, to be precise."

His nephew bowed his head in tribute to the fallen Meyores, and emanated despondency.

"I know very little about this race, Uncle," he said. And his head raised, eyes clear, but pained. "Was this done as a security measure, or do you think they were simply reducing the number of mouths to feed?"

"Probably both, Nephew," Zechkreeshrrprhkq admitted, sighing deeply. "Either way, the Hshtahni have much to answer for. This day will be recorded as a dark one for them, requiring a reckoning."

"The Hechktar will not forget," Achkptrrshkqk said very solemnly.

"No, we will not," he agreed, and closed his eyes to find badly needed rest.

Aboard the Egelv Destroyer Mountain Edge

"Give that anomaly a wide berth, but let's get on the Egelv territory side of it," Captain Rost Fott said grimly. "It's getting stronger every moment."

"Yes, Captain," Van Dono said grimly, "The gravitational pull is very strong, but we're far enough out to be able to stay free of it."

"How long until we have help, Second Officer Rel Steen," Rost Fott asked, more for the benefit of the automatic recordings being made than a need to sound official. "Where are Raging River and Comet's Tail?"

"I can't see around the anomaly, Captain Rost Fott," Rel Steen answered, giving him a grim smile as he adopted his captain's verbal protocol. "But based on our last communication, I would think they're close enough to see it for themselves."

"Mountain Edge, this is Raging River." Commodore Mit Obet's voice was dry and cynical. "We're within detection range of the anomaly you reported. I guess this lets you off the hook, Captain Rost Fott."

"Simply following up on what our instrumentation tells us, Commodore," Rost Fott said, wondering if he was being exonerated or set up for future blame. "This is looking more and more like a black hole opening. I've ordered my crew to battle stations, all departments, as a safeguard. Our shields are fully powered and extended, and all weaponry and security personnel active and in place."

"Don't you think that's a little bit of overkill?" Mit Obet asked, humor in his voice. "It's a gravitational force, not an enemy."

"Simply taking precautions, Commodore Mit Obet," Rost Fott said evenly. "If gravitational forces are random and rapidly changing, debris and other possible dangers could emerge when the anomaly fully opens. If we have the crew manning all defensive stations, we might as well have the security forces geared up as well. They don't need to be sitting around, drinking wine and heckling the rest of the crew."

"Your decision," Mit Obet admitted reluctantly. "But your precautions seem unnecessary. We see you coming around the anomaly. Form up with us as soon as you are able."

"I see them," Rel Steen said in relief, and put the display up on the screen. Rost Fott could see the two ships approaching, slowing as they neared, to avoid being pulled into the gravitational pull.

"We see you as well, Raging River and Comet's Tail," Rost Fott acknowledged. "We are giving the anomaly a wide berth to avoid being sucked in, but will form up with you presently."

"Very good, Mountain Edge," Mit Ober answered. "Safe sailing."

Before Rost Fott could answer, the anomaly opened widely, and two ships emerged. One was huge, some sort of population mover or generation ship, the other a very deadly looking fighting ship.

"Full power to weapons and shields," Van Dono barked out, and then looked confused as he remembered they were already at that stage. He looked up ruefully at Rost Fott, who shrugged.

"Better safe than sorry." He turned to Rel Steen. "Any ideas of who they are?"

"The big ship?" Rel Steen shook his head. "No idea. The other is Hshtahni, a heavy cruiser. A very formidable foe, if they choose to fight. From what I've heard of them, that could be their first choice."

Rost Fott opened his mouth to comment, but two things happened at the same time to make anything he was going to say irrelevant.

The anomaly literally collapsed in upon itself and disappeared in a matter of moments. And the heavy cruiser opened fire on Raging River and Comet's Tail.

Aboard the Hshtahni Generation Ship Muschwain

Azimoth leaned over his helmsman, watching his efforts to hold the Muschwain on course. At first, he'd thought his crewman was just being lazy, and not doing his job, but it was now clear that some gravitational force was dragging both ships to the right.

Sensors showed some sort of gravity fluctuation or anomaly was occurring ahead, and to the right. Something was dragging them off course, and potentially into a dangerous situation. He saw that the Clonoschk was also off course.

Azimoth came to a decision and turned to his lord.

"Lord Bakhtochk, I wish to put both ships on full alert and bring all our defenses to full readiness."

"What is causing this gravitational anomaly?" his lord asked ominously. "Can you provide full power to get us free?"

"No, my lord," Azimoth admitted. "We're already at full power and still being drawn in. Clonoschk has just confirmed they are in the same situation."

Even as he spoke, a circle began to take form in front of them. Azimoth checked, and saw that it was in the very center of the anomaly.

"What is that?" he said, standing and staring at the large screen on the wall.

"It appears to be a phenomenon called a black hole," Lord Bakhtochk said, and Azimoth turned to stare at him as he heard doubt in his voice.

"Is this a natural phenomenon or artificial?" Azimoth asked, his mind racing.

"We have heard theory on this, and it is possible to occur naturally," his lord said slowly. "For it to be artificial, it would have to be someone with the ability to control massive power, far more than anything we have or use currently."

"But it's possible that someone could have created this situation?" Azimoth asked, and didn't wait for an answer.

"Second Officer Zoun, bring the ship to full alert, including arming all Mba not at a ship's station." He looked at the screen again and winced.

The circle was now a broad ring, with what looked like a tube running away behind it. Azimoth would never admit it, but looking into the circle frightened him. It was blacker than the emptiest space, and yet, it looked like a cauldron of motion, but all colored the same darkest of black.

"Contact Clonoschk, tell Commander Fizrald to bring his ship to battle stations, same instructions as we have here," Azimoth said, unable to tear his eyes away from the black hole. "Lord Bakhtochk, I believe we are about to be drawn into that black hole. What effect will it have on us?"

"There are three theories," his lord said slowly. "And they are all only theories. There are stories of ships seeing this phenomenon in a large enough form to swallow a ship, but we've never heard of a case of it happening. First, it should have such a heavy gravitational field, any ship would be crushed instantly. This is the most likely result."

Azimoth didn't like the sound of that.

"Second, with this much power, it could send us into another dimension, possibly warp time and space, sending us anywhere and any when."

"But we wouldn't have any control of the where or when?" Azimoth asked, and his lord nodded his massive head.

"No," he admitted.

"What is the third possibility?" Azimoth asked, wondering if it could get any worse.

Lord Bakhtochk laughed, and Commander Azimoth was unnerved by his deep, booming, rumble that passed for laughing with the Hshtahni.

"It pulls us in, shoots us through and spits us out the other end."

Azimoth looked at the screen and saw they were so close to the phenomenon it consumed the entire screen. They were about to be pulled in. All questions would be answered very shortly, he thought dourly.

"Battle stations, repair crews be ready, we do not know what kind of stress this will put on this old tub," Azimoth said, and checked his sidearm to be sure it had a full charge. He saw that the cruiser was going to precede them slightly.

"Be ready to come out firing, Clonoschk," he said, and someone acknowledged him. He looked at Zoun. "The same with us. If there are ships waiting, they are almost certainly part of this. We must use any advantage we can seize."

Azimoth watched in awe and horror as Clonoschk disappeared into the blackness. Muschwain was close behind. He glanced up at Lord Bakhtochk.

His lord nodded to him.

"You've done what you can, Captain Azimoth," he said, and then they were drawn into the void, almost too fast for the Mba captain to realize his Lord had called him by his true rank.

Azimoth staggered, wondering how long they had been in the black hole. He felt a little dazed and very thirsty. That all was forgotten as he stared at the screen.

Clonoschhk was dead ahead of them, and as he looked, it began firing its weaponry as fast as it could. Ahead of it were two ships, and as he watched, they began firing back. For the moment, they were ignoring his ship, and he quickly realized why.

A third ship, identical to the first two, was approaching fast from starboard.

"Direct all weaponry at the third ship to the right," he said, and Zoun responded sluggishly.

"Fire!"

❖ ❖ ❖ ❖ ❖

Aboard the Egelv Destroyer Mountain Edge

Captain Rost Fott watched as his pilot veered to the left sharply, causing most of the shots from the large egg-shaped ship to miss. The few that connected were stopped by their shields.

"Aim at their weaponry, and try and disable their propulsion units," he said, and his orders were acknowledged by the weapon stations. He looked at Rel Steen. "What can you tell me about the ship?"

"It's very old, been altered so many times, the origin is impossible to discern without actually boarding it," his second officer said. He hesitated, then muttered profanity under his breath.

"What is it?" Rost Fott asked, frowning. Rel Steen was usually so even-keeled, he wasn't sure he'd ever actually heard him swear before.

"It is definitely a generation ship, and it looks fully utilized," Rel Steen said, his voice sounding strained.

"How many cryo or stasis units on a ship that size?" Rost Fott asked, knowing he wasn't going to like the answer.

"About ten thousand stasis units, all currently in use." He looked at Rost Fott. "It's big enough, there could have easily been between thirty and forty thousand units."

Rost Fott fought the urge to swear himself, and connected to Raging River. He quickly explained the situation to Commodore Mit Obet, who had no problem swearing, and with some vigor.

"We will attempt to disable, then take the generation ship," Rost Fott said, and half expected Mit Obet to argue with him.

"The heavy cruiser we're fighting is Hshtahni," Mit Obet reminded him. "Have you ever seen one of them?"

"Not in person, but I've seen pictures and analytical data on their physiology," Rost Fott admitted. "Any suggestions on how to kill them?"

"Stay at a distance, if possible. Our hand weapons have a longer range than theirs." Mit Obet hesitated. "They won't fall down at the first shot. Or the second or third."

"Noted," Rost Fott said. "Out."

He turned to Rel Steen, who was still scanning the ship.

"You heard that?"

"Yes, I did," his second officer glanced up at him. "There are two medium sized Hshtahni and one very big one on that ship."

"Three?" Rost Fott kept the dismay out of his voice. "Do you have more good news for me?"

"Sure," came the response. "There appears to be around a hundred and fifty beings, race unknown, in a large hold. They're bipedal, but we know nothing of their capabilities, or why they're all in one hold, or even on board. But they appear to match the physiology of the bipeds in stasis pods."

Rel Steen brushed his long white hair back away from his face.

"There also appears to be more than sixty Mba on board as well." His second officer shrugged. "They're probably crew from that cruiser, and extra security troops for some purpose unknown to us."

"Anything else?" Rost Fott said in a mild voice as he checked his side-arm again.

"No, that's about it," Rel Steen said, watching him. "You know you can't be part of the boarding party, don't you? You can't leave your post. I'll tell Security Chief Zard Win to prepare for when we grapple. He has twenty-four security force troopers on board."

"That's too few," Rost Fott argued, knowing his second officer was right. "We'll need to send some armed crewmen as well."

"I should be the one that goes," Rel Steen said. "I'm the most expend-able, in case we have to separate from the world ship and destroy it."

"You're also the least experienced in combat," Rost Fott said, and shook his head. "You are too valuable here on the bridge."

"Officers, please quit arguing," his first officer, Van Dono said brusque-ly. "We all know I'm the one that's going. I've already contacted Security Chief Zard Win, and he's forming an assault team."

Rost Fott saw that the generation ship was still returning fire.

"Come, my officers, we still have a ship to disable. We can resolve who leads the boarding party when it's time."

"It'll be me," Van Dono said, and both of the other men ignored him.

Chapter Fifteen

Aboard the Hshtahni generation ship Muschwain

The floor shook beneath them, and Myrina looked at Gelon in fear. He understood her fear well. Once, when he was younger, he'd felt the ground buck and shake just like this. Portions of seashore cliffs had separated and fallen into the sea. This had happened far to the south and west of where the People now lived.

Or had lived, he thought solemnly.

He reached out and pulled her to him, supporting her as he worked his way over to one of the walls.

As quickly as the shaking started, it stopped.

Gelon held his wife's shoulders, looking at her, trying to generate a positive level of comfort. He wanted to remove her fears, take away the anxiety that had to come when the very world around you shook and cried out in pain.

"I am better, husband," she said, and he exhaled in relief. Her voice was strong, and determined. She was already looking around the room to see if anyone needed her aid.

"You are my purpose in life," he said in a thick voice, his emotions threatening to show themselves.

"I am one of your three purposes in life," she retorted, and he had to smile. Myrina tried to smile and almost achieved it. "And if Scyles was skilled, Arga is fertile, and we are lucky, you may soon have four."

"Give the boy a break, wife," he laughed, wondering at how she always made him stronger. He looked searchingly until he saw Arga and Scyles.

They were reassuring her parents. Gelon was glad to see little Serlotta standing next to his older sister, safe and undamaged.

Scyles seemed to feel his stare. He turned and saw them, and relief was clear on his face. He said something to his new wife and walked over briskly.

"Are you ready to escape this prison, and take our lives back?" Gelon said, and his son gave a cautious smile.

"I am, Father." Scyles looked into his face searchingly. "Do you have a plan?"

"That door slides to the right to open," Gelon said, nodding his head at it. "Surely we have enough strong men to force it? Then we kill the guards, if there are any."

Scyles looked at the door thoughtfully, and shrugged.

"It's as good as any, and sound in its simplicity," he said, a small smile coming to his face.

They both turned and watched Targitai approach.

"Are you fully recovered, old friend?" Gelon asked him, and Targitai snorted, glanced at Scyles with a sly look.

"More importantly, young prince, are you?" His grin was very suggestive. "Women can drain you."

"Or they can give you the strength to carry on and win the day," Gelon said, and gave Targitai a warning look. Then he was all business. "Get as many big men as we can muster to try and push that door open. And spread the knives out amongst us."

Gelon watched Scyles loosen his necklace and make it into a sling. Then he pulled a knife out of his boot, and glanced at him. Behind him, Arga pulled two knives out of concealment and crouched behind Scyles.

He opened his mouth to protest, and then closed it again. He would not shame his son's wife that way. Orik came over to stand next to him, one of his wife's knives in his hand. Their wives were right behind him, both with knives as well. He nodded at Myrina, and quickly told them the plan. Orik and Opis looked hopeful, but Myrina gave him a skeptical look.

Targitai got men lined up, shoulder to shoulder, with half a dozen men with knives in a second line behind them. Scyles and Arga were to the left of the door, and he had his sling swinging in a deceptively lazy fashion.

"Go," Gelon said, and the men strained, trying to use their hands to slide the door to the right. It didn't budge. "Again!"

Scyles caught his stone, and stepped closer to inspected the wall to the left of the door. The men stopped trying to slide it, and a couple of them looked at him. His son bent over to look at a spot closer, then straightened. He looked at the men against the door.

"Be ready to charge," he said softly. He glanced at Gelon and inhaled deeply. Gelon leaned over and saw two circular spots, one above the other. He wondered what they were.

Scyles pushed the bottom one and his sling came up, swinging swiftly. Nothing happened.

Scyles muttered something, and Arga actually leaned forward and slapped him on the buttocks. She got him squarely and it made a loud sound. He flinched, turned and saw her, and grinned sheepishly.

He nodded to the men, and pushed the top one.

The door slid open.

There were two of the dog men on the other side, both carrying the weapon that could knock them out.

Scyles let the stone fly, and it hit one of them squarely in the forehead. His head shot back, and he staggered, looking like he would fall.

Before he could, both he and the other guard were overwhelmed by men with knives. Gelon heard the weapon sound once, then both of them were on the ground, unmoving, multiple wounds all over their torsos.

Two men fell to the floor.

"Are they breathing?" Targitai asked brusquely, but Gelon could hear the concern in his voice.

Skulis knelt next to them, felt their necks, then put the back of his hand in front of one of their mouths, then the other. He looked up and nodded reassuringly.

One of the men handed Targitai the two weapons. He handed one to Gelon, and hefted the other, looking at it curiously.

Gelon backhanded his son on the shoulder.

"Why didn't you tell me you knew how to open it?" he asked, and felt Arga stand close to him to watch Scyles' face as he answered. He also saw the pride in her eyes.

"I didn't know I did," Scyles admitted. "I know where the weapons are. Let me have some men and we'll go get as many as we can carry."

"Men and women," Arga said, and tapped her two blades against each other.

"As she says," Scyles said in a fatalistic voice, and Gelon had difficulty keeping from laughing out loud. He motioned for Targitai to come to him.

"Pick about eight or ten men," he began, and felt her eyes upon him. "Or women," he quickly added. "Scyles and Arga know where the weapons are stored. Bring back as much as you can."

"We should go, too," Orik said, doubt in his voice.

Gelon shook his head.

"Better we wait here," Gelon said softly, and glanced across the room to where the Caitiari were sprawled lazily. Their king pointedly had his back to them.

Gelon shook his head and looked at his swordmaster.

"Go."

Targitai nodded, picked out eight men and two women, and Scyles led them away.

Arga trotted alongside Scyles in a gait that was easy to maintain. She hadn't paid as close attention as Scyles when they'd been led this way. She hadn't seen any weapons, and wondered where he had.

Behind them, the men and women trotted along, breathing easily. A couple of them sounded like they hadn't needed to run for quite some time. But most of them were fine.

Scyles led them around a corner, down a smaller concourse, then another turn to the left. She thought she remembered where the belongings were stored, but they passed right by the door. He slowed and came to a halt about ten horse lengths past the storage area.

He found the round spots next to the door and pushed the top one. It obediently opened, and they all gave a collective sigh of relief at the sight of swords, bows, spears, and more, piled high on several platforms, and messily stacked over against the far wall.

She picked out two short swords with Auchatae colors on the handles, and strapped them around her waist. As she found a bow and a gorytos, she saw Scyles examining the base of one of the bins of weapons. He stood up and walked around to the other end, and slid his hands around the edges.

She jumped back, as did the other men, as the large bin of weapons rose into the air as high as her knees. Scyles pushed against the side of the bin, and it floated a few feet.

"Clever boy," Targitai said, and stopped cold as Scyles stared at him. Their eyes locked for a moment, and then the swordmaster nodded grudgingly.

"Clever, my prince," he said. "You've proven yourself a man many times over this last couple of days."

Arga suddenly understood what those looks between them involved. Without thinking, she spoke up.

"He certainly proved it to me," she said, hoping her face wasn't too red. "And when we get all this dealt with, he can prove to me again a few more times yet this eve."

Now it was Scyles' turn to blush as the men chuckled. He covered his embarrassment by pointing at two of the men.

"One of you on either side, push and steer it like it was a wheeled cart," he said, and pointed at a third man. "You go with them and keep your bow cocked and your eyes open. Do you know the way back?"

"I do," one of the two men pushing the bin said. "Here, you push, I'll lead and watch."

The two swapped places and they pushed their way out the door. Scyles noticed that the bin was mostly full of swords and spears, along with a couple stacks of shields.

Then they were out the door and gone.

Targitai was organizing another team of three men to push another bin, but couldn't figure out how to make it float. Scyles showed all of them the two buttons to raise and lower it.

None of them knew the way back, so Arga reluctantly agreed to go with them. She cocked an arrow, held it in one hand and let Scyles give her a quick hot kiss. She noticed the bin was as the first, mostly swords, shields and spears.

"Scyles, make sure the third one has plenty of bows and every shaft you can find," she said, and pointed her men to the left. "The first two didn't have hardly any."

He nodded to her, his eyes glowing with pride. Then he was busy piling more bows into the next two bins.

"Ha, found mine," Arga heard her husband cry out as she led their bin away, and smiled at his enthusiasm. Then she blinked.

My husband, she thought in wonder. I am married, and a woman.

It was too much for her to deal with at the moment, so she put the thought away and kept the men moving along at a brisk rate. But the sweet phrase, my husband, kept coming to her lips, trying to escape them. Somehow, she kept quiet as she led them back.

As they neared the final turn, she heard noises ahead and signaled the men to stop the bin. She crept forward to look around the corner, and saw Caitiari warriors streaming out of the room they'd been imprisoned in.

They all had swords and shields, and some carried a spear in their shield hand, in addition to the shields. She saw King Agathyrsus turn to the left, and his men, as well as his wife, follow him down the concourse.

Arga turned to the men and quietly told them to wait until the Caitiari were farther away. She didn't want to fight them off for the weapons. She looked again, and saw them turn down a side hall and disappear.

"Good, let's go," she said, and stepped into the concourse, bow raised.

They brought the bin into the room, and a quiet cheer went up. Arga was happy to see both Gelon and her father wearing swords, and shields resting near them. A good number of the men closest to the door also had weapons.

"Father," she called out, and saw a look of relief appear on his face. She frowned at him. "Why did the Caitiari leave?"

"They were waiting and caught us by surprise when the first cart arrived," her father admitted ruefully. "They'd gradually moved closer to the door, so when the weapons arrived, they took theirs first."

"But where did they go?" Arga asked, bewildered. "Why didn't they wait until we all returned, so we'd have strength in numbers?" A thought occurred to her. "And there were no bows in the first bin at all. Scyles is close behind us with the bows and arrows, and more of everything."

"Scyles is here," her husband said as he entered the room. He had his two swords on his back, gorytos at his waist. Two bins floated in behind him, people stepping aside to make room for them. The men and women warriors began scavenging through the three bins, looking for their own weapons, or something close to them.

Arga walked over to him and gave him a hug. She was glad Scyles didn't hurry to end it.

They finally pulled apart, reluctantly.

158

Targitai and Ariapithes walked over to the two kings, and nodded.

"We've posted archers to watch the concourse for the enemy," Ariapithes said.

"King Gelon, are you ready to make a plan to kill every one of these dog men and any big lizards we come across?" Orik asked, and Arga pulled Scyles closer so they could listen.

"It will be a pleasure to tear the entrails from every one of those creatures," Gelon admitted. He pulled the men over to a side wall, away from the crush of the crowd. His eyes strayed to her and Scyles, and he hesitated for a moment, then sighed and nodded.

"I think the bows will give us an advantage," he began, and everyone leaned in closer to listen.

"Commander Azimoth, the primitives have broken out of the containment area," Second Officer Zoun said, and looked at him with concern. "At least half of them are still in the area, but there are several independent groups uncontained."

"Where are they?" Lord Bakhtochk asked in a deceptively mild voice. "It looks as though the Egelv will be trying to board us shortly. We don't need to have multiple groups of hostiles wandering around the ship."

Azimoth looked at Zoun questioningly, and he quickly tracked them down.

"There are about twenty-six heading this way, from the look of it." He frowned as he looked at the heat signatures, then compared them to the schematic floor plan. "It would seem they found where we stored their weapons. There are several primitives in that hold, and more pushing an antigrav raft between there and the hold we put them in."

"Can we simply stun everyone in both holds, and possibly the ones on the concourse?" his lord asked, as though he were explaining something very simple to a pup.

"We could on our ship, but this one was never used as a slaver ship, and has no anti-personnel features for controlling the occupants," Zoun said, and Azimoth winced at his choice of words.

But his lord let it pass.

"Deal with them," he said to Azimoth, and turned back to watching the Egelv ship close on their position.

"Send eight warriors to intercept the group approaching, stun them, and then proceed to the hold with most of the conscious populace, and stun them all." Azimoth hoped eight would be enough. He had a feeling he'd need every soldier he had if the Egelv managed to board them. "Round up any stragglers, and report in."

"Yes, Commander Azimoth," Zoun said.

Azimoth sighed. Being recognized at his true rank had been nice, if too brief.

He pulled up the visual on the concourse and quickly found the approaching band of primitives. They all had swords and shields, and a couple had some longer spears or pikes. None of it would be a threat to his men.

He found the eight Mba warriors trotting down another concourse parallel to the one the primitives were on. He quickly estimated the best path, and told the squad leader to turn left on the next connecting passageway.

Azimoth directed them to a position where, once the primitives had gotten close, his men could fan out in front of them and easily stun all of them.

It went almost exactly as he expected, and none of his warriors suffered any injuries. He told them to continue on the concourse towards the holding area where the remainder of the primitives were. He would direct them when they got close.

Azimoth started to pull up the cameras where the primitives were, but alarms began to go off, and he saw that the Egelv ship was closing.

First things first, he thought dourly. Deal with the Egelvs, then help his squad subdue the primitives, if they needed any direction, which he doubted.

Scyles watched his father talk to King Orik. They had a plan, but the two kings were having a hard time agreeing on who was going to carry it off. They both agreed that both of them could not be risked on the same mission, but deciding who would go and who would stay here with the balance of the people was turning out to be a challenge.

He watched his father nod at him and Arga and winced. He hoped that didn't mean he was being suggested as a proxy for his father, and she for hers, to stay here. He knew he would be of value, and had a feeling their bows and skills would be a deciding factor. And he was the best archer in either tribe.

Arga had made it very clear they were partners in every way, and that where he went, so did she. He suspected that was a big part of the problem with the two kings working out the details, but even after only a day or two of re-acquainting themselves, he knew better than to try and order her to stay here.

Scyles caught Arga's eye and nodded to the door. They went out into the concourse, and he went through the motions of checking the twenty men to see they had plenty of arrows, and that their bows weren't damaged by the careless handling of their captors.

Targitai came out and saw what he was doing. He raised an eyebrow questioningly.

"We are ready, Scoloti warriors," Scyles said, letting his eyes sweep across the faces of the sixteen men and four women. "Today, we take back our freedom, and destroy these monsters."

He walked over to his teacher and smiled, a little grimly. Arga stepped next to him, and slapped him on the back.

"That was a good talk, Husband," she said, and Scyles wondered at the thrill he got from her calling him that. "They like and trust you."

"What makes you think you're going along?" Targitai asked pointedly, and gave the warriors a visual inspection of his own. Something he saw made him look back at Scyles approvingly. He apparently saw something in both their faces that made him immediately continue. "You are. But it wasn't a given thing, for you or Princess Arga."

"I am the son of a king," Scyles said evenly. "I will be a king someday. Our children will be kings and queens. And I will die," he admitted, and his arm crept around the waist of his wife.

"But not this day. This day, I help you and my father lead these men and women into a battle to free our people."

"How do you know it will be your father that leads us?" Targitai asked pointedly. "King Orik has an opinion on the subject. And I am very sure he has an opinion about his only daughter going into battle this day."

"They both know that my father is the fiercer fighter, and with you at his side, almost invincible." Scyles searched for words to give both kings the proper respect they deserved. "King Orik has the faith of the people, and is the obvious choice to lead them from this situation to safety and prosperity. My father is the obvious choice to kill large lizards with a bow, an axe, a sword, his teeth, if need be. Just as you are the obvious choice to be at his side, helping him do this."

Scyles' voice hardened.

"His only daughter is now my wife and partner. She and I will decide the actions she takes. Or I take, for that matter." Scyles had a premonition, and hurried to continue. "We both know King Orik is wise, and will recognize that we now must make our own decisions. He will respect our right and trust our judgement."

"But will her mother?" King Orik said dryly as he and Scyles' father walked into the hall. He turned to look at Targitai. "Did you give him a sign I was close?"

"No, Sire," Targitai insisted, then continued, his eyes dancing with humor. "But he does have remarkable hearing."

King Orik grinned crookedly as he looked at Scyles and Arga. Then his expression became very serious.

"The two of you control the fates of both tribes," he said. "Destroy our enemies, but keep your head about you."

"Yes, Papa," both of them said at the same time, and looked at each other, startled. Then Arga stepped forward and hugged her father tightly.

"Don't tell Mama until we're well away," she suggested, and King Orik snorted.

"I learned even before you were born, that I am incapable of fooling or deceiving your mother about anything," he admitted. "Be safe. Both of you. All of you," his voice rose in volume, and he turned to Scyles' father and waved a hand down the concourse.

"Go find and destroy our enemies, King Gelon." He sighed as he looked back into the room. "And if you see about two thousand of our people, please bring them back with you."

He and Gelon embraced, and then they were away, trotting down the causeway. Two men ran ahead to scout the way.

Scyles watched them go, and sped up, speaking to his father quickly as he began to pull away.

"I will go with the scouts and make sure we stay on the path to our goal," he said, not looking at Arga. He didn't know what her reaction would be, but he instinctively knew this was the right thing for him to do.

Scyles caught up with the two warriors quickly. They looked at him and grinned.

"Are you going to lead us on a chase, as you did last night?" One of them said. He recognized them both as part of his tribe, and he grinned back at them.

"No, I am going to keep the two of you from getting killed or knocked out by these dog creatures," he said, and they all shared a quiet laugh, then fell into a comfortable pace. Their soft-soled boots made nearly no sound as they ran.

Scyles glanced back and saw they'd opened quite a lead on the main party. As they approached an intersection, he raised a hand, and they all slowed to a halt. Scyles crept forward, to a point just short of the side hallway. He listened for a moment, whirled, and came back to the other two men.

They trotted back to the previous intersection, choosing quiet over speed. Scyles pointed to the hall to the left, and motioned for one of the men to go into it. He pointed back down the concourse to the main group, barely visible in the distance.

"Go warn them the enemy approaches," Scyles said quietly. "Tell King Gelon we should split our forces into two lines, one well ahead of the other. We don't know the range of their devices, and if the first line falls, the second can still fire at them from extreme range. Now go!"

The man gave him a curious look, and was off, racing down the concourse as fast as he could without being too noisy.

Scyles hurried into the hall across the concourse from the other man. He looked over and nodded at him. They both notched arrows, and prepared to fire. He waved to get the other man's attention.

He raised his hands and gestured that they represented the two of them, and made a firing motion with his right hand, to the extreme left, did the same think in reverse with his left hand, then again with his right, but not quite as extreme.

The other man immediately nodded, understanding they were to fire crisscross, so as not to duplicate targets. It would also give them a slightly safer angle to use the corner of the hall as cover as they fired. Also, shots coming from both sides might make it difficult for the enemy to judge the numbers they faced.

Sycles looked down the concourse, and saw the runner had arrived, and they were forming into two lines. The back one waited, giving the first one time to get well ahead before starting to trot forward at the same speed as the first group.

He leaned as close to the corner as he could without giving his position away and listened. He could hear voices, and suddenly, he could hear them in his own ear. Whatever they did to allow him to understand their language also told them when they spoke, and from their words, Scyles could get a better feel for their location without looking. He saw the other man's head shoot up and stare over at him. He held his hand up to his mouth, signaling silence.

Scyles could hear them now, in person. They couldn't be more than three or four horse lengths away.

He took a couple deep breaths, controlling his breathing, then smoothly leaned out from the wall enough to let an arrow fly. He followed it immediately with a second, then a third, then leaned back against the wall, hoping whatever the devices did, it didn't work through the walls. He saw the other man get a shot off, and then another, before he had to duck back out of sight.

Scyles thought he'd heard three bodies fall from his shots, but only one from the other man's shots. He was about to try to get a couple more of them when a volley of arrows flashed past, closely followed by a second, then a third and fourth.

He listened and thought he heard more bodies falling, as well as the sound of arrows hitting the floor, far down the concourse, and sliding on the smooth surface.

He popped out to shoot, and then eased up on his bow. There were eight bodies, either still or twitching in their death throes. He saw no sign of any retreating enemy, and thought there might have been only eight to begin with.

"Scyles! Scyles!"

He smiled as he heard his wife's voice, trying to contain her worry.

"I'm here," he said, stepping out of the hallway into the concourse.

Arga was only a few horse lengths away, the rest of the first line with her. The second line were hurrying to catch up. She saw him and slowed to a walk, trying to look casual and calm, but she didn't fool anyone. He was glad she didn't hug him or talk about her fears for his safety as most women would.

She made a show of looking at the fallen enemy, and pretended to count them.

"So, you were only able to shoot three of them?" she asked, and shrugged. "I guess that's not too bad."

The men in hearing range chuckled, among them his father. He looked at the fallen dog men and nodded his approval. Then he was King Gelon again, and checking his men for injuries, making decisions.

Three men had fallen in the first row, and he pointed at two other men.

"You two stay with our fallen," he said. "One of you, that is. And one of you needs to run back to the main room and get one of the floating carts, along with some more men, to get our downed men to safety until they awaken, and to replenish our numbers. When you have them on their way back, both of you, as well as three more men, follow us and try and catch up."

They nodded without speaking and turned and ran back to the three fallen.

Scyles nodded to the man he'd sent back to warn them.

"That seemed to work," he said, and the other man shrugged, grinning.

"I was trying to decide whether King Gelon should be getting advice from our most junior warrior, and he directed them into the exact same formation you suggested," the man admitted. "You're definitely your father's son. I won't hesitate again."

"Good," Scyles said evenly. He'd been about to lose his temper that the man hadn't automatically done as he'd told him to. But this, overheard by the others, was probably a more effective way of proving his worth as a tactician and leader in battle.

He looked at his father questioningly.

"Scout ahead?"

His father glanced from the man to Scyles, and nodded his head, satisfied. Scyles had a premonition that had the man not said what he did, it would have been a race to see who berated him first, he or his father.

"At least one of you take one of these devices that make men sleep," he said, and motioned for one of the men that had helped gather up the enemy's weapons to give him one.

Scyles glanced at it quickly, and tucked it into his gorytos.

"Go," his father said, and Scyles turned and ran, tapping the same two men on the shoulder as he passed them. They fell in step with him easily.

Scyles and his father had discussed the route earlier, and he watched for the few landmarks that denoted where they needed to turn off this concourse. They made the turn and just as they reached the point of crossing another main concourse, they saw bodies lying on the floor ahead.

It was the Caitiari, and as far as Scyles could tell, it was all of them. They checked the king and queen, and they were both breathing comfortably, but in a very deep sleep. The rest all looked in the same condition, and Scyles looked at the unconscious bodies and frowned.

He couldn't just leave them here, but there were three in his party, and twenty-six Caitiari. He didn't wish to waste time dealing with them, but decided he knew what he wanted his father's men to do when they arrived.

Scyles leaned over and started to grab the queen's hands, and stopped. He shook his head, and picked a warrior at random and pulled him across the floor to the nearest door. He opened it and saw there were containers almost filling the room. But there was enough space to put twenty-six bodies, he decided with a smirk.

He pulled the man inside and away from the door.

"Leave that one halfway in, so the door will be open," he said, and the other two men nodded, grinning as they figured out what he was doing.

They started down the concourse. Scyles could see that it ended, not too far ahead, and they all slowed instinctively.

"We grow close," Scyles said in a low voice. "From here on, we favor quiet over speed.

Both men nodded, and they trotted on.

Chapter Sixteen

Azimoth swore as he looked at the screen. The team he'd sent out had managed to stun a large group of the primitives, and continued towards the main body of primitives. But they hadn't checked in on time, and he was having trouble finding them.

He clicked from camera view to camera view, wishing mightily that Muschwain had better surveillance capabilities. He could feel his lord's eyes upon him, and knew his patience was diminishing.

"Infra-red?" his lord asked shortly, in his deep, rumbling tone of disapproval.

"The only signs of groups emanating heat are all of the primitives."

He forwarded quickly through a number of views, then swore and backed up several cameras.

The eight Mba warriors lay on the floor, multiple shafts sticking in most of them. He saw why there was not a significant heat signature. They were all dead.

"I found them," Azimoth said, raising his voice to be sure his lord heard him.

"So I see," Lord Bakjtochk rumbled, his disapproval evident. "I am beginning to see how these primitives would prove useful."

"They seem to be fearless warriors," Azimoth said, through his clenched teeth.

"We shall see how they match up against two Hshtahni," his lord said, and his progeny gleefully headed towards the hatch off the bridge. "Send ten more of your warriors to accompany them."

"Yes, my Lord," Azimoth said, and glanced at Zoun, who nodded.

Azimoth saw another alert appear on his screen. He investigated and resisted the urge to whine in frustration.

"My Lord, the Egelv have destroyed the last of our weapon pods, the engines are disabled, and they appear to be about to grapple near the aft airlock."

Lord Bakhtochk nostrils snorted loudly, in what Azimoth assumed was frustration.

"That airlock is closer to us than the primitives," he said, his voice booming and showing his anger. "Char Lakhmoshk and Charna Piquhkh shall deal with them first. Then they will destroy any primitives running loose around the ship. Those still in the hold, may be allowed to live, my children may eat them. Either way, this ends now."

Azimoth nodded and focused on finding which cameras could be brought to bear on the pending action. He couldn't tell his lord what he thought, but he was pretty sure it wasn't ending quite yet. And if it was, it would not be to their advantage.

Aboard the Egelv Destroyer Mountain Edge, grappled to the Muschwain

Captain Rost Fott nodded for Second Officer Rel Steen to connect him with Raging River. A moment later, he heard Raging River respond.

"Commodore Mit Obet, we have disabled the generation ship's engines, and destroyed their weapon pods. We're grappled to their aft airlock and will board immediately." He hesitated a moment, and, making a face at his officers, continued. "We will send our security forces, as well as ten crewmen to begin subduing any resistance. We may need additional forces before we're done."

"Understood, Captain Rost Fott," Commodore Mit Obet said, his voice sounding a little strained. "We're getting the upper hand with the Hshtahni cruiser, but it might take time to get reinforcements to you. I'll do what I can."

"Thank you, Sir," Rost Fott said, not liking the lack of a time frame, but he knew there wasn't much else Mit Obet could do. "We'll keep you informed of updates as we can."

He stood and turned to look at Van Dono.

"First Officer Van Dono, what progress?"

His first officer looked up at him and nodded in satisfaction.

"We're secured against their airlock, and will breach it shortly. Zard Win has gathered his forces, and is ready to move as soon as it's open. We've set all energy weapons on maximum fatal settings. No stun level would have sufficient impact on any Hshtahni, and we will be facing at least two of them, almost immediately."

Rost Fott had a sudden thought. "If they get past you, would the Hshtahni be able to enter our ship?" He certainly didn't want to fight those huge lizards on his own ship.

"No, the corridor from the main concourse to the airlock is too small for them to fit, and our airlock is even smaller, as well as our own corridors." Van Dono looked relieved, although his smile was strained. "Thankfully, our warships are designed specifically for our race, and size. No huge beasties will be running amok on our ship."

Rost Fott nodded in satisfaction. He spoke to his security chief.

"Zard Win, are you ready to board?"

"Yes, Sir. My team is at the lock, as well as the ten crewmen, and a medical officer." He hesitated. "I told her she should wait until we secure at least part of the ship, but she insisted, and quoted regulations to support her argument."

Rost Fott resisted the urge to smile at the frustration in his voice. The only female medical officer on board was Shae Apon, and this was her first tour on Mountain Edge. He doubted she and Zard Win had met before this. She lived and worked by the regulation book, and she seemed to know it better than anyone else on the ship.

"Knowing her file, I bet she is frantic to inspect what we suspect is a new species in these bipeds that are running loose on the ship." Rost Fott grinned at Van Dono. "Keep her at the back of your forces until you secure the ship."

"I have a feeling that is easier to say than it will be to do," Zard Win said darkly. "We are opening the airlock."

"Good, any luck on mounting the spare energy blaster on an antigrav raft?" They had one in storage, in case one of the ship's outside armaments broke down or was damaged. "You do know these aren't designed to be used inside a ship. In fact, the idea is highly discouraged. One poorly placed shot can breach the hull from the inside, where it's more vulnerable."

"I know, and we will not use it unless we have one of the Hshtahni at point-blank range," Zard Win promised. "And there is a better than fair chance they will place an energy weapons null field over the entire ship, if we begin to gain the upper hand."

"We overrode the airlock controls and are opening the hatch," Van Dono announced.

Rost Fott nodded his satisfaction.

"Good hunting, Zard Win," he said, and hoped he wasn't sending much of his crew to their deaths.

Zard Win watched the two scouts forge ahead as he led the body of his forces down the corridor. Far ahead of them, he saw several figures appear in the juncture to the main concourse. They started to bring their weapons to bear, but his scouts were faster, and their aim was true. The two figures collapsed.

"I hope those were Mba warriors and not this new species," a female voice spoke behind him accusingly.

"Silence in the ranks," he said, and she fell silent.

Zard Win hoped so too. When they caught up to where the two scouts crouched over the fallen figures, he was relieved to see they were indeed Mba warriors.

The two scouts suddenly brought their weapons up and began firing as rapidly as they could. One of them fell, and the other dodged back into the corridor, flattening against the wall to the right.

"Hi low," Zard Win hissed, and the first two security men to reach the corner, stopped and leaned into the concourse far enough to get shots off.

A loud roar sounded from not very far away.

Zard Win was chagrinned as he realized they'd lost the advantage of the longer range of their weapons. If they could have reached the corner even a couple minutes earlier, they could have picked off the Mba, and done damage to the Hshtahni before they were close enough for their weapons to reach them.

He checked the fallen man, and was relieved to see the Mba still had their weapons set on stun. Of course, as soon as they realized the Egelv were using lethal force, that would change. The Hshtahni that had been hit had probably already warned them.

His men shot again, but even as they did, the voice of Lema Azod came over their transceivers.

"An energy weapon null field has been placed over the entire generation ship," he said, and Zard Win hurriedly warned his men.

"Null field in effect, switch to crowd control rods."

Zard Win was worried now. Since the rods didn't release energy, they still could shock and stun opponents very effectively in hand-to-hand combat. Egelv security forces were every bit as deadly as the Mba, so the odds would have been in their favor, if not for the Hshtahni.

But their presence changed the entire scope of the battle.

"Grab our fallen and move back down the corridor, out of the reach of the Hshtahni," he said, and as they all heard the scrambling feet of something very large rushing forward, his man jumped to obey.

As it was, they barely got beyond the reach before the head and neck, as well as the arms of a red Hshtahni pressed into the inadequate space, trying to reach them.

One of his men slapped his energy rod across the back of a paw, and the Hshtahni snarled, ignoring the pain and redoubling its attempts to reach any of them. A few Mba warriors rushed in, but were quickly dispatched by Zard Win's men.

"Move back a little more," he said, and they were just in time, as the Hshtahni backed out of the corridor, and the tail of the other one appeared, this one blue, swinging wildly from side to side, trying to reach them.

Zard Win watched the Hshtahni move back out, and the head of the other appear at the juncture. He snarled at them, as if daring them to come forward. His forces stood their ground, and didn't take the bait.

Stalemate, he thought glumly.

Scyles held up a fist, and pointed to the adjoining corridor to the right, and then to the one going to the left. The two men he was with split, one just within each corridor. He went to the left as well. Both men knelt, and pulled their bows back enough to provide tension to their arrows.

"Stay here, be ready to shoot as soon as you see a sign they've noticed us," Scyles said quietly, and the older man nodded. Even though Scyles was so young, and his beard was still scraggly and patchwork, neither man seemed inclined to resent taking his orders. "Make sure he understands and is ready as well. When the shooting starts, I want them looking down the concourse towards the two of you, and the rest of our men when they get here. I think we're out of their range at this distance. When I'm well ahead, both of you start creeping forward, from corridor to corridor. When our main party gets close, the real battle will begin."

"May Ares guard your flank, Prince," he said, and Scyles smiled his thanks.

"And yours as well," he said, and without waiting for a response, began striding forward, bent over, loaded bow ready to pull back and let arrows fly, as he watched the dog men milling around, looking down a corridor three intersections away. The two winged monsters his father had described, dragons, he'd called them, were both intent on whatever down that corridor, but even from here, Scyles could see they were too big to fit.

He made it to the first corridor, and stopped to check the men behind him, and see if the rest of the force were in sight yet. There was no sign of anyone behind him, and he nodded in satisfaction. He wanted to be as close as possible before the main party arrived. His plan was to disrupt the dog men's defenses as much as possible while his father's group closed with them.

As plans went, it wasn't much, but there was no natural terrain to use for cover, and a warrior of the People didn't moan about less than ideal conditions for a battle. They dealt with what they had.

Of course, a horse would have been nice right about now, he thought, smiling grimly, as he started working his way down the concourse to the next intersection.

Scyles' luck held until he was at the last corridor before the enemy's position. He stared at the giant flying lizards in awe. The closer one was a brilliant red, and looked as though its skin was as thick and durable as armor. He wasn't sure an arrow would penetrate, even at point black range.

The farther one was the color of the sky on a bright, sunny day. It was a very beautiful blue, although he could see in some places, it seemed to have some darker shading. They were both showing their fury and frustration with whatever was down the corridor.

There were several of the dog men down. They looked dead or unconscious. There was no sign of what had disabled them, and he assumed it was the same kind of weapons the dog men used.

Scyles was almost to the point where he could duck out of sight when he more sensed than heard that his father and his fighters were getting close. He resisted the urge to hurry to the next corridor, not wanting his movement to catch any attention.

His luck ran out as the closest giant lizard, the red one, turned to stare down the concourse. Scyles froze and watched the monster look past him down the concourse, and snort, almost as if in derision.

Then his eyes turned to look directly at Scyles, and the large red head reared back in surprise.

Scyles didn't hesitate. He drew back and fired an arrow, reloaded and fired another as fast as he could, then another. The beast somehow blocked the first two arrows with a swipe of its arms. But the third, which he fired anticipating where it would move, went directly into its right eye.

The dragon raised its head and screamed in fury and pain. Scyles took advantage of the move to send a volley of arrows at the newly exposed throat. Several lodged, and several deflected away, but he could tell he'd hurt it.

Several of the dog men fell from arrows from the two men behind him, but he ignored them, leaving his men to deal with the lesser threat.

The red dragon glared at him with one baleful eye, and roared again.

Scyles immediately fired as fast as he could, two at the yawning maw, one at an eye, then repeating, over and over, all the time, running forward as fast as he could.

Two of the dog men saw him and started to charge, but dropped immediately, impaled by the arrows of his men's accurate fire. A roar came from behind him, and he recognized his father's battle yell. The rate of arrows aimed at the few remaining dog men and the blue dragon increased dramatically.

The blue one shook off the arrows, none hitting it anywhere critical. The red one, on the other hand, was staggering, and a dark, viscous fluid poured out its mouth. It turned away from him, towards the blue one, and Scyles didn't hesitate.

He ran up the tail onto the back of the first dragon, which appeared to be on the verge of collapsing, and managed to fire one arrow into the mouth of the blue dragon as it snapped at him. He threw himself off the lizard, to the left, using it as cover from the jaws of the blue one.

The blue dragon was in such a fury, it snapped down on the arm and shoulder of the red one, as it missed him. The dying lizard screamed, and the blue one immediately released its bite, its eyes widening in surprise.

Scyles fired as quickly as he could, and at least one went deep into an eye. The other men were now concentrating their fire on the blue lizard, and it realized it had threats from more than one source now. It turned back towards them, and Scyles kept firing, using the prone red dragon for cover.

He heard someone roar, very close, and saw Skulis charge forward with what had to be the longest pike in the tribe. Its point caught the lizard in the neck, and actually seemed to slip in between the scales.

Scyles jumped back onto the now-dead lizard and continued firing. The blue one looked around in puzzled agony and another of his arrows penetrated the other eye. He kept trying to fire down its throat, but it was shrieking now, and its head was twisting back and forth.

Targitai rushed up an arm of the blue dragon, axes in both hands. He swung at the mouth, trying to cut the thick grotesque tongue, or any other vulnerable part. Skulis let go the pike and pulled out his own axes, following the swordmaster's lead.

Without hesitation, Scyles leaped from the shoulder of the dead lizard to the back of the blue one, and began firing nonstop into one of the eyes. With one last scream of pain and despair, it slumped to the floor, either dead or very nearly so.

Scyles stopped firing, steadying his footing as the beast collapsed. He stared at his father, now standing next to Targitai, the rest of the group crowding forward behind them. He saw Arga in the middle of the pack, looking at him with both pride and concern. He saw her eyes flick across his body, as if looking for injuries, and he smiled at her, raising his bow with his left hand.

The men responded by brandishing their own weapons, roaring their excitement and exhilaration. Several went around, checking the dog men, making sure they were all dead, sticking two with swords to be sure.

One of his tribesmen gave a shout of warning and pointed down the corridor that had been the object of interest of the dog men and lizards.

Scyles stared, even as he hurried to climb off the dead lizard.

There were several dozen strange-looking men, most of them holding thick sticks with knobs on the ends. Most wore dark green garments, the pants shamefully tight to the shape of their legs, their jerkins form-fitting as well. Others wore the same type clothes, but in a deep blue. There was some sort of markings on the chest and shoulders of all of them, although Scyles noticed it was different on some of them.

One of the men in blue took a step forward, and said something, but Scyles couldn't understand him.

His father straightened to his full height, squared his head, and spoke solemnly.

"I am King Gelon of the tribe Auchatae, of the Scoloti. Are you friend or foe?"

"Father, they were the target of the dog men and monsters, so I think they may be friendly," Scyles said, although his eyes never left the strange-looking men in front of them.

They were taller, on the average, than the People. Most were at least as tall as his father, although much leaner. Their skin was a deep brown, which made their long, straight, white hair, braided down to their waists, all the more startling. They had dark eyes with piercing gazes, thin lips, and their noses were prominent and pointed, as were their ears.

One of the strangers in blue said something, and several of his fellows gave a very People-like chuckle. The one in front turned and stared until they all looked nervously at the ground and grew silent.

The stranger, which Scyles decided was their leader, turned back to them and nodded his head slightly.

His father glanced over at him, and Scyles met his eyes and gave an imperceptible nod. They both turned back to the leader, and returned a nod, offering respect.

The stranger waved a hand, as if to signify all of his group, and carefully said a word.

"Egelv."

"What did he say? Elf?" Targitai asked cautiously, and Scyles answered.

"No, he said Egelv," he said, then ducked his head and looked at his father, wondering if he was usurping authority he didn't have.

His father smiled faintly and then looked at the stranger. He did the same motion with his hand, gesturing broadly to their group.

"Scoloti."

The Egelv nodded and pointed at himself.

"Van Dono."

"Gelon," Scyles' father said, and continued before Targitai could complain. "King Gelon."

The Egelv called Van Dono nodded his head, and said something to his men, and one in blue stepped forward.

Scyles realized this one was a female. It appeared these Egelv were very similar to the People, at least as far as their physical traits went.

She said something, and he nodded, then looked directly at Scyles.

"Van Dono," he repeated, and looked at him in expectation.

"Scyles," he said, suddenly feeling more nervous than when he'd charged the two giant lizards. "Son of Gelon."

Van Dono pointed past him at the two dead lizards and smiled in a very satisfied fashion that felt very much as one of the People would have. He clapped his hands together, and the rest of his party joined in.

Scyles felt his face go bright red with embarrassment, which didn't escape their attention. Several made comments and got laughter as a response from other Egelv. But he could tell they weren't mocking him. They were impressed with his fighting skills against the lizards.

"Better tell them you're married, young Scyles," Targitai said. "I think the Elves are in love with you." Arga pushed her way through the people between them, and inserted herself close to Scyles. He instinctively put an arm around her waist as she spoke.

"It just shows these Egelvs have good sense," she said archly, correcting Targitai, and shoved lightly against Scyles with her shoulder. "But let's be clear with them. Arga," she said, pointing at herself, and smiling in a very possessive manner.

"Wife of Scyles."

Chapter Seventeen

Zard Win watched Van Dono introduce himself to the primitive race calling themselves the Scoloti. He called Rel Steen on his transceiver.

"You getting this?" he asked, and winced at the enthusiastic response by the second officer.

"I have," he said, talking very fast. "I've queried Scoloti and there are no records of them at all. But we have learned the word for their position of authority. Of course, we don't know the basis of the title, if it's earned, hereditary, a rank. Oh, did you hear that? I guarantee that younger voice is of his son."

"Yes, I think you're right," Zard Win agreed, listening to both the conversation happening in front of him, and the rapid babbling of the second officer, who was the specialist in communication and technology.

"Ooh, that is either the mother, sister, or wife of Scyles," Rel Steen said, and reconsidered. "Or is it an adolescent boy? That high tone could be age related."

"It's his wife," Zard Win said dryly, watching her attach herself to the boy. "Actually Scyles and his wife, what did she say her name was? Oh, Arga. Both of them are very young-looking. We don't know the racial characteristics, but I would bet both of them have only achieved adolescence in the last few years."

"Primitive cultures often mate at an early age, and are known to wait for years until both are mature enough for parenthood to consummate the relationship," Rel Steen said, and Zard Win laughed.

"Trust me, they're beyond that stage," he said, watching the young girl's fierce possessiveness. "If they aren't mated, I'm a..."

Zard Win thought better of finishing that sentence the way he'd planned to.

"Well, they're married," he finished lamely. He remembered what he'd really called about.

"I know you have the computer analyzing their conversations, or at least what you can hear of them. I scanned them, and they all have embedded transceivers in their skulls, but they're connected to this ship's system. Any way you can access and redirect the feed, or tie us into it somehow?"

"We'll have to break into their ship's computer system, and that could take a while," Rel Steen said cautiously. "I would say hours, at the very minimum."

"We're about to try and take the bridge, and there is at least one very mature Hshtahni there," Zard Win said. "Communications between us and our new allies might be a critical factor. The only other solution I see is to implant them with our transceivers."

"That won't help us get the translation," Rel Steen pointed out. "I don't know that the Hshtahni have any translations of our language, so I don't think that would help immediately, in any case."

"Right," Zard Win said, and shook his head. "Gar forbid anything be easy."

He stepped forward and cleared his throat. Van Dono turned to him questioningly.

"We should probably head towards the bridge. The Hshtahni lord and the Mba still control this ship's functions. And we don't really want them escaping in a shuttle while we're standing around."

"Any ideas how we can communicate with our new friends?" Van Dono asked, glancing over at Gelon and nodding his head.

"Gestures and shouting comes to mind," Zard Win said, wincing at his whimsical answer.

"That was about what I came up with, as well," First Office Van Dono admitted, and turned to the leader of the Scoloti. He pointed at Zard Win, and spoke slowly.

"Zard Win," he said. "Security Chief."

The big barbarian calling himself Gelon turned to him questioningly.

Zard Win had an idea and pointed at the fallen blue Hshtahni. He then pointed in the general direction of the bridge, and held one finger up.

The younger man named Scyles said something, and Gelon motioned him forward. The young girl, and up close, he saw she really was a young girl, followed him. He saw her glance over at Shae Apon with misgivings, and pressed his lips together to keep from grinning.

These Scoloti aren't so different, he realized. They get jealous, anyway.

One of the Scoloti stepped up to Scyles and handed him an armful of the pointed shafts he'd fired at the Hshtahni and Mba, with such amazing accuracy. He was almost positive the only ones that didn't strike home were the ones the Hshtahni managed to block, or turn enough that the shaft bounced off their nearly impervious hide.

On a whim, Zard Win stepped closer to Scyles, and pointed at one of the shafts and looked at him questioningly.

Scyles handed him one without hesitation, and kept inspecting the rest, wiping some, and putting them in the open-ended long box he carried at his side.

"Arrow," he said, and held up the weapon that fired them. "Bow."

Zard Win handed the arrow back to him, repeating the words, and Scyles nodded in satisfaction. His eyes shifted to the side for a moment, and a quick little flush of color came to his face.

"Scyles," he said, pointing at his own chest. "Zard Win," he said, pointing at him. Then he stepped aside and gestured at the young girl. "Arga," he said, and something that looked pride filled his face. "My wife," he continued, flicking a hand at himself, then pointing at her.

"Arga, wife, Scyles," Zard Win said, and bowed his head to her.

The girl's face changed color as had Scyles', and she bowed her head exactly the same amount he did.

Zard Win had a sudden inspiration. He pointed over at Gelon.

"King Gelon," he said, and then pointed at Scyles. "Scyles?" he said, nodding his head and then saying the boy's name with a questioning look.

He got it immediately and grinned a very Egelv-like grin.

"Prince Scyles," he said, and turned to Arga. "Princess Arga. Wife of Scyles."

Zard Winn grinned back at him, and winced as Van Dono called to him. He nodded at Scyles, who smiled as he recognized the summoning Zard Win was getting.

"Sir?" he asked, and First Officer Van Dono looked at him in exasperation.

"I'm thinking we should take the bridge before anyone dies of old age," he said, and then relented. "Did I see you talking to the son of their leader?"

"Gelon is a king," Zard Win said with total confidence. He saw and felt Shae Apon staring at him with interest. "And the boy is Prince Scyles, and that's his wife, Princess Arga."

"How can you be sure?" he asked doubtfully.

"I just got my first lesson in Scoloti," Zard Win said, and laughed as Shae Apon jumped into the conversation.

"I want to learn their language as well," she said, and then blushed in what Zard Win thought was a very Scoloti manner.

"First things, first," Van Dono said dryly. "We have a Hshtahni and a couple dozen Mba warriors to kill first."

Azimoth watched the primitives meet the Egelv, and shook his head in dismay. For a moment, he'd had the wild hope they might mistake each other for the enemy and fight. The primitives would almost certainly win as long as the energy weapon null field was engaged.

Another screen gave him yet more bad news. He slowly turned to face Lord Bakhtochk.

"My Lord, it is with regret that I must report that, not only have your younger two children been killed by the primitives, but the Clonoschk has also been destroyed, resulting in the death of your heir, Char Pohkclaushkclt. The two Egelv ships both survived the battle, and are maneuvering closer."

Azimoth saw that the primitives and their new allies, the Egelv, were making their way on a direct path for the bridge. He knew what the answer would be, but had to ask.

"My Lord, the Egelv and primitives will be at the hatch to this bridge very shortly. Do you wish to try and escape via your shuttle?"

The shuttle was big enough to carry all four Hshtahni, so Azimoth knew everyone on the bridge could fit, although the odds of their eluding the Egelv warships were not good. Of course, as bad as those odds were, they had to be better than staying on board, and trying to defeat the forces approaching.

"No," his lord said, his voice booming, although after so much time around his lord, Azimoth could recognize the pain in his voice as he dealt with the death of his brood. "I believe I will try and deal with them right here. You and your warriors should put your helmets on now."

Azimoth hated this part. He'd felt the attacks his lord was about to mount, and even with the helmets designed specifically to block out the effects, this was always painful.

He picked his helmet up, eyeing it in distaste. It was awkward and heavy, and fighting while wearing it was difficult. He would have most of his functional capabilities, but if it came to fighting an accomplished foe, the helmet made it more difficult. His agility and maneuverability were limited, no matter how much he practiced with it on.

His warriors followed suit, and everyone checked their stun rods to make sure they had sufficient power, and were set to kill, not stun.

Killing all the Egelv would be a pleasure. And they had more than enough of the primitives in stasis to achieve everything they wished.

His lord could easily afford to kill this batch off.

Scyles looked at the heavy door as they approached.

"That's the way in," his father said, nodding. "I remember thinking it was very strong when they brought us here." He pointed at it and nodded to Zard Win.

Zard Win nodded, and motioned them to step back by where most of both groups had stopped. They watched as several of his men poured some very thick liquid up one side, across the top, down the other and along the bottom of the heavy door. Scyles leaned forward, wondering what it was. It seemed to have already dried.

The men moved back quickly, and Scyles was startled when hands gripped both his arms and yanked him back hard. He looked down at Arga, more curious than annoyed. She kept pulling him back, but nodded to his other arm. He saw it was the female Egelv in blue, he'd noticed earlier.

"What?" he asked, beginning to get annoyed.

Before anyone could say anything, the stuff they'd poured around the door, whatever it was, flashed in a brilliant array of bright colors, and the deck and very air around them shook with the shock.

All three of them stumbled, but hands caught them and pushed them back upright.

"Pay attention to the beastie, Son," his father said in his ear, and released him, as did the other hands.

They watched in awe as the large, heavy door slowing fell into the room beyond. Then they were all running forward, some men running across the door, others jumping over the corners to either side.

Scyles was mortified. If Arga and the stranger hadn't pulled him backward, he probably would have been injured by whatever forces could do that to the massive door. He put that thought away for future consideration, and dashed across the door, veering to the right as he did.

He saw what his father said was the last of the beasties, and was shocked at how much larger it was than the first two. His coloring was mostly black, with dark greys interspersed, making him look almost more like a large pile of rocks than a lizard.

A very large pile of rocks.

A number of the dog men were scattered around the room, and just as Scyles noticed they were all wearing some sort of heavy hat, he felt a wave of fear sweep over him.

Scyles stumbled, and almost fell, staggering like he'd drunk too much fermented mare's milk. The dragon was so large, powerful, and frightening, he wanted to run away. Anything that large could tear him apart with ease.

They'd all fought their way to this room, only to die, torn apart by a foe too big to defeat!

Scyles looked around, searching for a way out. He saw his father stumble and fall, Targitai trying to get to his side, but collapsing on the floor with his arms wrapped around his head.

He saw that the Egelv were as overwhelmed as the People. Of course they were! It wasn't like they were superior or anything. Not like that giant, black lizard. He was so large, so strong, his might shone like the full moon on a cloudless night.

He started to scramble across the floor, and saw the enormous tail of the dragon sweep around, striking the people and Egelv alike, sending them across the floor.

The enormous room was too large to ever find his way out before the giant lizard tore his entrails out of his body and ate them. He stared around, finding himself unable to tear his eyes away from the slaughter around him.

Scyles saw the deadly tail sweep past Arga, barely short of hitting her. Surely a blow from the overwhelming force of the tail would have crushed her like an eggshell. He wanted to get to her, protect her, but knew if he tried, the tail, or the mighty jaws of the dragon would get him, tearing and rending his body to pieces, right in front of his wife.

The lizard roared, and he watched in horror as its mouth opened wide, revealing rows of jagged, deadly teeth, chomping down on one of the People, tearing off the top part of his body. He wanted to stop the lizard, to help his people, but it was too big! And he was so small.

He'd always been small, too small to compete. Even his parents thought he was too small. Why couldn't he be bigger and stronger, like his older brothers? He knew his father had been devastated when he saw both die in battle six years ago. Now, all he was left with was the runt of his third son, too small to compete, too small to live, the moment he wasn't under the protection of his tribe.

He's always been too small, and today it would be the cause of his death.

Because he couldn't beat anything bigger than himself, and almost everything in the world was bigger. He saw Skulis on his hands and knees, arms covering his head as he screamed in fear. His size wouldn't save him, Scyles knew. The dragon was too big, like everything else in the world.

Bigger than Scyles.

The thought threatened to freeze him into a curled up ball on the floor, when he remembered he'd beaten Skulis, in battle. In the common yurt. Skulis was big enough to pound him to death, yet he'd beaten him in battle. He'd beaten the bigger man.

In fact, for most of his life, he'd found ways to beat the bigger foe, to win in the end.

Because he never, ever conceded. He never gave up, and always thought his way to victory. And his body was just fast enough, just strong enough, to help him do so. He focused on building a wall between him and the waves of fear pounding against his thoughts, trying to paralyze him to inaction.

"No!" Scyles shouted, and found he still held his bow. Somehow, even with all the scrambling around in fear, mindless terror, he still held the one thing that had never failed him.

He pulled an arrow out of his gorytos and fired it at the head of the dragon. The very act seemed to free him from the waves of terror, and he quickly followed the first shaft with two more.

The dragon, as if it could see his intentions, had blocked the first arrow with a giant paw. It was so large, how could he get an arrow past, he despaired, then shook his head.

No! He wasn't weak, and he wasn't going to give in to his fears. But how could he get arrows past its guard? It was as if it could read his thoughts!

Could it be? He gaped at the idea, but shifted his aim to one of the dog men. He shot him, then another, then suddenly fired a volley at the lizard's eyes, and then the mouth. He heard a scream and knew at least one got through to its target, but he was too busy firing at the dog men again.

The secret was not letting the dragon know what he was about to do by acting instinctively, mixing his targets so the giant monster couldn't anticipate his aim. After killing one of the dog men, he let his instincts take over, and fired where he felt the lizard would be.

The lizard moved towards him, but he stood his ground, firing as fast as he could. The head of the monster snapped back, it turned its face away, and he knew he'd hit an eye again. He took advantage of the moment to run quickly to the left, firing at any part he could see that seemed like it might be a weak spot.

The tail slammed down where he'd just been, and an Egelv screamed, and abruptly stopped. Scyles managed to put two shafts into the dragon's yawning maw, and it shook its head, trying to dislodge them.

Scyles kept firing.

He became aware the others were no longer screaming in mortal fear, or scurrying around in panic. Most seemed dazed, but a few seemed to recover enough to start attacking the source of their earlier pain and fear.

He saw several of the dog men go down, and off to the side, five or six of the People firing at the lizard. His father had his sword out, and Targitai had axes in both hands. They looked like they were trying to figure out the best way to use them to advantage.

Scyles saw the dragon notice them, and immediately charged onto the tail and ran up its back towards the head. He nocked two arrows as he climbed, and as the lizard reared back, he rushed forward and, planting a foot on the top of its head, leaped over it, twisting as he flew, releasing both arrows into its right eye. He fired another arrow, this time right down its throat, and then tried to land rolling, but got caught up in the dog man bodies strewn around the floor.

The air whooshed out of him, and he watched the head swing back and forth as the lizard blindly searched for him. He managed to get another arrow loaded, just as the dying lizard seemed to realize where he was.

Its mouth opened wide, and he brought it down, directly at Scyles. He fired the arrow and tried to get another out of his gorytos, but it was pinned underneath him.

Skulis slid across the blood-covered floor, and braced the base of a pike on the floor next to Scyles with his foot. Scyles gave up on the arrow and swept his long sword out of his scabbard and held it up high.

The cavernous maw came down, impaling itself on the pike, driving the spearhead deep into the lizard's skull. The head slid down the pike until it reached Scyles' sword, and finally stopped, his sword barely penetrating the roof of the creature's mouth.

Skulis looked at the sword, then at Scyles, lying next to him, his arm stretched out as far as he could reach. A big drop of ochre or blood, or whatever flowed in the dragon's veins, oozed around the sword tip and fell between them.

Skulis sighed and shook his head in mock despair.

"I suppose you're going to claim that your sword made the fatal wound," he said, and Scyles snorted, trying to suppress a laugh.

They looked at each other, and both started laughing as they worked their way from beneath the giant head. They both tried to stop, and burst out again, leaning against each other for support.

The rest of the People, the ones that still lived, crowded around them, slapping them on the backs, joining in the laughter. His father pushed through the crowd and stood before them a moment, watching them laugh. Scyles tried to stop, sure his father thought he'd gone insane, but that only made him laugh harder.

Scyles became aware that the Egelv were standing in a semi-circle around them, staring at their reaction to the fierce battle. He didn't know if he was correctly interpreting their expressions, but at the moment, he thought the Egelv might both be in awe, and horrified by them. That only made him laugh harder.

Targitai pushed through to stand next to Scyles' father, and held up his axe.

"You think that little stick, and your sword did any more than clean that beastie's teeth for him?" he said with derision. "Now with this hand axe, I clipped his toe-nails pretty severely, I did. Obviously the killing blow."

"But you were rolling on the floor in fear, just as I was. As everyone was, until Scyles managed to break free of its spell and hurt it," Skulis pointed out, and Targitai shrugged, but his eyes were thoughtful.

Arga slipped between several of the men to stand before him, viewing his blood-covered body critically. She moved back when he reached for her.

"You're cleaning that smelly mess off before you drape yourself all over me, dear husband," she said, holding her nose with one hand. "Have you had a bath this year?"

The men around them roared, and Scyles couldn't help but grin at the Egelv, hanging back, not afraid, but not understanding them, either. The ones wearing blue began to scatter around the room, inspecting the various devices.

Scyles turned back to Arga with a deadpan expression on his face, then looked behind her, startled, letting his eyes widen in apparent shock. She gave a little whoop, and took a step towards him, even as she drew her short sword as she turned towards the dead lizard.

Scyles swept his arm around her, turning her to press tightly against him. She gave him a good cursing, kneeing him in the process. He knew she intentionally hit him in the stomach instead of his manly parts, but it still knocked the breath out of him.

The laughter around him renewed, and she gave him a victorious look, even as she looked at the smears all over her front in disgust. She looked at his father and shook her head in mock despair.

Then she took hold of his kurga with both hands and pulled him back tight against her, giving him a very passionate kiss. He didn't argue. He ignored the lewd remarks of the men around them. And of the warrior women as well, he noticed.

Their lips finally parted, and they looked at each other without speaking.

"Thank you for not dying this day," she said quietly. "You fought like the white bears of the north."

She looked down at herself, and sighed.

"And now, we both smell like them, as well." She made a face, and shrugged. "Now we both need baths."

Scyles started to argue. The people didn't usually fully immerse themselves to bathe, like the Greeks, but he caught a whiff of himself, leaned forward quickly to sniff her, and grimaced.

"You do smell," he admitted, and she slapped him.

Scyles grinned at her.

"Well, if we find a place to bathe, at least we can do it together."

"Wash first, play after," she said firmly.

Scyles looked thoughtful.

"Or, maybe wash and play, at the same time."

They both grinned at that.

Azimoth coughed, and a thin spray of blood added to the growing pool on his chest. It was slowly growing outward from the arrow embedded in his chest. He knew he was dying, and cursed the day his sire sold his entire litter to the Hshtahni.

He took some small comfort in knowing his lord would soon follow him into the void.

Azimoth watched in awe as one of the primitives ran up the back of his lord, leaping over the head, firing arrow after arrow into the few vulnerable areas his lord possessed. Even as it looked like his lord might take his tormentor with him, another primitive saved him from the powerful jaws with a long spear.

He saw the rest of the primitives, screaming and cheering their excitement and exultation, as his lord finally slumped in death.

He saw one of the female primitives checking each of his fallen warriors, using an axe on any she found still living. She would chop their head off at the relatively narrow neck, and throw the head over her shoulder. It seemed like he was observing from a distance, but she was only a body or two away.

Azimoth watched as she saw his open eyes and chortled in glee, calling out to her companions. Several gathered with her to watch as she pulled his head hard to extend his neck.

The last thing he saw was the faces gathered above him as the bloody axe head came down.

Chapter Eighteen

"So, is Van Dono getting the primitives under some kind of control?" Captain Rost Fott asked. Zard Win shook his head, and remembered his captain couldn't see him from the bridge of Mountain View.

"I wouldn't call it that," he said cautiously. "He's trying to get access to the ship's computers, but the Mba erased so much. Fortunately, the translation files seem intact, so it's just a matter of time until we download their data, and have their transceivers conforming to our system. Rel Steen is helping quite a bit, but we might need him, with actual hands on the computer to get this right."

"I hate depleting our own ship of all her officers," Rost Fott said doubtfully. "Maybe once Van Dono has the bridge and the rest under control, he can turn the day-to-day operations over to you. Congratulations on successfully taking the ship."

"As much as I would like to claim credit, the Scoloti did the bulk of the work, clearing the ship of living threats," Zard Win said, picturing the final battle for the bridge. "Of course, their methods ended up with the bridge looking like a slaughterhouse scene in one of our classic historical ent-vids."

"Blood everywhere?" Rost Fott asked, sounding very happy to not have seen that firsthand.

"You have no idea, even with the footage we sent to you," Zard Win assured him. "We're lucky our casualties weren't much worse. As it is, you're going to be short-handed most of the trip home. A few of the men, after a couple day's rest, should be able to return to duty. But we lost three men each, and are lucky it was only that."

"I'll send Rel Steen over immediately, and talk with Van Dono," Captain Rost Fott promised. "I'm afraid you may have to quarter on board the generation ship until we reach Egelv Prime, if that's where we're taking this monstrosity."

"How many of my men should I keep over here?" Zard Win asked hesitantly. "We'll need to keep some sort of force on hand. And I think we should turn the energy weapon null field off as soon as possible."

"How many do you feel you need?" Rost Fott asked, and he could hear the cautious tone of his captain.

"Well, with everyone from all three ships, I might have a decent chance, if the null field is lifted," Zard Win said sardonically. "But I wouldn't promise anything."

"Are they really that fierce?" The captain sounded like he didn't really believe that.

"Wait until you see the footage," Zard Win promised. "I think you'll see my viewpoint. They fight with total abandon."

He hesitated, but felt it too important to lose track of.

"I think the Hshtahni have some ability, or possibly a weapon, that projects fear to their enemies," he said, remembering the chaos right after they entered the bridge. "And the Mba all had some sort of helmet on. It wasn't to protect their heads in battle, it was something else."

"Possibly to block a psionic attack?" Rost Fott asked. He looked worried at the idea.

"Possibly," Zard Win conceded. "I intend to discuss this with Shae Apon. She has multiple degrees, and may have studied the appropriate fields to understand this better than I. I'll have both her and engineering examine the helmets."

"Include this in your report," the captain said, and Zard Win nodded, concerned. If Prince Scyles hadn't somehow shaken off its effects, that battle might have ended quite differently.

"I think we should split your team in thirds," Rost Fott said, sounding thoughtful. "Have eight on duty, and we'll rotate four at a time out of two shifts of eight on Mountain Edge."

"That was what I expected to end up with," Zard Win admitted. He remembered something. "Oh, and Shae Apon is completely immersed in learning about the Scoloti, and their normal habits and customs. She also wants to inspect the stasis pods."

"I can't say I'm surprised," Rost Fott admitted. He hesitated, and then went on. "Can you make sure she eats at least once a day? She gets so caught up in her work, she forgets normal niceties, like eating and sleeping. Try and keep an eye on her, if possible."

"I will," Zard Win said, and felt a pang of guilt. He didn't have time to chaperone an officer. He had a feeling keeping tabs on the Scoloti would occupy all his time. "Tell Rel Steen I'll meet him on the bridge. Tell him to wear his old uniform."

"Right," Rost Fott said.

Gelon sighed, and reached over to take Myrina's hand. He let himself relax enough to recognize how comfortable the seat he sat in was. He was used to sitting on wooden chairs, stools, upended logs, large rocks, the common element being the hardness of the seat.

Two of the Egelv, the leader of the ones wearing green, and the lone female non-warrior that wore blue, had led him, Orik, and Agathyrsus and their families to a room with a large table and many of these comfortable chairs to sit on. The three swordmasters, as well as their apprentices were also present, standing back by the wall behind their perspective kings.

The Egelv were trying to explain the situation, but Agathyrsus either wasn't comprehending, or simply didn't care. All he could talk about was that he wanted his two children found, and that they wanted to leave, as soon as they did.

The time of the gathering was upon them, and he intended to carry out his plan to consolidate all the major tribes under one common ruler, himself.

The voice in their head that translated the words of the dog men that he now knew were called the Mba, and the giant lizard, which was a Hshtahni, also translated the words of the Egelv. It also, apparently, translated their words to the language of the Egelvs.

Mostly.

There were still points in the conversation that one or the other race didn't have a word that matched with what was being said, and that usually led to confusion. But it was an improvement on hand gestures, and Gelon was grateful it worked as well as it did.

It worked better than his ability to fully understand what the Egelvs were trying to explain to them. And King Agathyrsus, his queen and men understood even less than he did.

While leading the Egelvs, along with Targitai, Scyles and his new wife, and enough of his men to provide an escort, back to the main room his people were being stored in, they'd heard the Caitiari pounding on the door and walls of the room they'd been left in. Gelon and Targitai had looked at each other in surprise, followed by guilt, and then grins of humor.

He stopped and the group stopped around him.

"I forgot about them," Gelon admitted, and tried to keep a big smile from his face.

"As did I," Targitai agreed, not even attempting to conceal his grin.

Gelon turned to their new friends, Zard Win and Shae Apon, and gave them an apologetic look.

"There are three tribes of the people here, and one of them you will find annoying." He decided honesty was the best policy. "You will find myself and King Orik of the Paralatae very content to work with you to discover what options we have, for the future. And you will find us very grateful for your assistance. I'm afraid you will not find that attitude with King Agathyrsus and the Caitiari. You will find him quarrelsome and eager to portray himself as the king of all three of our tribes. This could not be less truthful. I apologize for the abusiveness you are about to endure."

"I'm sure it won't be that bad," Zard Win began, and both men shook their head in unison.

"You are kind, and we will allow you to make your own judgement on this," Gelon said, and shrugged. "Perhaps I will be proven wrong. Just know that this comprises all the Caitiari that we have seen. The rest must be in this sleeping spell you mentioned. Including his two children, who he will want awakened immediately."

"We need to study the controls and methods," Shae Apon said quickly. "We've never used this particular design, and to be safe, I need a little time to study it."

"Do yourself a favor, and tell him it will take longer than you expect it to," Targitai said, and looked at Gelon for confirmation. "He will push you to hurry, and will probably want you to awaken more of his men to give him an advantage in numbers."

"Is there a conflict between you, or that you anticipate we will have with them?" Zard Win asked quickly. He looked concerned.

"No, only that it is in his nature to push, and try to dominate all situations," Gelon said, and shook his head dourly. "He will almost certainly want separate quarters for his people. Right now, all of us are in one large room, along with the livestock."

"Would giving each tribe its own quarters, uh, place to sleep and eat in, be a good idea?" Shae Apon asked.

"For sleeping, certainly," Gelon agreed. "As for gathering and eating, a common yurt, or place to meet, eat, and drink, is useful."

"I couldn't agree more," Shae Apon said quickly, and Gelon saw Zard Win look at her curiously.

"I suppose we should let them out," Gelon said reluctantly, and Scyles grinned at him as he went to the door and pushed on the top button.

The door slid open, and the Caitiari poured out, looking for a foe to battle. Their attention immediately centered on the two Egelv, and Gelon and Targitai had to step between to keep them from being slaughtered on the spot.

"King Agathyrsus, thank the gods you live," Targitai said quickly, showing relief that, had Gelon not known him for so many years, would have believed to be real. "We saw no bodies, and hoped for the best, but found no sign of where the beasts took you."

Scyles suddenly turned away from the Caitiari, biting his lip, and Gelon was hard-pressed to hide his own grin.

"These people are not in league with the beasts that stole us from our encampment," Gelon said quickly, trying to avert an accident. "They arrived and have helped us defeat the dog men and the giant dragons."

He quickly introduced the two Egelv to King Agathyrsus, who, once he realized they weren't foes, mostly ignored them.

"Where are the rest of our people?" he demanded of Gelon, who shook his head to the negative.

"We don't know," he admitted. "We're going to search for them, but we found out, just before the last of the scum died, that everyone that wasn't in that room when we woke, are safe, all in one place. But they are asleep, and can't easily be awakened, without risking killing them."

"How do we know this is true?" Agathyrsus demanded to know. "And where could they hide six thousand people?"

"This is a very big ship," Gelon said solemnly. "Remember the one in the sky that we saw? As large as that one was, the ship we are on is much bigger. Much, much bigger."

"How can this be?" the Caitiari king asked, feeling the floor with his feet. "I sense no movement as if we were on water."

"Remember, the ship flew in the air like a bird, but much higher," Gelon reminded him. "This ship is so much bigger, even breezes and storms in the air do not affect it."

"That is impossible," Agathyrsus said bluntly.

"Excuse me, King Agathyrsus," Zard Win said slowly, and the king stared at him in frustration and anger, but let him speak. "It is more complicated than what King Gelon says. Please, let us reunite you with the rest of your people, possibly have a meal, while we find a suitable place to meet with the leaders of all three tribes. And in the meanwhile, we will search for your family and fellow tribesmen."

Queen Latoreia stepped forward, placing a hand on her husband's arm.

"Husband, this is good advice. Let us return to the room we sleep in. I don't know how long we were unconscious, but my stomach tells me we've missed at least one meal, perhaps two."

"You are very wise, Queen Latoreia," Zard Win nodded, bowing his head. "I will find a suitable room very close to where you've been sleeping, as well as find separate rooms more suitable for sleeping, for all three tribes."

Gelon had been impressed at how easily the two Egelv had manipulated the Caitiari, and vowed to pay close attention during any interactions with these clever elves, as Targitai called them.

As it turned out, they all ended up eating, with the exception of the two Egelv. They politely refused, and said they were going to figure out sleeping arrangements.

And now, here they were, sitting in these soft chairs, around a table made of some unknown material, that was perfectly smooth on the top, listening to the two Egelv, understanding very little of what they were saying.

Gelon made himself listen to the confusing words being spoken, and suddenly realized Scyles and Arga were also paying close attention, and seemed to have a better understanding than any of the rest of the people at the table.

Orik and Opis were listening intently, but their brows were furled, both with concentration and puzzlement, from their expressions.

Agathyrsus and Latoreia were, as he'd already noticed, not interested in explanations or excuses. They wanted their children back, and to be back in the surroundings they were familiar with, and they wanted it now.

He and Myrina were trying to understand, but the concepts were so far beyond anything they'd ever had to think about before.

Were they really in a very large ship, flying in the sky, far above the ground? Why had they never seen such a ship before, and where was the ship going? And what happened when they reached the ends of the world? Did they simply turn around and fly back?

Targitai, Ariapithes, Koloksai, Skulis, and Lik, all seemed more interested in watching the actions of the kings and each other than actually listening to what was being said.

But Scyles and Arga were both nodding in apparent understanding.

Scyles saw him watching, and probably the confused expression on his face. And on his mother's face, as well.

He reached under the table, fumbled for a moment, and pulled his hand out.

"Zard Win, may I speak for a moment, both to help our parents understand this better, and for you to tell me if I'm right or not?" he said to the Egelv.

Zard Win nodded, looking relieved.

Scyles held out a closed fist and opened it, showing one of the round stones he always coveted for his sling. He picked it up between his thumb and middle finger, and held it up for all to see.

"This round stone, is like our 'world', as you call it." He pointed at the stone. "Our world is much, much bigger than this, but in the same round shape?"

He looked at Zard Win for confirmation, and the Egelv nodded reluctantly.

"More or less," he said. "All worlds have mountains, seas, flat areas, and more, but all roughly round in shape."

"Why don't we fall off if we go too far to the south then?" Orik asked curiously, and Gelon silently applauded him. He'd just wondered the very same thing. "And does that mean Hades is below our world, and when we fall off, we fall to Hades for all eternity?"

195

Zard Win winced and shook his head.

"No, there are reasons you don't fall off, but they are scientific in nature and would take much explaining." Zard Win gave them all a strained smile. "For the moment, can we not worry about such things as falling off the world, and an imaginary place you fall to when you die…"

"Zard Win, this is their religion you speak lightly of," Shae Apon said gently. "We do not wish to argue the merits of something you believe in with conviction. Instead, let us start with the idea this world of yours is so big, you could spend most of your life walking, and not walk completely around it and come back to where you started."

She'd been looking at a small box that had been sitting on the table when they'd come in, and now pushed something on it, causing part of one of the walls to change.

It now showed a round object, and it was spinning, surrounded by nothing except what looked like the night sky.

But not their night sky, Gelon realized. He tried to find the gods in the sky, and they were gone, replaced by unrecognizable gods he didn't know. He looked at the Egelv, confused, and with more than a hint of fear.

"This is not your world," Shae Apon assured him. "But like yours, it is surrounded by the night sky, as you call it, and circles its own sun, providing the light of day."

"Wait, our world circles the sun?" Arga asked, wonder in her voice. "Are you sure?"

Gelon watched the woman try to hide a smile as she nodded.

"Very sure, Princess Arga." She bit her lip in a very people-like way. "I do not mean to laugh or mock you. I simply like your enthusiasm and willingness to ask questions. I know we ask you to take a lot of things as true, and trust we are not leading you astray."

Arga blushed and nodded her head in acquiescence.

The Egelv woman turned to Scyles.

"Prince Scyles, would you have another stone I might borrow for a moment?"

"Of course," he said, digging another one out. It was almost the exact same size, Gelon noted.

"Hmm," she said, inspecting the stone with interest. Then she was back to the topic at hand. She placed the new stone near the other, and began moving the other in a circular motion around the new stone. "This stone in the middle is your sun. Your world circles it once a year. You mentioned your gathering at harvest earlier." She nodded to Agathyrsus. "Both your sun and world are in the night sky, and it is so much larger than you can imagine or believe."

She set the small flat box that had been on the table near the stone denoting their world.

"Think of the stone being much larger than this, and this being so much smaller than your world, but far bigger than anything you've ever seen. When you were captured and taken, you were put into the ship, and it flew up until it was in the night sky."

She had the box move farther and farther from the two stones.

"The ship passed many suns with their own worlds, systems, we call it, and was voyaging back to the home world of the Hshtahni, the large lizards that ruled this ship, as well as the one that made you all fall unconscious."

She thought for a moment, and Gelon was fascinated with her determination to explain their current situation in a way they could understand. Zard Wan had struggled with his explanation, and it had done nothing but confuse them. But he actually understood her words, mostly.

"Their ships were caught in a very large storm, unlike anything you've ever seen before. It swept the two ships far off their path, and when they emerged from the storm, they were at the outer edge of our night sky."

"So when they intruded, you attacked them?" Scyles asked, and Gelon liked his guarded tone. This might be a very important thing to know, because it showed much about the normal thinking processes of these Egelv.

"Oh no," Shae Apon rushed to say. "At most, we would have asked their intentions in our night sky, and did they require assistance." She looked at their skeptical expressions and hurried to continue. "It was a very big, very dangerous storm. They were lucky to survive it at all. But before we could even identify ourselves, their ships fired their weapons at us."

"Weapons like those?" Scyles asked softly, pointing at the stun device on her hip.

"Yes, more or less, but much bigger," she said, seeing their doubt. "Both their ships and ours have weapons that can destroy other ships, or damage them enough that they must either surrender, or we board them, taking their ship, as we did this one."

"With your help," Zard Wan said quickly, before anyone pointed out the obvious. "We could have destroyed this vessel at any point, but when we realized it carried so many beings in stasis, we wished to try and save them, if we could."

"Zard Wan means your people and livestock sleeping in the stasis pods," Shae Apon continued. "We now know where they are, but there are ten thousand pods to investigate, and the only way to tell who is in which pod, is to look inside. It will take some time."

"This should be your highest priority," Agathyrsus said firmly. "We should be doing that now." He stared at Zard Wan. "After you have found and awoken all our people, how long will it take for you to return us to our world?" He gestured at the stone on the table.

"That will be a problem," Zard Wan admitted, and Gelon perked his ears up. The Egelv was about to admit something he did not wish to, and it was probably the most important item in this long, yet interesting conversation.

"We can't wake everyone, because there are insufficient stores aboard to feed them for more than a short period of time."

"How long could it take to return us?" Agathyrsus asked rudely. "We've only been gone several days at the most, and half of that time was right here, fighting for our freedom."

"But your ship was caught in the storm, and it took you far away from where you were supposed to be," Zard Wan reminded him. "And finding the way back to your world is going to be a challenge. We have no idea where it is."

"But you can find it?" Agathyrsus leaned forward in his chair, as if to threaten him physically.

"I don't know," Zard Wan admitted. He clearly wasn't intimidated, and Gelon wondered why. "It isn't just like retracing your steps in a forest. And the distances involved are so great."

He turned to Gelon.

"King Gelon, you didn't recognize the gods in your sky, did you?" he asked, pointing at the large display of the night skies on the wall. "This is outside our ship right now. If the night skies aren't the same, we have no trail to follow. We will have to try other methods, which means we can't awaken too many of you at once, or we will run out of food for you."

"But you will wake my children," Agathyrsus said belligerently.

Zard Wan nodded, and Shae Apon spoke.

"We will, after we find them, and after we are sure we can operate the machinery safely," she said, and Zard Wan nodded his agreement. "They use a different method than we do, and it is very old. Instructions on how to use it will have to be found and studied. But we will be able to do it soon."

"How soon?" he pressed her, and Gelon was impressed that he didn't intimidate her any more than he did Zard Wan.

"As soon as we accomplish all the things I just listed," she said. "I can't put a definite time to it, but I would think, with some of your people to help us find them, it should only take several days."

"For now, I would recommend you all get some rest. We will start searching in the morning. Some of my people have found sleeping quarters nearby for all of you." Zard Wan smiled at them. "We found comfortable quarters for all three royal families to sleep in, several larger dormitories for warriors of each of the clans, and a few other rooms that several families can sleep in, giving everyone a little more privacy and comfort."

"The Auchatae tribe will need two royal quarters," Arga said, and her face turned bright red, but she stared at the Egelv boldly. Boldly, but not risking a single glance at her own parents, Gelon noted, grinning at his old friend.

He decided stepping in here would ease much stress and embarrassment around the table.

"Princess Arga and my son, Prince Scyles, only married this morning, when we were all being held in that large room," Gelon explained to the two Egelv. "I believe they may have some unfinished business to attend to."

All the people around the table laughed boisterously at the obvious discomfort of the young couple, with the exception of Agathyrsus and Latoreia, and Koloksai. That didn't go unnoticed by either of the Egelv, Gelon noticed with satisfaction. The sooner these strange elves understood the difficult dynamics of the People's relationships, the better.

"Well, I think we can arrange that," Shae Apon said briskly, standing up. She looked at Arga. "Would you like me to show you what we found?"

"Please," Arga said, and grimaced. "Is there a place we can clean ourselves? My husband killed the Hshtahni, and even though we tried to wipe their blood off, the stench doesn't seem to go away. He also felt the need to hug me hardily to share the aroma," she finished, wrinkling her nose as she sniffed herself.

"Let me show you," Shae Apon said, smiling broadly at her, and they left the room.

Zard Wan walked with the Caitiari, talking fast and clearly trying to reassure them that their children were a high priority. Koloksai walked behind them, hand on his sword.

Scyles scooped up the two stones and made them disappear in his clothing. He looked at Gelon, and something about the seriousness of his son's expression made Gelon stop.

"What is it?" he asked softly.

Orik and Opis saw them stop, and joined them. Serlotta was standing in front of the screen of the night skies, looking at it intently.

"Did you notice they weren't very concerned about how angry King Agathyrsus was, and how neither of them seemed afraid of us?" Scyles asked, keeping his voice low. Gelon nodded and saw Orik do the same. "After the battle, they were all very nervous, and seemed afraid of us."

Orik shrugged.

"They had a chance to know us better, and wish to be friends. Not surprising that their fear lessened."

"It didn't lessen, it left," Scyles said sharply, and immediately bowed his head. "Excuse my tone, King Orik. I meant no disrespect."

"Speak your piece, Son," Orik said, and Scyles blinked in surprise. Orik grinned and slapped his shoulder. "You are my son now, just as Arga is Gelon's daughter."

"The reason they show no fear now, is their weapons work again," Scyles said, and pulled one of the stunning devices out from under his kurta. He pointed at the end that fit so nicely into a hand, and Gelon saw a tiny yellow light. "That wasn't lit when these didn't work. I had it in my hand when the light came on. I haven't tested it, but I would bet three horses it works now."

"Three horses are too much," Gelon began, and flinched as Orik and both women turned to stare at him. "Well, it is," he finished gamely.

Myrina shook her head at him with affection and turned to Opis.

"Come with me, Opis. Since we weren't included in the son and daughter recognition, I guess we don't matter." She grinned at her old friend. "Let's go find two young and able stallion warriors to help us occupy the evening."

"Or two lusty women," Opis said nonchalantly, and Myrina laughed.

"We'll see," she agreed, and they left, arm in arm, Opis snagging Serlotta as they passed him.

Gelon watched Scyles stare at his mother as she left with Opis. He seemed to feel their eyes on him, and turned back to them, making the stun weapon disappear under his kurta.

"Father, King Orik, I had better go find my, uh, wife," he said, sounding both excited and more than a little nervous. "She says we both need a bath." He looked at Gelon with genuine apprehension. "I thought the Grecians were the only people that bathed," he said, and hurried out of the room.

Gelon and Orik stared at each other, and laughed.

"Don't look at me," Gelon said, shaking his head. "He gets that from his mother."

Chapter Nineteen

Zard Win watched Commodore Mit Obet discuss the state of the bridge of the Muschwain with Captain Rost Fott, and Rel Steen. Thankfully, they'd gotten the body of the dead Hshtahni lord moved out and into a storage hold. It had been difficult, even with the use of anti-grav platforms and a heavy-duty crane they found in storage in one of the cargo bins.

What had surprised all of them was how helpful the Scoloti had been. First, they were far stronger than they looked. Second, they were willing to get their hands dirty, and weren't sickened by the sight of blood or dead beings.

He was happy to see this, because he didn't see any way they were going to find a way to return them to their home world. Because of the black hole, there was no path to follow to do so. But although physically, they were remarkably well suited to hard and messy labor, it didn't necessarily mean they were mentally and emotionally so.

The People, as the Scoloti constantly referred to themselves as, were a very proud and confident race. Zard Win didn't want to think what their reaction was going to be when they realized that, on Egelva Prime, they would be looked at as menial labor material.

"So, we have full access to everything they didn't wipe, and that includes all ship operations," Commodore Mit Obet said, and Captain Rost Fott nodded his agreement. They both looked at Rel Steen.

"We have accessed everything of consequence they left us," he agreed. "It's unfortunate that they wiped any information regarding the Hshtahni, or the primitives, as they called the Scoloti, or the location of their home planet."

"We should be realistic," the commodore said. "It's not like we're going to return them to their home planet, in any case. Their best hopes are that we find a useful purpose for them, and they become a productive part of the Egelv Empire."

"That is not going to be received well," Zard Win observed hesitantly. "They are used to being the strongest force in their world, and the mightiest."

"Perhaps a place in our security forces might be an answer," Mit Obet said, shrugging. "That would be a considerable step up from being sold en masse to another race as slave labor."

Zard Win winced at the idea.

"I don't want to be around when that gets said."

Commodore Mit Obet shrugged. "Sometimes, the truth is painful. It's not like they're going to have any say in the matter." He sighed. "Let's go see what the stasis pods look like. I guess it's time I met some of these 'Scoloti', as well"

Zard Win walked behind the Commodore and his captain, with two of his security guards. He was uncomfortable with the Commodore being around the People too much. He could be blunt, and even though the null field was off, and the stunners worked again, he had little or no illusions that the five of them could defend themselves adequately, if the People got the idea they were to be sold into slavery.

And they wouldn't be, he was sure of it. They had abilities, even if they weren't trained.

Trained for anything besides fighting, he thought grimly. They seemed born for warfare. Look at young Scyles. He had the impression this was the boy's first battle, and he'd ended up leading the fight directly to an over-whelming enemy.

And defeating them.

The door to the first huge room of stasis pods was open, and as they got close, they could hear King Agathyrsus shouting and cursing his men to find his children. Zard Win was already tired of dealing with him. The other two kings were shrewd and strong-willed, but they were much more reasonable to work with.

Why couldn't this Agathyrsus, his wife, and his people have been among the People put into stasis, Zard Win thought wistfully.

They entered the room, and Zard Win stared. Row after row of stasis pods spread out across the hold. His eyes scanned the rows, and quick math told him there had to be close to a thousand pods, in this hold alone. Which made sense, he reminded himself. There were ten holds dedicated to the pods.

There was a small view screen on top of each pod, and the Caitiari were scattered out in a line, working their way across the hold. With only about twenty people searching, it was going to take a while, Zard Win could see.

He noticed Shae Apon standing off to the side, looking at him. He walked over to her.

"Any luck?"

She made a face.

"We just started. I tried to get him to wait until tomorrow, but he insisted. I was trying to get an accurate idea of what housing needs his family and tribe members need, but he insisted that I show him the pods. I dare not leave them alone. If they find their children, they will try and get them out, and not following proper protocol will almost certainly get the children killed."

"Do you know how to operate the pods?" Zard Win asked curiously. "I can have one or both of these men stay here, and keep an eye on them, freeing you up to do more important things."

"That would be wonderful," Shae Apon said, looking relieved. "I got the newlyweds and their parents set with sleeping quarters, as well as all the Caitiari." She made a face. "Not that they're using them."

"We probably need to take a look at provisions for them as well," Zard Win suggested. "I doubt the Hshtahni put any thought into long-term conservation of their resources. I got the impression they use different animals for different purposes. And we may need to have more brought out of stasis to provide them the numbers necessary to reproduce more of each species."

"There is so much to do," Shae Apon said, and looked at him hopefully. "Can your men really cover this duty?"

"Of course," Zard Win said, and called the squad leader on duty aboard the Muschwain. He told him to allow for at least two guards to escort the Caitiari when they were in the stasis pod holds. In fact, he wanted them discreetly watched whenever they weren't in their quarters, sleeping. Shae Apon quickly showed his men the procedure to view who or what animal was in each pod without disturbing them. She cautioned them that if they found the children, she was to be called immediately. No one was to try and bring anyone out of stasis, and that included the livestock.

He saw his captain and the commodore finish their talk with King Agathyrsus and head towards the door. He could tell by their expressions and body language that they found him every bit as annoying as the rest of them did.

"Why don't you come with us now," Zard Win said to Shae Apon, smiling at her. "My men will watch the Caitiari from here on out. We're going to the main hold the Scoloti are currently quartered in. Maybe after we get the Commodore and Captain on their way, I can help you with sorting these people out."

She looked grateful, and smiled back at him.

"I would like that," she said, and suddenly looked awkward. "What I mean is, I could use the help."

"Of course," he said, and they turned to meet their superiors at the door.

"We don't have any more stasis pods on this ship? None at all?" Commodore Mit Obet asked in a testy voice, and Zard Win hid a smile. The commodore looked at the captain. "What about our ships? Do we even have any stasis pods?"

"Only for medical purposes," Rost Fott said, and Zard Win could hear the honest regret in his voice. "In fact, the ones on our ship are in use with the casualties from the battle. There are only two," he admitted.

"Your ship will be staying moored to the Muschwain," the commodore said, and the captain winced. "I know towing this huge hulk back to Egelva Prime will make your trip three times longer than usual, but we don't have any alternatives."

The commodore looked at Zarn Win and Shae Apon.

"The two of you will have to be our connection with these Scoloti," he said, and tried without success to sound sympathetic. "I would imagine dealing with these barbarians constantly will be a test of your endurance and patience, but it only makes sense. No matter what they ask of us, we will not be bringing any number of their people out of stasis any time soon."

"I've found King Gelon and his family, as well as King Orik and his, to be fairly easy to work with," Shae Apon said, and glanced at Zard Win.

"Security Chief Zard Win has been very helpful as well, with implementing actions we need taken to get the ones not in stasis into adequate quarters, and their livestock and foodstuffs organized so they're completely self-sufficient in regards to taking care of themselves."

"That's fine. I leave it in you and your people's hands, Captain Rost Fott," the commodore said, glancing at him. "Keep them happy and occupied, if you can, until we're home, and then we can turn this entire mess over to whoever gets stuck dealing with it."

They turned a corner, and the main hold was in front of them. Several armed male Scoloti stood guard, standing across the hall from the door. They saw the Egelv approaching, and stiffened. Then they recognized himself and Shae Apon, and they relaxed. One of them stuck his head inside the door, and called out to someone.

The other guard waved them inside with an expansive gesture of one hand.

They entered the giant hold, and Zard Win noticed it didn't seem as crowded as it had. He turned to Shae Apon and commented on that.

"I was able to get some of the families assigned rooms to give them a little more privacy," she admitted. "I promised them that when I got back from taking the Caitiari to the pods, I would finish the task."

"It looks like they're making this the mess hall," Commodore Mit Obet said, and nodded to the long tables that had been moved in and laid out in neat rows, with one row slightly separate from the rest.

"Yes, that was their wish, if they could get everyone into their own yurt, I believe they called it." Shae Apon looked at Zard Win mischievously. "I finally ascertained that a yurt is a tent. Apparently, they are nomads and the closest thing they have to houses are small huts on carts that they pull with the animals they call horses."

King Orik and Queen Opis appeared from the storage area off to the left, along with some more of their people, carrying benches, bags of what Zard Win suspected was grain or something similar, and some cooking utensils.

Zard Win and Shae Apon looked at each other.

"We can't have them starting fires to cook over," he said, and she nodded, giving him a slightly aggrieved look.

"I know that," she said, and looked around the room. "I think we'd better see what resources any of these holds have for preparing food. And soon."

The king and queen saw the Egelv and set what they were carrying down and walked over to them. Right about then, King Gelon and Queen Myrina appeared, he carrying a long bench, and she several pots.

"I would like to introduce you to the commodore of our squadron," Zard Win said, and quickly made the introductions. He was glad to see that, although the commodore had expected two more annoying royal families, he quickly noted that they seemed much more reasonable and courteous than the Caitiari.

"It is looking like the voyage back to our home planet will take about twenty days," Commodore Mit Obet said, and looked relieved when they didn't automatically start complaining. "I wish to thank you and your warriors for helping us defeat the Hshtahni."

King Gelon looked more than a little amused by the commodore's interpretation of the battle for the Muschwain. Zard Win knew they would still be trying to defeat the Hshtahni if the Scoloti hadn't attacked on their own volition.

The Auchatae king looked past them and a huge grin came to his face.

"Here's the lad you should be thanking," he said, and nodded past them. "Without my son, I think the Hshtahni might be dining on Egelv tonight."

They all turned to see Scyles and Arga pause as they realized they were suddenly the center of attention.

Scyles looked uncomfortable, and Arga seemed self-conscious, and Zard Win's smile broadened as he realized it wasn't because of the praise his father was heaping upon him.

He knew Scyles and Arga had been shown a room that had very simple furnishings in the way of a sleeping platform, bedding, and, of course, running water and toilet facilities. They had a sink, and a good-sized shower, as well.

Last time he'd seem them, they were filthy with Hshtahni blood and guts all over him, and smeared fairly heavily on her as well. Their hair had been matted and filthy looking, even braided as it was.

They looked like they'd just stepped out of the shower, loosely braided their hair, and stepped into different clothes, moments ago. But Zard Win knew for a fact it had been at least three hours ago, that Shae Apon had found them their room, showed them how the facilities worked, provided them with some ship's stores of soap, shampoo, and lotions for both their skin and hair.

It looked like they had taken full advantage of everything, too. Their skin was clean and almost glowed with a healthy hue.

The two mothers walked up to them, and inspected them closely. As Zard Win watched, their skin began to acquire a reddish tone, darkening as he watched.

Queen Myrina pulled her son into a hug, and Zard Win watched her sniff him curiously. She looked startled, and then pressed her lips, as if to hide a smile.

"You look and smell very nice, Scyles," she said, and kissed his cheek. Her eyes widened, and she looked at Shae Apon. "Does our yurt have the same..."

She paused, as if trying to decide how to word her question. Shae Apon had mercy on her.

"Yes, I'm stocking each room, er, yurt, with basic soaps and..."

"Mama, it is wonderful," Arga said, and Queen Opis looked at her with an innocent look that fooled no one.

"You will have to show me, daughter," she said, then looked puzzled. "But is it difficult to use? Were you trying to get clean all this time. It's been three hours."

Arga's face and neck quickly turned darker red, and Zard Win realized what Queen Opis was implying. He kept his face blank.

"No, we got clean first thing," Arga said, and she glanced towards but not at Scyles. "We helped each other get clean, but that led to other things, so we had to get clean again." She straightened her back boldly and stared at her mother. "Three times."

Gelon and Orik burst into laughter, as did any of the Scoloti within hearing range. The two queens looked at each other, and then smiled with pride.

"I believe I will leave them with their tales to tell, and give them a little privacy," Commodore Mit Obet said, clearing his throat, obviously embarrassed by the earthy comments flying around them.

Apparently, the Scoloti were not prudish about sexual matters, Zard Win thought, and without thinking, glanced at Shae Apon. She looked as embarrassed as the commodore sounded, but was also finding it funny.

Zard Win decided that she looked very attractive when she was embarrassed. He immediately banished the thought from his head. He enjoyed working with her, and the last thing he wanted to do was make her feel uncomfortable in his presence. She was from a very influential family back on Egelva Prime, and his had a long history of military tradition. Any dream of his forming a relationship with her was just that.

A dream.

Myrina nudged her husband, with more than a little strength.

"Husband, we will have to experiment with this 'shower' that our children have discovered. I have an urge to see what lies beneath the layer of oils, dirt and sweat that coat my body, and would be happy to assist you in doing the same," she said, slipping an arm around his waist.

Gelon eyed her with caution.

"I've always found the sweat-yurt to be more than sufficient," he said nervously. "It's not healthy to strip our bodies of their natural protection."

"Dirt isn't a natural protection, Husband. It's dirt." Myrina smiled, knowing full well she would get her way on this. "We are not out on the steppes, and we will be interacting with other kinds of people. I, for one, look forward to this experience. Look at Scyles and Arga. They don't look in danger of their health failing them by scraping the earth and sweat away."

She gave him a not so little shove with her hip.

"And look at how happy they are." She looked up at him, and gave him that look. "Our helping each other with this experiment might just give Scyles a little brother or sister. That will give their firstborn someone to play with."

Gelon stared down at her, then his head shot around to stare at the newlyweds. Myrina looked at them as well. It was very cute the way they were fully aware of each other, no matter who they were talking with, and their hands kept finding each other's.

Myrina knew that Arga was a very strong girl that would be a force to reckon with, but right now she looked exactly like what she was. A young girl, newly married, and madly in love with her husband. Unless their timing was bad, odds were very good she was already with child.

A thought occurred to her, and she went over to Opis. The other woman saw her coming, and stepped away from her husband, looking at her enquiringly.

Myrina smiled and spoke in a quiet voice.

"Opis, may I ask where you are in your bleeding cycle?" She saw the speculative look in the other woman's eyes, and shook her head, laughing. "No, no, don't get your hopes up. My body is for my husband alone."

Opis got it and turned to look at her daughter, then back at Myrina with a smirk.

"If those two have been as energetic in their love-making as they are in almost everything else either of them do, I think we can expect the sound of crying babies well before the next gathering." Opis got a funny look on her face as she realized that was probably a thing of the past. "Or when there would be a gathering, were we still on our home world," she finished awkwardly.

"You're at the right point?" Myrina asked, with excitement. "You and Orik should try this shower thing out together. Gelon and I are going to, tonight. No matter what he says. Who knows how many babies we might hear crying to be cleaned in nine moons."

"You too?" Opis laughed out loud. "Well, the longer we are around each other, the more our times merge. We'll have to talk in the morning, and see what progress has been made."

They laughed and spontaneously hugged.

Myrina noticed their husbands were standing together, watching them with misgivings. She nodded in their direction.

"Who would think two women could strike such fear in the hearts of noble warriors and kings," she said, and Opis laughed. Then Myrina grew serious.

"We have much to do today, before we can retire to our yurts," she said. "We need to go through everything the Mba had brought aboard of ours, sorting out what is property of who, and deciding how many more sheep and horses we need to awaken."

"We should have a feast," Opis said thoughtfully. "Perhaps invite Zard Win and Shae Apon. Let them see how we live, when we are free. I know I saw some casks of Grecian and Persian wines. We have much to be thankful for, and to celebrate."

Myrina nodded and looked at the two Egelv, and then looked at them closer.

"I think those two are fighting nature, and I believe nature will win," she said, and Opis got her meaning. She looked over at them, standing next to each other, supposedly listening intently to Orik go on about something. But their body language screamed a desire, no, a need, to be close to each other.

"I see what you mean," Opis said, and smiled at her. "We should see what effect our wines, and maybe a little fermented mare's milk has on their inhibitions. Allow nature to run its course."

"Let us go plant the idea of a feast in our husband's minds," Myrina said, and nudged her fellow queen. "Make them think it's their idea."

Opis laughed, and pulled her along.

"That won't be difficult."

Arga smiled to herself as she watched the Egelv enter the large yurt room. They looked around, clearly torn between discomfort at being out of their element, but yet very curious about how the People lived. Or, at least, how they had lived before being taken captive by the Hshtahni.

Zard Win, in charge of the warriors aboard the ship Mountain Edge, pulled a box that floated behind him. Arga, not for the first time, wondered at the amazing things the Egelv took for granted. She wondered idly what was in the box.

When King Gelon and her father declared there would be a feast to celebrate their breaking free of the yoke of the Hshtahni giant lizards and their Mba minions, they'd invited the Egelv officers they knew. Zard Win, Shae Apon, the Science Officer/Doctor, as she called herself, Captain Rost Fott, and the First and Second Officers, Van Dono and Rel Steen, of the Egelv warship Mountain Edge, and Commodore Mit Obet.

Shae Apon had said she would need to test whether the People and the Egelv had compatible digestive systems, to make sure food for one race wasn't poison to the other. That was yesterday. She took samples of the sheep that had been slaughtered, the grains, the fermented mare's milk and wines, anything that would be part of the meal. She also took blood samples from several of them. Arga wasn't sure why.

Captain Rost Fott said one of his officers needed to stay on the bridge of their ship, so the first officer couldn't attend. The commodore had agreed to attend, although he hadn't sounded very enthusiastic. He'd brought four men from his own ship, Raging River, as an escort, but they were evidently staying out in the concourse. Arga was pretty sure that if she went and looked, there would be at least two, and probably four more military escorts from Rost Fott's ship, out in the concourse as well.

"Friends, welcome to our yurt!" Her new father-in-law's voice boomed out. "Come, we have seats here for all of you."

Her mother and Queen Myrina, her new mother-in-law, had hatched the idea that a feast was needed, and it was easy to convince their husbands.

King Agathyrsus and Queen Latoreia had initially been against the idea. They wished to keep their warriors searching for the twins. They'd spent the remainder of yesterday, and all of today looking at the pods, one by one. Arga heard they were in the fourth hold, when they stopped for the feast. He briefly entertained the idea that his guards keep searching during the feast, but after seeing the initial resentment, had backed off that idea.

Their men and women, with the exception of their Royal Bodyguard, sat with the combined Paralatae and Auchatae tribes.

A large royal table in the middle had Kings Gelon, Orik, and Agathyrsus sitting in the middle of one of the long sides, with Koloksai, the Caitiari Royal Bodyguard next to his king, followed by Ariapithes, and Targitai sitting on the end, facing the length of the table.

Scyles sat next to his father, with Serlotta, and then his mother on the other side, and Opis across from her. Queen Latoreia sat at the end, facing Targitai at the far end of the table.

Arga sat next to her mother, and places for the five Egelv filled this side of the table.

Her father looked at Zard Win inquisitively.

"What do you bring?" he asked curiously, and all of them looked at the floating box. Her mother made no bones about looking beneath it.

"How do you make it float in the air, like a cloud or a mote of dust in the yurt?" she asked, passing a hand beneath it.

"We've brought an offering to the feast," Zard Win said, looked around the room. "I'm afraid there isn't enough for everyone."

There were one hundred and fifty men and women from the three tribes in addition to the royal families.

King Gelon and her father glanced at each other, and nodded. King Agathyrsus shrugged.

"They wouldn't expect to have any of it anyway," he said dismissively.

"We'll try a sampling and see how far the rest will go," her father said, and Gelon nodded, and looked at Zard Winn.

"We've roasted a sheep, and made a stew with some of it." King Gelon nodded at Shae Apon. "With her help, we figured out how to cook, and even bake, safely, in a connected room. Since we can bake, we have bread, as well."

He held up his goblet.

"And we do have a goodly amount to drink, since we were planning on feasting already."

Queen Myrina sighed and shook her head at him.

"Manners of a boar," she said, and the queens all laughed, Gelon and father with them. She turned to the Egelv. "Please, be seated. Commodore, perhaps you'd like to sit across from King Orik?"

Arga was impressed at how her and Scyles' mothers were so adept at handling people. In no time, they had the captain to the right of the commodore, across from King Agathyrsus, and the Second Officer, Rel Steen, to the right of him.

Shae Apon chose the seat next to Arga with a questioning look. She nodded her head enthusiastically.

"Yes, please, sit next to me. Do you need help with that, Zard Win?" Arga asked, and the Egelv smiled at her.

"We have some platters of cheese, and something similar to your bread, as well as some meat that goes well with the cheese."

He and Shae Apon pulled covered plates, and as they set them around the table, the tops opened to show the contents. All of the Scoloti leaned forward curiously to look at the narrow loaves of bread that had been sliced thin, along with the perfectly square pieces of cheeses and meats.

Shae Apon took some bowls, also covered, out of the floating box and set them near the plates. They opened, showing some sort of pastes or gels, each with a small, dull, knife.

"These can be spread on the bread, and are flavors we enjoy. They compliment the meats and cheeses."

King Agathyrsus picked up one of the slices of meat and looked at it closely.

"You have square animals on your world?" he asked suspiciously, sniffing it. His eyebrows raised in surprise. "It smells like it might taste good."

"We think so," Captain Rost Fott said congenially.

Zard Win pulled some bottles from the box, and the women all oohed at how pretty they were. He smiled at them and pulled the top off one of them. He opened a small door in the side of the box, and started pulling out goblets. They were smaller than tankards, and had little pedestals on the bottom.

"We found that the milk we took to sample was fermented, and the wines had a variety of strengths." Captain Rost Fott said, and smiled apologetically. "We don't have anything on board as strong as your milk, but our wines are comparable to yours."

"They are very smooth, but stronger than you might think," Zard Win warned them. "You might want to sip this, not gulp it down."

He poured out glasses for everyone at the table. When he got to Serlotta, he hesitated, and looked at his mother questioningly.

"A small one," she said, and Scyles rubbed Serlotta on the head. He was clearly pleased, and Arga laughed at the excitement on his face. He was really too young to drink, but since this was such a special feast, Mama was stretching their rules.

Zard Win finished pouring cups for everyone else at the table, including Arga.

Shae Apon leaned over and whispered to her.

"It is early, so tonight in moderation would not matter, but if you truly do get pregnant, you should not drink anything with alcohol in it while you are carrying the child."

"Why not?" Arga asked, curiously. "Most women drink while they carry, except when the morning sickness hits them. And when they are very close to giving birth."

"Consuming alcohol can damage the unborn child," Shae Apon said quietly. "When they are still within you, they are susceptible to certain things. It can cause the bones to be weaker than they would have been, affect the thinking ability of the baby, and other things as well."

Arga looked at her in dismay. She purposefully didn't glance over at Scyles. She could sense he'd seen her grow serious and didn't wish to worry him needlessly. She might not even be pregnant.

"Yesterday, we did make love several times, three," she admitted. "And then again last night. And this morning," she admitted, her lips trying to fight forming a grin. "We'd just married earlier in the day, so we'd only had a chance to do it once before the fighting began.

Shae Apon looked at her, then over at Scyles, then back at her again, her eyes wide, and mouth slightly open.

"Oh." she finally said. "So you really want to get pregnant? Because I've never heard of anyone having sex six times in one day's time."

"Well, Scyles is a prince," Arga said with a straight face, then laughed when the Egelv looked confused. "No, we didn't really even think about my getting with child. It's just we fought the idea that our parents wanted us to marry so hard, and then we fell in love, and got married the next day. We're just very happy and enthusiastic."

"Enthusiastic," Shae Apon said, keeping her face expressionless.

"Very," Arga said, hearing the little girl in her voice, but not caring. A thought occurred to her that immediately made her solemn. "Last night, we did drink while we were, um, being enthusiastic," she admitted, worried.

"That would be too early to worry about," Shae Apon said, and Arga sighed in relief.

The Egelv woman looked at her a moment, as if debating in her mind.

"I don't think a glass or two would hurt anything the day after, if you did get pregnant," she said. "If you like, in a few days, I could run a test and probably be able to tell if you're pregnant or not. Was yesterday the first time for you?"

"Yes," Arga admitted, and felt her face go red. "Truthfully, I'm feeling a little sore."

"I wonder why," Shae Apon said with a straight face, and Arga looked at her confused. Then she realized she was being teased.

They both laughed, and Arga noticed that Zard Win was staring studiously across the table, his brown skin a slightly different shade.

"Shae Apon, do Egelv blush when embarrassed?" Arga asked innocently. The woman turned to look at Zard Win, and a grin came to her face as she turned back to her.

"Why yes, yes we do," she said, and both women laughed again. "Not quite as pronounced as your people."

Anything Zard Win was going to say was interrupted by her father, who was now standing.

He was holding one of the small cups by the pedestal, and raised it to everyone at the table.

"I offer a prayer to the Gods to protect our new friends, the Egelv. May our friendships flourish, and our children be fertile."

The room roared with laughter at Scyles and Arga's expense, and everyone drank. She blushed and looked over at Scyles, who was watching her curiously. He smiled, and she saw the love in his eyes, and felt warm inside.

They raised their cups to each other and took a sip. Arga was surprised at how light it was, both as a liquid, and in taste. It was very fruity, yet not sweet. And with only one sip, she could tell it was much stronger than it felt like it should be.

She saw Scyles look at his cup appreciatively, and smiled. They both sipped again, their eyes never leaving the other's.

Arga felt her mother lean over to her, their shoulders touching.

"Did I just hear you tell her that Scyles was successful in his husbandry duties six times?" Her mother sounded impressed, and Arga couldn't prevent a grin from turning her lips up at the edges.

"He was very eager to satisfy me," she said, and heard the almost dreamy tone in her voice.

"And did he?" Myrina asked from across the table.

Arga looked around in surprise, and realized that all the women had heard her clearly, as well as Serlotta.

She didn't dare look at Scyles.

"Oh yes, yes he did, very completely," Arga said, and wondered if she sounded too brazen, talking with her husband's mother about something like this.

"Who did what completely?" her new father-in-law asked, and she felt her face get very hot.

"Scyles and Arga, six times. Scyles and Arga, six times," Serlotta chanted, and everyone at the table turned to stare at Scyles, then at Arga, then back at Scyles.

She met Scyles' eyes. From the heat on her face, she knew she was blushing at least as much as he was.

"That is what I would call a consummated marriage," her father said in a boisterous tone, and her mother laughed, both at and with him. "May we see our grandchildren even sooner than we could have hoped!"

"Papa!" Arga said, her face still flushed, but secretly, she was pleased at the awe and admiration everyone was showing both of them. She shrugged and looked at Scyles with a devious grin. "It's really Scyles that deserves all the credit."

"New daughter of mine, trust me," Queen Myrina called out, laughing at her son's discomfort. "It may have been Scyles that found the reserves to perform, but he never could have done it without you inspiring his performance."

"Too true," her mother chortled, and nudged Queen Latoreia with a grin, and tapped her cup with her own.

They both raised their drinks and sipped, but Arga saw that the Caitiari Queen's eyes showed anything but laughter or enjoyment. She didn't dare look to see the expression on King Agathyrsus' face.

Women began putting huge platters of chunks of spiced mutton, and large kettles of mutton stew around the tables. One of them began ladling stew into bowls and another served them to everyone, along with thick wooden spoons.

Arga hid a smile as she watched the reaction of the Egelv to the foods being placed before them. One by one, they tried a taste. After the first bite, most of them ate with confidence, enthusiasm, in Zard Win's case. She noticed that after the first spoonful of stew, the commodore more played with his food than actually ate any.

Next to her, Shae Apon dipped a chunk of bread into the stew, after seeing Scyles' mother do the same. She smiled at Arga as she realized she was being watched.

"This is quite different than anything I've eaten before," she admitted. "But it's interesting. I don't usually eat very much meat, so I'll have to be careful not to overdo it."

She heard King Agathyrsus talking loudly with the commodore and the captain, and he sounded agitated. Both of the Egelv seemed to be listening to his every word, but Arga could see the captain's expression was strained. And at least once, she saw the commodore look at him with an annoyed expression.

Arga couldn't really be surprised. As far as she knew, King Agathyrsus was annoying to everyone. But he was insistent about both finding the twins and being returned to their world.

She couldn't be sure, but from what she'd seen and heard from the Egelv, there didn't seem to be a very good chance of their ever making it back to their tribal grazing grounds. She had a feeling they were going to be finding new lives here, far from home.

But she had Scyles, and together, they would be fine. And if their efforts bore fruit, their children would be born out here, wherever they were, here or in some new home.

She looked around the table, and was satisfied. With the exception of the Caitiari, everyone here was family, in one form or another, to her and Scyles.

As long as their family was together, where they were would matter little.

After all, she thought, we are nomads.

We are the Scoloti.

Chapter Twenty

"I had to tell him that some parts need to be scrubbed differently than others," Opis said, and laughed. Myrina joined her, and Arga did the same, then looked over at Scyles guiltily. Her mother saw her glance and leaned forward to put a hand on her arm. "It's okay, daughter. All men have to be told these things."

"You don't think you risk becoming ill, getting your entire body wet, and for such an extended period of time?" Latoreia asked hesitantly, and looked over at her husband, who was talking loudly with the other two kings, as well as the Egelv officers.

"My daughter looks so healthy, she glows," Opis said, and placed the back of the fingers of one hand on Arga's cheek. "And her skin is so soft." She smirked at the other women. "And what it did to my husband, who was already of a lusty nature, was nothing short of inspiration the Gods would show pride in."

Myrina smiled, remembering she and Gelon more or less going through the same transformation last night. He'd been difficult to convince, until she finally got fed up, stripped her clothes off, every bit, and stepped under the flowing water. The shock had been considerable until she discovered the knobs could change the heat, and then it became quite pleasant.

Her eyes had been closed when she sensed her husband had joined her in what the Egelv called a shower. They had spent a long time under the water, interspersing scrubbing each other, with reacting to the passions it induced. And those passions had continued through much of the night.

She knew they hadn't matched the fervor of their son and his new bride, but they'd been quite satisfied with what they did achieve. She discreetly watched Latoreia look at her husband, and the speculation on her face was clear to see.

She saw the woman look at Arga, having switched places with Serlotta, holding hands with Scyles, and a sadness came to her eyes. Latoreia felt Myrina's eyes upon her and after a moment of anger, her expression grew depressed.

"I had hoped they would marry our twins," Latoreia admitted, looking at her with resignation. "I fear that if we are not able to return to the rest of the People, we will never find them proper mates."

"Oh, I'm sure that between the tribes we have, we can find suitable matches for them," Myrina hastened to say. "There are many good men and women, and it will work out."

"Perhaps," Latoreia said, and drained her glass. "But none of them will be princes or princesses. I bid you all good night."

They watched her walk over to her husband, and wait until he paused in his diatribe, and then she spoke quietly. He listened, which surprised Myrina. An even bigger surprise was when he nodded, said something briefly to the men around him, and escorted her towards the door.

Myrina couldn't help but see the relief on the faces of the men he'd been talking to. Gelon looked over at her and grinned. She couldn't help but return the grin, and wondered if she'd get any sleep tonight. She rather hoped not. It had been many years since they'd had a night like the last. She was more than willing to try for two nights of passion in a row.

She watched Koloksai gather the men and women of the Caitiari, and after a few minutes of talking, then cussing, and finally cuffing one along-side the head, he got them on their feet and out the door.

Myrina noticed her son looking at Zard Win thoughtfully. He seemed to be trying to make up his mind about something, and the Egelv made it easy for him by sensing his attention.

"Did you have a question, Prince Scyles?" he asked, and Scyles nodded slowly.

"When we fought the great grey dragon, I found myself under some sort of spell that caused me to almost collapse with fear," he said slowly, his eyes not meeting anyone else's, intent on his cup of mare's milk. "It felt like everything was suddenly so large and over-whelming, that to try and fight it was impossible."

"It was your first time in battle, and your father says the dragon was fierce," Myrina hurried to say. She looked at Gelon, and was shocked to see him not meeting her eyes, or anyone else's, for that matter. "Husband, did you see Scyles falter? By all accounts, he led the attack, and his bravery carried the day."

"He didn't falter. And he did lead the attack," Gelon said shortly, but stopped short of saying more. She looked at him curiously. He was hiding something. She looked around the table, and was struck by the fact that all the Scoloti at the table that had been in that battle looked very uncomfortable, and their eyes were darting everywhere except focusing on anyone else.

Scyles looked at Zard Win finally. He looked haunted, and Myrina felt like dashing around the table to hug him, but made herself sit still.

"Do the Hshtahni have some sort of weapon that can cause fear, or prey on our own insecurities?"

"What do you mean by insecurities?" Shae Apon spoke up, alternating between staring at Scyles, and then at Zard Win. "You felt some sort of mental attack?"

"Weren't you there?" Myrina asked, curious despite her concern for her son.

"I was, but they made me stay back, since I am not a warrior," Shae Apon said, and looked thoughtful. "I found myself frightened, but I am not a warrior or soldier, carried no weapons, and the noise and carnage, and all the screaming was paralyzing."

"What screaming?" Myrina asked, wondering. She hadn't heard anything about this.

Shae APon shrugged.

"It sounded like our Egelv, and the People, as well," she said slowly. "From the sounds of it, I thought everyone was dying. Then, suddenly, it changed, and everyone began to sound like they had in the earlier battle, yelling and cursing, but not screaming."

Myrina looked around and saw every man, and even Arga, looking away from everyone else, embarrassment and, could it be, shame, on their faces?

She looked at her son again.

"Scyles, you say everything seemed so big, and so over-whelming," she said, encouraging him to continue.

"Best not to speak of such things," her husband began, and she hissed at him. His mouth snapped shut, and he looked at her, shocked.

"It was as if everything had grown much bigger and more difficult," Scyles said slowly, pain showing in his voice. "All hope had fled, I knew I was about to die, because I was too small, too insignificant, to defeat the huge dragon, the mighty Hshtahni, before whom all must fall. I was curled into a ball of fear, and couldn't move."

"Husband?" Opis spoke up for the first time. "Did you feel this?"

"I fear no one," Orik began, and stopped, his face crestfallen. He couldn't continue.

For long moments, everyone at the table, Egelv and Scoloti alike, sat, embarrassed, eyes averted. The three Egelv officers Myrina knew had been on their own ship looked mystified, but everyone else looked troubled, and shaken.

"We all felt it," Skulis said, standing next to Ariapithes, who glared at him.

"Well, we did," he said. "I felt the same sensations, and it knocked me off my feet. I saw all of you, and the rest of the warriors, everyone, on the floor, rolling around screaming, holding our heads. We were paralyzed with fear." He looked embarrassed, and nodded towards Scyles.

"If Scyles hadn't fought the fear away, we all would have died yesterday."

"You fought off the fear?" Myrina asked, staring at her son. "How did you do it?"

Scyles didn't speak. His face looked tortured, and Arga cupped her hand around his cheek. He stared at her wildly for a moment, and then seemed to pull himself back together.

"All my life, I've been the smallest," he said slowly. "My father and brothers were much bigger than I. All the other boys were always taller, and stronger. I was told I was too small to ever be a great fighter, or leader, or even survive, once I didn't have my father, or our swordmaster, to protect me. Yet, I learned how to do things, how to do things better than the bigger people around me. I found a way to succeed each time I had to. When Skulis came after me, he should have won. He's much bigger and stronger than I am, and an accomplished wrestler. But I'd always tried to learn ways to take away any such advantage, and I beat him that morning, so long ago."

"That was three days ago," Skulis reminded him, and many around the table laughed ruefully. Scyles allowed a small smile to appear and nodded his agreement.

"The waves of fear that kept washing over me made me so angry, I was able to block it long enough to get a couple arrows off, and after that, the fear seemed to go away."

"I remember," Targitai said quietly. "Suddenly, we were all able to think clearly again."

Myrina saw the captain and the commodore exchange guarded looks, and wondered what they knew about this ability to cause fear in the hearts of your opponent.

Myrina glared at her husband.

"You knew this, and yet let your son think it was his weakness alone?"

Gelon hung his head for a moment, then raised it to meet her eyes.

"I thought it was just me," he said woodenly. "I have never feared any man in battle, but that dragon… I didn't know he'd felt it too. Or that any of the others had."

"Aye, me as well," Orik admitted, and the other men around the table nodded their heads, emboldened by not being the only one who'd been felled by fear.

"And my son overcame whatever sorcery that dragon tried to use on us," Gelon said, smiling grimly. He looked at Zard Win intently. "So, do these dragons have some sort of ability to cause fear?"

Zard Win looked troubled, and glanced at Shae Apon. Then he looked over at his captain and the commodore.

"I felt it too, and wanted to talk with Shae Apon about the Hshtahni possibly having some sort of psionic attack capability," he admitted. "But there's been so much happening since we took the ship, I hadn't had a chance to, yet."

"You forgot," Shae Apon said quietly.

Zard Win winced, and nodded.

"I forgot," he admitted.

He looked over at Scyles.

"It was a real weapon, and wasn't a reflection of your own fears," Zard Win said, and Myrina was happy to see the relief on her son's face. Arga gave him a sweet, gentle kiss on his cheek, and rested her head on his shoulder.

Scyles looked at her, and she saw that although he was relieved, he wasn't totally beyond the shame he'd felt.

"Son, you take too much on your own shoulders," she said quietly, knowing he could hear her perfectly, because she was his mother. "You must learn to share the load, let those that love and honor you help."

She smiled at him sweetly.

"And remember, my son, it was you that defeated the mind weapon of the dragons, and the very dragons themselves. Others helped, but you were the one that carried the day."

She watched the strain slowly leave his face and shoulders, and he visibly relaxed, his eyes glancing down at Arga. He nodded his thanks to her.

The party atmosphere returned, especially the drinking, and the tension dissipated.

Commodore Mit Obet stood, and looked down at Captain Rost Fott.

"I leave it to you," he said, and turned his attention to the rest of them.

"Thank you for an excellent meal, and an entertaining evening. I must return to my ship."

He bowed his head slightly to both kings, then slightly deeper bows to Opis and herself, and left. Rost Fott, Gelon, and Orik walked to the door with him, and stood there talking after he left.

Myrina watched Rost Fott say something to her husband and Orik, and they both stared at him. Curious, she watched them exchange glances, and thoroughly enjoyed seeing their faces go through a progression of emotions and expressions. The two kings and the Egelv were very animated in their conversation, and she finally turned away, knowing she would find out what that was about later.

She saw that Opis was staring at the men, and turned to her, puzzled.

"Did you see their expressions?" she asked, looking baffled.

"I did," Myrina admitted.

"What did you see?" Arga asked curiously, and Scyles turned from talking with Zard Win and Shae Apon, looking interested.

Myrina didn't respond as she watched Gelon and Orik gesture to their bodyguards. Both men joined them immediately, and the four of them and Rost Fott, and Rel Steen, moved over to a far wall and commandeered a table. The men at the table took it with good grace, and moved over near the casks of wine and mare's milk.

"I wonder what they're speaking of," Arga said, and she wondered the same. She saw the expression on her son's face and started. He knew something. She was sure of it. Then she saw he wasn't watching his father and the others, he was watching the two Egelv sitting with them.

"You know, don't you," he asked Zard Win quietly.

"No, we don't have any..." Shae Apon's voice faltered as she turned and looked at the Security Chief. "Wait a minute. Zard Win, do you know what's going on?"

"Maybe," he admitted, grudgingly. "I heard them talking earlier, and something they said stuck in my head."

"What did they say?" Arga asked impulsively, and Scyles laughed.

"He can't tell you. It would be like us giving away our father's secret plan," he said. "Or telling something he told someone in confidence. It's a betrayal, of sorts."

"Our fathers have a secret plan?" Arga asked, and saw the expressions on their faces. Scyles began laughing quietly. She exhaled noisily, and set her cup down. "I have had enough wine. It is making me stupid."

"Never that, my wife," Scyles said, and she smiled at him. Myrina watched them and for the hundredth time, marveled that these were the same two young people that had threatened dire results, if they were forced into marriage.

Dire, indeed, she thought with amusement. I will almost certainly be a gra'mama before another year has passed. She smiled at the idea.

"What are you smiling about?" Scyles asked suspiciously.

"I'm wondering if it will be a boy or a girl, or one of each," she said mischievously, and watched for Arga's reaction. It was quick in coming.

"One at a time is plenty," Arga said firmly, and then looked alarmed. She stared at her mother. "How many times he succeeds, doesn't affect how many babies there are, does it?"

"One for each time, dear daughter," Opis said with a straight face. "When you give birth, it will be more like a litter than a birth."

Both mothers shrieked their laughter, although both Scyles and Arga were pale as the moon on a full night. Arga looked at Shae Apon, as if for verification.

The Egelv shook her head, smiling, and Arga looked crossly at her mother. Then she relented and joined them laughing, even as she pushed her wine cup farther away.

"That is not funny," she said firmly. Beside her, Scyles looked relieved, but also amused.

Shae Apon nudged Zard Win's arm with her elbow.

"So, were you going to tell me?" she asked, and stared at his face.

"Yes," he said, returning the stare.

Myrina watched with interest as the two Egelv seemed to both become frozen into place for what felt like was a very long time, but probably wasn't. Then Shae Apon, looked away, her brown skin acquiring a visible red hue.

There was shouting nearby, and Myrina turned to see Skulis and a large man from her own tribe squaring off, their kurtas and tunic removed, as well as their trousers and boots. Wearing only their loincloths, they circled, tentatively slapping each other, vying for an opening to put the other down to the floor.

"Skulis will win this," Opis said, leaning forward. "He's the best wrestler in either tribe."

"A bolt of that blue felt you've been coveting says Savlius takes him," Myrina said immediately. She didn't know how good a wrestler he was, but felt honor-bound to defend a member of her tribe.

"Bad bet, Mother," Scyles said casually. "Second best," he continued in an aside to Arga's mother.

Opis laughed.

They watched Skulis get a grip on Savlius, twist him enough to get him off balance, and bring him to the floor. They seemed to grapple with no plan or skill that Myrina could see, until suddenly Skulis had him pinned, and was slowly tightening his grasp, so Savlius couldn't get a breath. He finally slapped out, and they both rolled away from each other.

Rising, they stared at each other as their fury slowly subsided, then grinned, threw their arms around each other and went over to the fermented milk urn.

"How did you beat him?" Arga asked, looking at her husband with both awe and doubt. "He's very strong, and much bigger than you."

"But I was thinking, and he wasn't," Scyles said quietly. "He let his emotions block his ability to think. I didn't."

"Craziest idea I ever heard," Gelon said, and everyone at the table started. None of them had heard he and Orik walk up behind them. Myrina wondered how long they'd been there. It didn't matter.

"Come sit by me, husband," she said, holding out her hand to him. "I wish to beguile you, and have two things I need from you."

"Two?" Gelon asked suspiciously. He knew his wife only too well. "What two things?" He got a crafty look on his face. "Or is it the same thing, twice? I can manage that, I think, and maybe a third, if the Gods will it."

"However many times you manage, dear husband, they all add up to one thing," Myrina said, and watched him with amusement. She knew he didn't have the patience to wait her out. Not when he'd been drinking. She was glad to see they'd all recovered from their mortification over feeling the fear in the heat of battle.

"Ah, I know what you want to know, girl," Gelon said, nodding and looking at Orik meaningfully. "I told you they would notice."

"Aye, you did," Orik admitted, and everyone except Opis stared at him.

"Do you always sound like a Celt when you're drunk?" Gelon asked, and Myrina sighed, knowing she would have to wait until later to get him to tell her. Every now and then, he surprised her. She loved that about him.

"Aye. I do," Orik answered, and they both roared and downed their drinks. As one, they headed to the urn.

Eventually, the men came back to them, and they all moved over to the same table near the far wall. A couple men saw them approaching, looked at each other and sighed, picked up their drinks and headed to the far side of the room.

Targitai and Ariapithes had gone for a walk, supposedly looking for any stray drunks to steer back to the yurts for sleeping. Myrina was pretty sure that wasn't what they were doing.

"Did you notice how many people were looking at us tonight?" Opis asked, looking at the wine in the Egelv cup she held. She'd grabbed one of the bottles, as they called it, when Zard Win wasn't looking. Of course, eventually, she had to get his help opening it, but he'd taken it in stride, showing good humor.

She poured a little more in both their cups, and looked into the bottle through the hole in the top. She looked up at Myrina.

"It's getting low."

"That's a good thing," Myrina said firmly. "I'm not so sure anyone is going to be making babies tonight, after all this drink."

"Oh, judging from the looks we got, some of the looks and talk between some of them, I think some babies might well get made tonight," Opis said, and they both grinned.

Gelon finally sat down next to her. He watched Orik sit on the far side of Opis, and his eyes ran around the table.

Scyles was sitting quietly, watching, as he always was. His bride's head was against his shoulder, his arm around her, supposedly showing his love, but really holding her upright. Zard Win and Shae Apon were drinking something that Myrina didn't think was alcoholic, and both looked alert. That hadn't been the case a couple hours ago. Myrina had been positive they were going to try and sneak away together. Then he brought out another bottle, and Shae Apon got a forlorn look on her face, but nodded, and they began drinking that.

"So, everyone else is having a fine time of it, from the sounds I'm hearing from the sleeping quarters, but I doubt we'll be making any babies of our own this night," Gelon said, and looked at her apologetically.

Targitai and Ariapithes came in, saw them, got fresh goblets of milk, and came over to take seats between the newlyweds and the Egelv.

Gelon looked at them questioningly.

Targitai looked at him with a crooked grin on his face. He glanced at the women, then back at his king.

"I think everyone in both our tribes is enjoying someone's company right now, and all the sleeping quarters have water pouring in the showers," he said, and everyone except Scyles and Arga laughed. He continued. "The Caitiari are all back in their quarters. Agathyrsus had them go back to the pods after they left the feast. They worked until just about an hour ago, and the men and women went back to their respective quarters."

He grinned mirthlessly.

"The wine, milk and situation didn't change any of their preferences for sleeping partners, so the women are having fun, all the men except possibly two are grumbling in their sleeping robes, and trying to blot the sound of the two men out."

They all laughed, and Gelon looked at Targitai questioningly.

"And the king and queen?"

"I think she might have convinced him that water won't kill him," Targitai admitted, and glared in mock-anger at Myrina. "My wife said the same thing, and she probably dragged some poor boy into our quarters, after I told her I'd be doing king's business most of the night."

Gelon looked disturbed.

"Old friend, the Egelv will be doing most everything," he said. "Go to your woman, put a smile or two on her face, scrape the tundra off that thick hide of yours."

Gelon looked rueful.

"I hate to admit it, but it feels good, both while you're in the water, and afterwards."

Myrina made a show of having a heart attack, and there were smiles from most of them.

"I'll wait," Targitai said, shaking his head. "When I get there, she'll be all the more eager."

He looked at Myrina.

"You didn't happen to see if she'd found a young rider to drag out of here, did you?" he asked, smiling his usual crooked grin.

"No, she didn't have a young rider," Myrina admitted, and paused for a moment. "She had two."

When the table settled down again, Gelon looked at Orik, who nodded for him to continue.

"You tell stories so well, old friend. And I'm talked out, tonight," he said, and put his arm around Opis's shoulder as she slid her seat closer to him.

Gelon took a deep breath.

"Tonight, after everyone has settled into their quarters, the Egelv are going to bring that big weapon that floats, and use it to knock all the Caitiari out." Gelon hesitated, and looked at Zard Win for verification. "It can be set to make people sleep, or to kill them."

Ariapithes cleared his throat.

"I tried to bribe the Egelv, but they wouldn't set it to kill."

The laughter was much more muted now.

Myrina knew why. They knew what was about to happen, and it was to another tribe of the People. By a strange race from another world. By knowing, but doing nothing, they were siding against fellow Scoloti, and that rankled them.

Gelon continued.

"After they're stunned, they'll be moved to the pods." He looked at Myrina, then at Opis. He glanced over at Arga, and smiled. She was sleeping heavily, and Scyles was the only thing keeping her from falling to the floor. Her son gazed down at his bride, looked back up at them, and shrugged.

"We need you women to check our livestock, decide how many more horses and sheep we need to bring out for breeding purposes." Gelon saw her about to say something and nodded. "I know we'll need more eventually, but we can trade them in and out of the pods as we need to, which should secure the health of the herd."

He looked thoughtful for a moment.

"If we still need more pods for the Caitiari, we can take a mix of people out." He looked over at Orik. "I think most of them should be from the Paralatae, since we outnumber you by so many."

Opis looked at Orik, her brows furled heavily.

"Your Mama?' he asked gently, and she mutely nodded her head.

Orik turned to them and explained.

"Arga's gra'mama felt poorly the day we were taken, so she stayed at the yurt," Orik explained. "I was standing with Agathyrsus when he checked her pod. Until then, I wasn't sure they'd brought her, or that she'd survived the experience."

"I would like her to see that Arga has wed, and is a woman now," Opis said softly, and Myrina heard her pain.

"You need not ask," Gelon said, his voice firm. "King Orik, you would have been made the next Great King of the People, had things gone as expected at the Gathering. Well, you are our Great King, even if we only number three tribes."

"Or two," Targitai said, staring off into the distance.

Gelon looked at Shae Apon.

"You can do this?"

She nodded, looking very humbled by their emotions.

"Thank you," Opis said in a small voice, and Orik echoed her.

Gelon stood and stretched, looking at the few people still in the common yurt. He looked at loose ends, and restless.

"How long before you think your men will arrive with the big weapon?" he asked the Egelv.

Zard Win looked at a band he had around his wrist, and touched something on it.

"About three quarters of an hour, perhaps an hour," he said, and they all sighed.

Gelon sat back down, even as Scyles maneuvered himself to his feet, holding Arga upright. He grinned at them.

"I'm taking Arga back to our quarters, get her in bed. I'll be back shortly."

"You don't have to," Gelon said, and looked at Arga's face, so peaceful in her sleep.

"I want to," Scyles said, and Myrina wondered a little at how her son had suddenly developed what she called the voice of authority. He wasn't in charge of anything or anyone, except his wife, and Myrina knew he was too smart to think he was in command there, either.

But he could speak with authority, and people automatically obeyed, or accepted his words.

Myrina was pretty sure he couldn't do that a week ago.

She watched him dip Arga enough to pick her up in his arms, and start towards the door. She was impressed. Arga was as tall as he was, if slighter of build.

"You want help, son?" Gelon asked, watching him with interest.

"No, I have this," he said, and kept on walking.

"You drop her, she won't let you forget until your kids are your age," Gelon called out to his back, but then he was out the door and gone.

"Stubborn little bastard," her husband said, and grudgingly continued. "But he is far tougher than I ever realized."

He turned to her, and she could see the pride in his face.

"You should have seen him charging that big dragon at the end. Ran right up his back, shooting arrows all the while."

Gelon turned to watch the door for a moment, and Myrina knew he was getting his face back under control. She didn't say a word. Finally, he turned around and looked at Zard Wan hopefully, but the Egelv shook his head with amusement.

"It's barely been ten minutes," he said, and Gelon and Orik both sighed.

Ten minutes later, Scyles walked back in, came over and sat next to Myrina. He looked around, and apparently thought something looked odd, because he glanced across the room, then back at them.

"What?" he asked.

Everyone chuckled, but didn't answer.

Gelon looked at Zard Win.

"So, your people have a king? Is he a good king?"

"We call him our Emperor," Zard Win said. "His family has ruled the Egelv Empire for almost twenty-six hundred years."

"What is the difference between a king and an emperor?" Scyles asked, and Myrina smiled. She'd wanted to ask that herself.

Zard Win looked thoughtful. He glanced over at Shae Apon, but she smiled and shook her head. Myrina enjoyed watching the two of them together. Every interaction was almost a flirtation, or an invitation to come closer, yet they made no move to show a romantic, or even sexual interest in each other.

He finally nodded, and answered the question.

"You are a king, and rule a kingdom of people with common roots." Zard Win glanced at Scyles, then back to Gelon. "I assume Prince Scyles will take your place when you pass, so you have a hereditary position that is passed from family member to family member."

"If he doesn't get killed fighting monstrous lizards," Gelon said with mock anger, and there was laughter around the table. Scyles eyed his father, with a good-natured expression on his face. Myrina was glad to see he was no longer tormented by the memory of the battle with the dragon.

Zard Win looked at Orik.

"You and King Gelon were discussing your gathering, and that you would have been the "Great King" of your people, ruling over all the tribes, which are really kingdoms, ruled by kings. In essence, it is the same thing as an emperor and his empire."

"Emperor Orik," Gelon said, and bowed deeply. "You've got drool on your chest, my emperor."

All the Scoloti laughed, but Zard Win and Shae Apon looked at each other, clearly disturbed.

"What is it?" Myrina asked, sensing her husband had unwittingly broken a social more.

"In the Egelv Empire, there can only be one emperor, of any sort," Shae Apon said, sounding troubled. "If I may give you council, I would not call him that in the presence of any Egelv."

"I meant you and your people no disrespect," Gelon said, but there was steel in his voice. "But we are not part of the Egelv Empire."

"But we are their guests, husband," Myrina said gently, not wishing to embarrass him before the others. "And we are on the way to their world, so giving respect to their traditions does us no harm, and loses us no face."

"All Myrina says is true," Orik said, looking troubled himself. "And it's not like we've ever called anyone our emperor. I happily refuse that mantle, and will settle for Great King of the Scoloti."

He made a point of looking around the room.

"Or at least the Scoloti we have," he said, and they all lapsed into silence.

"Is your great king always from the same family?" Zard Win asked curiously.

"No," Gelon said, and looked at Orik. "When one falls or dies of old age, the tribes all gather to choose another to replace him."

"When was the last time one ever died of old age?" Myrina asked cynically, and Opis nodded, looking at her husband, disturbed.

"So the mantle of emperor always passes through succession in the royal family only?" Scyles asked, and Myrina looked at him with interest. She knew him well enough to know there was a reason for his question.

"For almost twenty-six hundred years, it has been the Deh family," Zard Win said, nodding. "Emperor Balco Deh has ruled for one hundred and eighteen years. He succeeded his father's throne, the Emperor Tebo Deh. Only the emperor can carry the surname. Before he became emperor, he was Balco Fal."

"And no one has ever challenged the royal family, in all those twenty-six hundred years?" Scyles asked, and Myrina looked at him again, wondering what he was thinking.

Zard Win looked troubled and hesitated before answering.

"Only once," he said, finally.

"Technically, that is not correct, Zard Win," Shae Apon said, and he looked at her, puzzled. Myrina saw his expression change as he understood her meaning. "Six hundred and four years ago, the princess that would eventually become empress, gave birth to twins, Sona Fe, a girl, and Rapar Tet, a boy. She was the first out of the womb, by eight minutes."

Myrina waited for them to continue, and wondered that they didn't. Finally, Gelon grew impatient.

"So, tell us the story," he said, and grinned around at everyone. "Are you waiting for us to die the elder death? I can tell you, few of us will go that way."

Orik laughed and nodded, taking a gulp of his milk.

Myrina didn't laugh, and didn't have to look to know Opis wasn't either.

"So, when the emperor died, Sona Fe lay claim to the throne?" Scyles asked, and both Egelv looked at him in surprise.

"That is exactly what happened," Zard Win admitted. "But the Egelv Empire is a patriarchy, and the throne passes to the oldest male, next in line for the throne."

"There have been occasions that the emperor died, and the empress carried on and ruled until the oldest son was ready to claim the throne," Shae Apon added, looking at the other Egelv. "But Sona Fe had been married off to, what was at the time, an obscure family halfway around Egelv from the capital. She claimed the throne for herself, but all the families stood by Rapar Tet, and her claim was denied."

"Every time there has been a succession ever since, the Quo family has laid claim to the succession, saying their head of family had just cause," Zard Win said, and shook his head in disapproval. "There have been five passings of the throne, and each time they try again."

"They could never successfully challenge, then?" Scyles asked quietly, and Myrina looked at him. She could see this subject had caught his interest. She shook her head, bemused.

Scyles couldn't be less like his father in this respect, Myrina thought, looking at Gelon. It was a trait he clearly had gotten from her.

Gelon felt her eyes upon him, and shook his head, his eyes flashing over to their son, and then back to her.

"He gets that from you."

Myrina laughed out loud, and then jumped when Zard Win and Shae Apon both rose.

They looked at Gelon and Orik.

"My men are just around the corner from the rooms the Caitiari are housed in," Zard Win said, and looked at them. "Are you ready?"

Gelon and Orik jumped up and reached for their weapons.

"Gods, yes," her husband said, and Myrina sighed, knowing they had a long night still in front of them.

Chapter Twenty-One

Arga opened her eyes, groaned, and immediately closed them again. It wasn't so much that her head hurt, but the bright light in their sleeping quarters made her flinch. She decided to lay for a moment and think.

We were in the common yurt, she remembered. And we drank a lot. We joked about how we were going to come back and try and make a baby, even if it took all night. She slid her hand down between her legs and touched herself.

No, she was pretty sure they didn't make love last night. But she couldn't remember getting back here from the common yurt. And, she realized, she was naked under the bedding. She didn't remember stripping, and if they weren't going to make love, she would have almost certainly put a sleeping robe on.

Or she would still be entwined with her husband, she thought, smiling dreamily. And they would both be naked, and most certainly would have made love.

She opened her eyes cautiously, and it wasn't uncomfortable this time. She didn't have a headache, so she wasn't hung over. As details of the evening came back slowly, she wondered why the gods had blessed her by not making her pay this morning, for the pleasures of the drink last night.

Arga slowly recalled the events of last night as she reluctantly threw off the covers and climbed to her feet. She made her way to the toilet, as the Egelv called it. As she passed the floor to ceiling mirror before the door, she paused and looked at herself critically. She'd never seen such a huge mirror before, and decided it was a mixed blessing.

She pushed her stomach out, wondering if she could tell if she was actually pregnant. She gazed at herself with a critical eye, and sadly had to conclude she didn't look as if she were with child yet. Her stomach was flat, and almost all parts of her body were firm, hard even.

She lifted her breasts up, hefting them as if they were potatoes, and sighed at their diminutive size. Her mother said they would grow a little bigger as she matured, and would be substantial in her latter days of pregnancy and while she breastfed her babies.

Her mother also recommended weaning her babies off her milk as soon as they were ready for solid food. She pointed out several women that feed their babies breast milk until they were two or three years old, and how low their breasts hung. Then she pointed at herself and said she'd stayed very active right up to childbirth, and then as soon as possible after birth. And she got them drinking mare's or goat's milk from a nippled goatskin bag as soon as they would take it.

Arga had looked at her mother's lithe figure, and knew only too well how nimble she was. She'd also noticed her mother's modest-sized breasts had never seemed to bother her father in the least. She vowed silently that she was a warrioress, and would look like one again, by the time her breastfeeding ended.

She went into the shower and began cleaning herself. Doing it without Scyles was a letdown, but it was her own fault for drinking too much. She'd taken Shae Apon at her word about alcohol being bad for an unborn baby, so she'd overdone it last night, knowing it might be the last time for months.

And as a result, she thought, scrubbing herself viciously, Scyles probably carried me back here, in front of everyone in the yurt, got me out of my clothes, and done the gods only knew what, for the rest of the night.

She instinctively knew he'd never slept in the bed, so where was he?

"If you spent the night with some harlot instead of me, I'll cut that thing right off you," she muttered, and was surprised at the echo in the shower.

"Well, then I'm glad that I didn't," Scyles said as he slipped his arms around her from behind. He kissed her neck and pulled her tight against him. But he didn't begin searching her body with his nimble yet firm fingers. He simply held her, letting the water pour over both their heads.

She slid around to face him, her eyes searching his face.

"You sound tired," she said, and as she looked closer, she realized, he looked tired as well. "Did you carry me back here with everyone watching me passed out, over your shoulder?"

"I carried you in my arms back here, and no one saw you except our parents, Targitai and Ariapithes, and a few stragglers still drinking," Scyles said, and pushed her hair out of her face so he could kiss her on the mouth.

His lips were rough, but he was so gentle, they felt like a caress.

"And a few Egelv," he admitted.

"And then you went back to the yurt?" she asked, and frowned at him. "What did you do all night?"

"We talked some, with Zard Win and Shae Apon," he said. "And when their troops were ready, we stunned all the Caitiari, piled them on one of the floating carts, and took them to the pod rooms."

"Oh, I missed that?" she breathed, cursing herself for being weak and passing out, thereby missing the excitement. She vowed to never again overindulge. She said as much to Scyles, and he laughed.

"We shall see," he said, cupping her cheek with his hand. "You were very attractive and funny last night. But when you fell asleep against me, it was very comforting. I truly felt we were an old married couple, familiar as could be with each other."

"You have a silver tongue, like a Persian," she said and kissed him.

Scyles looked at her speculatively.

"Is that a compliment or an insult?" he asked, a smile on his face.

"Yes," she said, and pushed him away. "Now, let me finish. I wish to get dressed and go see them put the Caitiari into pods."

"You don't want to go back to sleep?" Scyles asked hopefully, and she slapped his arm.

"No, you won't sleep," she said, and he looked sheepish. "You missed your chance last night. Now you'll have to wait until tonight to perhaps, get another opportunity to please me."

He faked a pout, and she laughed. They quickly finished and dried off.

Arga looked through their clothes and shook her head.

"I never noticed how our clothing could get so dirty until I got so clean," she admitted. "The Egelv always seem to have clean clothing on. We'll have to find out where the creek is to wash ours." She looked at him significantly. "I will teach you how so we may do it together."

241

"Can we do it without wearing any clothes?" Scyles asked, and she laughed again at his hopeful expression.

"You can, if you like," she said, sniffing. "But I'm not going to let you have your way with me in front of all those old ladies that usually gather together at the creek. With my luck Gra'mama would be there."

"Oh," Scyles said, and looked guilty. "I forgot you were asleep when we talked about this."

"About what?" Arga asked cautiously.

"To make room for the Caitiari, we need to empty as many pods as there are of them," Scyles said, and dressed faster. "About half or a little more will be livestock, but most of the rest will be from your tribe. And your mother asked if your Gra'mama could be one of them."

"When will they be doing this?" Arga said, and began searching through their piles of discarded clothing on the floor. She found some trousers that looked acceptable. She pulled clean undergarments from a bag. She was probably being wasteful, but after washing, she didn't want to wear the same ones twice between washings.

They were both pulling tunics over their heads, when a voice spoke in their ears. It was the same one that translated when they were talking to someone not speaking the Scoloti tongue.

"Scyles, is Arga awake yet?" It was Shae Apon's voice. "We've revived several horses and sheep, and are doing a man and a woman from the Paralatae. Assuming everything goes well, we plan to revive her Gra'Mama next after that. Opis thought she would like to be here."

"Yes, I do," Arga said, and then wondered if she could be heard. Any doubts were quickly settled.

"Oh, good, you're awake," Shae Apon said, with a hint of humor in her voice. "How do you feel today?"

"Mortified, but otherwise fine," Arga admitted. "We're leaving our sleeping quarters now, and will be there as quickly as we can."

"We won't start her procedure without you," the Egelv woman promised.

Arga and Scyles walked quickly down the hall to the main concourse.

"Do you know where they are?" she asked, and Scyles nodded.

When they walked into the giant pod room, Shae Apon looked at them in surprise.

"You must have walked very quickly," she said, and Arga smiled.

"I am excited we're waking her," she said. "I know she will be happy to hear about Scyles and I having wed."

"And with your efforts to produce another baby for her to spoil," her mother said, and Arga grinned, even as she felt herself blush. "How do you feel today, daughter?"

"I feel fine," Arga insisted. "I was just very tired."

"Tired," her mother said to her father, who grinned and looked at Scyles' parents.

"She was tired," he said, and King Gelon started laughing.

"Oh, she was that, alright," he said, and looked at his wife. "Your new daughter was tired."

"Quit teasing her," she said, and slapped King Gelon on the arm. He grinned at her, and she relented, and smiled back.

"Okay, the procedure is almost finished," Shae Apon said, watching the old woman through the view screen. She frowned as she looked at the little symbols and lines on the display. "She's struggling a bit. How old is she?"

"She has seen sixty-six gatherings," Arga's mother said, and her voice sounded tense to Arga.

"What is the average life span of your people?" the Egelv asked, and they looked at her blankly. "Um, about what age do your people live until? How many gatherings?"

"Oh," her father said, and looked at her mother. "Sixty gatherings are considered quite an achievement," he said, and looked at the pod with worried eyes. He moved over and put his arm around his wife's shoulders.

"She'd been feeling ill, during the journey," her mother said, and he nodded in agreement. "That was why she wasn't with us at lunch, or the feast the night before. She'd been coughing more than usual, and seemed to be very tired all the time, almost the entire trip from our home grazing lands."

The pod had a light come on, and the lid loosened.

Shae Apon lifted the lid, and looked at the strange symbols on the screen with concern. Arga wondered that they constantly changed and moved, as if alive.

She wondered if they were.

"Her readouts don't look as strong as the four people I've already revived," Shae Apon said worriedly. "I wish I knew more about your physiology."

They all watched as the old woman's eyes fluttered open, but didn't focus clearly. Shae Apon muttered to herself and felt Gra'Mama's wrist, frowned, and took something off a tray she had floating next to her. It looked like a reed with a hollow body you could see through. It was full of liquid. She put one end against the old woman's chest and did something, but Arga couldn't tell what.

It seemed to help.

Her eyes grew more focused, and she stared at the pod she was lying in, a puzzled expression on her face. She saw she wore no clothes, and looked surprised. Arga had never seen her totally naked before, and she felt bad that her gra'mama found herself in such an awkward situation, wearing nothing and surrounded by so many people. She looked up at the faces staring back at her. When she came to Arga's, and saw Scyles standing very close to her, his arm around her waist, she smiled.

Arga bent down so their faces were close.

"Scyles and I are now married, Gra'Mama," she said, and the old woman smiled in relief. She started to speak and winced. She cleared her throat and managed to speak, although she sounded very hoarse.

"Did you..." She seemed to struggle with the right words, and Arga helped her.

"I am a woman now, in every way," she said, and her gra'mama beamed weakly with pride. "If I am not yet with child, it isn't for want of trying. Very vigorously," she added, and the old woman's eyes danced with glee. "And many times. Scyles is very...enthusiastic," she finished, and felt her face heat up.

"Good, good," she managed to say. She looked at them, then up at Arga's mother, and a look of discomfort, and then wonder appeared on her face. Her eyes closed, and her body relaxed as life left her.

"Gra'Mama?" Arga asked, and put her hand on the old woman's wrist, where she knew she should be able to feel the life flowing through her. But there was nothing.

"No!" Shae Apon cried, looking shocked, then desperate. She looked at the screen, but the strange marking were now just straight lines, and she looked back and forth between that and the body, then finally over at Arga, kneeling next to her. "I am so sorry. She's not that old. I should have been able to bring her out of stasis safely. I'm so sorry," she repeated, and burst into tears.

Arga looked at her in surprise.

She was sad her gra'mama had passed on to the underworld, but she was old, and had been sick. It wasn't unexpected, or anything to be shocked by.

Mama and Myrina knelt on either side of the Egelv woman, and tried to reassure her. Mama glanced at Arga, and looked relieved that she was accepting the inevitable.

"She was old. She lived a full life, and was with the ones she loved as she passed to the underworld," Arga's father said in an even tone. "Her greatest wish these last several years was to see Arga married and beginning her life as a woman with a good man. And she did."

Arga felt Scyles' hands on her shoulders, and she looked up at him. He smiled at her, looking a little sad, but he too knew, that it had been Gra'Mama's time. She was too weak to resist Hades' call.

"I'm sorry," Shae Apon said, looking both sad and embarrassed. "It's just, all of you are so robust and healthy, I wasn't expecting to lose anyone in the reviving stage. Please forgive me."

"You brought her back, she saw all of us, and knew that Arga was taken care of," Orik said, gruffly, looking uncomfortable with the role of comforter. "We appreciate the few moments we had with her, and her with us."

"Do you wish to rest and recover before finishing?" King Gelon asked, and the Egelv shook her head. "No, I'll continue. I apologize for my unprofessional reaction. I've seen people die before. But it's always been expected, and not a surprise."

"Our people usually bury our dead, with belongings for them to carry to the underworld," Arga's father said thoughtfully. "If she'd died in our ancestral lands, we would have buried her with her husband, although that might have been difficult."

"Why is that?" Shae Apon asked, and Arga suspected she was asking, only because she was still trying to pull herself together.

"I come from another tribe, much farther to the east," her mother said, and frowned. "When my father was killed in battle, my oldest brother became king. Neither his wife, nor the wives of my other three brothers ever grew very close to her, so when Papa died, she was mostly neglected by everyone."

"That's very sad," Shae Apon said, looking down at Gra'Mama sadly. "Growing old alone had to be very lonely."

"It is how it was," her mother said, shrugging. "When I was carrying Serlotta, and we saw her and my old tribe at the gathering, we asked her if she would live with us until the next gathering, to help me through my birthtime."

Arga's mother smiled thinly.

"I really didn't need any help, but I didn't like the idea of how much time she was alone, with no one to watch over her, or help, if needed. So she returned with us, and the next year, they made no mention of her, and we didn't either. She has lived with us ever since."

She looked down at Gra'Mama pensively.

"May Hermes protect you until you reach the underworld, Mama."

She looked at Papa. He nodded, and lifted her effortlessly out of the pod. He looked around, as if wondering where to put her body. Finally, he set her down on an empty spot of the floating raft that had been full of unconscious Caitiari.

Arga watched Shae Apon revive a woman in her tribe without any complications. Then she did the same with the woman's husband. She decided she'd seen enough of this, and looked at Scyles.

Not surprisingly, he was watching her, nodded, and led her out of the pod hold, as Shae Apon called it. They walked down the main concourse, more just to walk than to go anywhere in particular. Seeing her gra'mama pass on hadn't upset her that much. They'd had the chance to tell her the important things. But it had definitely gotten her out of the mood to go back to their room, and to bed. Somehow, making love right after seeing her die didn't sound very appealing to her.

They walked hand in hand, the entire length of the concourse, talking most of the time, sometimes just walking together without speaking, comfortable with each other's company.

Arga noticed they were getting closer to the common hall, and realized she hadn't eaten anything yet today.

"Are you hungry?" she asked Scyles, and he smiled in relief.

"Yes, very much so," he admitted.

"Good," she said, and realized her earlier somber mood had dissipated. "Let's see what there is. It must be midday, at the very least. And then I think I might wish to lie down for a while. Are you tired?"

"Tired of walking," Scyles admitted, with a little smile on his face. "But not too tired to help you lie down."

"Help me lie down," she repeated, unable to keep her own smile off her face. "Interesting way to put it. I guess that means you're not very sleepy."

"I guess we'll have to check and see after we eat," Scyles said, and they managed to let their bodies brush against each other as they entered the common yurt.

Captain Rost Fott watched the shuttles return to their ships. One of them docked with Comet's Edge and, as soon as it was drawn into the landing bay with tractor beams, the hatch closed, and the ship immediately moved away, accelerating as it went.

In a matter of seconds, it was out of sight.

He knew Commodore Mit Obet had decided to send Comet's Edge ahead to the squadron waiting at the rendezvous point to relieve them, and fill them in on the current situation. He was impatient to return to Egelv Prime. They'd been out on routine patrol in the outskirts of Egelv dominated space for too long.

He suppressed a sigh as he turned away from the display, taking a quick survey of who was doing what on the bridge. Several techs were doing routine maintenance on equipment and software.

He let his eyes linger for a moment on First Officer Van Dono. He was talking with Second Officer Rel Steen, and they were both looking at the same screen, deeply involved in whatever chore they were addressing. Rost Fott didn't focus on them too long, not wanting his First to feel his gaze.

"I'll be in the lounge," he said and both officers nodded unconsciously. He went into the officer's lounge and poured himself a cup of Barza Tea. He'd asked one of the techs to prepare a pot of it just a little while ago, so it was hot, fresh, and soothed his raw nerves.

He had to admit, his First had the ability to irritate him and cause stressful feelings. He was young for his rank, and would almost certainly achieve the rank of Captain at a younger age than Rost Fott himself had.

There were benefits to being from a wealthy family with longtime ties to the stronger families that clustered in and around Egelva, the city of the Emperor, and the capital of Egelv Prime. His family had people in powerful positions, both in the military and the civil government that advised the Emperor.

Rost Fott had seen Van Dono walking with Commodore Mit Obet, and wondered what that was about. An obvious answer came to him immediately. It only took a moment's investigation on his handheld to see he was right.

Commodore Mit Obet was from the same family as Van Dono.

He idly wondered if his dallying that kept them in the area the wormhole appeared in was a topic of discussion for the two officers. He knew he pushed the limits on procedure on a regular basis, but firmly believed it kept his crew's attention firmly in place on the task at hand.

Rost Fott also knew that had he not been lingering out on the fringe, they would have missed the arrival of the Hshtahni ships. That had to count for something.

At least you hope it does, he thought grimly.

He shifted his handheld to the monitoring system for the generation ship Muschwain. Van Dono had an engineering crew seeing what, if anything, they could do with the power system of the huge ship.

Unfortunately, Zard Win was too good at his job, as were his gunners. They'd made a Googlon mess of most of the rear portion of the ship. Their shots on the weapon blisters had been precise, which meant if there was a problem, the Muschwain was basically a huge defenseless target, and they were firmly tethered to its side.

He shifted to the surveillance system, and took a look at the bridge.

Young Lab Toof, the most junior officer in the squadron was there, directing repairs. It was mostly cosmetic, except for the control panels, which had been sideswiped by the Hshtahni's tail swinging at the Scoloti that had delivered the fatal wounds with his bow and arrows.

He shook his head, trying not to be awed by their fighting prowess. Armed with only crude, primitive weapons, they'd somehow killed three

Hshtahni. Sure, two were young and inexperienced, but even so, those two had his security forces pinned down in a narrow corridor.

He shifted the view to the Scoloti common hall, and saw that there were about forty men and women sitting around, eating and drinking. He'd been told that after the first day or so, there was a sudden surge in their use of the showers.

Rost Fott was glad to hear about that. Something they'd all noticed immediately, was that the primitive race didn't seem to place much value in washing.

In short, they smelled.

Several nights ago, something had caused a revelation for them. The water recycling system was stressed to its maximum, for most of the night, and into the next morning. He didn't know what was going to happen to them, but at least they'd be clean when they reached Egelv Prime.

Zard Win and Shae Apon had been spending a lot of time with them, and he decided that was a good place to get a sense of what the Scoloti were capable of, to secure a place within the empire.

If there were fewer, he could see them being seeded on a planet that was already lightly populated. But more than six thousand was too many to casually drop into a social system not prepared for it.

He scanned through the most likely places to find people, and found Zard Win and Shae Apon in one of the pod holds. They were standing close, and he noticed Shae Apon talking in a very animated way, and even with the poor quality of the surveillance system, she looked upset.

Zard Win seemed to be trying to comfort her, and he idly wondered what had happened. The young Egelv woman was very calm and calculated in almost everything she did. He hoped his second officer didn't cross any social boundaries, spending so much time with her. They were both single, about the same age, and very smart and competent.

And they were both attractive, he admitted with a sigh.

It wasn't spoken of, but Zard Win was of the same family he was, and he felt a sense of responsibility to make sure the young man didn't do anything to jeopardize his career. Their family had a long tradition of military service.

Shae Apon came from one of the oldest, richest, families on Egelv.

Frankly, he was surprised her immediate relatives had agreed to her going into the military service, even if she was in the Spatial Science Division. Most of her family went into business or entered government service.

He wished the quality of the picture was better so he could see their expressions. He would simply have to hope they both had enough common sense to not do something that would anger their families.

Perhaps we didn't have enough issues and stress factors in this tour, he thought wryly.

Shae Apon felt a little foolish.

The old woman dying had shocked her far more than she'd believed possible. She'd lost patients before, but never under such intimate conditions. Zard Win had been kind, and she found herself looking at him in a different light. She knew their family situation made any sort of relationship impossible, but he really was a special sort of person.

He had stayed with her until the pod transfers were complete. They also checked with Queen Opis about dealing with her mother's remains. Since there was no way to appropriately bury her body, she and King Orik had agreed that the Egelv custom of sending the body into the void of space was preferable to incineration. They'd agreed to have a ceremony for her, and the casualties of the battle for the Muschwain, in the morning.

Once Shae Apon was sure all the revived Scoloti and livestock were not having any distress, and that all the pods had functioned properly, putting the Caitiari into stasis, they'd both agreed they needed food and headed back to Mountain Edge.

They were able to convince the chef in the officer's lounge to make them plates of leftovers, since they were between meal cycles. Once their initial hunger was dulled, they'd slowed down, as if they both felt that as long as they were eating, it was all business and routine.

"What do you think will happen to the Scoloti?" she asked, more because she couldn't think of anything else to say that didn't appear to open doors that needed to remain firmly closed.

"I don't know," he admitted, running his hand through his long, white hair. "Their real calling is violence, and their skills are so primitive, I don't see how they will find a place in our universe."

"I wish we could return them to their world, let them live their lives in the manner they always have," she said, and he nodded mutely.

"It's a shame they only know crude weapons, and nothing of the modern weaponry of our world," she said, hearing the sad tone of her voice. "They couldn't even be hired out as mercenaries, without having to learn drastically advanced technology and tactics. As is, they would be slaughtered the first time they went into a battle."

"Oh, I don't know," Zard Win said thoughtfully, and she looked at him in surprise. He turned to her, and looked startled, both at how close she was, and how intently she was watching him. He cleared his throat. "They adapted very quickly in the battles against the Hshtahni. And when there is an energy null field in place, their primitive weapons can be very devastating."

"That's true," Shae Apon said thoughtfully, and ran both hands through her own hair. She looked at him again, and this time he didn't shy away. They stared at each other, and she wondered if her expression was as troubled as his.

"I wonder who will take charge of their retraining to be functional and useful. Who will make the decisions on resolving their fates?" she asked, sounding as troubled as she felt.

"I wish I could be part of that," Zard Win said quietly, and she looked at him, amazed as she realized she felt the same way.

"As do I," she admitted, and they stared at each other again. She knew what she was feeling was a mistake, but it was undeniable. But, still, she would deny it, as much a lie as it was.

"I have a few ideas," Zard Win said thoughtfully.

"I would like to hear them, as well as tell you some of mine," she said, wondering if she was being foolish. "I want to help these people. I admire their courage and strengths."

Zard Win cocked his head to the side, in an unconscious gesture that was remarkably similar to something the Scoloti did. With difficulty, she kept the smile from her face.

"I was thinking the same thing," he said, and she leaned forward, sipping her refreshed hot Barza Tea.

"You don't seem like a typical security chief," she said, hoping she wasn't insulting him.

"Thank you," he said, smiling at her. "I consider that a compliment."

"With all your technical skills, and your family's background, I'm surprised you didn't join the Navy," she said slowly, picking her words carefully. "I would think it would have been a faster path to promotion."

"Possibly," Zard Win conceded. "But that isn't really a major concern of mine. And truthfully, I would have been bored."

"Bored?" she asked, not expecting that answer.

"So much of the duty in the navy is repetitious routine, and I don't need to be a naval officer to study the science and new advances in space travel and weaponry," he pointed out. "I am already an accomplished pilot, and whether it's an armed family pinnace, or a heavy cruiser, the principles, technology, and skills are the same." He feigned looking over his shoulder. "Even a Hshtahni generation ship operates on the same principles."

"But why security?" Shae Apon asked curiously. "You might have ended up in infantry, or other ground force units."

"With my family's long tradition of the navy, it wasn't too hard to get my career steered to the Marine Forces," he admitted. "There is a big difference in the mentalities of ground and ship military command."

"I know you had extensive advanced degree study," she said. "I assume you studied military science and strategy."

"I did," Zard Win admitted. "I have doctorates in both, as well as military history." He grinned. "And even with keeping my forces in trim shape, well-trained, and working well with each other, I have plenty of time to read and study. Since my first posting, I've added an advanced degree in practical molecular chemistry, another in quantum physics, as well as management and leadership, and a lower degree in communications."

"How old are you?" Shae Apon asked, very impressed.

"I have seen thirty-six gatherings," he said with a straight face, and she laughed involuntarily.

"So have I," she admitted, and he looked surprised. She smiled at him. "I'm told I look somewhat younger. Not quite as young as Arga."

"So, you're a doctor, and...?" Zard Win asked, making the last word stretch out.

Shae Apon sighed.

"I am afraid I am one of those degree addicts," she said, not at all sorry.

Focusing intensely on her education, and then her career, she'd managed to avoid the pitfalls of so many young Egelv her social level.

"I am a Doctor of Internal Medicine, Psychiatry, and Cellular Biology." She looked apologetic. "I also have advanced training in Trauma Treatment, Geology, and doctorates in Chemistry, Physics, Anthropology, and Sociology."

"Geology," Zard Win said slowly, and smiled at her. "I wondered at the way you examined those stones Scyles had."

"They're from a planet we've never seen, and probably never will," she said, and saw her intensity surprised him. "They look like very average quartz and granite, but almost certainly have traces of elements we've never seen before."

She took a sip of her cooling tea, and when she set the cup down, Zard Win poured more in, heating it up a little.

"Thank you," she said quietly, thinking about what they'd just shared. "We're both very reclusive aren't we? Hiding from the universe in our studies and degrees?"

"Before, perhaps," Zard Win admitted. "But there's nothing like being the first contact with a new race to bring us out of our shells."

They both chuckled at his words, and Shae Apon realized she'd already told him more about herself than she'd ever told a fellow shipmate. A few days ago, that would have bothered her, and probably caused her to find a reason to bury herself in her studies for months.

She was more than a little bemused to find she was enjoying the company, enjoying their opening up to each other. Even the quiet moments like this were pleasant. Zard Win was a very comfortable man to spend time with.

Shae Apon raised her eyes as she took another sip of tea, and saw Zard Win watching her casually. He wasn't staring, but was giving her attention. In fact, she thought with wonder, he seemed as comfortable as she was with just sitting together.

When they'd met, he seemed ill at ease with long silences, but no more. To be sure, he still seemed very nervous at times, but she suspected he was more concerned with chasing her away than anything else. She doubted he had much, if any, serious experience with women.

Not that she was any kind of expert herself. She'd avoided any serious contact with men, emotional or physical, her entire life. But she was pretty sure he liked her as much as she liked him.

The thought startled her. Where had that come from? She'd only met him a few days ago. She had goals, and none of them included a relationship. Better to steer their conversation into safe topics.

"So, tell my about your family," she said, and blinked.

This was a safe topic?

Chapter Twenty-Two

Scyles and Zard Win walked the length of the concourse. The Egelv security chief was directing a floating raft with several sets of clothes stuffed with some sort of fluid that hardened almost as fast as it was sprayed into the old clothes and bits of material that were his own crude attempt at making manlike targets.

Scyles couldn't get over how many devices the Egelv used to make labor-intensive chores simple.

How could you simply pour a liquid into clothes and have it instantly firm into a solid mud-like substance that held its shape so well?

Regardless, they would make perfect targets for the archers. And he would be the first to test it.

They arrived at a large door that he'd recently learned was called a hatch. It opened, and he abruptly stopped walking, and gawked at the huge open space behind it. He couldn't call it a room, because of its sheer size. Nothing could allow him to compare this to even the largest yurt he'd ever been in.

"Is this big enough to give you a worthwhile distance to shoot?' Zard Win asked, a mischievous expression on his face.

"Oh yes," Scyles said enthusiastically. He felt embarrassed at his childish glee, but this was amazing. "The only thing that would make it better would be if I could ride my horse, Earth Runner, while shooting."

"I hope your horse is one of the ones in stasis," Zard Win said, looking crestfallen. "I would hate to think it was an animal that was butchered for food. I don't think it occurred to any of us that the horses, as you call them, would be personal property."

"Earth Runner is my horse, but not my property," Scyles corrected him gently. "We work as a team. He knows me as well as I know him. He was gifted by the gods with exceptional intelligence, and a love of running. He practically flies on the open tundra."

The thought depressed him.

He wasn't naïve enough to believe there was any chance the People would be able to return to their way of life. He wasn't even sure they would ever set foot on what the Egelv called a planet again. How could he ever hope to ride Earth Runner on the endless steppes, or anywhere remotely like them, again?

Scyles realized Zard Win was directing the floating cart with the target away from them, and it was picking up speed. He glanced at the Eglev, who was dividing his attention between aiming the cart away from them and giving Scyles covert glances.

Scyles glanced at the floating cart, which was getting to be a good distance away. He casually drew his bow back and let an arrow fly. It hit the target almost exactly between the shoulder blades, had it been a real foe.

Zard Win gave a little whistle, showing he was impressed.

"Can you make it turn and try to evade my arrows?" Scyles asked, and the other man answered by swerving the cart to the right.

Scyles had correctly anticipated his move, and his second arrow hit the target in the side, almost certainly a killing shot.

Zard Win muttered under his breath and began to try to evade the shots in earnest. Scyles shot twice, very quickly, and the cart resumed its flight away. The first arrow flew by harmlessly, off to the left. The second buried itself next to his first shot.

"Okay," Zard Win muttered, and Scyles didn't try to conceal his grin.

Five minutes later, Zard Win sighed, and glanced at Scyles' gorytos, shaking his head. He still had about half his arrows, and although there were a few strewn about the vast area, shots he'd missed, the vast majority of his shots were sunk into the target.

"Enough?" he asked, and Scyles nodded, and gave him an innocent look.

"Do you grow tired?" he asked, and Zard Win shook his head in admission of defeat. He slowed the cart, and turned it towards them.

"Would you like to try shooting?" Scyles asked, suddenly struck with a suspicion.

Zard Win's eyes widened and the excitement was easy to see. He glanced at the hatch, and Scyles followed his eyes. There was no one in sight. They had the entire huge space to themselves, and no spectators.

Zard Win stopped the floating cart a short distance away, and looked at Scyles questioningly. Scyles kept the smile from his face as he saw how close it was. The first time a Scoloti boy or girl shot their first arrow, it was usually at a target twice that distance away, but he said nothing.

He showed his bow to the Egelv, and explained how to load the arrow firmly into place, keep his arm holding the bow clear of the path of the sinews that made up the bow's string, and pull the nocked arrow back to his face.

Scyles did it very slowly, to demonstrate, drawing the string back until his clenched fingers hugged his cheek. He held it in place while instructing Zard Win, and finally let the arrow fly. It disappeared into the middle of the target, buried up to the feathers near the nock.

He gave him his bow, and then handed him an arrow. Zard Win awkwardly nocked it and began to pull the arrow back. His eyes widened, and his hand holding the string began to vibrate a little from the effort to pull the arrow as far back as Scyles had.

"Don't try and pull it that far," Scyles said, keeping his tone neutral. He didn't want to embarrass him new friend, but were all Egelv this weak? "Start off easy, that's good. Now focus on your target. Aim at the middle, and let fly."

Zard Win let go the arrow, and swore quite convincingly as his arm shifted, and the arrow went far to the left of the target.

"Ow," he said, and looked at Scyles, embarrassed. "How do you shoot without the string striking your arm?"

"Practice, and control," Scyles said, keeping the grin inside at bay. "Here, try another, and try and keep your arm crooked a little, for now."

Zard Win pulled back the string cautiously, watching the target, as Scyles instructed. When his arm began to shake, he let fly the arrow. He missed again, but this time was much closer to the target.

Scyles bit his lower lip, and handed him another arrow.

"Try again," he urged, and this time the Egelv was rewarded with a direct hit that penetrated the target perhaps the length of a finger, not one of the longer ones. The arrow stuck for a moment, then sagged, and fell out of the target.

Five arrows later, Zard Win sighed and handed the bow back to Scyles. He ruefully rubbed his forearm where the string had hit, on more shots than not. He pulled up his sleeve, and Scyles could see, even with his dark brown complexion, redness where the string had repeatedly slapped him as he shot.

"This is much harder than it looks," Zard Win admitted, and laughed. "And it looks hard."

"It was your first time," Scyles said diplomatically. "You will improve with practice. And I think we can rig an armguard for you until you are a little more accomplished."

"In what lifetime will that be?" Zard Win said, and Scyles recognized it was a joke. He wondered if they believed in reincarnation.

"Let's retrieve the arrows," Scyles said, deciding it would be prudent to change the subject, for the moment. His friend nodded and pushed the button on the box.

An arrow flew past them, and buried itself just below the waistline of the now-ragged and torn figure of a man.

Scyles and Zard Win both turned to see Arga and Shae Apon standing behind them, near the hatch, his wife with bow in hand, another arrow nocked. She let it fly, then smiled sweetly at him.

"Playing without me, husband?" she said, and Scyles smiled back.

"Please, join us," he said, and looked at Shae Apon questioningly. She quickly shook her head, glancing at Zard Win, who looked embarrassed. Scyles also saw something else, and stepped to the side. He nodded towards the center of the room, and Zard Win looked curiously, and swore in Egelv as he jumped back just in time to avoid being run over by the floating cart.

They all looked at the only two arrows that didn't have Scyles' markings protruding from the front of the target, and Shae Adon laughed, even as her face reddened.

Zard Win brought the cart to a halt, turned it around and brought it back to them slowly, making it halt right in front of them, as the women joined them.

Arga's first arrow had hit just below the supposed waistline, dead center. The second arrow had lodged a bit below that in a perfect line at the target's crotch. Scyles winced as he saw their locations. He peered down at his wife, and pretended to be brusque.

"Are you trying to tell me something?" he asked, and she smiled at him sweetly.

"My mother wishes to be a Gra'Mama, and doesn't think you're spending as much time on this project as you could be," she answered sweetly, and both Zard Wan and Shae Apon turned away.

"I am finding ways for our warriors to practice their archery skills and stay at the peak of their abilities," Scyles protested. "Zard Win and I are working very hard. I was showing him the range of our weapons, so he will give me the best possible advice and assistance he can, and he was getting his first lesson in archery."

From the involuntary laugh Shae Apon gave before putting a hand over her own mouth in embarrassment as she glanced at Zard Win apologetically, Scyles decided they'd been watching longer than he'd realized.

"Hmm," Arga said, and walked around to the back of the target. "How long do you plan on this taking?"

"Oh, we'll be done before lunch," Scyles said, as he pulled his arrows out of the target, inspecting each one as he did so. They all went back into his gorytos. He handed her the two she'd shot.

"Well, perhaps you have an opening in your busy schedule this afternoon for a leisurely shower," Arga said, and happened to brush against him as she walked around the target.

"Oh, I'm sure of it," Scyles said, smiling at her.

They both became aware of the two Egelv staring at them, visibly embarrassed at the subject of their conversation.

"The water consumption peaked at an unusually high rate a week or two ago," Zard Win commented, clearly trying to find a new subject. "There have been a few days and nights that spiked, but there was a two-day period that actually approached the system's limits to recycle the water."

"Was that the night after Arga and I wedded?" Scyles asked, and knew he was blushing. "And the night after that?"

"Yes, it was," Shae Apon said, looking back and forth between them, curiously. "The second night after was the highest rate since we've taken this ship. I was wondering what caused it."

"After killing the last Hshtahni, my husband was covered with the blood and stench of the monsters," Arga said, then added coyly. "And then he hugged me very vigorously, so I was covered with it as well. We decided that trying the rainfall room was a good way to clean ourselves and each other. And that led to…other actions, which resulted in our needing to shower, as you call it, again."

"And again," Scyles said without thinking, and saw they were embarrassing the Egelvs.

"And again," Arga said in a dreamy voice. "My husband can be very, very, vigorous."

She laughed out loud.

"When we finally emerged from our sleeping quarters, every Scoloti wife saw how clean our skin and hair was. And you had our clothing cleaned as well. I think that night, and the next, every Scoloti couple not in the stasis boxes spent much time in the rainfall room."

"Starting with both our parents," Scyles said dryly, and Arga laughed and nodded.

"Oh," Shae Apon said, and Scyles noticed she kept her eyes on them, and glancing around the room. Everywhere, in fact, other than at Zard Win.

"I think you should assume there will be more than a couple babies born in nine months," Arga said, laughing, and Scyles nodded. "Many more."

"Um, would you like to shoot again?" Zard Win asked quickly, looking like he was desperate to find a new topic of discussion.

"I would," Arga said, and bumped her shoulder against Scyles. "He probably doesn't need the practice, but I certainly do."

"Would you like to try a few shots?" Arga asked Shae Apon, and she shook her head, looking a little apprehensively at the mutilated target.

"It's fun," Arga said, and Scyles hid a smile. He doubted fun would be the word used by Zard Win, after his first session.

"I think we should make them arm guards before either of them shoot again," Scyles said as diplomatically as he could.

"Right," Arga said, and grinned at him. He couldn't help himself, and grinned back at her. She had the most infectious attitude these days.

Zard Win sent the target across the hanger floor, and Arga began shooting, even as Zard Win tried to hinder her success by making its path as unpredictable as possible. She used about half her arrows before he moved it out of her range. Scyles was impressed. She'd sunk more arrows into the target than she'd missed, and it was in constant movement.

As she paused, due to the range, he began to fire, and Zard Win renewed his efforts to befuddle Scyles' shots. He shot in short bursts of two to four arrows, and at least one or more of every burst hit the target.

"Showoff," Arga said, under her breath, as he hit the target with three consecutive arrows, one in the head, one in the chest area, and one in the groin.

Behind them, they heard Shae Apon gasp.

"How can he anticipate so well?" Scyles heard her ask Zard Win, who professed he didn't know.

"As with most things, practice," Scyles said, and turned to them with a shrug. "This is all fine, if we're fighting someone, but I am at a loss to imagine what our purpose will be amongst your people, when we reach your planet."

He could tell by their somber expressions, both Egelv shared his concern.

"I do not know," Zard Wan admitted slowly. "You are untrained and ignorant of the universe around you, through no fault or weakness of your own. But most compatible planets are already occupied by races that will not easily give up space to an aggressive young race. With no home planet, and no powerful sponsor to stand up for you, I fear for the future of your people."

"Where will they take our people as they bring them out of stasis?" Arga asked, and Scyles could see the fear in her eyes. "Will they keep us on this flying ship?"

"I doubt they will bring any more of your people out of stasis until they decide on your fate," Zard Win said slowly, looking troubled. "We need to find some sort of useful purpose. The problem is, the things you are trained and good at, fighting, farming, raising herds of animals, we have little need of."

"We can learn new skills," Arga began hesitantly, looking at Scyles. He knew she could see his skepticism, and it obviously frightened her.

"You can," Zard Win said firmly. "We need to try and show that to our leaders."

261

"We know so little of this universe you say surrounds us," Scyles said bitterly. "And your leaders have no reason to help us."

He stared directly at the two Egelvs.

"Trying to make us slave labor will not go well," Scyles said, and Arga nodded, her face betraying her fear.

"We don't keep slaves," Shae Apon started, but stopped as Scyles shook his head.

"No, but for the right price, your people would sell our entire ship, with all of us aboard, to someone that does," Scyles said, and thankfully, neither tried to argue with him.

Scyles trusted them, and that would be lost if they started lying to him, even if only to sooth his fears.

"Well, technically it isn't your shi…" Zard Win started, and stared at Shae Apon, as she put a hand on his arm.

"Isn't it?" she asked, her tone showing she wasn't actually asking any of them, so much as posing what they called a hypothetical question. She looked at Zard Win, and Scyles saw he understood her thoughts. He got a very thoughtful look on his face.

"What?" asked Scyles, suspiciously.

"I don't know that it would make a difference, but I have a theory I'd like to investigate before I speak any further on it," Shae Apon said slowly, and Zard Win nodded in agreement.

"The Captain," he said, and she nodded.

Together, they turned to leave, and Zard Win seemed to suddenly remember what they'd been doing.

"Can you finish up here, yourselves?" he asked Scyles, who nodded, full of questions, but knowing better than to ask them. "Just leave the raft near the door, in case anyone else wishes to practice. I'll have some more targets made up and brought here."

"We'll see both of you later," Shae Apon said, absentmindedly. "Enjoy your showers."

Scyles and Arga watched them scurry out the hatch and disappear down the concourse. They turned and looked at each other, and shrugged.

"Would you like to shoot some more?" he asked, and she shook her head.

"No, I think I'm ready for that shower," she said, and shivered. "I want to feel your arms around me. To hold me."

"I can do that," Scyles said, and they turned to gather the missed shots scattered around the hold.

Rost Fott sat in his captain's perch and listened to Commodores Mit Obet and Spur Vot discuss the sequence of events that led to their having custody of the very large Hshtahni generation ship, and the thousands of refugees they'd inherited with it.

All the ship's captains were on the conference call between the ships, but only the two that also held the rank of Commodore were speaking.

"So, these primitives, these…Scoloti, as you call them," Commodore Spur Vot spoke carefully, keeping any personal bias he had, out of his voice. Of course, from previous contact, Rost Fott knew the commodore was a bigot when it came to what he called inferior races. "All they appear to be good at, is killing Hshtahni?"

"Not an insignificant feat, when there are no power weapons involved," Commodore Mit Obet pointed out. "I sent you videos of the battles. They killed two young ones, and one mature, relatively well-armored one, probably the younger ones' sire. And in the process, wiped out the Mba warriors as well, fifty or sixty of them, I believe."

Spur Vot snorted.

"All good and well, but I don't see the value." He looked down at his own screen, watching something for a moment. "They seem to get good value from these strung weapons that fire bladed shafts."

"They do," Mit Obet agreed, and leaned back in his own seat. "So, Commodore, since we're going that way, we'll escort and transport their ship to Egelv Prime. The emperor might like a look at them."

"Whatever," the other man shrugged. "It's your problem, or opportunity, in any case. I'll be taking Chilled Wind and the rest of my squadron to our station, as long as you think your three ships can handle things."

"I'm sure we'll get by."

Rost Fott carefully kept his expression blank at his commodore's words. The sarcasm went right over Commodore Spur Vot's head, but he wasn't stupid. A careless grin could cue him in to his being mocked, and the commodore was very well connected in the Emperor's court.

I do not need more enemies at home, he decided. Or in the ranks above me.

The six of them exchanged pleasantries, then Commodore Spur Vot, and his two captains broke contact, and even as he watched, the three ships moved in perfect formation away at an ever-increasing rate. Within minutes, they would be out of normal scanning range.

"So, captains, it's just the three of us again," Mit Obet spoke and seemed to focus on Rost Fott. "Will you be able to maintain the tow until we're close enough to Egelv Prime to commandeer a tug or two?"

"It will be no problem, Sir," Rost Fott said. "Actually, we're using this opportunity to learn more about the Scoloti, and what their skills and capabilities are."

"I'm sure you are," Mit Obet said vaguely, causing Rost Fott to wonder what he meant. But the commodore spoke again before he could ask.

"Captain Vail Low, with Comet's Tail, will provide escort and, since we're well within our own territories now, I will go with utmost speed to Egelv Prime, to alert Command of our new acquisition and its cargo." He glanced back and forth between the two captains. "By the time you reach the system, we should have a plan on where we're going to park you. Since he has the mobility, Captain Vail Low will be in nominal command until you reach Egelv Prime."

Rost Fott nodded and saw in his side screen, Vail Low do the same. He couldn't say he was surprised that the commodore didn't wish to travel at a less than optimum speed back home, and this would give the powers that be time to decide on a course of action.

"Sir, Security Chief Zard Win did mention something I found intriguing," Rost Fott said, and the commodore looked at him suspiciously.

"When people say something is intriguing, it usually translates to troublesome," he said, and Rost Fott nodded hurriedly.

"I know what you mean sir," he said, and hastened to continue. "But he pointed out that, technically, although we are, in essence, towing them in, the Scoloti took the ship, virtually unassisted, and might have a valid claim to owning the Muschwain as compensation from the Hshtahni for kidnapping them from their planet."

"Preposterous," Commodore Mit Obet scoffed, then looked thoughtful. Finally, he shook his head. "That's a question for the lawyers, not me. And they're welcome to it."

Rost Fott was beginning to relax again when the commodore fixed him with a stare.

"Are your men keeping the Scoloti well in hand, under control?" he asked, looking at Rost Fott intently. "We don't need them doing something stupid with that ship, like trying to escape and fly it away."

"We damaged the engines and weapons pods in our initial battle," Rost Fott said reassuringly. "And they've shown no sign of wishing to learn to operate it, in any case."

"There hasn't been any trouble between the Scoloti and our own crew, then?" Mit Obet asked, and looked relieved when Rost Fott said no.

"They actually get along quite well," Rost Fott admitted. "They're very rough around the edges, but generous and good-natured, almost to a man, and woman," he amended belatedly.

"Good. Keep it under control, then, and have a smooth voyage back."

The commodore looked off-screen and nodded, then turned back to them.

"If the two of you think you've got things covered, Raging River will be on her way."

The commodore didn't wait for a response. His screen blanked, and Rost Fott's own screens showed the destroyer accelerate rapidly, and begin to pull ahead of them.

"Let me know if you have need of anything," Captain Vail Low said, smiling thinly. "I'm going to try and catch up on my reports and mail." His smile broadened a little.

"And my sleep."

His screen went dark, and Rost Fott watched Comet's Tail move to a position behind and to the side of the Muschwain.

Rost Fott sighed, and turned to Van Dono, sitting at his own station, off to the left a bit.

"Which leaves us," he said, and smiled as he stood and stretched, feeling his ears tremble as they pointed at the ceiling of the bridge. "Well, you, anyway. I'll be in my cabin."

He hid his smile as he heard Van Dono mutter.

"Of course you will."

Gelon watched his wife make several adjustments on the pod, and the cover changed from being impossible to see what was within, to a clear surface where he could very clearly see a sheep. It lay as if dead, but he knew it merely slept.

No, he remembered. That wasn't quite right either. It neither slept or breathed, yet it didn't die. It was as if, in an instant, it was frozen in time, neither alive nor dead. But if they needed to, it could be brought to life faster than it would take to butcher it.

Myrina pushed several buttons on her handheld device, and touched it to the pod. A small piece of papyrus rolled out from a second device on a small floating cart. It had a crude outline drawing of a sheep, a symbol beneath it, and more symbols below that. The back side of the papyrus was sticky, and the woman standing between the table and the pod fixed it to one end of the pod, muttering something as she did so.

Gelon was impressed, as always, by the fact that the speaker could keep track of everything she was handling, and repeat it back to them at will. He could never have memorized anything so quickly as accomplished speakers did on a regular basis.

"How many sheep is that, Marpesia?" Myrina asked.

"Thirty-seven sheep, two rams, so far, my Queen," the woman said with sincere respect. She turned to the young children standing behind her, and pointed to a boy and a girl. "You two, take this pod to Queen Opis, in the room with the large sign of the sheep on it. She may have a pod ready for you to return here. Follow her instructions."

"Yes, Speaker Marpesia," the young girl said with deference in her voice. She nudged the boy next to her, and nodded at the pod with her head. Without a word the boy took hold of the pod and easily guided it between other pods to towards the door to the concourse. The girl grinned at the Speaker and followed him. Gelon knew this would have been the year of their ninth gathering.

Speaker Marpesia turned back to Myrina, and they shared looks of humor.

"Tell me again why we pretend men are in charge, Speaker?" Myrina asked, her voice whimsical and light.

Gelon sighed and watched the two young children disappear out the door with the pod.

"I'm right here, and can hear you, and so can the rest of these children," he muttered, and the two women tittered. "That boy might as well be one of these sheep."

"Don't be too hard on him, my king," Myrina said, and her tone belied her words. "I'm sure he'll grow up to be a fierce warrior, and leader of men, if not of women."

"Eurybia will be a force to reckon with, when she's reached womanhood," Speaker Marpesia pointed out. "Swordmaster Targitai and Greya have produced a very formidable offspring."

"All of theirs are, in their own ways," Gelon admitted. "Auric, their oldest, will someday be almost the warrior his father is."

"Almost?" the Speaker asked, looking curious.

"Every generation of the people has always had at least one avatar representing some aspect of the people," Gelon said, knowing she was already familiar with this concept. "Targitai is the closest thing to Ares you will ever see. He is literally, the avatar of Ares, the War God."

"Could you defeat him in battle, dear husband?" Myrina asked, curiosity in her voice. She knew him well enough to know he conceded fighting skills to no man or woman. Or most gods, for that matter. "Most of the kings of the people agree you are the most daunting fighter they've ever seen. None of them would fight you willingly."

"I fear no man in battle, and certainly none of the other kings of the People," Gelon said easily. "But I would never willingly fight Targitai."

"He is your swordmaster, as well as your friend, since you were both young children," Myrina pointed out. "Of course you would never willingly fight him."

"Because he is the one man I believe could defeat me," Gelon said slowly, finding it hard to say this, even to his wife. "If we ever fought, I would bet extra ponies on him, were I you."

"Hmm," Myrina said, and he glanced at her curiously. She felt his eyes upon her and a slight smile came to her lips. "I'm always glad to see my husband tries to keep both his feet firmly planted on the ground. I would hate it if you weren't still around when I'm an old crone, with wrinkles, warts, and most of my hair fallen out."

"You will never be that, my beloved wife," Gelon said gallantly, and she laughed at him, her eyes promising rewards later, for his words.

"And we will never finish this task if we keep letting ourselves get sidetracked," Speaker Marpesia pointed out, and made a show of looking at the next pod in the row.

"Yes, Speaker," Gelon and Myrina spoke in perfect unison, and burst into laughter as the Speaker made a face at them.

Gelon saw Zard Win and Shae Apon enter the room, see where they were working, and begin making their way to them. Myrina handed her device to Speaker Marpesia.

"Would you mind taking charge of this for a while, Speaker?" she asked with deference, and Marpesia smiled at them.

"Go, talk with our Egelv friends," she said, and leaned closer to whisper. "These two, I truly believe would be our friends. Some of the others, I wonder, but these two seem genuinely interested in our ways, and our future welfare."

"I agree," Gelon said, keeping any sign of worry out of his voice. He knew, from conversations with Zard Win and Shae Apon, as well as Orik and Opis, Targitai, and even Scyles and Arga, that their future was clouded, at best. Try as he did, he could see no clear path the People could take to keep control of their destiny.

It was no way for a king to reign, he thought bleakly.

Zard Win shook hands with him, in the manner he'd been taught was the Scoloti way, grasping each other's right arm, above the elbow.

"King Gelon, Queen Myrina, I see you make progress in this room," he said, looking around at the rows of pods with the sticky papyrus already attached.

"And how many more rooms have we to go through?" Gelon said with mock despair. In truth, having a task, no matter how mundane, made the time pass more quickly, and gave him at least some sense of accomplishing something.

"I wish we could speed the process for you, but I'm told you have no written records of your people." Shae Apon said, looking at one of the labeled pods. "These stickers only tell the basics, and have no names or ages on the stickers."

"We have no written language," Myrina said, and gestured at Marpesia. "That is why our Speakers are so important to us. They record the history of our tribes, our stocks, animals, everything we need to know."

"Right," Zard Win said, and nodded. "That is why you searched so hard for Speakers when we put the Caitiari into pods."

"In most cases," Myrina agreed, and Gelon looked at her sharply. As far as he knew, that, and trying to keep families intact had been their only goals. She felt his gaze upon her and smiled at him cynically. "Husband, you know I only tell you what I think you really need to know."

They all laughed, and stopped abruptly, embarrassed, when Speaker Marpesia shushed them.

"I am trying to teach these children what we are doing, and keep the progress going, and the four of you are acting like first year trainees," she said primly.

"I'm sorry, Speaker," Myrina said, and swept the rest of them before her as she herded them out of the large room, and into the concourse outside. Her expression was a mixture of glee and exaggerated mortification. "I believe we've been put in our places," she said in a deliberately loud whisper.

"I can still hear you," the Speaker called from inside the room, and the four of them smiled as they moved down the broad hallway.

"I have been talking with Prince Scyles and Princess Arga," Shae Apon said slowly, clearly looking uncertain how welcome her words were to the Scoloti. She looked at Gelon, and then at Myrina. "You had him tutored by some sort of learned scholar, he called a 'Grecian'? He learned to read and write their language?"

"That is true," Gelon nodded, wondering what her point was.

"If we were to use their alphabet, written symbols for sounds," she added, seeing the lack of understanding on their faces. "We could apply the Grecian alphabet to your language, and create a written language for your people."

"We have speakers. Why would we need a written language?" Gelon asked, skeptical there was any value in such a task. His wife lay a hand on his arm, and he looked at her in surprise.

"Husband, I could see advantages to our having such a way of recording information, and possibly even instructions," she said slowly, her eyes

269

staring into space, seeing something beyond Gelon's vision. "Think of it. What if we didn't need to find the correct speaker that knew the lineage of our horses, and which stallions should be mated with which filly, from which sire and mare?"

"Or what your stocks of grains were, currently, and instructions on how to operate the pod devices," Zard Win said casually, but it got Gelon's attention. He still wasn't convinced. Teaching most or all the people how to use this written language notion, as opposed to sending someone to find the correct Speaker with the information, seemed so much more difficult and time-consuming, but he could see his wife was intrigued.

I guess I could wait and see what she decides on this subject, since she always gets her way, he conceded glumly to himself.

Gelon saw Targitai coming up the concourse, with a group of warriors, all of them in full fighting gear. His eyebrows raised at his swordmaster, who shrugged.

"I don't want these lazy sheep to get fat as mares, and as docile," Targitai said and grinned. "So I thought I'd have them beat the crap out of each other for a while."

Gelon nodded in agreement. He knew he could always count on his swordmaster to not let the details slide when Gelon himself was caught up dealing with some situation.

Zard Win stepped closer to Targitai, and stared at his overlapping armor in his battle kurgi.

"Is that several rows of plates, overlapping?" he started to say, stepping close to Targitai, who instinctively took a step backwards, his hand automatically going to the handle of his long sword. The Egelv belatedly realized he'd broken some unknown law or rule of etiquette by getting too close.

"I'm sorry, I meant no disrespect." Zard Win looked at Targitai, "May I look closer at your jerkin? The method you use to insert the plates intrigues me."

Targitai looked annoyed, and glanced at Gelon, as if to ask if this was necessary. Gelon gave him an imperceptible nod, and the swordmaster sighed, conceding to the Egelv with a nod.

Zard Win thanked him and put a finger on one of the plates, feeling through the material to trace the plate, and feeling where it overlapped with the ones above and below it. He tapped a fingernail on the plate itself, and nodded to himself.

Gelon was happy to see he didn't stretch the moment out. As soon as he had a firm vision of the construction of the armored kurgi, he bowed his head in thanks, and backed away from Targitai.

"Thank you very much," the Egelv said, and glanced over at Shae Apon, then at Gelon himself. "I think I might have some ideas of a way to reproduce this in a stronger, yet lighter, version. I will let you know what I find."

Targitai nodded brusquely, and with a bow of his head to Gelon, then Myrina, was off with his men. He'd barely disappeared from sight down the concourse, when Scyles happened by.

"Son," Gelon said, nodding to him, and looked at him quizzically. "I don't see you often without Arga at your side," he said tactfully.

"She's sleeping," Scyles said, and a satisfied expression flashed across his face.

Myrina laughed out loud.

"Did you please her mightily, dear son?"

Gelon laughed as well, now understanding his son's jaunty air. He had the stride of a man well pleased with himself. And satisfied, at least for the moment.

"I believe so," Scyles said innocently, and they all laughed. Myrina gave Scyles a hug, and whispered something in his ear. He looked startled and looked at her questioningly.

"I like it," she said, and looked at Gelon demurely, then back at her son. "And I think she will, as well. And I know you will, if you have any of your father in you, which you do."

Gelon laughed as he looked at the Egelvs, and how embarrassed they were. Myrina followed his gaze, and a peal of laughter escaped her lips.

"I'm sorry if we embarrass you," she said to them, and shrugged. "But when it comes to sex, and many other things, it is a part of our lives, and one of the better parts, at that. I'm sure you know what I mean."

She stared at them, and Gelon saw from their expressions, that they might not know. How on earth did this race manage to reproduce, if they were so prudish about such a common thing as sex?

He watched Zard Win firmly keep his eyes from Shae Apon, as he searched for something, anything, to say. She said she was going to check on the speaker's progress, and disappeared into the pod room.

"I was just telling your father and swordmaster that I might have an idea to improve upon your chest armor," Zard Win said desperately, and Gelon was proud to see his son graciously help him.

"Really?" Scyles asked, and looked thoughtful. "Improve in what way?" he continued, gesturing to them to walk with him down the concourse.

"Well, strength and durability, as well as lighter in weight," Zard Win said, and Scyles nodded for him to continue as they went into the next pod storage room.

"Tell me more," Scyles said encouragingly as they moved out of hearing range.

Gelon felt his wife's eyes on him, and turned to her, amused.

"You know, if you embarrass them enough, they won't come around as often," he said mildly, and she snorted in a very unladylike manner. He found it very enticing. He reached out with a long arm, and swept her into his arms. "So, what did you whisper to Scyles?"

"I'd rather show you than tell you," she admitted, and he shrugged, smiling at her.

"I have time," Gelon admitted, and began herding her down the concourse in the opposite direction everyone else had gone, his arm around her shoulders, holding her against him.

"I thought you might," Myrina admitted, and her own arm went around his waist. "And don't worry about their not coming around because of embarrassment. Those two are destined to become one, and just don't see it yet."

"My wife, the witch," Gelon said lightly, letting his hand slip off her shoulder and downward.

"Your wife, the all-seeing goddess of love and lust," Myrina corrected him. "Now come, great king, help me travel forward in time, and wonder where this afternoon went so quickly."

"I can do that," Gelon admitted, and their pace quickened.

Chapter Twenty-Three

Rost Fott listened to Mar Ence, the Chief Engineer of Mountain Edge, give him a rundown on the repair efforts so far, on the engines and power system of the Muschwain. He winced as the list of parts needed to fully repair the ship kept getting longer and longer. They'd already done an analysis on the weapons pods, and at least that part was encouraging.

The ship itself had holds full of replacement parts and raw materials, and Mar Ence estimated they would have all the weapons systems fully functional by the time they entered the Egelv Prime star system. It looked like the story was about the same for the power systems. There had been relatively little structural or functional damage to the huge ship.

The engines, on the other hand, were another matter. The chief engineer wasn't even sure they could be brought back on line without copious replacement parts that were not part of the ship's repair inventory.

They were in the vast docking bay of the generation ship, and there were some Scoloti men and women training and working out about half way across the bay. He watched them fight with swords and was duly impressed. He saw a few of them practicing their archery, but after watching the king's son, Scyles, virtually destroy the target the first time Zard Win introduced the gel man figure, it would be hard to impress him now.

Rost Fott was impressed with the surveillance system built into the ship, and it had come in handy in a number of ways. He now knew, for certain, that the Scoloti weren't plotting to attempt to take the ship, or surge aboard Mountain Edge and try and seize it, and he was pleased to see them take their own initiative when they saw something that needed doing.

He had to impress on Van Dono that the cameras to the private sleeping and bathing areas of the Scoloti were not to be casually observed by the crew. Zard Win had come to him, commenting on some of the men abusing the system to watch the primitives procreate, both in their sleeping quarters, as well as in their showers. He'd only seen a brief example before he forbade any intrusions on the primitives' privacy, but their energy and enthusiasm had been impressive, to say the least.

He saw Zard Win and Shae Apon enter the docking bay, and returned their wave. They went over to where the Scoloti were practicing their swordplay, and watched as they examined the heavy outer jacket most or all Scoloti, men and women, wore on a daily basis.

Rost Fott wondered idly what they were up to. He wasn't sure it was such a good idea to become so immersed into the daily routines of the primitive race, but so far, there had been little or no problems within the ranks of the Scoloti, or between them and the Egelv, for that matter.

Things seemed to be going very smoothly, Rost Fott thought. And that made him very nervous.

Shae Apon looked at the list of letters Scyles had written down for her. She wished she could demand he spend every waking hour they had left before they arrived at Egelv Prime, working with her on creating a working written language for his people. Getting him to pronounce each letter clearly, in the same order as his written list, for her to record, had felt like a major accomplishment.

She had to admire the tenacity of his people, to rely on these Speakers to record their tribal history, keep records, and whatever else they found them useful for. She'd asked if the Speakers kept track of instructions on how to do certain things, and he'd looked at her strangely.

He'd said that's what people were for. If you wanted to know how to make a sword, you asked the metalsmith. If you wanted to know how to make a good bow, you asked older warriors that had mellowed, to show you how. Or you asked your father. Or another relative that was older, more experienced.

She stared at her screen with all the Grecian letters in one long column. It blurred a little, and she automatically checked the time. She was shocked to see how late it was. She risked a glance at Zard Win, working at a computer station, his eyes intent on the screen.

They'd taken over one of the conference rooms near the bridge of the Muschwain, some days ago, and, in many ways, it had become their second home. They'd discovered that having another person to bounce ideas off was much better than sequestering oneself and trying to figure everything out on their own.

There were also several couches that, at one time or another, both of them had utilized for naps. Whenever either of them did so, waking was an unsettling moment, mostly because it didn't feel awkward, which it should.

She liked Zard Win, and found working with him to be a very satisfying experience. She knew he felt the same way, although they hadn't really discussed it.

Shae Apon sighed, and stood, stretching to relieve aching muscles and joints, left in one position for far too long. As usual, she could tell he noticed, but he deliberately kept his eyes on his work, and didn't acknowledge her in any way until she initiated the contact.

At first, she'd wondered if he disapproved of her, or didn't particularly care for her. As they spent more time together, she realized it was a protective mechanism he'd adopted to keep them at a distance, for propriety's sake.

Spending so much time around the Scoloti made it difficult to keep things strictly professional. For one thing, they were not at all shy about sharing their intimate thoughts and actions with the Egelv. And since both she and Zard Win had developed the beginnings of genuine friendships with some of them, they got more exposure than any of the other Egelv to the raw sensuality of the primitive race. Shae Apon also knew that at some point, she and Zard Win were going to have to acknowledge that they might be developing personal feelings for each other. If they were unable to admit this issue, she knew it would be better if they quit working together at all.

But she didn't want that. She liked being around Zard Win, and even if she would never admit it to anyone else, she knew she was feeling an attraction to him. She knew he felt the same, if for no other reason than the extremes he went to, trying to keep them from finding themselves in a compromising situation.

She looked over his shoulder, and saw he was working on a three dimensional copy of one of the small metal platelets the Scoloti wove into their kurtas for armor. She looked at the composition of the intended platelet, and blinked.

"You're going to make a one molecule armor platelet to deflect the point or edge of a sword?" she asked, in awe of the audacity of his idea.

"I'm trying to," Zard Win admitted. He sat back in his seat and looked up at her. "This molecule is dynamically stronger than any metal the people have learned to make. If I can just figure out how to allow me to connect them into a vest-like garment, I think I have worked out the tensile strength issues, and dramatically reduced the brittle factor."

"What if you design holes in the platelets, and string them together?" Shae Apon said thoughtfully. "If they're part of the molecular shape, they would be as strong as if there was no hole. It wouldn't be hard to come up with a pattern of stringing them together where they overlap, just like the armor jerkins they wear now."

"Except, what kind of material will hold up to blades, and the edges of the holes?" Zard Win asked, despondently. "With the platelets so thin, the hole's edges will cut through any material, after a while, just by wearing it."

"What if you make the string from the same molecular composition as the platelets themselves? Research the actual length needed, depending on size, and make the thread a one molecule thread, as durable as the platelets themselves."

Zard Win stared up at her, and slowly shook his head.

"That is brilliant," he admitted. "I never would have thought of that."

"Of course you would have," she reassured him. "You haven't been getting enough sleep, so you're not quite as sharp as you normally are. I can tell." She smiled at him. "You should go back to the ship, get some sleep, and deal with this in the morning, when you're fresh and wide awake."

"Actually, I've moved into one of the crew quarters rooms nearby," Zard Win admitted, yawning. He looked at her guiltily. "Please excuse my crass…"

He stopped as she put a finger on his lips.

"Hush. You're tired, you yawned." She shrugged. "It's very Egelvan of you."

She took her finger away, suddenly aware of how that action had violated his personal space. She could tell he was very aware of it as well, and vowed to not let herself have such a weak moment again. She didn't want to make his life more difficult.

As if they'd both reached the limit of their ability to allow intimacy between them, they simultaneously turned back to the computer screen. She thought about his having a room to stay on board the Muschwain, and how much more convenient that must be.

"So, you go back to Mountain Edge for meals, and fresh clothes?" she asked, more out of a lack of anything else entering her mind. But silence was dangerous right now, and she would be strong and safe, for both of their sakes.

"I do for some meals, but as often or not, I go to their common hall and have whatever they're having," Zard Win admitted. "It's interesting, and I believe the time I'm there is well spent."

"Right," Shae Apon said slowly, wishing she'd thought of this first. If she mimicked him, she had a feeling people would talk, and she wasn't sure what he would think.

"As far as my clothes go, I've moved most of my belongings here," Zard Win admitted. "When necessary, I take a load back to the ship to do laundry, catch up on anything I need to do requiring my actual presence on board. Check in with my unit, make sure they aren't getting sloppy without me to push them."

He looked at her without speaking, and she realized he was debating internally about something. Finally, he took a deep breath, and spoke.

"There are several empty cabins near mine, should you decide it would benefit your work," he said, and immediately bent over his controls, and began creating something new that, even as she watched, began to resemble a Scoloti dagger.

"A knife?" she asked him, and he smiled without looking up.

"I took pictures and analysed one of Scyles' throwing knives, thinking I could make one with a much sharper blade," he admitted. "But apparently, weight is an issue on a throwing knife. I was trying to make it as light as possible, but he says they don't fly as accurately. He says it needs the weight for stability and the power to penetrate the target."

"A body," Shae Apon said, shivering. "I feel I should not approve of this, but I do," she admitted.

"I know," Zard Win agreed. "They think so differently, yet, who am I to say they're wrong?"

"These are brilliant ideas you're having, Zard Win," she said, envious of his ingenuity.

"I'm sure what you're working on is every bit as important," he answered, sounding very confident of her, which she found touching. "What are you currently working on?"

"Oh, I'm still trying to apply the Grecian alphabet to the Scoloti tribal language," she admitted. "I think it's very doable, but labor intensive. We'll need to come up with phonetically correct words in Scoloti, using Grecian letters. Scyles will be the only one able to read it, if I get it right. And there are so many words," she admitted, suddenly feeling the weight of her project and hopes pressing down on her. "But their young could learn it, and pass it on."

"Can't you have the translator computers use your Grecian alphabet to print out all the Scoloti words we've managed to translate, and even those we haven't?"

Shae Apon stared at him, trying to see what she was missing, because at first glance, that seemed like a very good idea.

"Let's see, what's a Scoloti word?" Zard Win asked, more to himself than her. "Translation program, use the Grecian letters in Shae Apon's files to make a written translation of Ares, the god of war."

They both watched his screen as a strange-looking word appeared. Zard Win looked up at her questioningly. She slowly sounded the letters out.

"Ares," she said, and gasped. She tried to remember any other Scoloti words she'd picked up in conversations with Scyles, or with Arga, who was fast becoming a good friend. They spent time together every day, and Shae Apon treasured those hours, or even minutes.

"Water God," she said, and watched the letters appear. "Avestan," she slowly read, and then clenched her fist in excitement.

"Kill," Zard Win said, and letters appeared.

"Pata," Shae Apon said, and looked at him. He nodded and grinned at her.

"Sun," he said, and she nodded as she quietly said "Khala."

"Scoloti," she said, and they stared at the letters that appeared.

"Egelv," he said, and she gripped his shoulder as the letters appeared and she sounded them out.

"Zard Win, you are a brilliant, lovely man," she said, and leaning over, gave him a big hug around his shoulders. His hand went to her arm, and it rested there for a moment, and then she straightened, trying not to seem in too great a hurry, to draw attention to their actions. His hand slid off her arm.

"I should probably get back to Mountain Edge, get some rest," she said slowly, and Zard Win nodded. His fingers flew across the controls, initiating commands, setting parameters, and then leaned back in his seat.

"Are you tired?" he asked casually, but she wasn't fooled.

"No, but that's the adrenaline pumping through my system," Shae Apon admitted. She came to a sudden realization. "However, I am suddenly very hungry."

"I am, too," he admitted. He glanced her way without making eye contact. "Want to see if they have anything set out at the common lodge?"

"Are we depleting their provisions, by eating their food?" she asked, pretty sure she knew the answer.

"No, not really," Zard Win said. "We've already cloned their lamb, mutton, and horsemeat, and they say they can't tell the difference. So we can make as much of their food as we want."

"Well, I am hungry," she repeated, and nodded her head decisively. "Shall we go see?"

"Certainly," Zard Win said casually, but she could feel the tension in his voice.

She went to her work station and gave her computer a couple instructions, and straightened up with relief.

"Good. I'm going to get some late dinner while my program prints out every Scoloti word the computer knows, as well as those it doesn't recognize." She smiled at him with satisfaction. "Good use of time. Very professional and efficient."

"And I'm having the computer print a few hundred 3-D one-molecule plates, with the holes you suggested. It will probably take a few hours."

"Then we should eat," she said, and gestured to the door.

"We should," Zard Win agreed, and they both walked out the door and down the concourse, trying to project confidence, and a casual manner.

She suspected any observers would agree they failed completely.

But it's a start, she thought, and struggled to not change her stride or facial expression as the strange idea.

A start at what, she wondered.

Scyles and Arga held hands as they walked into the common hall. He spotted some space at a table, and they made their way to it, reluctantly releasing their grip on each other's hands to sit.

He nodded to the men and women already seated, eating out of communal bowls. One of the old women that always seemed to be there brought them cups of milk, and he looked at her questioningly.

"No, no, it's just milk, fresh from a mare," she promised him, and gave Arga a lopsided grin. "Anyway, I've seen what effect fermented mare's milk has on Princess Arga. None this early for you, girl."

Scyles laughed, and Arga scoffed, but she didn't argue. Getting so drunk she passed out the night they put the Caitiari into the pods, causing her to miss the entire thing, had given her a determination to never let drink keep her from knowing what was happening around her.

He admired her determination, although he wondered how long her vow would last. The People weren't known for their abstinence or willpower to refrain from drinking too much.

Arga nudged him, and he looked at her askance. She nodded to a table over near the far wall, and he saw Zard Win and Shae Apon working on something. They were totally oblivious to anything happening around them.

"They've both been at it most of the night," the old woman said in a quiet voice. "When I came in early, Greta told me they'd stopped in for a late meal, then left, and came back in less than an hour, and have been at that table ever since."

She bent closer to Scyles.

"I don't know if what they're doing is so important, or the fact they're doing it together is what is so important, but they've not stopped in hours." She leered at them. "I think they should go back to that room he's been sleeping in, and get after each other. You can tell they want to."

"You think so?" Scyles asked, and both the old woman and Arga laughed.

"Yes, foolish boy," his wife said, and stuck her tongue out at him. "It's so clear, even you should be able to see it."

"Hmm," Scyles said, not convinced. He shrugged at Arga, and got up and walked over to them.

"I hear you've been here most of the night," he said, and they both jumped in their seats.

"We have this project," Zard Win said evasively, and Shae Apon gave him a scornful look.

Scyles looked at what they were working on. It looked like they might be making an armored vest or kurga, but without the material. Just the scales of armor.

But they didn't look right, he decided. He wasn't sure what was wrong or different, but they looked...odd.

Shae Apon startled him by holding out a handheld computer device so he could see the screen.

"Can you read that, and say it out loud?" she asked brusquely.

He looked closer and shook his head.

"Those letters are from the Grecian alphabet, but that's not a word," he said, sure of himself.

"Can you sound it out, and speak it aloud?" she asked, and he shrugged and looked at it again, humoring her.

As he began sounding out each word, he felt his eyes widen in shock.

"I am great the archer," he said, and repeated it again, only with the correct Scoloti wording. "I am a great archer."

He stared at them, and then her in particular.

"How did you do this?" he asked in wonder. "Can we do this with other words of the People?"

"We can put your entire language down in writing," Zard Win said, and there was real excitement in his voice. "Anything you or your people want to record, your family lineage, how many horses you own, the story of how you and Arga fell in love, anything," he ended, lamely.

Scyles stared at him, and he looked uncomfortable.

"This is Shae Apon's work," he hastened to say. "She came up with the idea, and should get all the credit."

"You helped," Shae Apon contradicted him. She smiled at him, and Scyles was intrigued to see him blush, visible even under his dark brown skin. "We did it together."

"Well," Zard Win said, his blush deepening.

Beside him, Scyles heard Arga giggle.

"You two are so cute together," she said, and both Egelv stammered denials.

"We're not together," she said, and Zard Win quickly agreed.

"Right, definitely not together," he said. "We work together on projects, that's all."

The last word was fervent, almost a shout, and Scyles looked at them with amusement, wondering if he and Arga had been so transparent when they'd first spent time together, back at the gathering site, an eternity ago.

"So, you're not together," Arga said, and Scyles couldn't help snickering. She nudged him and looked down at what they were working on.

"Is this something else, you're just…working on?" she asked innocently, and both Egelv quickly agreed with her.

"Yes, this project is…" Shae Apon began, but Zard Win cut her off.

"Scyles, could you try and cut this armor?" he asked, and Scyles felt the interlocked small platelets. He felt his eyebrows raise and picked up the armor.

It was light. Certainly too light to be effective. He looked at the two Egelv with an apologetic smile.

"I don't think this will hold up to any significant blows," he began, and was startled when Zard Win cut him off.

"Could you try? Try cutting it with your sword?"

"Of course," Scyles said, and looked around for something to set the armor on. He decided one of the wooden stools at their table would do. It wasn't like he would be trying to cut it with any intensity. The material was light, and would most certainly shatter under a blow using the weight of the sword itself.

He did that very thing, and was surprised to see his blade not only didn't break any of the platelets, it didn't even scratch any, or leave any mark at all. He did it again, hard this time, with the same result.

He picked up the armor and stared at the platelets. They were so light, and thin. How was it resisting his blade?

Well, it wouldn't be able to resist this time, he decided.

"May I use your butcher block," he asked the old woman, who'd joined the growing crowd of spectators to his efforts.

"That sword too heavy for you today, Prince Scyles?" a voice asked from the anonymity of the crowd, and there was laughter.

"Husband duties can wear a man down," another voice called out, and the laughter increased.

"Now don't you get shards of that all over the food," she snapped at him, and waved him to the large butcher block that rested nearby.

Scyles draped the armor over the top of the heavy wooden block, and without any ado, swung his sword as hard as he could, bringing it down on the platelets draped over the block of hard wood.

He could tell as his blade connected that the result would be the same. He sheathed his sword and picked up the armor and peered at it closely.

Not a mark. No sign whatsoever it had just been struck by a sharp metal blade.

Scyles shook his head, and turned to Zard Win and Shae Apon, ready to admit his defeat. He saw Skulis standing behind Arga, with a big grin on his face.

"Skulis, I offer you a chance to embarrass me, and to show off for the ladies," he said as he put the armor back on top of the wooden block. "Please, use your axe. Don't let fine Scoloti iron be defeated by little pieces of Egelv earwax."

Skulis stepped forward, drawing his hand axe, amid the laughter at Scyles' words. He didn't hesitate a moment, but struck the armor harder than Scyles would have believed possible for anyone other than his father or his older brothers, when they'd lived.

The axe head bounced back up, and Skulis swore vehemently as they both leaned forward to inspect the armor. It was without a mark.

Skulis shook his head in frustration, and looked around the room.

"My chance to get revenge for the thrashing he gave me back home," he said, longing in his voice. "But I can claim nothing from this, other than there is no weakness in our prince. The armor has defeated us both."

They grinned at each other and hugged impulsively.

Scyles turned back to Arga, and he noticed Skulis step to the side of one of the girls whose family had been brought out of the pods to make room for the Caitiari. He vaguely recognized her as being from his tribe, and thought she was the same age as Arga.

Agave, he remembered. Her name was Agave. Very pretty too, he thought, happy to see his friend moving past his infatuation with Arga.

Scyles handed the armor to Zard Win.

"So, what is it?" he asked, and the Egelv shook his head.

"Let us finish it first," he said, glancing over at Shae Apon questioningly. She nodded, and smiled at him. He turned back to Scyles. "Let us finish it, and let me get some sleep. I am groggy, and can hardly form coherent sentences."

Shae Apon nodded her agreement, and they began to gather their belongings together.

Scyles wanted to know more, but it was clear they were both exhausted, and it wasn't like they were going anywhere, anytime soon.

He and Arga returned to their seats, and he picked some meat and bread, out of the common bowl, and took a bite.

He nodded at the clever comments by the people around him on how spending so much time with his wife must be draining his strength.

One of the older men slapped him on the back as he walked by.

"So, Prince Scyles, is your young bride with child yet?"

Scyles sighed and looked at Arga, who shrugged expressively. He looked up at the old man.

"I don't know," he admitted, and stared at his wife in amusement as the laughter rose around them. He reached for another piece of horse meat.

"Good idea," the old man said, and guffawed. "Red meat to keep your strength up."

Chapter Twenty-Four

"Captain, we are being hailed by Raging River."

Rost Fott sighed at First Officer Van Dono's words, and glanced in the mirror. He decided he looked presentable enough for a captain off duty, on his own ship. Then he sighed and pulled a duty jacket over his casual shirt, and sat at his work station in his quarters.

He shook his head enough to allow his long, luxurious hair to fall over his shoulders, and told his first officer to forward the call to his quarters.

Commodore Mit Obet looked at him, and behind him, and nodded.

"Did I catch you off duty, Captain?" he asked soliticiously.

"Yes sir, but that is no problem." Rost Fott' screen split, and showed a schematic of the immediate space around them.

Generation Ship Muschwain was toddling along, with Mountain Edge firmly attached to its side, with Comet's Tail in proper formation.

The new addition to the situation was a heavy cruiser bearing down on them, with three accompanying destroyers of the same class as Mountain Edge. Rost Fott also saw Raging River and a troop carrier, as well as an armed freighter.

"You brought reinforcements." Rost Fott said in a mild voice, and the commodore smiled thinly. "Home and back in two weeks, with what had to be an interesting briefing at Egelv Command tucked between. Very impressive."

The commodore nodded his head modestly, and grew serious.

"This heavy squadron is under the flag of Admiral Shin Ver, aboard heavy cruiser Dark Void. It and the three destroyers will remain in station on the Muschwain, well off to the stern, but close enough to react if any more Hshtahni incursions into our territory occur.

Rost Fott debated pointing out that technically, they had been just beyond space claimed by the Egelv at the first encounter, but decided not to. He reluctantly nodded his agreement.

"Armed Freighter Safe Passage will dock at one of the cargo bays, and remove the Hshtahni carcasses and return to Egelv Prime, immediately."

"Have them approach the port bay, then," Rost Fott said, glad to have the dead aliens gone. "The Scoloti have some of their things in the starboard bay." He intentionally left it vague, having no desire to explain his logic to allow the Scoloti to practice their combat skills. "It keeps them busy," he said, and was relieved when the commodore didn't seem interested in details.

"I will be docking with your starboard airlock, keeping my ship from any danger of contamination from the Muschwain, and the Transport Cruiser Cold Fury will dock at the port bay." Commodore Mit Obet looked at him intently. "Egelv Command isn't comfortable with ten thousand alien warriors having control of a ship the size of the Muschwain approaching Egelv Prime without a strong military presence on board."

Rost Fott kept his face expressionless, but he was troubled. He'd seen Egelv shock troops interact with native populations before. Sometimes it was fine, sometimes it was not.

"There are a little over six thousand of them, including dependents, and all but about one hundred and fifty are in stasis, so they will be no problem," Rost Fott said in his most reassuring voice, but the commodore raised a hand, forestalling any further politicking for the Scoloti he'd intended.

"Not our call, Captain," he said. "They will inspect the ship, make sure everything is as it seems, and other than limited patrols, will stay in the bay area, or on their transport."

The commodore smiled at him, but there was something about the smile that raised alarms in Rost Fott's head. A transport cruiser like the Cold Fury could have four platoons of eighty heavily armed and armored troopers. One of the four would usually be mostly comprised of power weapon specialists, but those were for battle against fortified targets, or mobile armored units. In this situation, the ship would probably have four platoons, all troopers.

The connection ended, and Rost Fott dressed hurriedly, and made his way to the bridge. While he was briskly strolling down the corridor, he called Zard Win, and filled him in on the situation.

"Sir, these troopers won't try and disarm the Scoloti, will they?" his security chief asked, alarm clear in his tone. "I don't know that they would submit to that."

"Then they might find themselves waking up after an educational stunning," Rost Fott said, trying to sound firm. After all, he was supposed to support the policies of his superiors.

"You know them well enough to know it wouldn't go quite that way," Zard Win said, and the strain in his voice was easy to hear. "Our troopers would be stunning men and women that would resist. You know the Scoloti don't have any nonlethal weapons. It's not a given that they wouldn't get at least a few troopers before they went down. And then where are we?"

"Security Chief, you're not making this any easier," Rost Fott said, frustrated as his officer voiced his own concerns. "Your words actually support their being disarmed."

"They were disarmed when they were first captured, and that didn't go as expected," Zard Win pointed out. "I'm just saying, they're proud, and at this point, feeling that we are all good friends. This kind of action could take all that progress away."

Rost Fott sighed.

"Look, I'll send your men down to meet you. Where are you?" The security chief told him he was on the way to the common yurt. "Okay, I'll get them right to you. Keep everyone cool, if you can. But don't let yourself or your men get caught in a crossfire."

He walked onto the bridge and nodded to Van Dono. His first officer reluctantly got out of the Captain's chair, ofttimes referred to as the Captain's Peak. He saw that Dark Void and the three destroyers were already on station, and the heavy transport was approaching the loading bay on the port side. Raging River was already closing in, and one of his officers was guiding them to a secure docking.

The freighter was holding off, well clear, awaiting permission to dock, after the troopers verified the generation ship was secured.

What a muddled mess this is becoming, Rost Fott thought, sighing. He discreetly notified security to take all available forces to the Common Yurt and report to their chief. No one on the bridge noticed his action, and he sat back, wondering why he'd unconsciously thought that mattered.

No matter, he decided. This was probably not going to go well, no matter what he did.

Gelon nodded as Myrina gave him a detailed accounting of their progress organizing the stasis pods. He saw Targitai come into the common yurt and, being a masterful tactician, the swordmaster quickly assessed the situation and veered off to talk with some men sitting at a table, drinking their meal.

Traitor, Gelon thought, wishing he could join them.

Zard Win hurried in, saw him, and quickly walked over. Gelon took one look at his face, and held up his hand, stopping his wife in mid-sentence. She frowned at him, saw the Egelv, and a look of concern appeared on her own face.

"What is it?" Gelon asked, staring up at Zard Win.

"We may have a problem," he admitted, and Gelon nodded, gesturing for him to continue. "Ships from our home world have arrived to escort us to Egelv Prime."

"That's a nice gesture of your people," Myrina said, and Gelon could see she knew better, but was giving him the opening to give them details.

"If that's all it was," Zard Win said, almost wistfully. He took a deep breath. "They're military ships, and one of them is a troop transport. A ship full of warriors," he said, and Gelon nodded his thanks for speaking simply. "They're going to search the entire ship, assess the situation, and probably want to have your weapons locked up."

"What is happening?" Targitai asked, and Gelon resisted the urge to jump in his seat. His weaponmaster ignored his reaction, his attention on Zard Win.

"Oh, so now you show up," Gelon commented, and Targitai gave him a sardonic grin.

"I know when to avoid a situation, old friend," he said, and Myrina sniffed.

"Repeat what you just told me, to my old friend," Gelon said easily, and Zard Win looked at him in confusion. He knew they truly were old friends, and he was missing something, but shrugged and repeated what he'd just said.

Targitai looked at Gelon, and then, as one, they both looked at the Egelv.

"You might convince them that will be unnecessary," Gelon said mildly, and Targitai snorted. "We're all friends here. And the People never surrender their weapons."

"But these are combat warriors, and they will be heavily armed and probably in full armor," Zard Win said, looking very worried. "Their weapons will be on stun, but if one of them should fall, they would turn them to lethal, and not hesitate to use them."

"Even so, no Scoloti will give up his weapons willingly." Gelon's voice hardened. "And there is no reason for us to. We have raised no weapons against the Egelv. We were your allies against the Hshtahni monsters. Taking our weapons away would show a lack of respect, contempt, even. No Scoloti would submit to such a dishonor."

Gelon saw Scyles and Arga walk in, see them, and start to make their way over to them. He watched his son's face go from cheerful, to attentive, to thoughtful, to very wary, in as many steps. He casually clicked both his swords past the guard in their sheaths, making them faster to draw.

"What is it?" he asked as he took his bow out of his gorytos, strung it, and put it back.

Targitai gave him a cheerful nod, doing the same with his own weapons. Arga, watching them, hurried to follow suit. Gelon gave her a pat on the shoulder to show his approval. She blushed, but looked pleased.

Zard Win told him the situation for the third time, and Gelon was pleased to see Scyles tackle the problem without looking to him for help.

"We've had our weapons since we took the ship from the Hshtahni and Mba," he pointed out. "We took the ship, and killed them, not the Egelv. In fact, we liberated you from where they had you pinned down, wiping out the bulk of the enemy in the process."

Scyles looked directly at his father for the first time, as if assessing his reaction to his words.

"This is our ship," he said, turning his attention back to Zard Win. "We appreciate your assistance in helping us to a safe harbor. And I'm sure we can come to an agreement on paying for repairs, or perhaps selling it to the Egelv, should we find some sort of accommodations that would allow us to continue to live as we always have. And we would make excellent allies to the Egelv."

"Zard Win, we will not surrender our personal weapons," Gelon said gently, knowing the Egelv was a friend and ally. "They are as much a part of us as an arm, or a leg."

He watched the struggle on Zard Win's face, and didn't envy him. As strange as his people seemed, he was a friend to them now, and as familiar as one of their own. Zard Win touched something on his belt.

"Did you get all that, sir?" he asked, and nodded. "Yes, I will tell them."

He looked at Gelon, then at Scyles and Arga, before his eyes settled on Targitai, who was as solemn as a wolf on the tundra. He nodded slowly, deep in thought, and turned back to Gelon.

"My Captain is talking with the Commodore, trying to convince him all this is unnecessary, but meanwhile, the troop carrier, Cold Fury, has docked and a squad is making a sweep of the ship. They will reach this point within a couple minutes."

Gelon felt, rather than saw, Targitai go over and quietly tell the table of men to move near the wall, and watch their king, and be ready to act. Several of the women serving them hurried out the door. Targitai came back and stood nodded to them.

"I told them I'd kill anyone that fired the first arrow myself. But if someone else starts it, they'll be ready. The women went to roust any men or women warriors in their sleeping quarters."

"Good. Thank you, old friend," Gelon said, and sighed at how unnecessary all this was. Surely they'd showed their trustworthiness by now!

Four Egelv entered the yurt, and Gelon looked at them with interest.

The average Egelv stood at least half a head taller than most of the Scoloti, with the exception of Gelon and a couple others. They were taller, leaner, and moved with a litheness that Gelon envied. These Egelv were, on the average, a full head taller than the People. They wore heavily padded clothing, perhaps even armor beneath, and seemed more muscular than the Egelv from Mountain Edge.

They took one look at how many Scoloti were in the room, and of course, that every one of them wore weapons, and stopped abruptly. One of them spoke quietly, and Gelon assumed he was calling for help.

"Welcome, friends," he called out, gesturing to the mostly empty tables. "Some of us were just having our mid-day meal. Would you join us? We also have a fermented drink you might find you like."

That was probably the last thing they expected to hear, and they looked at each other questioningly. Then one of them stepped forward.

"We thank you for the offer, but we're on duty," he said, being polite, but firm. He pointed to the nearest empty table. "And part of our duty is gathering all weapons to put into storage for the duration of this trip. So we will need everyone to bring their weapons to this table. If necessary, we can give you receipts, but we must secure all weapons on this ship."

"We are the Scoloti," Gelon said in a full voice that carried to every corner of the large room. "Our people have travelled the frozen tundra of the north, fought through the deadly swamps of the south, sent the Persians fleeing home to the east, and held the Grecians at bay to the west. We have repelled tribe after tribe of barbarians from the north, east, and west. Our weapons are like our arms and legs. Our children begin to carry them as soon as they are able to walk or ride. No man or woman would feel proper or complete without their swords or gorytos, or their axes, belted around them. This is the way of the People."

He gestured at another empty table.

"So we will keep our personal property, where it belongs, on our person." He tried to look sincere. "We are sad we can not submit to your request, but it can not be. Please, come, sit and drink with us. We will put a freshly killed horse on the fire, and in the pots, and we will feast."

Two more groups of four soldiers showed up while he was speaking, then yet another. They looked at the one who had spoken previously, as if for direction.

Gelon turned enough to call out, but without letting them out of his line of vision.

"Bring out more food and drink for our guests," he called, and was gratified to see several women come out with baskets of bread and buckets of mare's milk. He gestured to the table and they started filling it with the bread and milk, and then platters of chunks of meat and vegetables began to appear. He turned back to face the Egelv directly.

"Please, sit, join us as friends." He forced himself to smile at them. "I am King Gelon, and one of your hosts. I bid you welcome."

291

The warrior who had spoken earlier looked bemused, but determined. He seemed to notice Zard Win for the first time, and stepped towards him. The warrior looked closer, and Gelon realized he was checking what the Egelv wore to figure out how important he was.

"You are the Security Chief of Mountain Edge, and you let them keep their weapons?" He asked, even as eight more soldiers appeared. They all moved deeper into the yurt, and began to fan out to either side of the door.

"They fought alongside us to take this ship," Zard Win said sharply. "In fact, they were really the ones that killed the Hshtahni and Mba and took the ship. They were already aboard when we arrived. They were prisoners, and broke free, got their weapons, and took the ship."

The warrior looked skeptical, and shook his head.

"This ship is bound for Egelv Prime. It is being towed by your ship, which makes it salvage, and therefore, property of the Egelv Empire. We can't allow armed forces to approach our home planet."

"This ship is a generation ship, and incapable of entering the atmosphere," Zard Win pointed out. "They are armed with swords, axes, and bows. Do you think they're going to shoot down at the planet from orbit?"

"They could use their weapons to take the ship, and fire energy weapons," the warrior argued, and Gelon was amused that they were able to keep these supposedly superior fighters at bay by talk.

"We have an escort that could destroy this ship in moments," Zard Win pointed out. "And my ship knocked all the weapons out in the battle. They don't even have functioning engines, and can only go where we take them."

Scyles stepped forward, and nodded to the soldier spokesman.

"There is no need for us to take what we already possess." He smiled, and Gelon thought it looked sincerely sympathetic. "This is our ship. We are accepting assistance from our friends, the Egelv, and we are very appreciative. We are happy to give you free rein to roam the halls, we have extra rooms for sleeping quarters, if you're tired of your bunks on your own ship. My father has offered you food and drink, which makes you our guest. And it makes us responsible for your safety. You are in our new home, and we welcome you. But we can't give up what makes us who we are."

The warrior stared at Scyles. Gelon actually believed he wanted to agree, but knew he couldn't. He shook his head, as if to clear it.

"Enough," the warrior said, and placed a hand on what Gelon now knew was called a stunner on his hip. "All of you will place your weapons on these tables now."

"No, I am afraid that is impossible," Gelon said, regret in his voice.

Even as he spoke, armed Scoloti appeared in the large doorway, hands on their swords, carrying shields, behind the Egelv warriors, too numerous to count from where Gelon stood.

The Egelv had made a serious tactical error, and Gelon could see their leader recognized it. They were all in close quarters, which negated much of the value of their weapons. The Scoloti thrived in close battle, and were now intermingled with the Egelv warriors. Close enough for him to see these were hardened warriors that had been in battles, acquired the scars to prove it, and had that look of tough men that wouldn't yield easily, if at all.

Zard Win stepped forward, raising his arms to try and calm everyone down.

"Everyone, please relax and no one do anything foolish," he said, and looked at the Egelv soldier that spoke for them. "Check with your ship. You have new orders."

He turned back to the room as a whole.

"Commodore Mit Obet has agreed that there is no reason for the Scoloti to give up their weapons, and cause them dishonor. They are loyal friends of the empire, and will be presented to the Emperor when we reach Egelv Prime. This matter is closed."

Gelon watched the expression on the Egelv soldier's face as he listened to someone on his ear voice. Anger changed to relief, then to annoyance, and finally to one that he recognized only too well.

This warrior knew that the men who commanded him might not be as decisive and competent as he and his own men. But they still had authority over him.

His expression finally settled for chagrin. He turned to Gelon and nodded.

"It would appear my commander has changed her mind. Please accept my thanks for your gracious attitude and patience."

"It is forgotton," Gelon said graciously, and couldn't resist. "Women are like that, sometimes. Would you like to stay and have lunch?"

"No, no, I think I would like to finish our sweep, and return to my ship, where I know what to expect," he said dryly, looking at the Scoloti settling in around the tables, and all the food and drink that was appearing before them. He shook his head as he gathered his men and left.

Gelon noticed Zard Wan assigning some of his men to accompany them. The Egelv noticed his observing and shrugged. "I don't want a repeat of this, and having my men with them will keep them focused." He winced. "And they will show them where the Hshtahni carcasses are, so they can get them off this ship. They stink."

"They do," Gelon admitted, feeling a relief he wasn't used to. Usually, he relished a good battle, but he knew, even if they'd won here, the consequences would probably be severe, if not terminal. For all of the People on board.

Orik and Opis separated from a group of his tribe members, and approached him, Ariapithes following closely.

"I'm glad you waited for us," Orik commented, and both men laughed and embraced, slapping each other's backs robustly. "Let us eat."

Soon, both families and their swordmasters were sitting at the table slightly removed from the rest, eating, but most of them looking grim.

"I do not think the Egelv are as unified as we thought," Scyles said thoughtfully, and Gelon nodded in agreement.

"Aye, we have allies in Zard Win and Shae Apon, and many of the crew of Captain Rost Foss's ship, but as a people, I think they are not all in agreement on many things," Myrina said, and Gelon smiled his approval at her.

She frowned at him.

"Don't give me that 'come to bed' smile, dear husband, after your comment about women being like that," she said tartly, and slugged his arm with a balled fist.

"You heard that?" Gelon asked, dismayed. He had been teasing the Egelv, and knew his wife too well to ever say something like that to her. "I was…" He stopped as Myrina started laughing. He snorted and turned his attention to his drink.

"So, we are going to meet their emperor?" Scyles asked, and Gelon heard doubt in his voice.

"You think that was a lie?" he asked, and Scyles shook his head.

"No, not if Zard Win said it, I don't." He looked grim. "But I don't think the Egelv are all fighting with the same battle plan. I don't know what it is, but there is something off. And I can't see what."

"Don't stay awake nights, worrying it," Myrina said. "The answers will appear to you when it is their time."

"He can stay awake nights, as long as he's using the time wisely," Arga said casually, and Gelon almost snorted his drink. Scyles' shy, young wife, had a bawdy side to her, and he appreciated her sense of humor. It reminded him of the relationship he and Myrina shared.

"Zard Win said that ship could have as many as three hundred or more soldiers on it," Scyles said, and Gelon frowned, looking over at Targitai, questioningly. His swordmaster shrugged.

"Perhaps we should bring some more warriors out of the pods, not letting the Egelv know," Targitai said.

Gelon looked at Myrina. She nodded.

"Opis, Arga and I have all assisted bringing people out of what they call stasis, and we know how to do it ourselves, as long as there are no complications," she admitted.

"We will wait, and see if anything becomes clearer," Gelon said slowly, thinking it through. "One or two warriors, no one will notice. But any significant number, and at the very least, Shae Apon, and probably Zard Win, will know."

"We should have some of the small children watch the new Egelv, see if they try to do anything they shouldn't," Orik said, and Gelon nodded.

"Good idea." He picked up his mug, and the other king did the same. "May our new friends, remain our friends. And may we find good fortune when we reach this planet of the Egelv."

Everyone at the table drank, but Gelon noticed there were few cheerful expressions.

Zard Win paced the floor of their work room, and Shae Apon watched him with interest. He impressed her in so many ways. She knew that should be a cause for concern, but she had already decided she didn't care. A union with him was impossible, but the more they worked together, the less those things mattered to her.

But that was a problem for another day, she decided.

"We're only four days from Egelv Prime," Zard Win said, and Shae Apon couldn't resist.

"From the system, but five days to reach an orbit around Prime," she corrected him gently.

"Right," he said, not really reacting to that, and she suspected he hadn't even heard what she'd said. He was totally focused on the current situation.

"There was something so strange, and so wrong, about today, with the soldiers," he said, and for the hundredth time, she regretted missing the confrontation. "I can't see what it is, but there was something that happened, or that I saw today, that I don't understand."

"But you don't know what it was," she said, not asking a question, and he nodded.

"Exactly," he said. "How is the mail armor for Scyles coming along?"

She got it out of the box she kept the loose materials for the construction in, and showed him.

"I'm almost done, and I would like to have him try it on, to see if it fits him properly."

Zard Win looked at it closely, and she could tell he was impressed. Then he looked up at her, excitement filling his face.

"Want to see what I've been working on?" he asked, and she nodded, enjoying his enthusiasm. He was like a little boy, and she liked him this way, very much.

He went to his personal bag and pulled a sheathed knife out of it.

"I'm making two, if he thinks this one works well enough," Zard Win said, and pulled the knive slowly out of the sheath.

She stared at a very slim, double-edged knife with almost no handle to speak of. The point looked very sharp, as did the edges.

"Don't you need some sort of hilt, so his hand won't slide up onto the blade?" she asked, and he shook his head vigorously.

"These are throwing knives," Zard Win said, and hefted it before handing it to her.

Shae Apon was surprised by how light it was. She could tell the blade was a bit heavier than the handle end, and looking closely, she saw that it seemed very sharp.

"And it's really only one molecule?" she asked wonderingly. "How were you able to expand the size of the molecule without losing the strength, durability, and cohesion?"

"I used the same techniques we used for the plate armor," Zard Win said. "It took a few attempts before I think I got it right. And a few more before I figured out how to make it with the blade and point already sharpened. Thank Gar I solved the brittle factor with the platelets, and it's just a matter of manipulating the molecule."

"I wonder if the military already have blades like this?" she said, and he shook his head.

"I don't think so," he said, and grinned. "The only reason I thought of it, was when I saw Targitai's armor that day. It looked so heavy on him, and the jacket it's attached to is a coarse, heavy material. I bet in the hot season, fighters would drop from over-heating. And that led to the knife."

"Scyles is going to have the most advanced weaponry his race has ever seen," Shae Apon said, and Zard Win grinned at her.

"I was thinking about those wooden shields they have," he began, and Shae Apon gasped.

"That would be one huge molecule, if you were successful," she said, and he smiled at her, his hands on her arms.

"If we're successful," he said, correcting her. "We've been doing this together. It's your background in science that helped me past some pitfalls. This was a team effort."

He seemed to suddenly realize he was holding her arms, and that they were very close. He released her and, looking for something to change the direction of their focus, took the knife from her, and threw it at the wall.

His throw was wobbly, but the point hit first, and she was shocked to see it sink a third of its length into the wall.

They looked at each other in awe, and she wanted to jump up and down, scream, kiss him, or, or what? Kiss him? Where did that thought come from?

Shae Apon knew she was on new ground on so many levels right now. The single molecule technology, the application of it for the chain mail and the knife.

And, she thought with trepidation, her feelings for Zard Apon.

She tried to think of something, anything, to say, to get their minds away from each other. She glanced at the knife, and grinned at him.

"Can I try?"

Chapter Twenty-Five

Zard Win leaned back and stared at his computer. It currently showed the bridge of the Muschwain. Currently, there were two crewmen manning the monitor systems. Theoretically, he was the officer on duty, but since there were no functioning engines, all weapon systems were down, the skeleton crew was responsible for making sure the power stayed on, and the atmospheric system was operating properly.

And the water recirculation system, he thought with a smirk.

"What is so funny?" Shae Apon asked, and he turned to her with a smile. He was glad she'd shifted some of her belongings to a crew cabin next to the one he was using. It meant they spent even more time together. She was going through the pod data, checking all the shifting around the two queens had done.

Amazingly enough, they were well over half way done with their task. Most of the Caitiari had been moved into four of the stasis holds, along with a good number of the sheep. Both the Auchatae and the Paralatae had a complete hold, and when finished, the balance of their numbers would split a third hold, along with the personal horses of those not in stasis.

Both he and Shae Apon had seen when Scyles found his stallion, and had been shocked to see the young man fight off tears of joy.

"I was there at his birth," Scyles had admitted, and accepted a hug from his wife. Arga, on the other hand, had been noncommittal about her own mount when they found it, and moved it next to Earth Runner. Yet she'd shown excitement when a red filly named Scarlet Sky, which Scyles had brought for her to ride on their first true 'date', had been found. It earned a spot between the other two horses.

His thoughts returned to the present as he saw Shae Apon patiently awaiting his answer.

"I was checking on the bridge crew, and it reminded me how important it is we keep the water recycling system operating at full capacity," he admitted, and she gave a peal of laughter.

A double knock sounded on the door, and they looked at each other guiltily.

"We speak of them, and they appear," Zard Win muttered, and she laughed again, more quietly this time.

The door opened and Scyles looked in.

"Everyone dressed?" he asked in an innocent tone.

Both Zard Win and Shae Apon immediately began to talk, assuring him that they were working, and that there was nothing inappropriate happening.

Scyles looked amused.

"For two very educated, sophisticated higher life forms, as you call it, both of you are easily flustered," he pointed out, and entered the room. "You wanted to show me something?"

Zard Win looked at Shae Apon, and she opened a drawer in her work area and pulled out the linked mail jerkin they'd been working on.

"We're not quite finished, but we want you to try it on and see if we have your correct size," she said, and held it up for Scyles to see.

"Oh, this is the same type of material you showed me before," Scyles said, and took it from her.

He held it up in front of him, and whistled under his breath at the lightness of it.

"And this is as strong as what you had me try to destroy?"

"It is," Zard Win said. "Try it on. It goes underneath your tunic."

Scyles nodded and quickly stripped to the waist. He held the jerkin and looked for the fasteners to undo it so he could slip into it.

"You have to pull it over your head," Shae Apon said, and Zard Win glanced at her. Her voice sounded strained, and he saw she was trying to avert her eyes. He stifled a laugh and turned back to Scyles.

"It should be flexible enough to pull over your head," he told the young Scoloti. "We didn't want it to open, because it might leave an area a blade or arrow could fit into."

Scyles nodded as he pulled it down to cover most of his torso. He played with the small platelets, seeing how much they would shift. Not much, Zard Win knew.

"It should deflect any blade, and even an arrow shouldn't be able to slip between the platelets," Shae Apon said. "But there is enough flex in the shirt that it shouldn't hinder your movements."

Scyles lightly ran his fingers down the front until they reached the end of the platelets, and felt the smooth cloth, wonderingly.

"It's so soft," he said, and Zard Win saw he was deciding if the platelets stopped too soon, leaving his midrift vulnerable.

"It's not finished," Zard Win said, and looked at Shae Apon. "We wanted to see how it fell on you. We want the platelets to cover you far enough, but not bunch up under your belt."

"It fits me well," Scyles admitted.

"You will probably not fight large, pitched battles, but being able to be armored without it being obvious will give you an advantage in tight quarters, or if you are ambushed."

"We could also make you a larger one, that will act as your kurga, should you wish it," Shae Apon said, hesitantly. "But it will take longer, and we'll have to learn what material to use for the kurga, and how to blend the platelets with it."

"And you would probably need assistance to put it on," Zard Win said apologetically. "It will be bulkier, and less flexible."

"I have a wife," Scyles said, grinning, and they all laughed.

"She may want one as well," Shae Apon pointed out, and Scyles laughingly agreed.

"Oh, she most certainly will," he agreed.

"How many knives do you carry?" Zard Win asked suddenly, not wanting to forget something he wanted to check.

Scyles hesitated, and Zard Win realized he'd unwittingly asked a very personal question that almost no Scoloti would ask another.

"It doesn't matter," he began, and Scyles shook his head and pulled out the two knives he almost always had strapped to his thighs. He handed one to Zard Win, who took it gingerly.

It was a vicious looking blade, with a slight haft. It was double-edged, and the point was like a needle. They were heavy, and clearly meant for close fighting. He supposed they were designed to do as much damage as possible, as quickly as possible.

He handed it back to Scyles, and looked at the younger man's soft boots. The Scoloti seemed surprised he knew about those, but with one motion, the original two knives disappeared back into their sheaths, and he leaned over farther and pulled two more blades out.

As he straightened, Scyles twirled both of them, spinning them so fast, it was difficult to see either knife clearly. Abruptly, the knives stopped, one gripped with the blade extended, the other reversed, so a swung fist would also drag the blade across a foe.

Scyles extended the second knife to him, handle first. It was lighter than the first two knives, but heavier than he expected, and he frowned. He looked at Scyles.

"You usually throw these, correct?"

Scyles nodded, looking amused.

"The weight is important?" Zard Win asked, and Scyles nodded.

"It helps the knife fly true, and will make a deeper impact when it strikes my target," he said, and cocked his head to the side. "Why?"

"I've been working on something else," Zard Win admitted, and removed his prototype from another drawer. "It's from the same material as the platelets."

"That would make it too light to penetrate, or even fly true," Scyles said, and took the offered blade. His eyes widened as he hefted it, checking the balance.

"The center is a little too far back in the handle, and it's too light to penetrate," he said, spinning it around. "But it's very nice. And sharp."

Shae Apon picked up a thick square of Polic root, and carried it to the far wall. It was still too close for a serious test, but it would have to do for now. She grunted as she went to hang it on the wall.

Zard Win moved to help her, but Scyles was faster. He seemed to glide across the room and took it out of her hands before she even knew he was helping her. He lifted it, frowning as he tried to see how it would attach. He stopped, lowered the Polic root, and looked at two holes in the wall, one much bigger than the other. He looked back at them and grinned.

"It looks like they do fly true," he said as he lifted the block back up. He blinked as it seemed to leap out of his hands to attach itself to the wall. He stared at it a moment, then turned to them, a questioning look on his face.

"Magnetic plates on the back, attach to more plates on the wall," Zard Win said, and resisted the urge to laugh at his expression.

"I will introduce you to magnetism at your next class," Shae Apon said, and Scyles nodded.

"Next class?" Zard Win asked, surprised.

"I'm trying to give some of them a crash course in technology, before we reach Egelv Prime," Shae Apon said, and looked sad. "I'm not sure we'll be able to see them much, if ever, after that, so I'm trying to prepare them any way I can."

"Brilliant," Zard Win said in wonder.

"Let us hope our paths stay on the same trail," Scyles said wistfully. "I have grown to enjoy our time together, and call you my friends."

"As do we, Scyles," Shae Apon said, stepping closer to Zard Win to give him space to throw. "As do we both."

"She speaks the truth," Zard Win said, trying to form his words into the structure their language seemed to lean towards.

Scyles nodded, and quickly turned, throwing one of his own knives. It stuck firmly into the Polic root block, slightly to the right of center.

"As you see, the weight of the blade and handle give it more strength to sink into the target," he said as he threw the second. It mirrored the first, slightly to the left, this time.

"I can compensate a little, but this blade is actually a little smaller, and much lighter, so it will not fly as true, or kill as easily."

The mono-molecular knife flew out of his hand and stuck firmly into the block, a little above dead center.

Scyles seemed surprised at the result, and walked over to the wall to inspect the blade. He pulled it out, and seemed surprised at the strength it took. He inspected the blade closely, and hefted it, his eyes never leaving it.

"Could you make it the same length as these blades, move the center back a little, and add any weight at all, and perhaps a hint of a hilt?"

"I could," Zard Win said, trying not to get too excited. "It would probably increase the width of the blade by about half, but it would add some weight, mostly right where you want it. Could I keep one of your blades for a day or so?"

Scyles hesitated.

"I freely trust you with my most prized weapons, but I fear I can not part with either, at this moment."

"Something wrong?" Shae Apon asked curiously, and Scyles grimaced.

"Perhaps, perhaps not," he admitted. "Something about the new guards makes my hair lift every time we pass on the concourse. I sense something ominous about them, but could not tell you what."

"I feel the same way, and feel threatened by them, for some reason," Shae Apon admitted, looked at Zard Win. She misinterpreted his look to be skepticism. "I just do!"

"No, no, I agree with both of you," Zard Win said, and realized he hadn't really noticed it until they brought it to his attention. "I don't trust them, but they're imperial troops, some of the best fighters in the universe, and we should feel safer with them aboard.

"I'm afraid I do not share your view," Scyles said slowly, and finally looked at Zard Win slyly. "Especially your assessment of their fighting skills."

They all laughed at that. The Scoloti didn't try to hide their pride in their fighting prowess. They had fought the finest empires on their world to a standstill, time and time again. A few hundred soldiers that relied too heavily on their magic weapons didn't frighten them at all.

"I'll scan and weigh one of your blades, Scyles," Zard Win said, and Scyles handed one of them over. "That should give me everything I need to work off of."

Scyles nodded and looked Shae Apon, and then at him.

"You know, Shae Apon, if you get nervous, there is a door between your new sleeping quarters and Zard Win's." He grinned at them. "Perhaps you should leave that unfastened, or even open, for safety's sake."

Zard Win carefully didn't look at Shae Apon as he went to scan the blade.

"Swordmaster, I wish to focus on my sword-fighting," Arga said, and Ariapithes stared at her.

"Princess, I taught you the basics of swordplay when you first began your training," he said, and she could see she'd surprised him. "I would council you to work on your archery skills, and not let the enemy get within swords-length of you."

"I practice my archery every day," she replied tartly. "My husband is the finest archer of the People, and he can point out any bad habits I acquire. But in close quarters, I need more skills to protect myself and my unborn son."

"You're with child?" Ariapithes said, and stepped back to give her a hard look. "And you pray to the gods for a son, but can't know for sure, until the birthing."

"I think I am with child," Arga insisted, and felt her face heat up. "Gods know we've done our part often enough since our marriage to fill a raiding party. And Shae Apon says that soon, she will be able to perform a test to see if I'm pregnant, and whether it is a warrior or warrioress."

She saw Skulis enter the giant hold, walking with a young girl. He could tell by the way they walked together that they'd had sex. She felt an irrational bit of jealousy. She'd only married Scyles a moon ago, and Skulis was already over her and had found someone else!

She saw it was Agave, from Scyles' tribe. She remembered hearing their mothers talking about possible choices for Skulis, and her name had been mentioned by Queen Myrina.

But, this quickly, and this seriously?

She turned back to the swordmaster, and saw he was watching her closely, and probably correctly interpreting her thoughts. She drew her long blade, and he reluctantly drew his own. She slapped her sword against her shield, and he did the same, and they engaged.

Ariapithes didn't try to press her, but let her try the moves she knew, easily blocking her blows, countering her attacks.

"What, you expected to get to have them both?" he asked shrewdly, and laughed when she shook her head violently, and renewed her assault. "Oh, you're just mad because he's not still pining for you."

Arga cried out and renewed her attack, actually surprising him with her ferocity. He turned her blade away, time and time again, until she wore down, and struggled to get a deep breath. She finally stopped for a moment, and stood facing him, still in a defensive position. He'd taught her that lesson years ago, and if one looked at her back cheeks, bared, the hairs-width scar from his sword not quite swatting her squarely was still visible.

She remembered Scyles laughing so hard his ribs hurt when he saw the scar and found out how she got it.

Arga grinned at the swordmaster, and shrugged.

"I am a princess. I'm supposed to get anything I want."

He guffawed, and then was backing away, using his considerable skills to counter her sudden assault.

Arga grinned again, showing her teeth, as she kept the pressure on him.

Chapter Twenty-Six

"Captain, we have entered the home system, and Egelv Prime Traffic Command is requiring we respond to their hailing," Second Officer Rel Steen called out.

Rost Fott sighed and nodded. Rel Steen nodded to him, and he faced the main screen in front of him.

"Egelv Prime Traffic Command, this is Captain Rost Fott, of the Egelv Destroyer Mountain Edge, towing generation ship Muschwain, previously of the Hshtahni Dominion. We request orbit parking instructions for the Muschwain. It currently has no propulsion abilities, and will require a tow."

A female Egelv officer appeared on the screen and smiled at him apologetically. He didn't remember having seen her before, but she was stunningly beautiful, even in uniform.

"Mountain Edge, I've been instructed to inform you that you're performing the tow more than adequately, and you will receive instructions on where to place your salvage into orbit. You will remain on station with the Muschwain, providing logistical aid until further notice."

She leaned forward, and gave him a sympathetic smile.

"Sorry, Captain Rost Fott. It appears the upper ranks wish you to continue your current responsibilities regarding the generation ship's contents." She shrugged. "The price you pay for doing a good job, it appears."

"I have the coordinates for our orbit, Captain," Rel Steen said quietly, and the woman on the screen nodded.

"It is a pity you won't be docking here, Captain," she said, her voice softer now. "I would have enjoyed hearing the story of your voyage in person. Captain Lans Pre out."

The screen changed to a view of the orbiting station, and Rost Fott blinked.

Her invitation to contact her couldn't have been clearer, and wasn't the reaction he usually got when meeting attractive women. His dedication to his ship and crew before all else didn't exactly make him prime partner material, either for romantic or upward mobility purposes.

"Where are they putting us?" he asked Rel Steen idly, and nodded as the projected orbit appeared on his personal screen.

Mountain Edge was to bring the Muschwain into an orbit outside the orbits of the two moons, Migain and Fluen. It was about what he'd expected, but he really thought he was going to finally be clear of being responsible for the Muschwain.

"Captain, Raging River is requesting a docking valve for Commodore Mit Obet," Rel Steen said, and Rost Fott sighed.

"Take care of it, and have services bring some refreshments to our conference room," he said, and stood. He had enough time to slip into a fresh uniform. He wouldn't want to look sloppy for the commodore.

Thirty minutes later, Rost Fott sat at the table in the conference room, sipping hot T'Clomo, watching the commodore cautiously. Van Dono was also present, which surprised him, since his first officer was off duty, and he hadn't requested his presence.

They sipped in silence for a minute. Courtesies observed, the commodore set his cup down, and both he and Van Dono followed suit.

"Thank you for meeting me on such short notice," he started, and Rost Fott resisted the urge to raise an eyebrow questioningly. It wasn't as if he had any choice when his superior officer requested a meeting. He glanced at Van Dono, but his eyes were on the commodore.

Thoughtful, he turned back to Mit Obet.

"I will be going planet-side shortly, and I plan to request an opportunity to present the Scoloti to the Emperor," he said, watching Rost Fott close for his reaction.

He was surprised. An introduction to the emperor was a rare event, and he wondered what had sparked this idea.

"I know, it's highly irregular," the commodore said, laughing a little. "But we've only recently crossed paths with the Hshtahni, and technically, the Scoloti have had more contact with them than any Egelv."

"Other than a very brief introduction, the contact was mostly the Scoloti killing them and their Mba underlings," Rost Fott said dryly. "I don't think they had much opportunity to talk."

"Heh, I suppose you're right," the commodore nodded his head to show his appreciation of his humor. "In any case, the Scoloti are a singularly unique case, and deciding their fate isn't something to rush into. Any contact with the emperor could pave the path for a positive fate."

Commodore Mit Obet leaned back in his chair.

"Can you perhaps have them wear their finest clothing, and make sure everything has been radiated and cleaned?" He smiled thinly. "Emperor Balco Deh is a bit of an eccentric, and dirty, unkempt attire or personal hygiene will make him want to flee."

"How many of the Scoloti did you have in mind?" Rost Fott said thoughtfully. "You don't mean everyone that isn't in stasis?"

"Oh, spirits no," the commodore grimaced, even while shuddering at the idea. "Just the royal family, or families," he corrected himself. "There are two, or three tribes, all with kings and their families?"

"One king and his men had to be put into stasis, you'll recall," Rost Fott admitted.

"Oh, I remember him," the commodore laughed, and nodded. "So, none of his people are walking around, causing mischief?"

"No, we stunned all of them," Rost Fott said, and the commodore nodded, satisfied.

"Ambushed them, did you?" he said, looking at Rost Fott slyly.

"I did," Rost Fott admitted. "With the assistance and blessing of both the other kings."

"Well, good then," the commodore said, and stood. Rost Fott and Van Dono immediately got to their feet as well. "So, the members of the two royal families, maybe a guard or two to make them feel comfortable and safe."

The commodore turned to leave, then swung back around.

"Captain, make sure they have their weapons with them. A demonstration of their skills might entertain the emperor. He loves that sort of thing. It might help with deciding their fate."

"A new race having their weapons when they have their first audience with the emperor?" Rost Fott asked, shocked. "I can't believe his personal guard would authorize such a thing. Or that the emperor himself would allow it!"

"Well, they have, and since I don't believe you've had the honor of meeting the emperor in person, you have no idea what he likes or allows," Commodore Mit Obet said blithely. "Tell them to polish their swords, or whatever, to make them look as impressive as possible."

Rost Fott was preoccupied all the way to the airlock. Van Dono came with them as well, and after the lock closed, and separated from Mountain Edge, he turned to his first officer.

"Well, this is highly irregular," he said, and Van Dono nodded his agreement. Rost Fott looked at him curiously.

"How did you know about the meeting?" he asked. "You were off duty."

"I saw one of the duty officers in the corridor, and they told me what was happening." Van Dono shrugged sheepishly. "I thought I should be there. The more he sees my face, the more he might remember me at an opportune moment, sometime in the future."

Rost Fott couldn't fault his logic, and nodded.

"Well, good that you were there, then," he said. "If nothing else, having you witness he insisted on their being armed is comforting."

"What could go wrong?" Van Dono said, and grinned at him. Rost Fott was surprised at the jocular mood of his First. They'd never really bonded closely. Perhaps the unique nature of this last mission had opened the door for a more personal relationship. It would be nice to have a first officer he felt comfortable confiding in.

His mind came back to the pending introduction, and he winced.

"What could go wrong, indeed?" he asked himself as he made his way back to the bridge.

Shae Apon looked through the diagnostics for the pods, and was glad to see all were functioning properly. They weren't of Egelv origin, and when it came to medical equipment, she was very particular. Glancing over the readjusted map of locations and contents, she was amazed at how much the Scoloti had accomplished in such a short time. She'd intended to oversee the process of sorting and grouping the pods for the three tribes, and livestock.

It quickly became clear to her it would be a laborious process and, considering her limited free time, would take time to accomplish. But the queens and princess, with their stable of helpers, had identified all ten thousand pods, and were in the final stage of shifting them around.

A double knock on the door startled her. She didn't have anyone scheduled, and if it was Zard Win, he would have just called her on her transponder, as would the ship.

She looked at the screen and saw it was the subjects of her recent thoughts. Arga stood in front of the door, and was flanked by her mother, Queen Opis, as well as Queen Myrina.

"Please come in," she said, and they all flinched and their hand went instinctively to their ear. The door slid open and they entered cautiously, looking around the room she'd transformed into a clinic.

"Welcome to my office, ladies," Shae Apon said, and realized they almost certainly didn't know what an office was. "Welcome to my medical clinic, queens and princess."

They all smiled and nodded, although Arga looked very nervous.

"Princess Arga is very interested in knowing if you've divined whether she is with child or not," Queen Myrina said, and Queen Opis nodded her agreement, putting her arm around her daughter's waist.

"You'd think it was her first," she said innocently, and both women laughed. Arga smiled, but Shae Apon saw the strain in her face. She decided to quit torturing them. But the calm lack of curiosity in both the queens had her puzzled.

"So, neither of you are curious?" she asked, looked from one queen to the other, and back.

"I know I am with child," Queen Myrina said confidently. "And I believe it to be a girl."

"What makes you say that?" Shae Apon asked curiously. She was taken aback a little at the woman's confident manner.

"Because I know the kick of a baby boy," she said, and Queen Opis nodded. "I swear they arrive running, and don't stop until the midwives pull them out."

"Which is how I know mine is a boy," Opis said. "He may be very tiny at this point, but he's already swinging an axe inside me."

Both queens laughed, and Shae Apon saw that Arga had no such past experiences to draw upon, and was watching them joke with growing impatience.

"I would like to hear my results," Arga said in a strained voice. "If you would, please."

"I'm sorry, Arga," Shae Apon said contritely. "We're being cruel." She nodded to both older women.

"You both have it right, a boy," she said, looking at Opis, and shifted her gaze to Myrina. "And a girl."

"What about me?" Arga cried out, and Shae Apon flinched.

"You're with child, and it will be a boy," she hurriedly said.

"Only one? We were hoping for twins," Myrina said and Opis laughed.

"Maybe you were," Arga said darkly, but then her excitement and happiness won out.

Her smile was beautiful, Shae Apon thought, watching her seem to glow as she hugged her natural mother, then her new one. She put her hands on her stomach, as if she could feel the baby, but of course, it was far too early for that.

"Can Scyles and I still have sex without it hurting the baby?" Arga asked anxiously, and both mothers burst into laughter.

"For a girl that was a virgin before your marriage, you seem to have welcomed that duty without reservations," Opis said, nudging Myrina.

"I really, really enjoy it, and don't consider it a duty at all." Her eyes gleamed with mischief as she looked at Myrina. "Scyles is very good at pleasing me, while performing his duties. Very good, yes," she said, her eyes softening for a moment, and then the mischief returned. "Would you like details?" she asked, and Shae Apon flinched as they both nodded their heads vigorously.

"You would?" Arga asked, taken aback.

"You thought that would embarrass us?" Myrina asked incredulously. She put her arm around Opis and gestured towards the door. "Let's go get full tankards, and you can tell us everything the two of you did, in detail."

"In detail," Opis agreed, and they turned towards the door.

Shae Apon remembered a previous conversation she'd had with Arga and winced.

"Ladies, before you go, may I tell you something?" she said, her mind racing on how to say what needed saying without losing their faith in her.

"Would you like to come with us?" Opis asked, and winked. "From what I can tell, our bodies are similar enough, that her stories will probably interest you as much as they do us."

"Well, thank you for asking, but I am on duty," Shae Apon said, stalling, trying to keep herself from blushing. From the looks the two mothers gave her, and then each other, she thought they could read her body language far too well. She hurriedly continued.

"I told Princess Arga that we've found that drinking alcohol while with child can lead to health issues for the child later on," she said slowly. "And I know your people enjoy smoking and consuming a mild drug called cannabis or hemp. I analyzed the plant, and it contains a drug that can affect the health and development of the unborn child."

"Scoloti women have always smoked hemp," Myrina challenged her. "It has always been that way."

"Do you have many cases of stillborn children?" Shae Apon asked softly, and blanched as both Myrina and Arga turned to look at Opis. The woman looked crestfallen, and her eyes began to fill. She fought the tears, and held them back, but was clearly shaken.

"There are some, and always have been," she said, her voice weak, but rebellious.

"I must tell you," Shae Apon said, very quietly, and as inoffensively as she could. "Your race is strong and healthy by nature. Barring some sort of genetic flaw, stillborns should be extremely unusual with a healthy female, and no obvious defects in the father."

"But we are different races," Opis said, but her pain was clear to see, despite her words. "Sometimes the babies are just not strong enough, or the gods have found them either unfit, or have another purpose for them."

"I do not intend to insult or offend you," Shae Apon said carefully. "But the gods tend to leave the baby-making to the parents. May I ask if you've had a still-born child? I mean no offense," she rushed to say.

"You make no offense," Opis said weakly. She blinked back tears, and Myrina swept her into her arms, hugging her close, letting her release her tears on her shoulder. Arga stood next to them, then slowly put her arms around them both, and leaned her head against her mother's shoulder.

"Two," Myrina said quietly to Shae Apon. She clearly shared the pain of her friend. "She had two, before Arga. Both would have been boys."

"Orik and I were living life," Opis said, slowly pulling herself away from the other two women. "He was not yet king, and we knew that our lives would soon become very complicated and we would need to be more responsible. We smoked and drank constantly, even as I was with child, both times."

"We all do, dear friend," Myrina said, consolingly. "Our people have always celebrated life every day we could. If we had drink, we drank it. If we had hemp, we smoked it, or sweated in the steam of it, or cooked it into our food."

"We have always done this," Opis agreed, and Shae Apon knew she would see the pain in the woman for a long time to come.

"Did you smoke when you carried Arga?" Shae Apon asked, realizing the young girl was as healthy a specimen as any young girl she'd ever seen, of any race.

"Before I became pregnant with her, the hemp began making me cough," Opis said slowly. "My throat was always sore, so I stopped smoking." She looked startled. "And I found that drink was making my morning sickness worse, so I barely drank while I carried her, either."

"Mama, I…" Arga started to speak, but stopped, as if not knowing what to say.

"Praise Demeter I did," Opis said fervently. "It must have been her doing, to allow me a daughter that rivals the gods for her beauty."

"Hardly, Mama," Arga said, blushing furiously, but looking pleased at her words.

Myrina looked at Shae Apon with a serious expression on her face.

"Friend Shae Apon, do you attest what you've told us to be true, not simply an attempt to frighten us into following your instructions?"

Shae Apon was startled, and on the verge of being annoyed at the question. Then she realized how she'd shaken their core of beliefs of allowable behavior.

"I do attest that everything I've told you, or advised you, to be true. These are well-known medical facts to us, and I advise you because I wish you only the best." Shae Apon sighed. "I am sorry my words have caused so much pain."

"But you may have saved many future lives," Myrina said, and the other two women nodded.

314

"I will follow your instructions, Shae Apon," Arga said boldly, and a tiny smile broke on her face. "As it happens, I don't appear to have my parent's ability to drink and stay conscious, so this is not a difficult decision for me."

Both mothers nodded in agreement, and the mood lightened some, much to Shae Apon's relief.

"I will, as well," Opis said heavily. "If I were to ignore your advice and give birth to another stillborn, I do not think I could live with that shame."

"We will do it together," Myrina said, and they hugged.

Shae Apon sighed in relief, and tried to change the subject.

"This is your first child, Arga," she said, looking at the young girl. "How old are you?"

"I have seen fifteen gatherings," Arga said proudly, and Shae Apon blinked.

"You're only fifteen?" Shae Apon tried to hide her shock. "In our culture, that would be considered very young to be married and a mother."

"Your people don't live on the steppes," Myrina said tartly, and Opis nodded, her mood lightening by the minute. "We must start everything as soon as we can, because we will leave too soon, and have much to do first."

"Fifteen doesn't give a girl much of a childhood," Shae Apon mused, and both mothers laughed.

"Yes, she is still developing, physically, and will be shocked at how large her teats are by the time she gives birth," Opis said, smiling at her daughter, who looked down at her modest breasts in doubt. "But I married Orik and became pregnant at the same age."

"As did I," Myrina said, and laughed at the expression on Opis' face. "Except it was to Gelon, not Orik."

"Right," Opis continued, and shrugged. "If she didn't marry now, she would grow curious and experiment with some of boys her age anyway. In fact, I'm surprised she didn't earlier."

"I did, but just the once, with a girl," Arga said, leaning toward Shae Apon, as if telling her in confidence. "It was pleasant enough, but I found I desired my mate to have more between the legs."

"As did I, new daughter," Myrina said, and Opis shrugged.

"I liked women quite well enough, that if I hadn't met Orik, I would probably have a woman mate, and be satisfied with her." She looked around at them with a leer. "Women don't shrivel up when you want them the most. Shae Apon, can I safely assume you are more attracted to men than women?"

"I...am not attracted to women that way," Shae Apon hurried to say. "Nothing wrong with it. A certain percentage of our population is sexually attracted to the same sex."

"Oh, right," Myrina said, looking amused. "You forget, Opis. Shae Apon is with Zard Win. She definitely prefers men."

"We're not 'with' each other," Shae Apon said, feeling her face heat up. "I mean, we're not, I've never..." She stopped, aghast with herself for having slipped. She liked these new friends very much, but they could be merciless when teasing.

"You've never?" Opis said, her shock easy to see. She looked at Shae Apon closely. "You must be...well, somewhat older than Arga, anyway. And you've never...with anyone?"

All three of the Scoloti began talking at once, and Shae Apon sighed. This day had taken a sudden turn for...for what, she didn't know. But she was pretty sure her slip of the tongue was going to be the cause of much more embarrassment before it became a memory.

Chapter Twenty-Seven

Scyles walked down the concourse, feeling good about life in general. He'd just practiced his archery, and any doubts among the observers in his and Arga's tribe about his being the finest archer in either of their tribes were erased.

He felt a little less secure after a long, hard, sometimes painful session with Skulis, practicing traditional swordplay with shield. He suspected that would never be something he would excel at. At some point, he would unveil his own personal sword-fighting style that Targitai had helped him hone, but it was a skill that best be left unknown for as long as possible. His mentor was sure that once his unorthodox method of swordplay was known, potential enemies would study his style and develop techniques to counteract its effectiveness.

In the meanwhile, he would take the bruises. And who could be sure that someday the gods wouldn't grant him sudden upper-body strength to supplement his natural speed and tactical shrewdness.

He decided he'd earned a cup or two. And then, after dinner, perhaps he and Arga might go back to their quarters and practice baby-making for an hour, or a night. He smiled to himself. Arga had certainly embraced the long, tender, vigorous, sometimes frantic, sometimes teasing, bouts in their sleeping quarters, with a passion that matched his own.

He saw her walking with both their mothers and Shae Apon, about the same time they saw him. His mother's head perked up, and she looked like she was about to call out to him, but Queen Opis took her by the arm, and they disappeared into the common hall.

Arga stared at him, and her jaunty stride changed to a hesitant shuffle as she walked by the common room entrance. Shae Apon stopped at the door, but didn't immediately enter. His wife's eyes were wide, and she opened her mouth to greet him.

"Hello, husband. How was your training?"

Her voice was shaky, and she looked nervous. Shae Apon had a genuine smile on her face, and Scyles looked back and forth between the two of them. Suddenly, with no warning, Arga was in his arms, her face buried in his shoulder. He automatically closed his arms around her, bewildered.

"What is it? What's wrong…?" he started to ask, and immediately knew the answer. He gripped her shoulders and gently pushed her far enough away to see her face. "Are you with child?" He looked at Shae Apon for confirmation. The Egelv woman shrugged her shoulders and went into the common hall.

"I will deliver you a future king, husband," Arga said, and he felt weak in the knees. "Please, Scyles, don't faint like a Persian girl," she teased, and then they were holding each other tightly, their lips planting kisses all over each other's face.

"Are you sure?" Scyles asked hesitantly. "She can tell if it's a boy or girl?"

"She says she can," Arga said, and grinned playfully. "Because of her, we also know you will have a sister, and I will have another brother."

Scyles stared, and staggered. He righted himself, but couldn't quit staring at her.

"All three of you, all pregnant?" he asked, but it wasn't a question, it was a statement of wonder.

"I have another bit of news, and it's not bad, but it is a little disappointing," Arga said, and told him about the issue with alcohol and hemp.

"None until after you've given birth?" Scyles asked, and felt her disappointment. It would have been fun to celebrate their success with a night of serious debauchery, accompanied by copious amounts of fermented mare's milk and time in the sweat tent, wearing nothing more than his wife. But it was what it was.

"You can do it," he said confidently.

"And so can you, dear husband," she said sweetly, and he gawked at her. "Oh, yes, if I'm going more than a year without, so are you."

"A year?" Scyles stared. "Why a year?"

"She said we should not partake until the baby is weaned off my breast milk," Arga said, and Scyles shook his head. It just kept getting…well, worse wasn't the right word. Arduous, stressful, strenuous, felt closer, but not quite right.

They walked into the common room and the room erupted in applause, and cheering.

Both Scyles and Arga were embarrassed, both by all the attention, and the bawdy comments flying around the room.

"Show us how you did it, young lord!" Targitai shouted out, and laughter rang out across the room.

Scyles noticed his parents weren't cheering as much. The four of them were sitting at a table, and it looked like they were arguing, and Scyles knew why. From the look of it, neither Gelon nor Orik thought their abstinence was a required condition, but from the look on both women's faces, Scyles was pretty sure he knew who was going to win this battle.

Like either of them ever had a chance, Scyles thought, amused despite his own situation. He decided to help the resolution settle so there might be something resembling peace in three sleeping quarters tonight.

"Father, Father Orik, I have just found out that we will have the chance to show our love and support for our wives by joining them in their vow of abstinence to guarantee the good health of our as yet-unborn children," Scyles said cheerfully. He made a point of pouring himself a mug of mare's milk, unfermented, and taking a big swig.

"What in Hades are you talking about?" His father didn't quite bellow as he stood up, towering over Scyles. In days past, Scyles would have taken off running at this point, but those days were finished. He was a prince, and soon, a father. And someday, a king. It was time to act the part.

"Are you on their side?" Orik asked, crestfallen. Scyles could see he was counting on numbers, knowing that on their own, their wives would pick them off, one by one, like an assassin archer, hidden in a tree, greeting an enemy scouting party. The only hope they had was strength in numbers, stay together, hold their ground, keep their shields high.

"I want my son to be as strong and healthy as his Gra'Papa, either of them," Scyles said quietly. "I want to hear the sound of his coming into this world, screaming and crying, at the top of his lungs."

Gelon looked at him, and he could see his father knew he'd lost the battle. Next to him, Orik looked like he was in battle shock. He slowly turned to Scyles' father, shaking his head in resignation.

"I don't know which of us will be the Great King," he said, slapping Gelon hard on the shoulder. His father hardly even noticed. "But I damned well know for sure, who will be the next one after us."

"That would be my son," Scyle's mother said, and kissed him on the cheek.

"My husband," Arga said, and slipped under his arm, hugging him around the waist, her other hand on his chest, pressed tight to him.

Targitai stepped forward, hand on his sword, and stared at Scyles. He suddenly wished he was somewhere else. The swordmaster wasn't usually the sentimental type. What could he be going to say?

Targitai cleared his throat, and his solemn expression turned into a grin. "About that demonstration, young lord?"

The room erupted in raucous cheering, and he could feel his wife's shoulders shaking with laughter.

Skulis walked by in front of him, chugging the entire contents of his tankard, his eyes dancing, and Scyles vowed to introduce him to his personal sword style, first opportunity he got.

Zard Win heard the roar of voices and mugs slamming on tables, and several voices singing a song that would have made him blush, if Shae Apon was present. Since she wasn't, he allowed himself to enjoy the bawdiness of the words.

He stepped into the crowded common hall and decided that every single Scoloti not in stasis was in this room, probably drinking. He laughed at the physical impossibility the song was describing in vivid detail, right about the same time he saw Shae Apon sitting with the two queens, holding a mug, and staring into it, as if trying to decide whether drinking it would kill her or not.

Scyles and Arga were sitting next to her, and clearly amused at her indecision. Zard Win made his way around clumps of singing Scoloti to them, and sat down across from Shae Apon. She was talking to several women standing next to her, and they walked away as he approached.

He looked at her quizzically. She looked embarrassed, and yet, very excited. Her eyes almost glowed with energy.

"Surely all this isn't just because Arga is pregnant," he said, and Shae Apon actually smirked at him.

"I believe the Scoloti would celebrate like this for almost any reason," Shae Apon pointed out, and Zard Win had to agree. It had become clear, early on, that the People were a cheerful folk that tried to live life to its fullest. And anything was worth celebrating.

"To give them credit," she continued, and Zard Win watched her, amused. He wondered how much of the alcoholic milk she'd drank. "To give them credit, they're celebrating the union of two royal families, and a pregnant princess that will give birth to a future king of the Auchatae tribe. And to top it off, both queens are also pregnant, Queen Myrina with a girl, and Queen Opis with a boy."

"All three of them managed to get pregnant at the same time," Zard Win mused. "What are the odds of that?"

"About the same as about forty other women all pretty sure they're carrying, as well," Shae Apon said, leaning forward to whisper conspiratorially. "I've been besieged with women wanting to come have me examine them and tell them if they're pregnant, and if so, with what."

Zard Win sat upright, and looked around, doing the math.

"That's close to two thirds of the woman not in stasis," he said slowly, his eyes coming back to her. "How is that even possible?"

"Well, first, they almost certainly aren't all pregnant," Shae Apon admitted. "But it appears it isn't for want of trying. The Scoloti are experiencing a surge in sexual activity."

She shook her head, chagrined. "A rather sustained surge, at that." She looked at him, her face flushed. "It's like we walked into an entertainment establishment full of Albi on leave. Everything they say and do is so charged with sexual energy, it's very, well, almost, it's, it's…"

"Contagious?" Zard Win said, keeping a straight face.

"Yes. I mean, no!" Shae Apon blushed even redder. It made her already dark brown skin a very interesting shade. "No, not contagious," she stammered. "I meant to say…disconcerting."

"Of course you did," Zard Win said, trying to sound sincere. He didn't want her to be so mortified she would feel uncomfortable around him.

"No, of course I did not," she admitted, the flush not abating a bit. She kept her eyes on her hands wrapped around the mug. She suddenly took a drink, and then another, bigger one, shuddered, and set the mug down.

He noticed she didn't let go of it.

"Contagious is the word I was thinking of," she admitted, and furtively looked up at him. "I can't believe how unprofessional I am being, letting the sexual atmosphere of a primitive race affect me."

"Their enthusiasm is very inspiring," Zard Win said, hoping he didn't sound like he was trying to take advantage of her temporary vulnerability. "Everything they do, they jump right in, give it all their attention and do the best possible job they can."

He decided that didn't sound quite like he'd intended, but she seemed to find solace with his words. He tried to find another topic to try to shift the conversation. He nodded at her mug.

"How do you like fermented mare's milk?" he asked, and she shuddered, even as she smiled.

"It's horrible," she admitted, then made a face. "But, somehow, it seems the appropriate drink for the occasion." She grinned at him, and he was glad to see she seemed to be recovering her self-confidence. "You wouldn't believe how upset they were when I told them they should abstain from alcohol and hemp until they've weaned the child off breastfeeding."

"I didn't think of that," Zard Win admitted. He looked at her hands clenched tightly around the mug. She saw his gaze, and her face started to flush a little again.

"Want some?" she said brightly, pushing it across the table at him.

He put both hands out to block the cup, and they closed around hers, still holding the mug. They both froze, staring at each other.

"Lady Shae Apon, we'd like to come see you tomorrow, if you've time, to see if we're carrying a new brat," a Scoloti woman said, and the two women behind her nodded.

All three of them looked at Zard Win's hands closed around Shae Apon's, and the cup.

"We don't want to interrupt your own celebrating," the woman said, and all three of them grinned widely at the two Egelv. "Can we come to your meeting room by your sleeping quarters? We could wait until after the midday, so we don't intrude on the two of you."

Both Zard Win and Shae Apon began protesting they weren't sleeping together, and the women watched them gleefully, even as they listened to the hurried disclaimers.

When they wound down, the woman leaned forward and whispered at a volume that would have carried across the room, if everyone else around them weren't talking, singing, and generally being loud.

"Look, don't worry your heads if your rules or laws say you can't roll around together in private," she said, and continued before either of them could respond. "Your secret is safe with us. It's not as if you're about to go into battle, or one of you is royalty, and the other's a farmer. It's clear how you feel about each other, and rolling in the bed sheets is to be expected."

She winked at them, and turned to Shae Apon.

"We won't come by too early," she promised, and the three woman turned and blended into the crowd.

"We're not..." Zard Win started to call after them, and Shae Apon squeezed his hands and shushed him. He looked down, startled. He hadn't realized they were still holding hands around the cup.

"The more we protest, the more certain they are," Shae Apon said, sounding resigned.

"I'm sorry," Zard Win apologized, wondering if she was about to retreat, both back to their ship, and away from him. The thought depressed him.

"Don't be, Zard Win," she said, and squeezed his hands again. She smiled at him, a little hesitantly. "There are many worse fates I could suffer than being in a relationship with you."

Zard Win blinked, and stared at her.

"What are you saying?" he asked softly, not daring to hope.

Shae Apon didn't answer right away. She stared at the mug, and he tried to curb his impatience, and wait for her response.

"I don't know," she finally said. She suddenly looked shy, which was very out of character for her. "I know what concerns you, and I know it is valid, according to societal mores and customs. But I don't know that I care about any of that."

She met his eyes boldly.

"I truly don't know what I think right now," she admitted, shaking her head. "But what my family might think, or how some people might view our actions, is very low on my list of concerns."

"You mean…" Zard Win wanted to ask, but was terrified it might cause a result he didn't want.

"I mean I don't know," Shae Apon said, pulling her hands and the mug free of his hands, and took a healthy swig. She winced, then took another smaller sip. "But, in my mind, nothing is off the table. I am here to work, to break new ground on studying and assisting a young race to learn to survive the plight they're in. Any sort of relationship was never part of my plans."

She smiled apologetically at him as several more women approached. But her words were sure and firm.

"But as I said, nothing is off the table. I enjoy your company, and would miss you if our ways parted." She smiled. "Now, let me do my work with these women, and we will talk later."

Zard Win nodded, and wanted to tell her many things. Instead, he left her to the women, and decided to do what he'd originally come here for, if he could just find Scyles.

As he turned away from her, he saw Scyles and Arga, surrounded by friends, watching him closely, even as they joked with their friends, laughed, and seemed to be bonded at the hip.

Scyles motioned with his head, and Zard Win walked over to them.

"My congratulations to both of you," he began, and Scyles laughed.

"As with everything, I did the best I could," he admitted, and several of his friends guffawed and made lewd jokes. Arga slugged him on the shoulder, and looked at Zard Win with a cynical expression on her face.

"You men always think it's all about you, but as you know, he couldn't have done it without me."

Zard Win couldn't help but smile at how comfortable they both were with all the bawdy behavior around them. He caught Scyles' eye.

"Could I show you something?" he asked quietly, raising the bundle he'd been carrying around, waiting to catch him alone. "In private."

Scyles eyed the package with clear excitement. He glanced at his wife, and Zard Win nodded.

"Princess Arga, I think you might want to see this as well," he said, and they both rose and followed him out into the main concourse. A few ribald shouts followed them. They walked down the concourse until there was a side corridor, and stepped into it.

Zard Win unfolded the materal covering his work, and handed Scyles the jerkin within. The individual platelets were a dull, nondescript color, and he saw the disappointment in both their eyes.

"This is a neutral color because this armor goes beneath your kurga and tunic," Zard Win told them. "The idea is to not attract attention to it, so if someone wants to cut you, ideally they will choose for convenience, not to avoid your hidden armor. Chances are better than fair they'll strike you in an armored spot."

Scyles held it up, and looked at the platelets closely. He eyed the sleeves with distaste.

"Most men do not have armor extending down their arms," he said, hefting the jerkin, and letting Arga take it out of his hands. She held it up in front of herself, and her lips pursed, as if trying to decide if it was too big for her.

"Most men look better with arms on each side," she retorted sharply. "If this helps you in that way, I don't see the problem. It's very light," she admitted, hefting it herself. She looked at Zard Win and hesitated.

He knew what she was going to ask.

"If you'd like, we can make one for you, as well," he assured her.

Scyles shrugged.

"If she likes, she can have mine," he started, but she was having none of it.

"Or, we could both have them," she said in a sharp voice.

"Shae Apon and I are working on a design for one that goes on the outside," he admitted. "It will be heavier, and very similar to the one Targitai wears. It will also be the same, bright color as his, even though this material is not metallic."

"This will stop a sword thrust or slash?" Arga asked, holding it against her.

"It will," Zard Win said confidently. He hesitated. "Of course, it will only diffuse the power of the blow so much, so although you might not get cut, you could still get your arm broken, or cracked or broken ribs," he admitted.

"They heal," Arga said, shrugging. She turned to Scyles. "Off with your tunic. Be quick about it. I want to see how this fits you."

He started to protest, and abruptly shut his mouth. They stared at each other, and he finally sighed heavily, conceding the battle.

"I give up hemp for you. I give up drink for you. Now you wish to dress me in women's undergarments," he muttered, taking his belt with the two swords and the gorytos off and setting them on the floor.

Arga smiled at Zard Win in triumph, and then murmured very softly to Scyles as she took his tunic as he pulled it off.

Zard Win stared at his chest, even as the young man turned to take the armor from his wife. He blinked as he saw his bare back. Arga saw his stare.

"We all have tattoos, Zard Win. You know that," she said, and raised an eyebrow, even as she adjusted the jerkin as Scyles slipped it on. "You want to see mine?"

Scyles stopped what he was doing, and looked at his wife with a speculative gaze.

"All of your tattoos?" he asked, teasing, and Arga shook her head, looking at Zard Win apologetically.

"If I show you some of my tattoos, Scyles will have to challenge you, and beat you to within an inch of your life," she said simply. "And we wouldn't want that."

"I know I wouldn't," Zard Win said slowly. He thought it funny that they both assumed Scyles could take him in a fight. But then, they didn't really think about the fact that he was the head of security of Mountain View, and could be a very dangerous man when he needed to be.

Then he remembered watching Scyles attack the Hshtahni in the battle for Muschwain, and wondered if maybe they didn't have a point.

Scyles smoothed the armored jerkin down his chest and flat stomach, and his eyebrows rose. He moved around, and a small smile came to his face.

"It's so light, almost as if I wore nothing," he admitted.

"But it'll actually stop a blade," Arga said, sounding a little skeptical. While Scyles was admiring himself, she'd pulled out her own short sword and without warning, slashed him across his side.

"By the gods," Scyles swore, wincing as he pulled away from her, glaring at her. She looked at his side, then his face, looking thoughtful.

"You want to know if it works, don't you, husband?" she asked innocently. "Are you bleeding anywhere?"

"No," Scyles marveled, rubbing the offended side. "He's right about it still hurting, though," he admitted.

"How does it feel? The jerkin, not your side," Zard Win hastily clarified his question.

"It's a good fit," Scyles admitted, and looked at his wife. "Do you want this one?"

Arga sighed, and shook her head.

"No, that is designed for you, and it looks like a perfect fit," she said, nodding her appreciation to Zard Win. "But I am afraid my size will be changing over the next, oh, nine moons or so. And then it will take me a couple more to get my fitness back."

She smiled at Zard Win.

"You can make me one then."

"I would be honored, Princess," Zard Win said formally, and she smiled at him.

"You should call me Arga, and my husband, Scyles," she said, impulsively giving him a hug. "We are friends. There is no reason for formalities. May I call you Zard?"

Zard Win blushed, and shook his head, embarrassed, even though there was no way either of them would know Egelv customs.

"I'm afraid you could only call me that if I'd actually seen those tattoos you mentioned, and it was because we were bonded." He looked at them. "Egelv always use both names except when they have bonded or are either mated, or about to be."

"So Shae Apon calls you…" Arga began and paused, waiting for him to finish the sentence. Scyles looked at her, disapproving her boldness.

"You embarrass our friend, wife," he said. "You know he wishes it, but they have taken no steps, even though she also wishes to."

"You are right, husband," she said, bowing her head to Zard Win. Her eyes raised, and he saw the mischievousness was still evident. "Please accept my apology, Zard Win."

"I am not offended, you could not know," he said, and hurried to clarify. "Shae Apon and I come from families that are far apart in social circles. It would be inappropriate for her to ever become involved with someone from my family. And presumptuous of me to think she would."

"Hmm," Arga said, helping Scyles pull his tunic over the armor. It was loose enough that you couldn't tell he had anything on under it. "Still..."

"Arga," Scyles said, warningly. Zard Win smiled, seeing that they were playing to each other. He wondered what it was like to be that young, in love, and able to act upon it. These Scoloti were so different, and he felt close bonds to them.

"Zard Win, Captain Rost Fott wishes you to come to the conference room on Mountain Edge," First Officer Van Dono told him through his transponder. "Commodore Mit Obet will be boarding shortly, and has requested a meeting with the two of you, as well as the captain."

"On my way," Zard Win said, and quickly handed Scyles a second package he had tucked into a small stack of printouts. "See what you think about these, but please don't show them around yet. They take a while to make, and I really need better facilities than I have on hand. When we get a chance, Shae Apon and I are going to try and requisition a number of tools and other things we think will be handy. Let me know what you think, as far as how the balance is."

Scyles opened the package and stared at a matching set of the throwing knives. Zard Win left him to it, and hurried down the concourse. Shae Apon was just coming out of the common hall, and they looked at each other apprehensively.

"I guess the meeting with the Emperor is on," Zard Win said, and heard the nervousness in his own voice.

She nodded and smiled.

"He doesn't bite, you know," she said reassuringly. Then she gave him a sly look. "Of course, his guards do..."

Zard Win winced.

The Emperor's Guard were notoriously loyal and very protective of the emperor. They would probably be out in record numbers if a contingent of the Scoloti were going to meet with him.

Five minutes later, they stood next to the captain at the Mountain Edge airlock, welcoming the commodore aboard. Five minutes after that, they were back in the conference room, seated around the table, the commodore and captain relaxed and comfortable, Zard Win and Shae Apon apprehensive, and more than a little nervous.

"I have managed to arrange an introduction to Emperor Balco Deh for two days from now, mid-morning Egelva time," Commodore Mit Obet said, and looked from the captain to the two of them.

"Did you discuss this with the Scoloti?" he asked, and Captain Rost Fott turned to Zard Win questioningly.

"Yes sir, I had a meeting with King Gelon and King Orik, and they are looking forward to it," he said, and anticipated the next question. "I had ship's house-keeping introduce them to the radiated cleaning equipment, and give them a tutorial. Queen Myrina, as well as Queen Opis have assured me everyone in their party would be dressed in their finest, and their weapons and shields would be clean and shiny, as if they were about to do battle."

Everyone at the table looked at him, and he smiled weakly.

"I think they were teasing me, but I have learned enough about them to know they will want to look their very best for this introduction, and will make their menfolk do the same."

"So, in this very rigid patriarchy, the women have secretly taken control?" the commodore asked, smiling as if they were confiding in a secret conspiracy.

Zard Win looked at Shae Apon. Her face was expressionless, but he could see the twinkle in her eyes. The captain watched him with amusement of his own, clear to see. Satisfied, he turned back to the commodore.

"Yes, sir, I would say that sums it up nicely."

"So, two kings, two queens..." the commodore began and looked at him to continue.

"King Orik has a fifteen-year old daughter and a son that looks perhaps five," Zard Win said.

"Or six," Shae Apon added, and he nodded his agreement with her, then continued.

"King Gelon has a sixteen-year old son, which brings us to seven. Both kings have their right hand man that is really more of a bodyguard, which makes nine, and then each tribe wants to have two additional guards, which makes thirteen."

"That's a lot of swords for an introduction to the Emperor," Commodore Mit Obet said hesitantly, but then shrugged. "But, three of them are children, and two are women, so we're really just talking about eight men."

Zard Win opened his mouth to correct him, and Shae Apon jumped in before he could say a word.

"Yes, sir, that is correct," she said, and didn't look at Zard Win.

He kept his face blank, and nodded when the commodore looked at him for confirmation.

"Well then, that's set," he said, satisfied. "We will send up one of the palace shuttles to pick your party up, right after breakfast hour, Egelva time, day after tomorrow."

He looked at them.

"You will both be attending as well, of course. I assume you have dress uniforms aboard?" He smiled at them cynically. "Technically, at the moment, the two of you are the universe's premier experts on the Scoloti."

He was laughing at his own joke as he walked out with Captain Rost Fott.

Zard Win looked at Shae Apon, and she gave him a serene smile.

He felt like he was in shock. Shae Apon smiling at him like that, and he was about to meet the emperor. He couldn't imagine there could be a better moment in his life.

Rost Fott watched the shuttle break away from Mountain Edge and move quickly back to Raging River. He was glad that meeting was over. The commodore could be very unpredictable. And for someone with his rank, his moods varied widely.

He nodded absent-mindedly as he passed crewmen in the corridors. He felt uneasy about the pending meeting with the emperor, but he couldn't decide why. Between that, and the troop carrier still docked at the port landing bay, there were too many things he had no control of. He was just honest enough with himself to know he didn't deal well with not being in control of everything around him.

Not for the first time, he rued playing around when they were preparing to return to Egelv space. Had he not caused the minor delay, the squadron would have been far away by the time the Hshtahni came through the black hole.

He returned to his cabin, and decided to look around both ships and see what was happening. He pulled up the directory of cameras aboard the Muschwain and winced. Gods, that was a big ship. He looked for views with motion and the first one to catch his eye was the common hall for the

Scoloti. It was packed, and he wondered what they were talking about. A lot of them were drinking, and there seemed to be a very spirited discussion going on. He watched as Shae Apon and Zard Win entered, and immediately became the center of the discussion.

She seemed to be the focus, and he winced as he saw how animated some of the Scoloti were. Then she began to speak, and the room quieted and they listened. Rost Fott saw the look Zard Win was giving her as he stood at her side, and winced.

That boy was free-falling in a very thin world suit. If her family got the slightest hint he was attracted to her, there would be hell to pay. Especially if she returned the attention.

He winced at the idea.

Shae Apon would come through fine. She was of the higher class, and brilliant. Not to mention, right now, she was the more indispensable of the two. He was popular with the Scoloti, but she'd been studying them, and knew more about them medically, sociologically, and probably psychologically as well.

But Zard Win's career would be ruined. Rost Fott felt some responsibility to the young man, and decided that when they returned from Egelv Prime, he would sit the lad down, have a talk with him. He was his senior officer, and an elder in the family, and it was his responsibility to try to protect the young man, even if it was from himself.

He wondered what Shae Apon was saying, but before he could turn the volume on, he saw several of the troopers making their rounds, and took a closer look at them. He thought one of them looked familiar, and that seemed surprising.

The cruiser troopship carried four platoons, which was over three hundred men and women, but he could swear only one platoon was handling all the duties, which was crazy. But, maybe it was coincidence. But something about them rang an alarm bell in his head, and he didn't know why.

And that bothered him.

All the senior Scoloti leadership not in stasis were going planetside, which would leave someone much junior, in charge of the Scoloti on board. That, coupled with the constant patrols of the troopers, made him nervous.

He saw Van Dono just outside Mountain Edge, past the airlock. He was talking with one of the patrols, and although there was nothing suspicious about that, it still bothered him. He'd seen Van Dono talking to the soldiers, several different times, and that was odd. Ship's crew and troopers were almost never a good mix, especially when the troopers weren't even from their ship. What could Van Dono find to talk about with them?

Probably some sports team, or female celebrity, he thought, deciding he was becoming more and more paranoid as he grew older.

More like my father every day, he thought, grimacing. Not good.

Van Dono nodded to the troopers and they continued their patrol. He returned to the ship and was clearly headed back to the bridge. That path would bring him very close to Rost Fott's cabin, and he decided to accidentally cross paths with him.

He left his cabin and began to leisurely make his way towards the dining hall. Just as he'd planned, Van Dono came down the corridor towards him.

"Captain," Van Dono said, nodding, and Rost Fott returned the gesture. "Checking to see if the chef has afternoon snacks out yet?"

"I thought I might give it a look," Rost Fott lied. "You on your way to the bridge?"

"Yes sir," his first officer said, nodding. "Second Officer has the bridge now, but he's due to check in on Muschwain in a bit, so I'll be covering."

"Good," Rost Fott said, trying to think of something to extend the casual conversation. "Just firmed up details of the Scoloti jaunt planet-side. Can't pretend I'm not a little envious. I thought we would have been released from this duty by now, but it looks like we may be up here a while before they give us leave."

"I suppose it's a tradeoff for the positives we'll reap for discovering a new race," Van Dono said, and smiled at him in a more personal manner than they usually had towards each other. "That's a shame for you. That woman at High Command seemed quite interested in you, and she certainly is beautiful."

"She is, at that," Rost Fott said, and watched his first officer continue on down the corridor until the curvature of the ship took him out of sight.

He walked on to the galley, knowing no snacks were out yet, but wanting to act consistently with his words, for Van Dono's sake.

Captain Rost Fott entered the galley, nodded to the chef, and pretended to look over the man's shoulder to see what he was preparing. But he couldn't have said what he saw, because his mind was back in that corridor, and at the same time, on the bridge.

As if he didn't have enough things that felt off on board his command, he'd just added another, and it was going to bother him until he solved it.

How did Van Dono know about the pretty woman at High Command, when he hadn't been on the bridge at the time?

Rost Fott wanted to think he was being paranoid, or just getting a bit crazy after so long on board. He knew he needed some shore leave. But he also knew there were things happening on his command that he couldn't explain.

At least, not yet.

Chapter Twenty-Eight

Zard Win watched the Scoloti with some amusement. He'd asked the crew of the shuttle if the large screens in the transport hold could show the view of the external cameras, and show their approach to Egelv Prime.

At first, the image of the planet slowly growing larger had caught their interest, but other than the three youngest Scoloti, they'd quickly lost interest. Scyles and Arga were interested, and pointed things out to the younger boy, Serlotta.

He was impressed at how much both of them had retained from back when they first met, and he used videos from the ship's library to illustrate that they'd lived on a planet, and what that actually meant.

As far as he could tell, the Scoloti were all dressed in their finest attire. Both men and women wore remarkably similar clothing. They all had kurga over tunics on top, and what would be considered too loose trousers and comfortable-looking soft boots. The women tended towards the brighter, more flamboyant colors, and the men, even though the colors were strong, wore more muted shades.

Normally, all of them would have worn some sort of hat or other head apparel. Due to the fact that once put on, they didn't remove them for anyone, and that it was considered an insult for anyone to have any sort of hat or helmet on, in the company of the emperor, it was decided they would forego wearing their usual helmets.

They'd compromised, and the two kings and queens wore beaten metal headbands that shone brightly. They were designed to pass for casual crowns as well. Scyles, Arga, and Serlotta all wore similar headbands, made of beaten metal, but much more plain, with the exception of a precious jewel insert that rode in the middle of the forehead.

The Paralatae jewel inserts were all purple, Opis' purple sapphire, and Orik, Arga, and Serlotta all wore purple amethyst.

All three members of the Auchatae royal family wore garnet rubies.

Egelv Prime now filled the entire screen as they moved into the outer atmosphere. If they were aboard Mountain Edge herself, they could ride down through a tropical hurricane, and disregard the buffeting winds of the upper atmosphere. Between her artificial gravity, the gravitational compensation capability, sheer size, as well as her force field technology, weather simply wasn't a factor.

However, the Emperor's palace landing field permitted no ships capable of star travel, or with typical armaments to land, or even approach the palace. In fact, only the Emperor's own personal ship was allowed within the actual palace perimeter. The shuttle and ferry landing field was outside the powerful force field projector's range, and everyone arriving on them still had to go through the security checkpoints, with extensive scanning, and physical searches, when deemed necessary or prudent.

So they would be landing at the palace field, and riding a shuttle raft through the security points, submitting to searches and scans where necessary.

Zard Win hid his grin as he watched the royal families stir uneasily. Their bodyguards and the warriors accompanying them did little better.

Queen Opis went white as the shuttle lurched a little. Princess Arga leaned forward enough to look at her mother. She glanced down at Serlotta, sitting between them, and said something to Scyles, who nodded. She quickly undid her harness, then that of Serlotta, stood, and helped the child to his feet.

Scyles had hold of him and was strapping him in almost before his behind hit the bench. Arga carefully lowered herself into the area vacated by Serlotta, and strapped herself in, showing no fear or concern and, after making sure Scyles had her little brother safely in place, took his hand in her own left hand, and grasped her mother's in her right.

Queen Opis stared at her, wide-eyed, and the princess smiled at her reassuringly, and Zard Win saw her squeeze her mother's hand, and murmur something to her.

Whatever she said seemed to work, Zard Win saw, impressed.

In fact, he decided, her quick and fearless action to sooth her mother and little brother seemed to settle almost everyone down. Kings Gelon and Orik exchanged chagrined looks, and both started laughing. The other men seemed to take their relaxing as a personal challenge for them to do the same.

Targitai said something that Zard Win couldn't quite make out, and both his and Ariapithes' men chuckled, elbowed each other, and visibly relaxed.

Zard Win heard a couple of his men make jokes about fearless warriors, and he gave them a glance. They felt his look, and fell silent. One of them seemed obliged to say something.

"Security Chief, we're not mocking them. Even their young girls seem tougher than almost any non-military Egelv we know, Sir," he said, and leaned back in his seat. "I've seen government officials look as though they were going to be sick in less turbulence than this."

Zard Win nodded, and looked over to where Scyles was pointing out the mountain ranges visibly increasing in apparent size, as their altitude dropped. The boy didn't seem at all nervous, or uncomfortable, and clearly Scyles and Arga were fine. He knew they'd been spending some time on the educational computer terminals, and he thought they'd all taken advantage of the program simulations that were available, on everything from a landing similar to this, to a deep sea exploration in a underwater vessel.

Their descent started over high, rugged mountains, all with snowy peaks, even this time of year. They ranged most of the length of the main continent that included Egelva, the capital of the Egelv Empire. As their altitude dropped, the cities, surrounded by wide swaths of natural forests, meadows, and rolling hillsides, grew more detailed, and all the Scoloti unconsciously leaned forward in their seats.

Zard Win could see the longing and desire in their eyes and posture. He heard a sound next to him, and looked over to see Shae Apon, quickly put her hand down from her eyes. He thought she'd actually teared up, and was touched by her apparent love of the beautiful world.

It hadn't always been that way. It had taken centuries to repair the damage done to the ecology by the Egelv, in their industrial boom era. This was all millennia ago, but every Egelv child was taught the lesson of not disturbing the natural state of things any more than necessary, and to repair when damage was done.

"It's beautiful," he said quietly. "I guess you're homesick? You went to Empire University, here in the capital, correct?"

"I did, but that's not what I find so moving," Shae Apon responded. She sighed, and quit pretending as she openly dabbed her eyes. "Look at these people, and the longing when they see all that open ground. Remember, this race is a migratory people, accustomed to being in the wide open expanses of their own world, following the seasons and the best grazing and hunting areas."

"And pillaging and conquering cities and tribes in their path," Zard Win added, and immediately regretted it when he saw her face harden. He winced, hoping she didn't think him heartless, but pressed on, wanting to be honest. "It doesn't make them bad, but it is part of what they are. And of what makes them so admirable in their adaptability, and capabilities. Without this background, they wouldn't have taken the Muschwain, killing three Hshtahni in the process."

"That is true," Shae Apon agreed slowly. She gave him an appraising look. "You don't think it makes them evil, or bad people?"

"Their ruthlessness is what has allowed them to survive, to succeed, and control their environment," he said, and grinned, despite himself. "Except when it comes to being mass incapacitated, and kidnapped by strange creatures from other worlds."

"Well, it is hard to plan for such exigencies," Shae Apon admitted, and allowed herself a rueful smile. "Knowing and liking them, should be a contradiction, but doesn't feel like it."

"Products of their environment," Zard Win muttered, and nodded at one of the screens.

They both watched as Egelv Prime grew to fill the screen. There were tall, spiraling buildings, all beautifully designed, yet very functional. They reached the boundary of the city and the palace grew in size and detail on the screen.

The palace was an interesting blend and contrast in beauty and functionality. There were some high spires with turrets atop them, but Zard Win also knew they housed force screen projectors, as well as surface to air defenses. The rounded, more squat main buildings went many stories underground, he knew, and the most average looking portions were the most important.

From the outside, the part of the palace Zard Win knew housed the Emperor and his family, as well as portions of the Emperor's Guard barracks, were simple and unaffected.

All screens went dark, per protocol, during landing.

The Scoloti looked at each other, uncertain what that meant.

"It is standard procedure to turn all scanning devices off, when landing at the Palace Landing Field," Zard Win said loudly, and they visibly relaxed. He watched his own monitor, and saw they were settling down on the tarmac.

He unfastened his restraints, stood, and addressed the group.

"We are going to disembark from the shuttle and be admitted through security stations. It is common for weapons to be trained on anyone approaching these stations, and throughout the procedure. Once we're through, and have boarded ground transport, the defenses will be relaxed. But please do nothing to draw any alarm or sense of danger from the security forces. They have an important duty to keep the emperor safe, and take their work very seriously."

The Scoloti seemed to accept that as reasonable. He hid a grin as King Gelon turned to Targitai.

"Please follow our own protocol, and keep anyone from sticking a dagger in my back until we've passed through the checkpoints," he said in an official-sounding voice. His swordmaster grinned at him. "And after that, you can keep anyone from sticking a dagger in my back as well. It wouldn't feel any better getting stabbed in the palace than it would outside."

The Scoloti snickered and jostled each other good-naturedly, and turned as the back hatch door opened.

As they exited the shuttle, Zard Win was gratified to see it was a beautiful spring day, bright sunlight, minimal breezes, and almost no sign of clouds.

He also saw Commodore Mit Obet waiting for them, with two squads of the Emperor's Guard, eight men each, lined up as if in honor guard. They directed the Scoloti across the short stretch of tarmac to the checkpoints.

They passed, one at a time, through the gates of scanners, and he watched Scyles pay close attention to the screens that showed any metal on their bodies. It would show all their weapons, even the arrowheads in the gorytos every one of them carried.

The scanner screens also showed everything from buckles to jewelry, or anything else with a metal content, or power source. Of course, only he and his own men had power weapons, since that was their standard arms.

Zard Win nodded to the officer directing the procedure, identified himself, and asked that copies of all scans, and notations be forwarded to his personal device. He mentioned he was surprised there wasn't more concern about the Scoloti all having personal weapons.

"We already received pre-approved exceptions for the Scoloti," the officer told him. "Straight from the Emperor's Guard, with your commodore, and the Emperor's own approval. As long as they have no power weapons. Of course, your men do, but they're legitimate security forces, and standard procedure."

"Well, good," Zard Win said, disconcerted by how smoothly things were going. Egelva authorities were not known for being easy to work with.

"Anyway, their weapons are primitive, both in nature and construction," the officer said, giving him a knowing look. "Not the sort of thing that would hold up against the Guard, with all their weapons and toys."

"True," Zard Win said, wanting to end the conversation. He passed through the scanners, and caught up with Shae Apon as they all boarded a large floating raft. The Guard kept most of their men to the back, allowing the visitors a good view forward, as they approached the palace. But he noticed their attention never wavered, and they were alert, regardless of how primitive their visitors were.

It took less than five minutes to arrive at the palace. The raft floated to the left of the building and came to a halt, sinking to the ground.

"The Emperor is in his personal gardens and expects us," Commodore Mit Obet told Zard Win, and gestured to the wide open walkway that wrapped around the palace.

Four of the guard led them, along with Commodore Mit Obet, and Zard Win saw that the remaining twelve guards were fanned out behind them. He had to give them credit for taking their duty seriously.

They rounded the corner of the palace and very soon, Zard Win saw a small gathering of people working in the gardens near a very ornate, white gazebo. As they neared, the gardeners became aware of their approach, and one of them called out something to the others.

Zard Win saw that the gazebo contained a simple dais, and a man ascended to sit on the carved stone bench atop it. He climbed the several steps, turned and sat, awaiting their approach.

"That's the Emperor," Shae Apon breathed, and Zard Win realized that, even though she'd seen him before, at one of her graduation ceremonies at Empire University, seeing him in person, and up close, was still a novel experience for her.

Emperor Balco Deh wore plain, light green, loose-fitting pants, and a darker green tunic, also loose-fitting, with sleeves that fell just below his elbows. His shoes were plain, but practical, and he wore a light-weight golden crown that was really more a headband. He pulled gloves off his hands as he watched them approach, reaching out to hand them to an attendant.

His long, white hair had several thongs tied around it, holding it to a rope shape down the middle of his back. As with all Egelv, he had no facial hair, and his smooth, brown, skin looked young and healthy, even though Zard Win knew him to be well into his second century of life.

There were already four guardsmen attending him, two on each side, but they stayed in the background. Zard Win noticed that didn't keep them from watching the newcomers like hawks, their eyes noting the swords in their scabbards, and the gorytos full of bows and arrows. He saw one of them looking at a handheld, and realized he already had the scan reports from the security station.

All in all, Zard Win was very impressed with their casual, yet very thorough and competent professionalism, and attention to detail.

Commodore Mit Obet paused, well before the dais, and the emperor waved him forward. The four guards peeled off, two to each side, and without looking, Zard Win knew the other sixteen had formed a line behind the Scoloti, staying far enough back to not seem intrusive, yet close enough to immediately respond to any threat to the emperor.

An attendant, his long, flowing robes showing clearly he wasn't one of the gardeners, stepped forward, off to the side of the Emperor.

"Emperor Balco Deh, fourteenth ruler in the Deh Dynasty."

Zard Win risked a quick glance to the side to see Shae Apon next to him, her face full of wonder and respect, as they both bowed low. And perhaps a little hero worship, he thought with envy. Beyond her, Arga and Scyles stood, holding hands, looking at the emperor with interest, if not awe.

King Gelon and Queen Myrina looked as though they were having trouble deciding whether to look at him as an equal, or to visibly acknowledge him as their superior in rank. King Orik and Queen Opis seemed to be having the same problem, and both couples shared glances showing their uncertainty.

Young Serlotta seemed to have no difficulty putting everything into a perspective he could understand. He was too young to have been alive at the time, but he was more than aware that throughout the time of the People, there had been one condition present, more often than not.

"Papa," he said in a quiet voice that, unfortunately, carried clearly to everyone present. "Is this the Great King?"

Rost Fott watched the shuttle descend towards Egelva Prime. He knew this should be a fine moment, both for the Scoloti, and for his own career, as well as his officers.

The patrol had been a resounding success. Of course, Commodore Mit Obet would get the lion's share of the credit, but that was fine. He was the senior officer when the Hshtahni came through the black hole, or space tunnel, or whatever they ended up calling the phenomena.

But something at the back of his head kept causing an itching sensation, and he had no idea what was causing it. He'd learned over the years, that when he got these sensations, his subconscious, or unconscious impressions, were trying to tell him something. And he was sure this was another case of that very thing.

But what was the catalyst?

He sighed and told Van Dono he was going to take a walk to clear his mind. He found four of Zard Win's security troopers on duty in the lounge, watching training vidoes. He suspected they had an early warning system that an officer was approaching, and the moment he left, they'd be back to whatever mischief they'd been up to moments before he arrived.

On a whim, he told four of them to suit up, arm themselves with traditional power weapons, as well as their non-powered crowd controllers. He'd meet them at the airlock in ten minutes, and they should plan on spending the balance of their shift on the generation ship.

Fifteen minutes later, they were in the common hall, as everyone now called it, and he was talking with a young Scoloti named Skulis that had been left in charge, along with another young man from Gelon's tribe named Lika.

Rost Fott felt embarrassed that he was trying to warn them to be ready for something, but yet he had no idea of what, or when, or why. Oddly enough, they didn't seem to find that peculiar.

"You are experienced at what you do, you feel a, what do you call it?" Skulis asked Lika, who promptly responded.

"A premonition."

"Yes, that's it," Skulis agreed. "A premonition. They are real. We will have our people quietly gather their weapons, and have them close on hand."

"Most of them do, anyway," Lika pointed out, and Skulis nodded.

"True, you never know when strange beings from another world are going to attack you," Skulis said with a straight face.

Rost Fott laughed with them, and to be honest, felt better about things afterwards. He watched Lika begin circulating around the room, murmuring a few words, to people here and there. After a discreet amount of time, people began to move around, bringing their swords and gorytos to tables and begin to clean or sharpen them.

"This is about those soldiers, from the other ship, am I correct?" Skulis asked quietly, and, after a moment, Rost Fott nodded. "We've had the same premonitions. We will watch them closely. I will go now, and speak with the Warrior Women. They are some of our fiercest fighters."

Rost Fott nodded and said he was leaving two men here, supposedly on break, to grab a bite to eat. He glanced at Skulis, and decided to take the plunge.

"Can I ask you something?" he started off, wondering how to word it.

Skulis exhaled heavily and pretended to glare at him.

"You want to know if Scyles really defeated me in a fight, and if so, how, without killing me with arrows, right?"

"More or less," Rost Fott admitted.

Skulis sat back down for a moment, and propped his feet up on a stool.

"First, he cheated," he said with a straight face. "Second," and he paused and smiled sincerely. "That little bastard has the fastest hands I've ever seen, and he's always thinking. Always." Skulis shook his head. "That should work against him. If you're thinking, you aren't acting. But he's also the fastest thinker I've ever met. He does things even as he thinks of them."

Skulis laughed.

"In battle, that should get you killed," he admitted. "But it works for him. I have thought about this much, since the day we were taken. And I can tell you, he will never beat me in battle again. You know how I'll do it?" he asked, leaning forward.

"No, how?" Rost Fott asked, intrigued.

"I'm never going to fight him again," Skulis said as he stood up. He was still laughing when he reached the back of the hall to talk with the Warrior Women.

Rost Fott went to the bridge of the Muschwain, and left the other two security officers with Third Officer Lace Ray. There were four crew members there, two that had just arrived, and two about to get off duty. He told them to stay on the bridge, monitor everything they could, and to be very careful. He gave them several extra stunners he had taken from the armory of Mountain Edge.

He hurried back to his own ship. He found Second Officer Rel Steen in the galley, and quickly gave him the rundown of his concerns.

"I can't explain it, but something is eating away at the back of my brain, trying to warn me of something," Rost Fott said, and Rel Steen nodded.

"I know what you mean, sir. I've had the same sensation."

"Really?" Rost Fott asked, and Rel Steen nodded again.

"Look, don't make a huge deal about it, but find all of Zard Win's men, and tell them to arm up, and that everyone is on duty until further notice." Rost Fott looked at him intently. "But I don't want them chattering about it. Let's not worry the ship's crew about this, except for those we absolutely have to keep in the loop."

He frowned and looked at Rel Steen speculatively.

"Do you think a couple security men could bring the mobile stun blaster near the airlock, perhaps in a room very close, without the crew noticing?"

Rel Steen nodded, smiling.

"I know exactly who to sneak it there," he said, and Rost Fott felt reassured.

"I wish I could at least figure out who the threat is," Rost Fott said, frustrated. "Weird things keep happening, coincidences occur, but I can't put my finger on it."

"Does Van Dono know about your concerns?" Rel Steen asked, and looked shocked when Rost Fott, after hesitating a moment, shook his head. "You suspect him of something?"

"Not really," Rost Fott admitted, and shrugged. "Oh, I know he wants my ship, but every first officer in the fleet wishes his captain would retire, or get promoted, or have a heart attack."

"He certainly thinks he can do the job better than you," Rel Steen said slowly. "He's come close to being insubordinate talking about you with some of us," he admitted.

"Really." Rost Fott wasn't surprised. But it did anger him. "And I think he's got the ear of the commodore, as well. When he came aboard before going ahead of us, on the return trip, Van Dono was at the meeting that I thought was going to only be us and Zard Win. I didn't even know he knew about the meeting, but he was there before me. Said someone on the bridge had mentioned it to him."

"That never happened," Rel Steen said flatly. "I was on the bridge that day, and no one on duty informed him. If he knew about it in advance, that wasn't how."

Rost Fott sighed, knowing he was about to take a big risk. And by doing so, he was going to jeopardize another officer's career as well.

"Keep him out of the loop about this premonition of mine," he said, and Rel Steen nodded mutely. "And about our preparations and precautions we're taking."

"Yes sir, Captain," Rel Steen said, shook his head, as if to clear it, and hurried down the corridor.

Chapter Twenty-Nine

"Emperor Balco Deh, I would like to introduce you to two very important officers of Mountain Edge," Commodore Mit Obet said, and Zard Win's head shot up, and he stared at the commodore in confusion. His surprise didn't go unnoted, and both the emperor and the commodore looked amused. "They will introduce you to our newest friendly race, the Scoloti. They work with them every day, and their insight and experiences are invaluable."

Zard Win didn't dare look over at Shae Apon, but from the jerk her body gave, when the commodore began speaking, she clearly had no more advanced warning than he did.

"Zard Win is the Security Chief, and he and his men were at the forefront of the battle for the Hshtahni generation ship Muschwain," Mit Obet said. "Their bravery was exemplary, and Zard Win showed exceptional ability to adjust to the situation as it developed."

"My Lord," Zard Win said, bowing very low again.

"And this is Shae Apon, Science Officer and Medical Doctor for Mountain Edge. She has Doctoral degrees in Medicine, Psychology, and Chemistry, as well as a number of lessor degrees. She has been invaluable as liaison between us and the Scoloti."

"My Lord." Shae Apon bowed as low as Zard Win.

The emperor looked at the two of them, and his eyes sharpened, and then he smiled. For a moment, no one did or said anything, and Zard Win belatedly realized they were supposed to be introducing him to the People.

"My Lord may I introduce King Gelon and Queen Myrina of the Auchatae tribe of the Scoloti, and their son, Prince Scyles, who led the assault on the Hshtahni on board Muschwain," Zard Win said, wondering if they were angering the Scoloti by chosing the order to introduce them. Before he could say anything more, Shae Apon smoothly picked up where he'd left off.

"And, My Lord, may I introduce King Orik and Queen Opis of the Paralatae tribe of the Scoloti, their daughter, Princess Arga, wife of Prince Scyles, and their son, Prince Serlotta."

All the Scoloti bowed their heads politely, but none bowed as low as he and Shae Apon had, and he wondered if the breach in etiquette would become an issue.

The emperor smiled slightly, not missing a thing, Zard Win suspected. His eyes flipped back and forth between the younger Scoloti.

"So, your marriage connects the two tribes," he said, and smiled reassuringly at them. "You look so young to be married already. Was this something arranged and done long ago, for alliance purposes, or for true love?"

Zard Win watched Scyles evaluate the question, and knew he was deciding how he would respond. Arga didn't have his inhibitions about casually disclosing anything on her mind.

"Originally, our families wished us to marry for the sake of the tribes, and we said no," Arga said, and looked at Scyles shyly. "We both agreed and spent time discussing how we would proceed. But that time only showed us we loved each other, so we declared our love and Scyles proposed to me."

"The morning we were abducted by the Hshtahni, Emperor," Scyles said with a thin smile. "Once we were committed, our families thought we should marry immediately, but the attack came at that moment, so we waited until we regained consciousness, and then married later that day."

"You married, while prisoners of the Hshtahni?"

Zard Win suspected it was difficult to surprise the emperor, but Scyles and Arga had managed. Now, he thought, as long as they don't...

"And consummated it, as well," Arga said boldly, and there was an audible gasp from some of the emperor's gardening staff. She patted her stomach. "Shae Apon tells me I carry the next king of the Auchatae. After Scyles, that is," she finished brightly.

There was a long, shocked silence, and Zard Win began regretting the once in a lifetime experience of meeting and speaking with the emperor.

Then the emperor began to laugh. Everyone in attendance relaxed, and the Egelv staff laughed politely, even though Zard Win could see they were still in a state of shock at the bawdry turn in the conversation. The emperor looked at Orik and Opis, and then at Gelon and Myrina.

"She is precious," he said, laughing so hard, it was hard for him to get the words out. "The four of you have raised treasures for children. She so bold, he so brave. I love my children, and hope they grow to become as impressive as yours."

Zard Win took a step backwards as the emperor began to chat with the Scoloti. He watched Shae Apon standing nearby, and she must have felt his gaze, because she turned to look at him, amusement on her face. He grinned at her, and they looked at each other for an eternity, which was probably all of five seconds. Then a question from the emperor pulled her away.

He looked around at the large group of Egelv and Scoloti, and was struck by how different they suddenly were.

The People looked relaxed, comfortable with themselves, even in the presence of the most powerful being in this part of the galaxy. The Emperor's Guards, on the other hand, held to their posts. He noticed Commodore Mit Obet standing back a bit, off to the emperor's left side, watching everyone, and looking down at a handheld. The two pairs of Guards held to their posts on either side of the emperor, and two more had approached the dais that acted as the throne of the empire for the moment.

Sitting on the Dais, the emperor's head was about level with everyone else, except the Scoloti, who were all at least half a head shorter. Scyles, in fact, was a full head shorter than any of the Egelv, including Shae Apon. He stood back a bit, and Arga, seeing him, made her way to his side.

Zard Win looked around again, wishing he could figure out what was causing the subconscious alarms that wouldn't quit going off in his head. Everything seemed to be going smoothly. The emperor seemed to be enjoying his first encounter with the Scoloti, which was amazing in its own right.

He'd been introduced to the emperor! And actually spoke with him!

So, what was wrong?

The emperor's gardening staff were scurrying back to their duties, although Zard Win was pretty sure most of their duties consisted of catering to the emperor's current hobby.

The two Guards closest to him, to the emperor's right, ignored them and kept their eyes on the crowd. He idly noticed they both wore the patch of the Quo family beneath the Emperor's Guard emblem. No surprise there. All the families provided recruits to the academy that churned out Emperor's Guardsmen as needed. There was always a broad mix among the guards on duty, to keep any one family from acquiring favor through their guardsmen.

Zard Win glanced to his left, and saw, with a little surprise, that he was also of the Quo family. As were the guards on either side of him. He didn't want to turn around and look at the rest of the guard, first, because it was considered offensive to turn away from the emperor, except at certain distances, and under specific circumstances.

Second, he didn't want to attract any attention from them. He didn't know if he'd subconsciously noticed the common badge of the guard on duty, but it certainly qualified as unusual and somewhat alarming. He saw that the two guards behind the commodore were also from the Quo family, and began to get very alarmed.

The two Guards to the Emperor's left were from other families, he saw, and watched with fascination as one of them suddenly frowned and muttered something very quietly to the other Guard. They both began look intently at the other Guards, and the one that first noticed something quietly asked one of the Guards on the other side of the Emperor why the roster of Guards on duty had changed, and why so many were of one family.

Zard Win knew that was going to get a reaction, but before he could even move, or utter a word, the commodore nodded and all the Guards except for the two drew their weapons and trained them on the Scoloti, the two Guards not from the Quo family, the gardening staff, Shae Apon, Zard Win's men, and unfortunately, himself as well.

"No one will do anything foolish," Commodore Mit Obet said firmly, stepping behind the two captured Guards to stand next to the Emperor. "All weapons are set on kill, not stun. Everyone will place their weapons on the ground at once."

Emperor Balco Deh stood, raising himself to his full height. He stared at the commodore.

"What are you doing?" he demanded to know, and then his eyes fixed on the commodore's own family badge. He shook his head in disgust. "Are you really fool enough to think that a coup will put your family on the throne? Even if you kill me, my heir will become Emperor. Every member of your family will be hunted down and killed. Or exiled, if they are able to prove they weren't part of this conspiracy."

"Emperor, you will sign papers relinquishing your claim, and your family's claim to the throne, and acknowledge the Quo family as the rightful heirs, or every member of your own family will be executed." Commodore Mit Obet said coldly. "I have Guards loyal to me already in the royal quarters, holding your wife, as well as the rest of your family. One way or another, your reign ends today, and the Quo family will provide the next Emperor."

"You?" the Emperor asked in scorn. "You are not fit to rule the Egelv Empire."

"Actually, I am sixth in line to the throne, once you've signed the papers," the commodore said, and turned to face the rest of them.

"Scoloti, this is not your fight," he called out. "Place all your weapons on the ground. You will be able to prove that you had no part in any of this, and your people will be safe. The only alternative is that my men will shoot you down." He stared at Zard Win. "The same goes for you and your men, Security Chief. Stand down, or die."

"How can you hope to get away with this?" Zard Win asked, and then his eyes widened.

It had been the commodore that suggested the Scoloti bring their weapons to give a demonstration. If he was telling the truth, their not having any weapons on them would have been the smarter choice, both for them, and for the commodore's chances of success.

He planned to blame the Scoloti, which meant that everyone here, except for members of the Quo family, must die this day.

"Weapons on the ground," Commodore Mit Obet said, his voice louder now. "Or everyone dies."

Scyles watched as Zard Win and his men slowly placed their weapons on the ground. The two Guards not part of the rebellion hadn't moved yet, but they smelled of surrender to him.

The Scoloti all looked at Gelon and Orik to see their reaction, and for guidance on what to do. Surrendering wasn't an option any Scoloti ever easily chose, because usually, the victors killed all the defeated. So surrender was really a form of suicide.

Other than their insanely optimistic enthusiasm they exhibited when they went into battle, the Scoloti didn't commit suicide. Scyles watched his father look around at his wife, and at Arga, and knew he was weighing the odds.

To Scyles, there was nothing to consider. They were pawns in a battle far bigger than themselves, and one that started long before they arrived. Surrendering his weapons was not only suicide, but taking an active hand in killing his wife and unborn child.

Gelon undid his belt and lay the two swords and the gorytos on the ground in front of him.

"The rest of you, throw them farther away," said the man Scyles knew as the commodore. "And we scanned you, so we know about your hidden knives. Out with them. Now."

His father sighed and pulled out two daggers and tossed them forward. Orik began to toss his own weapons forward, and after a moment, so did his wife and daughter. The other Scoloti slowly followed suit. Targitai and Ariapithes were the last, and they hesitated. Two Guards stepped forward, raising their weapons and pointing them at their faces.

The two swordmasters threw their weapons forward, one by one. Scyles was impressed, despite the seriousness of the moment, at how many weapons they both carried.

Finally, everyone had thrown their weapons forward, except for Scyles. The Emperor spoke up, glaring at the commodore.

"You intend to blame this on the Scoloti. You will kill me, no matter what I do, as well as my family and the palace staff. You will say the primitives attacked without warning, and although the loyal guard was able to defeat them, not before they achieved their goal, my death."

"Silence, old man," Commodore Mit Obet said scornfully. He looked at Scyles. "You're next. Don't make me kill your family because your ego wouldn't yield."

The Guard in front of Scyles raised his weapon, pointing it at his head. Scyles tried to see a way out, but knew the Egelv would kill him with no regret, and no hesitation. He untied his belt and set his scabbarded swords and gorytos on the ground right in front of him.

"Throw them forward, animal," the Guardsman snarled at him, taking a step forward, and gesturing with his weapon.

Scyles felt the blood flowing in his veins begin to pulse with anger, and he stared at the guard. Zard Win suddenly began speaking.

"The moment any power weapon is discharged in or around the palace, the entire palace and grounds has a null field activated, as well as force fields to prevent anyone from entering or leaving the area. This means, after the first shot, the weapons no longer work."

The Scoloti stirred, and Scyles saw his father's back stiffen with rage. He knew what Scyles intended, and was raging inside at the sacrifice he was about to make. Scyles knew it would only take a moment for him to realize that anyone starting to fight would result in a weapons discharge.

"Aim weapons," the commodore said crisply. "If anyone tries to fight and is shot, shoot your target immediately. We will get most of them before the null field takes effect. We will then kill the rest with crowd controllers or their own weapons."

"I strip you of your rank, and remove you from active duty in the Egelv Space Navy," the Emperor said. "I also place a bounty upon your head of one hundred million dracoons."

"You can't buy these men, Emperor," Mit Obet said, and raised his own weapon to point at the Emperor's head.

Scyles unstrapped the two knives from his thigh scabbards, and let them fall directly in front of him.

"I said throw them forward," the Guard snarled, and stepped closer, his hand firm and steady holding the weapon to Scyles' head.

"These are my own personal weapons, and heavy. I don't wish them to get scratched." Scyles smiled at the Guard, wondering why he wasn't terrified. "And I'll need them back in a moment to kill you and the rest of this scum."

"Really?" the Guard said, and for a moment, Scyles thought he'd pushed him too far. But he pulled himself together and reached down and picked up one of the knives."

He stepped close to Scyles, holding the knife at his chest.

"Down on your knees, animal!" he snarled, and Scyles somehow found the strength to smile without any twitching showing his frayed nerves.

"I am Scoloti. We don't kneel to anyone," Scyles said, his eyes never leaving those of the Guard.

"Then die!" the Guard said vehemently, rearing back and stabbing Scyles in the midrift.

Scyles bent forward over the knife, gasping in pain as he felt the impact of the heavy blade. He crumpled to his knees, trying to breath, the agony in his gut trying to override any attempt to think. From a distance, he heard Arga cry out his name. Underneath that, he could hear his father swearing, and the gasp of his mother.

Somehow, he stayed focused and drew both of the new throwing knives from his boots. He thrust upward with his right hand, gutting the Guardsman, pulling the blade upward as he staggered to his feet, stabbing the already dying man in the throat with the knife in his left hand.

Without hesitation, he pulled the knife free of the dead man's torso, and whirling, threw it. His aim was true, and the knife embedded in the exposed forearm of the commodore that held the raised energy weapon.

Mit Obet screamed and his arm swung to his right from the impact, involuntarily discharging the weapon he held to the Emperor's head. It was aimed too far to the right to kill anyone, but alarms immediately started going off. Scyles hoped that meant the null field was in effect.

He had tossed his scabbards down so that the long blade would carry forward a little from the momentum. It had slid partway out of the scabbard. Scyles hooked a foot behind the guard and kicked hard. The sword flew straight, handle first, until a hand reached out and grabbed it.

Targitai went into action, but Scyles had no time to watch. He hooked his gorytos to his belt, even as he drew his bow and several arrows. He started aiming at the guardsmen that hadn't been close to the Scoloti or Zard Win's men, and kept firing as he walked forward until he reached the Emperor.

Emperor Balco Teh stared at him as he approached. Scyles dropped his bow into his gorytos, and stepped forward, pulling his knife from the arm of the commodore. With his free hand, he pulled him close.

"You talk too much," he said, and stabbed up into the throat, the blade sinking deep into the base of the skull. He pulled the blade out, knowing the commodore was dead before he hit the ground.

Scyles smoothly threw his two blades into the ground on either side of him, and pulled his bow back out and began searching for targets. He kept his body in front of the Emperor, firing as quickly as he saw an enemy.

And then there were no enemies left to kill.

Scyles looked around, finding his family and the others, seeing who was still alive.

One of Targitai's men was down, either badly hurt or dead. Two of Zard Win's men were the same. He looked unharmed, which made Scyles happy. Of course, Targitai was unmarked, except for the copious amount of enemy blood splattered on him.

One of the two loyal Guards was dead, but other than that, the only other bodies on the ground were those of the Quo family.

His father was checking on his mother, who looked fine. King Orik and Queen Opis were untouched, as was Serlotta. He was relieved as he saw his wife, her arms red almost to the elbows, putting her gortos and scabbards back in place. She cleaned her two short swords on the tunic of a dead guard, and sheathed them.

She felt his eyes on her, and turned and marched over to him. He grinned and held his arms out. She marched between them and slapped him hard enough to almost spin him around.

Scyles staggered, hearing the oohs and ahs from almost everyone still standing. He turned back to face her and she tried to slap him again. He caught her arm and held it tight. She glared at him, pulled her arm loose, lifted his kurga, and tore his tunic enough to look at his stomach, searching for any sign of a wound.

"You knew I wore the armor," he reminded her. "You watched me put it on."

She sniffed, pulling up the armor to reveal a bright red and purple splotch on his lower ribcage.

"You hadn't put your trousers on yet. I wasn't looking at your armor," she said tartly, and he couldn't help but laugh. A moment later he was groaning.

"I bet that hurts," Targitai said, fingering the armor, even as he looked at the bruised area.

"Especially when I laugh," Scyles gasped, and watched the swordmaster show the armor to his father. He fingered it as well, and Scyles saw he was purposely allowing himself to be distracted until his battle fury abated.

"This stopped that knife thrust?" he asked gruffly, and Scyles nodded.

"That was a very good thrust, I thought," Targitai said, looking at his father. "That man knew how to use a sword."

His father nodded his agreement, and Scyles stared at them, and realized they were baiting him.

"Ah," he said, and turned back to face his wife. He looked at her arms. "It looks like you kept busy."

She shrugged.

"I don't think the Egelv are used to woman warriors," she said scornfully, and a voice behind her made her jump.

"Some of us certainly are, now," Emperor Balco Deh said, startling them both.

"Oh, excuse me, Emperor," she said, suddenly flustered. Scyles watched with wonder as the woman warrior became an impressionable young girl again.

"My family is still being held in our quarters," he said, and Scyles was struck by how vulnerable he looked.

"Not only that, there is a battle going on in the air space around us," Zard Win said, putting his handheld into an inner pocket. "We're safe from that unless there are Quo family members holding control of some of the palace defenses. We just don't know yet. Emperor, your guard is dead, except for one man. I have two men and myself, as well as Shae Apon. But she is not trained for battle. We don't know if there are any of the Guard in their quarters, but I suspect Mit Obet wouldn't have missed dealing with such an obvious loose end."

"We need to rescue my family," the Emperor said urgently, and Zard Win shook his head.

"We can't take you into a possible battle zone with so few men to defend you. We need you to stay out of the palace, until we've cleared a path to the safe room. And we can't be sure they haven't already booby-trapped that."

Zard Win turned and looked at Scyles' father. He nodded his head thoughtfully, and looked at Orik for confirmation.

"Emperor, we would be honored to stand at your side while a rescue party retrieves your family," he said. "We could send a small party with my swordmaster, while we protect you here in the gardens."

Targitai looked rebellious, and Scyles knew why. He also knew what he needed to say and do.

"Targitai, I will want you by my side while we rescue the Empress and the children," he said firmly, not looking at his father. "Ariapithes will be here with my father, King Orik, and the men and the queens, as well as my wife."

"I will be with you," Arga said firmly, and Scyles sighed. He stared at her, but she gave him no chance to argue. "The children will be frightened. You warriors will make it worse. They will find a woman less threatening, and more reassuring."

"They'll find two women even more so," Queen Opis said. She checked her weapons and finally looked at her husband.

"The baby," he began, and she shook her hand dismissively.

"Don't even," she said. "This baby isn't as big as a pimple on your ass yet. I can fight, as you well know, and I can calm frightened children." She looked at Scyles. "Let's get to it."

"My men must stay at the side of the Emperor, but I should be the one leading this," Zard Win started, and Shae Apon stepped close, hugged him, and pushed him back towards the Emperor.

"You know you can't leave the Emperor's side," she said. "And anyway, you've never even been in the palace. I've done the tour many times."

"Really?" The Emperor looked intrigued, despite the circumstances.

"I've always been fascinated by stories of the royal family, and wanted to be able to picture the setting better, back when I was younger," Shae Apon said, looking embarrassed. She looked around and picked up an energy staff that was Emperor's Guard standard issue for null field close-in fighting.

"We need to go," Scyles said, and nodded to Targitai. They both pulled out their bows, as did Opis, and finally, Arga. They began to trot towards the palace. Shae Apon caught up to them and trotted alongside Arga. She pointed at a smaller servant's entrance off to the side, and they veered that way.

"So," Arga said, glancing over at the Egelv woman. "You came to the palace as a child, fascinated with how these emperor types lived?"

Scyles looked at his wife. She was playing with a thread. He wondered what it would unravel.

"When is the last time you came here?" he asked, trying to picture her as a small Egelv. He hadn't actually seen any of their children yet, and didn't really know what to expect.

"Last year," she muttered, and Arga and Opis both snickered.

Chapter Thirty

Rost Fott sat on the bridge, looking at a summary of what Rel Steen had just noticed. There was something happening planetside, near the Emperor's Palace. He had crew and alien passengers at the palace this very moment. He didn't believe in coincidences.

He opened his mouth and it snapped shut again as Rel Steen stepped over into his view, looking at him intently. He held some sort of handheld that was very different from the standard ones issued to communicate with the ship's computers. But he held it so it was almost invisible to anyone not looking for it.

Rel Steen extended his hand, setting it on Rost Fott's console for a moment, and a resigned look appeared on his face. He met Rost Fott's eyes and signaled to the back of the bridge. He gave an almost imperceptible nod, and tried not to watch his second officer walk to the back as if to leave the bridge.

He stopped just shy of the exit, and stepped to the left. Rost Fott went to take a sip of his charna, and looked in the cup, as if surprised to see it was empty. He stood, even as one of the junior technicians hurried over, apologizing for not noticing.

"Not a problem," he said easily. "I need to stretch my legs anyway. Is it fresh?" he asked, walking to the back wall where hot and cold beverages, as well as relatively healthy snacks were available.

"Yes, sir," she said, and went back to her station.

Rel Steen didn't move. He gave a slight hand motion, and as Rost Fott reached the counter, he veered to the left, and went over to his second officer and looked at him questioningly.

"There are spy devices planted at your work console, Sir," Rel Steen said, his voice revealing his anger. "Give me an hour, and I can trace the path the data is taking, and who it is going to."

"I don't think we need to bother with that," Rost Fott said gravely. He remembered something. "And now I know how he knew about the attractive woman at Control. He wasn't on the bridge when I got the call."

"What do we do?" Rel Steen asked, and started. He pulled out his normal handheld and cursed. "There is a ship's battle going on over the palace. The force fields are up, but at least one ship appears to be trying to penetrate them."

"Find the first officer, place him under arrest, stun him, kill him, I could care less," Rost Fott said grimly, as they hurried back to their consoles. "And take us to full alert. Prepare to separate the ship from the Muschwain, if necessary. And have us ready to go to battle stations, but not yet. We need to find our errant first officer."

As if he was waiting to make a dramatic entrance, the back hatch opened, and First Officer Van Dono walked in, flanked by two crewmen with stunners in their hands. They saw Rost Fott and Rel Steen, and they raised their stunners.

Both of them began to go for their own stunners, but Rost Fott saw they were going to be too slow.

Val Dono and the two crewmen stiffened and fell to the deck. Two of Zard Win's men strode in quickly, their stunners fanning around the room, looking for targets. One of them casually shot the junior officer that had jumped up to help Rost Fott mere moments ago.

The other came to a halt before him.

"Captain, we just received a top priority message from Security Chief Zard Win, saying the Quo family is attempting to overthrow the Emperor. He and the Scoloti managed to thwart an attempt to use the Emperor's Guard to kill the Emperor, and the Scoloti are helping take back control of the palace."

"The Scoloti?" Rost Fott repeated, and wondered why he was surprised. A thought occurred to him. "Second Officer, did you happen to notice if the troops patrolling the Muschwain are Quo?"

"They are," the security guard said confidently. "I noticed the entire platoon was Quo a few days ago, but didn't think anything of it."

"Close and secure the airlock," Rost Fott ordered, and the security guard nodded and turned away for a moment, speaking quietly.

Rost Fott sat at his console and began pulling up screens. He could see that, on the Muschwain, four different squads were converging near the corridor that led to the air lock of Mountain Edge. He quickly checked and saw two more approaching the huge ship's bridge.

He looked at Zard Win's men.

"We need to do two things. First, we're going to need the portable stunner moved to just inside the airlock. Second, we need to find anyone on this ship that is a member of the Quo family, and place them under arrest. We also may be involved in a ship's battle very shortly, so we need to bring the ship to battle stations. All very discreetly," he added, and the security man smiled thinly.

"I have men at the airlock already. I'll have them prepare the stun gun," he said. "The Chief told me to detain all Quo immediately, and all my men have a list of who they are. We've taken all of them except one that is on the bridge of the Muschwain. Ensign Trib Pha."

"I put two of your men on the bridge less than an hour ago," Rost Fott said, and the security guard nodded that he knew. "Have them take him into custody immediately."

"Yes, sir," he said, and walked away, already speaking to someone via transceiver.

Rost Fott thought a moment, and nodded, smiling a little. "Let me know when they've secured the bridge," he said, trying to remember the name of the security guard.

Rel Steen leaned towards him and quietly said "Marl Tac." Rost Fott laughed, and nodded his head appreciatively.

He had a thought, and couldn't help but grin. He shouldn't be getting a kick out of this, because he knew it would cost at least a few Scoloti lives. But they would probably thank him for the opportunity to do something they considered constructive.

"Skulis, can you hear me?"

The answer came swiftly.

"When you shout like that, yes, I can hear you better than I'd like," he said, and Rost Fott rolled his eyes.

"We've just discovered a plot to kill our emperor, and along with him, your kings, and everyone else that went planetside," he said, and continued before the Scoloti warrior had a chance to question him. "They're all safe, and the rebellion at the palace was thwarted by Zard Win and your tribesmen and women."

"What do you need?" Skulis asked brusquely, and Rost Fott winced at his bluntness.

"I need help dealing with the patrols of soldiers on the Muschwain." Rost Fott took a deep breath, knowing his next words would mean the deaths of any number of Egelv and Scoloti. "You can consider them all enemies, and deal with them as harshly as you need to."

"Well, that should be no problem," Skulis said, sounding excited. "We think our bows have a longer range than their weapons that knock us out."

"I would assume they're set on kill," Rost Fott said grimly. "But if you wait five minutes, there will be a null field over the entire ship."

"We can do that," Skulis said confidently. "I've had trackers shadowing them all day, keeping track of where they are. I have warriors ready to attack, whenever you give me the word."

"I'll be right back to you on that," Rost Fott. "Prepare your men."

"And women," Skulis said dryly, and he nodded his head, resigned.

"And women," he said.

Rost Fott looked at the security man, who was watching a monitor on an unoccupied computer console.

"Marl Tac," he said, and the security guard looked up in surprise. "Please tell your men on the Muschwain bridge to place a null field over the entire ship."

"Done," he said, and grinned. "The four squads are massed at the airlock, and I think they're about to attempt an assault on Mountain Edge."

"Please use the mobile stunner, and subdue them," he said, and turned to Rel Steen.

"Take us to battle stations," he said, and his second nodded. "And be ready to seal the airlock and detach from Muschwain at a moment's notice."

"Put me on a system-wide channel," Rost Fott said, and after a moment, Rel Steen nodded.

"This is the captain of Mountain Edge, and I am issuing a system-wide alert," he said, his mouth suddenly very dry. He took a deep breath and continued. "The Quo family has attempted a coup, and tried to assassinate the Emperor. The plot has failed, however there are still some members of the Quo family resisting arrest. All ships and facilities should immediately place any Quo family member under arrest, by order of the Emperor. If you are a crew member of a ship captained by a member of the Quo family, relieve them of duty, peacefully, if possible, and place them under arrest. Route all status reports to Command Central. I am Rost Fott, captain of Mountain Edge, and attest this accounting to be truthful, and these orders are to be carried out by the command of Emperor Balco Deh. End transmission."

Rost Fott sat down at his station, letting his body fall heavily into his seat. He looked at Rel Steen, who shook his head in awe.

"Do you really have authorization to order all that?" he asked, sounding excited, but more than a little frightened, as well.

"Maybe," Rost Fott said, and his second's eyes grew wide.

"Maybe?"

"Zard Win said the Emperor was ordering him and everyone we could trust to take immediate action to stop the revolt, and regain control of the fleet."

"Well, that should do it," Rel Steen said, and plopped down heavily at his own station. He got a vague expression for a moment, and nodded. He looked at Rost Fott with more than a little awe. "Our men that are with the roving Scoloti warriors said they just slaughtered all the squads roaming around Muschwain, killed the bunch that were about to assault the bridge, and heard some of them bragging about all the throats they slit near our airlock."

"Oh," Rost Fott said, and stared at Rel Steen, wondering that he wasn't more horrified.

"They also decided to assault the troop carrier, took it, even though there was no null field on that ship," he recited. "They'd taken power weapons from the dead troopers, and took the entire ship, killing everyone aboard. They lost five Scoloti, four men, one woman."

"Oh," was all Rost Fott could manage.

Opis ran easily along with the rest, happy to see she hadn't grown too old to run and fight. She decided Scyles and her daughter would be able to provide enough firepower that she could use her favorite weapons of choice, two short swords.

She noticed that Targitai had both his swords out as well, one long, one short.

Two of the Emperor's Guard came out of a side door and rushed them. Scyles and Arga took them out before they took three steps. My daughter, she thought proudly. She would have grown into an excellent Woman Warrior, but being a fighting princess, and someday queen, was a goal worthy of her.

They approached an intersection of hallways, and half a dozen Guards charged them from the left side. Scyles didn't hesitate. He fired two arrows at a time, twice, and two guards fell. Arga got a shot off, even as Opis and Targitai engaged with the remaining three. The guard she attacked looked so surprised to be battling a woman, he was easy prey. With Targitai, it didn't matter. He ran by two of them, swinging his swords in a weaving flurry of death, and they both fell, blood pouring from multiple wounds. Scyles slashed the throat of the guard Arga had wounded, and they ran on.

Shae Apon pointed with her staff at a broad archway, and Targitai raised his hand. They all slowed down to a walk, and entered what had to be the personal quarters of the Emperor and his family.

They'd found the royal family, and eight Guards holding them prisoner.

There were several bodies on the floor, and four female Egelv, and three smaller ones, against the far wall. Two guards stood near them, both holding shocking rods and what looked like edged weapons. When they saw the Scoloti, they both turned to the prisoners, and Opis had the angle to watch Scyles spring into action. He kept walking forward, but drew back and fired six arrows so fast, she couldn't believe it.

The Guards appeared just as amazed. The ones closest dodged, thinking they were the targets, but the arrows buried deep into the two Guards securing the prisoners, three each. They both dropped without a sound.

Opis charged two of the other guards, while Targitai engaged the last four. One of her opponents staggered as an arrow appeared in his chest. She basically overwhelmed the other, knocking his lighter weapons aside with one sword, cutting him to the bone with the other. She saw Targitai had killed two of his opponents immediately, even as Scyles took the last two down with arrows. The swordmaster slashed their throats to make sure they were dead.

Arga finished off the other Guard, and they stepped over the bodies and approached the royal family.

"Do not fear us, we are friends," Opis said, but they stared at them in horror, and the three small children, which she could now see were two boys and a girl, were crying. She wasn't exactly sure how old they were, but doubted they'd seen ten harvests yet.

"Empress Lasa Sheen?" Shae Apon walked past her, approaching one of the women. Now that Opis took a good look at her, she could have guessed she was the empress. It might have been the finery she wore, the gorgeous gown that shimmered and changed colors with no apparent pattern. Or, it might have been the light crown, Opis thought wryly.

"Empress Lasa Sheen? I am Shae Apon, Medical Officer of Mountain Edge, and you are safe now. These warriors will protect you until the Emperor gets here." Opis was impressed with how calm Shae Apon sounded, and it had an immediate effect on the royal family and their retinue. "Zard Win, we have the empress and the three children, as well as some of her servants, here in the dining hall of the palace quarters."

Shae Apon smiled at the Empress again.

"The Emperor is coming," she said reassuringly.

Opis watched the woman pull herself together, and wondered if this was the first time she'd ever been in physical danger. She looked the four Scoloti over, more than a little suspicion on her face.

"You are warriors?" she asked cautiously, looking at them, and Opis nodded reassuringly. The empress looked puzzled. "What race are you?"

"We are the People," she said, bowing her head slightly. "We are the Scoloti."

"But, you are women," one of the little boys said, and Opis smiled at him.

"Yes, young prince, we are women warriors, when need be."

He looked at his mother uncertainly. She didn't seem to have any better idea of how to deal with them either. They were all saved from potential embarrassment when the rest of the Scoloti, along with the Emperor and Zard Win and his men came through the archway.

The children all shrieked and rushed the emperor. He looked embarrassed at their lack of decorum, but Opis also saw his eyes glint with moisture. All three swept against him, hugging his legs and waist. The Empress managed to look more stately until she got within arms reach, and then her strength fled her and she allowed him to sweep her beneath his protective arms.

Emperor Balco Deh looked around the room at the bodies on the floor and nodded. He looked at Targitai, and then at Scyles, gratitude in his face, and yet, a spark of humor.

"We followed the bodies," he said dryly, and watched one of the Scoloti warriors hand Scyles and Arga separate handfuls of arrow shafts. They'd already removed the arrows from the dead men in this room, and accepted the rest with thanks.

The Emperor shook his head, and turned to Gelon and Orik.

"I owe you a debt of gratitude," he said, and the other Egelv stared at him. "The empire owes you much."

There were loud booms and crackling outside the large, open windows, and Opis walked over to look. Overhead, above a visible dome that seemed to stop anything from entering, a battle raged between two ships. Then two more ships suddenly appeared, and one of the first two exploded, almost immediately. She turned and saw that nearly everyone had joined her to watch, but it looked like the battle was over.

She noticed that Scyles still held his bow, with an arrow nocked. He stood near the Emperor, back to him, watching the far entrances to the large dining hall. Arga stood next to him, but held her bow loosely, and not loaded.

The Emperor stepped next to Scyles, holding his two son's hands.

"Thank you for the lives of my family," he said so quietly, Opis could barely make out his words. "My wife says you shot and killed the two Guards that were tasked to execute them."

"That is what it looked like, when we first appeared," Scyles admitted. "Protecting the young ones is a duty we all must accept."

The Emperor stared at him for a long moment, before turning to his sons.

"Prince Scyles, I would like to introduce you to my two sons. This is Crown Prince Draw Ask, and his little brother, Prince Stem Eco. Boys, this is Prince Scyles, heir to the throne of the Auchatae Tribe, of the Scoloti People."

Both boys stood straight before him, and nodded to him.

"We are pleased to meet you, Prince Scyles," they said in perfect unison. "Thank you for rescuing us from the bad guards," Prince Stem Eco said, and his older brother nudged him.

"No, your brother is proper to thank him, Draw Ask," the Emperor said, admonishingly. "He stopped the two men that would have hurt you. He also saved my life, out in the gardens. He killed a traitor, many in fact. But, in particular, the one that intended to assassinate me."

"Thank you, Prince Scyles," they both said, again in perfect unison.

"I am told that Prince Scyles is the finest archer in the Egelv Empire," the Emperor told them, and Opis suppressed a laugh as Scyles began to redden.

"Are you the only archer in the Empire, Prince Scyles?" and she bit her lip, and felt her shoulders shake a little.

"Not quite, Crown Prince Draw Ask," he said, smiling.

"What is an archer?" the smaller prince asked, and both the Emperor and Scyles smiled at him.

"An archer is someone that can shoot this," Scyles said, holding up an arrow," with this, from a distance, very accurately," he finished, holding up his bow with his other hand.

"Show us," Crown Prince Draw Ask said imperiously, and the Emperor made a low rumbling sound in his throat.

"Please," he finished, hurriedly.

"Can you show us how effective this bow is?" the Emperor asked, and Scyles nodded.

"Is there anything in this room you don't mind having a few arrows stuck into?" he asked, and the Emperor looked around the hall.

"Well, I'm particularly annoyed at that far guard, near the couches," he said, pointing at a body almost twenty-five horse lengths distant.

Scyles raised an eyebrow as he looked at the Emperor.

"He's dead, Emperor."

"So he is," the Emperor responded, and Scyles nodded, glancing at the two boys.

Opis coughed and Orik immediately turned to look at her. She nodded with her head at Scyles, who walked off to the side, about a horse length away from the Emperor and the two princes.

Abruptly, he drew and fired six arrows so fast, she doubted most of them could have correctly said how may he shot. The boys gasped and stared at the arrows in flight. Then, every Egelv watching, with the exception of Shae Apon and Zard Win gasped as the arrows struck the body in a straight line, the first burying itself in the shoulder of the facedown body, and each after slightly lower in the body, the last sticking firmly in the corpse's hip.

She heard the Emperor exhale slowly, his eyes slowly shifting from the arrows to Scyles.

Opis looked at her husband, but they'd gotten the hint. Both Orik and Gelon walked over and nodded deeply to the Emperor. Zard Win and Shae Apon joined them, and the five of them began to speak in earnest.

Myrina walked by her, and hooked her arm through hers.

"Come, girl, if we don't step in and moderate this, our men will have the People working for mare's milk."

"Good point," Opis admitted, and let herself get pulled along.

Behind her, she heard her daughter give Scyles a loud smacking kiss on the lips.

"Showoff," Arga said, and she heard Scyles laugh quietly. Then she asked the question they all wanted the answer to. "How big a number is one hundred million, and what is a Dracoon?"

Opis smiled, satisfied that, despite the stress and danger, this day would prove to be a very important one in the annals of the Scoloti.

Chapter Thirty-One

Commodore Rost Fott coughed, and could still taste the fermented mare's milk. At first taste, it was abhorrent, and left a sour taste in his mouth. But he was glad he'd accepted the mug from King Gelon. As odd as it seemed, he was going to miss the Scoloti. Newly married First Officer Rel Steen had just verified that Muschwain was now in a stable orbit, and occasional adjustments by the generation ship itself would keep it that way.

He skimmed down the long report on the monitor, checking off details in his mind as he went. He was proud of what had been accomplished on this mission, but it was probably just as well his part of it was finished. He was developing too much empathy for the plucky race that called themselves the People.

Zard Win and Shae Apon walked into the conference room and greeted him warmly, saluting him one last time. He watched them get settled into seats next to each other, and couldn't help but notice their chairs were much closer together than they would have been a few months ago, under similar circumstances. He hoped Zard Win knew what he was doing. He wouldn't have an older, more established family member to back him if he committed a social gaff his superiors weren't willing to accept.

"Congratulations, Commodore," Zard Win said, and Shae Apon smiled, nodding her agreement. "Nothing more than what you deserved. It's been a pleasure serving under you."

"It has, Commodore," Shae Apon said in that quiet, soothing voice she had most of the time. "Thank you for giving me a free hand when the Scoloti fell into our hands."

"Are you both absolutely sure you wish to make this move?" Rost Fott asked, knowing what their answer would be. "I could pull some strings and make your assignment requests disappear."

"No, Sir, I think we're both happy with where we're headed," Zard Win said, looked at Shae Apon, who simply smiled back at him, and then nodded to Rost Fott.

"Well, you're seriously understaffed at the moment," he said, and looked at Zard Win. "Captain Zard Win, your crew consists of one ensign, and four technicians. Enough to cover skeleton crews with some stretch for leaves and such."

He looked back and forth between the two of them.

"I was able to finish all critical repairs and updates on the Muschwain," he said, sliding a printout across the table to Shae Apon. "Muschwain has full engine capabilities, although she's still a tub, and won't outrace anything faster than a rock. All weapon pods are replaced or repaired, and fully functional." He looked at Shae Apon. "And I did manage to find a couple hundred stasis pods in storage for who knows how long. They're in the lee storage hold near the airlock, tucked in between the raw materials and equipment for mass production of the armor platelets, knives, and whatever else you come up with."

"Thank you Commodore," Shad Apon said, and looked at Zard Win. "And thank you for the six cargo holds worth of river bottom gunk you left me in the starboard airlock."

They all smiled at that. She had the idea they could transform that giant hold into a combination of crops and grazing areas for the livestock. Rost Fott had a mental picture of her out in the middle of the massive load of muck, with a handheld gardening tool, spreading it out across the airlock's deck. He couldn't help but grin.

They both looked at him curiously, but he shook his head, and got his facial features under control.

"It's my pleasure, and the harbor maintenance chief was happy to oblige, Station Master Shae Apon," he said, and they all smiled, although she looked thoughtful.

"I don't know that Station Master is the appropriate title or ranking, if all propulsion units are functional," she said, and smiled. "Perhaps I should have the rank of captain."

"That is something that may get addressed sooner rather than later,"

Rost Fott admitted, and then relented, smiling. "Technically, Captain Zard Win is in charge of ship's functions. Remember, a ship can not have two captains," he said, smiling. "I worked hard to get two parallel departments on one ship, so neither of you is the other's superior."

Shae Apon glanced at Zard Win, and a hint of a smile flashed across her lips.

"And we thank you, Commodore," she said, and the hint of a smile returned. "Although I don't see any issue with that."

Rost Fott started to stare at her, and realized she was actually making a joke. A month ago, she would have been incapable of that. Zard Win looked back and forth between the two of them, probably horrified that they were casually joking about his manipulating the system to allow them to pursue a relationship, should they so choose. So much good has come of this last voyage, he decided, even as he realized she was still smiling at him.

"So, Commodore, how is Captain Lans Pre?"

Zard Win stared at her, shocked, and Rost Fott was glad they were leaving his command. They were both becoming just independent enough, that trying to perform in a staid, structured chain of command would be difficult, if not impossible, for either of them. He wanted them to be very successful, and happy, hopefully with each other. But if they stayed under his command, he would have made their lives hell.

"She's doing well, and very happy with her administrative position at Egelv Prime Traffic Command," he said evenly. "You both will probably see her more often than I do."

"Very sad to hear that, Sir," Shae Apon said sincerely, and Zard Win nodded his agreement.

"I feel I learned much from you, Sir," Zard Win said quietly. "And I wish to thank you for that opportunity. I think what we're going to be doing, and Shae Apon's plans to help the Scoloti adapt to this new universe they've been thrust into, will be critical to their development, and their long-term security."

"I admire your energy, and desire to help the Scoloti, but I don't envy the relative isolation you'll both have, here on the Muschwain, with a minimal Egelv staff and crew, within visual range of Egelv Prime, and yet so alone with all these Scoloti. What will you do to remain sane?"

Shae Apon laughed. "I will be busier than I ever have been." She glanced quickly at Zard Win. "And I have no complaints with the company I will have."

Rost Fott smiled at her openness. He looked at Zard Win, wondering if he'd even realized what she'd just told him.

"And you, Captain?"

Zard Win grinned, and rubbed his hands together.

"I'm going to learn to shoot a bow, and use a sword like the Scoloti."

Myrina stood in front of the open hatch to the interior concourse, looking across the vast airlock hold everyone was now calling the Steppes. Beside her, Opis breathed in deep, and sighed.

"Can you smell that?" she asked, sounding both sad and ebullient. "That is the smell of the world we left, even if it is not soil from our world. I missed it so."

"Do you want to go roll in it?" Myrina asked innocently. "I'll wait, if you like."

"Not today," Opis said, and didn't surprise her with her next response. "Unless you'd like to strip down, and roll with me."

Arga walked into the Steppes from the corridor just in time to hear them. She rolled her eyes.

"Do you two ever talk about anything else?" she asked, and held up a hand. "No, no, please do not answer that."

She looked out across the hold.

"Do you really think we can get grass, and grains, and crops to grow here, on this hard metal surface, with no day god to encourage the seeds?"

"Shae Apon says we can," Myrina said, and felt confident in her own words. "Everything she and Zard Win have promised us was possible has come to pass, and I think she knows how to do this. I do not pretend to understand it, but if we can't trust the two of them to help guide us, we are doomed."

"Can we please guide them into one bed together, soon?" Opis said, and they all laughed. "It pains me to see them fumble about with their feelings for each other. They've done so much for us, surely we can assist them with this."

"Some things can not be forced," Myrina said, and stopped cold. Both she and Opis turned and looked at Arga, who sniffed.

"No one forced either of us," she said, rubbing her stomach, and both women laughed. "Truth, I think they are finally figuring it out themselves."

"We shall see," Opis said, and frowned. "No, we won't. And it's a shame. I would like to watch how Egelvs perform under the bedsheets. See if they know anything we don't."

"I'd watch that," Arga said, and giggled. "Watching it with Scyles would be the best way, but getting him to agree will never happen. In some ways, he's very shy."

"He is, that," Myrina said, and grinned. "I don't think he gets that from either of us."

They walked back to the common hall, stopped in front of the open hatch, but didn't enter.

"Sitting in there, and not being able to have a mug or two, just doesn't feel the same," Myrina said, and sighed. She looked at the other two women. "Are you both ready for tomorrow?"

"Aye," Opis said, and nudged her daughter. "Poor Skulis. He and Lika will have to stay here on Muschwain, keep everyone busy. They will all have tasks, but someone will need to keep them focused."

"Skulis will be focused on Agave," Arga said dryly, and both of the other women nodded in agreement.

"He will want to," Myrina corrected her. "I had a talk with Agave, and he will find that diversion unavailable while he is supposed to be in command."

Opis turned to them.

"There is so much to do," she said. "All the things to make this ship our home, so much to learn. We are never going back to our tribal homelands. We must learn to live in this new world, with strange creatures none of us could have imagined, mere moons ago."

"Learn to live, and to thrive," Myrina said. "Our children will inherit what we accomplish. They already are," she said, looking at Arga, who blushed.

"We have so many questions, and no answers yet for most of them," the young girl said, and Myrina listened to her, smiling as she thought how hard both the girl and her son fought against what they now would fight to the death for. Each other. Her attention came back to Arga's words.

"One answer must be decided now, because time is short, and we can not make an error on such an important decision," Arga said, and Myrina wondered what looming difficulty had her attention. Their needing to learn how to use things, how they would raise their newborns in this new world, which king would assume the mantle of Great King?

Arga sighed heavily.

"What do we wear tomorrow?"

"We should talk," Shae Apon said, and Zard Win looked at her cautiously. They were walking back to their quarters after watching Mountain Edge cast off and disappear towards Egelv Prime.

"About?"

"Many things," she said, and began counting them off on her fingers.

"First, unless we decide to develop a true love for sheep and horse meat, and little else, we need to quit taking the easy path, and eating at the Scoloti common hall. We need to come to a decision on how to deal with providing meals. Someone needs to know how to prepare meals."

"I can cook," Zard Win said mildly.

"Really?" Shae Apon looked at him in surprise.

"Really," he said, and then smiled at her. "However, I have a commissary ship scheduled to dock tomorrow morning. They will make one of the larger conference rooms near the bridge into a kitchen and dining area. They will then install a complete galley based on Scoloti cooking methods in the other large airlock, on the port side, with proper ventilation and easy cleanup systems to deal with the smoke and grease, and other byproducts. It will be large enough to prepare meals for large groups, up to three hundred people."

He looked at her uncertainly.

"We will need to look through the purchasing online catalogs for suitable tables, benches, and such. Right now I'm using that airlock to store things, so it will need to be cleared out. And we will need to disable the airlock from being opened, permanently. Both of them, actually."

"Look at you. These are great ideas," she said, and slapped him on the arm with the back of her hand. Then she looked startled, and Zard Win began to laugh.

"We are both turning into Scoloti primitives," he said, and she nodded ruefully.

"We need to decide where we are going to have a manufacturing and assembly area, and get the equipment to make the platelets set up," she said, counting another finger. "We barely were able to make enough for tomorrow. Everyone else will have to wear their old, iron plated armor, until we get production rolling."

"I've got our new ensign and six Scholitoi to help him move everything where it needs to go," Zard Win said. "I might have accidentally told two of your technicians to be ready to help him assemble the hardware, and test the software."

"I believe I am the one with the authority to tell my technicians to help him," she said, and he heard her playful tone. It wasn't how she usually was, and he didn't quite know how to deal with this quixotic version of her.

"You can order some of my crew around tomorrow," he said.

"Okay," was her only response. "Third, we need to make plans to start a school of some sort, and decide what they need to learn first. Of course, they will want to continue with their training in fighting, but there is much they should know about their immediate surroundings, and about the universe around us all."

"A school is good, but we might want to start small, and maybe give them some basic knowledge that applies to their current lives. Like what gravity is, what electricity and neutron power cells are, basic math skills, why going out of the ship without a forcefield or spacesuit around you is a really bad idea..." Zard Win paused.

Shae Apon gave a little laugh, and stopped short.

He was surprised to see they were already back at their quarters, in front of her door. She looked at him, and he decided she didn't want their discussion to end any more than he did.

"Are you hungry?" he asked, and she sighed.

"Not for sheep," she admitted, and looked guilty. "I don't mean to complain," she said. "We can eat in the common hall."

"I have a better idea," he said, and gestured back at his door. She looked at him a little suspiciously, but walked with him.

"Make yourself comfortable," he said nervously, as his door closed behind them.

She chose a comfortable chair, and sat on the front edge of it, looking nervous. Both their rooms had received furnishings more suitable for an Egelv than whatever race had owned the Muschwain before the Hshtahni.

He went around behind the short bar he'd insisted on. The acquisitions officer had sniffed about it, but he'd said he would need to entertain visitors to the ship occasionally, and this was the most economical way. He didn't know if it was, but it seemed to satisfy the officer. He opened a bottle of wine and poured them both glasses. He set them on the small dining table, in front of two of the four chairs around it. He set the bottle between the two glasses.

"Would you, please?" he asked, gesturing for her to move to the table. He had the glasses at two settings that faced each other, across the round table. She got up, went to the table and moved one of the glasses over, so they were sitting next to each other, and then sat.

He hadn't expected that, and suddenly, he was very nervous. He went back behind the bar and pulled out two medium-sized thermal bags. One was to keep things hot, the other, to keep things either chilled or frozen, depending on which compartment you used.

"Where are your plates and utensils?" she asked, and he pointed mutely at a cabinet, and the drawer beneath it. She placed two settings properly. He opened the heated bag and pulled out several medium-sized covered bowls, and then a platter, also covered.

She sat back down and watched as he pulled the cover off the platter. She gasped, and stared at him.

"Is that Krensil?" she asked faintly, and he nodded.

"I hope it's prepared the way you like," he said, and began to remove the covers from the bowls. They held Egelv vegetables and a casserole. He also had rolls.

"How?" she asked, her voice, if anything, sounding even weaker.

"It came up on the Mountain Edge," Zard Win said, his throat very dry. He coughed. "I had it delivered before they departed, and Rel Steen made sure it got here safely."

"Delivered?" she asked, and he almost laughed at the look in her eyes. She wanted to ask so badly, but wouldn't. He decided to have mercy on her.

"From Fernicki's" he said, and she gasped.

"Isn't that place very expensive?"

Zard Win shrugged. It was like buying a long vacation at a very good resort, expensive, but he wasn't going to tell her that.

"It was worth it," he said, and finally looked into her eyes. "And I thought the occasion warranted it. Oh, and we have fresh fruit, fixings, and cheese for dessert."

"Special occasion?" she asked softly, staring back at him.

"Well, yes," Zard Win said slowly, stalling. What could he say that wouldn't make it obvious he was totally smitten with her? "The first day of the assignment of our lives. The beginning of a project, or even mission, that is all either of us could ever have asked for, and the beginning of a very successful, and long...working relationship between us."

Zard Win winced. That wasn't really what he'd meant to say. What did any of that even mean? It meant he was babbling, he decided. He became aware that she was still watching him.

"You should eat, while the Krensil is hot, and the spices activated," he said, feeling panic at her lack of a response.

Her eyes never left him as she took a bite of the fish. They widened at that point, but stayed fixed on his. He automatically took a bite himself, and blinked at how delicious it was.

"This is so good," she said, and he heard the awe in her voice.

"I know," he answered. "I had no idea," he admitted, as they both took another bite.

Oddly enough, it had gotten easier to keep eye contact with her. You would think their eyes would tire, or water. But he couldn't look away from her smooth brown skin the shade of Xarol wood. The way her face was framed by the luxurious, white flowing hair, parted in the middle on the top, and flowing down over her shoulders, hanging below the seat of her chair. He didn't know when she'd taken her hair restraints out, letting the thick cord of hair flow free.

"You're beautiful," Zard Win said, and even though he realized he'd just made the classic blunder, and she was probably moments from giving him a fake apology, and leaving his quarters, probably forever, he didn't try to repair the damage he'd just done.

To do so would have required ending their eye contact.

Just as he realized she still held her side of the gaze, she finally spoke. "Are you going to kiss me?"

The Muschwain stopped dead in orbit, as did every planet, even Egelv Prime. The atmosphere was also sucked out of the room entirely, including what was in his lungs. Breathing was no longer possible.

Somehow, Zard Win chewed and swallowed the bite of Krensil, and was finally able to speak.

"I don't want your food to get cold. It's Krensil," he said, and felt like an idiot. She considered his words, her eyes never leaving his. Their home sun aged until it cooled, and a planetary nebula formed. It eventually turned into a white star, then a black star before it finally died. This took several billion years, which passed very slowly, before she finally responded.

"Good point." She took another bite and eventually, after the acceleration caused by dark energy eventually became so strong that it completely overwhelmed the effects of the gravitational, electromagnetic and strong binding forces, causing the death of the universe, she swallowed. "Before cheese and fruit?"

Zard Win opened his mouth, but nothing would come out.

She sighed and quickly stood up, stepped over to him, and gave him a very thorough kiss. She went back to her chair and sat.

"Before cheese and fruit," she said, and he nodded mutely.

They both took bites of their fish.

Chapter Thirty-Two

Aboard the World Ship Kchoatkhakh, on the outskirts of the Egelv Prime star system

Zechkreeshrrprhkq slowed the progress of the sensor probes, and the large screen showed a visual of the generation ship Muschwain. The screen fragmented into multiple smaller views, one showing crews working on the outside of the world ship, several showing heat images spread throughout the the generation ship, others showing telescopically enhanced views of the palace grounds on Egelva Prime.

"I know," he nodded his massive head. One view, showing the same heat images, grew to dominate the screen for a moment, before shrinking back down to a smaller size. "It's amazing how so many sentient beings can be piled into such a small vessel."

His nephew, Achkptrrshkqk, pointed out that both the Eglev and the Humans considered the generation ship to be enormous. He laughed.

"It's all a matter of perspective, right old friend?"

Both Hechktar looked to the left wall, where a large tank extended out into the room. The constantly moving, writhing mass of appendages, and tendrils both filled and barely occupied the tank with the Trixmae.

His nephew leaned forward, and the screens readjusted to show the views of the palace grounds from several perspectives. The action centered around a recently constructed stage with an extensive arrangement of stands in a large arch around it.

There were many Egelv already seated, and many times more still moving towards the setup. The stage itself was mostly empty, with the exception of a few Egelv troopers spaced around it.

"It would appear that events have marched on without us," Zechkreeshrrprhkq said, and sighed a voluminous exhalation. He accompanied it with a resounding release of pressure, and his nephew accordingly followed suit. "The fate of these Humans appear to be set, but at least their home world is still unknown, and relatively safe for the time being."

"Do you think these Humans will thrive in this setting, Uncle?" his nephew asked. They both turned to the Trixmae and nodded, as if choreographed.

"We shall return in a handful of centuries to see how they fare, dear nephew," he said, and the smaller Hechktar nodded his agreement. "We bear responsibility for this situation, and I fear our assistance will be required to remedy it, when the time comes. Until then, these Humans that call themselves the People will have to deal with the situation without our help. They must grow, and can not, if we rescue them at every step."

"I look forward to our return," Achkptrrshkqk said, and he turned back to watching the tiny figures move around the palace grounds.

"Indeed," Achkptrrshkqk said, and without glancing at the Trixmae, nodded his massive head, tendrils writhing in near unison with the Trixmae.

"Indeed," he repeated.

Gelon watched the men and women of his tribe mill around the palace grounds, admiring each other's new armor and clothing. They all had new clothing, complete with platelet armor that covered their entire torso, as well as their thighs, and helmets.

He couldn't believe how light it was. And yet, it was so much stronger than his old iron armor. The chest armor, which actually hung all the way down to his own personal equipment, as he liked to call it, also protected the shoulders, the lower neck and entire back, and was all one piece. The platelets were woven into a jerkin, using thread of the same material as the platelets themselves. The waist area was fitted a little tighter, so the entire jerkin didn't just hang loose, from his neck to his crotch. His pants had the platelets woven into the thigh areas, as well as over the shins.

They all had platelet armored helmets that matched. They went straight across the forehead, and then down in a series of flaps that covered ears and neck, as well as the back of the neck. It did leave enough gap in the back for their thick braids. The top was also more rounded and didn't jut upward as high as many of their old helmets had. He thought it made them look very dull and boring, even though all the platelets, whether on helmet or armor, were bright silver that looked as if it had just been polished.

Gelon had fought having so much body area covered, not wanting to burden his warriors with so much weight. But the entire ensemble of armor didn't weigh as much as his old helmet with the iron platelets did. And it was so much stronger. In fact, they hadn't been able to break one yet.

And it wasn't for want of trying, he thought with amusement. Poor Skulis was all the poorer, due to his cocky arrogance that he could break anything.

One thing had caused more dissension than he would have expected. His tribal colors were a dark red that Myrina called maroon, whatever in Hades that was. And Orik's tribe, the Paralatae, wore purple, which looked a lot like maroon to him. The Caitiari wore bright blue, but who cared?

Word had come down to them, straight from the Emperor, that all their cloth, whether it be the armored jerkins, the long-sleeved tunics beneath, the trousers with the armored inserts, even their boots, would be a dark grey.

They all thought it boring, and there was much grumbling, until the last couple days, when they finally received their armor and casual clothing. Even the non-armored clothing they wore when they weren't on duty were the same dark grey.

There had been much complaining, until they tried them on. The grumbling died, and one by one, a comment, here and there, the men, and even the Women Warriors, began to admire each other and themselves in those strange walls called mirrors.

The first time they'd gotten the warriors fully in uniform and in something resembling a line, Gelon had been speechless. Orik stepped over to him and whispered.

"If you tell anyone I said this, I'll call you a liar, and split you like a melon. But we look pretty good in these dull rags."

Gelon watched Orik get a thoughtful look on his face.

"Well, except for Lik. He's still ugly as the boar of Thessaly."

Gelon smiled at the memory, and automatically put his hand on the haft of his long sword. He slid it out of its scabbard, also dark grey, as was his gorytos, and held it up. It was about the same weight as his old iron sword, and the same shape, of course. But the similarities stopped there.

His new "steel" sword literally glowed a shiny silver in the sunlight. He'd been told that in the dark, it would stay a dull dark grey, but he kept forgetting to check at night. His short sword was the same. As was his new shield. It was lighter than his old wooden one, but held up to swordplay far better than anything he'd ever seen.

He was told that, in theory, both the swords, their new knives, and the shields could be scratched, which they'd proved, but should be very difficult to damage, and nearly impossible to break, using similar weapons to theirs. If they chipped a blade, he was told that it could be resharpened and functional, until it was replaced.

He put his sword away and stared up into the sky, wishing he could see their ship. He'd been told that, at night, at certain times, if the weather was clear, the ship was visible to the naked eye.

The Muschwain would remain in the same orbit, beyond the two moons, and that would be their permanent home for the People. When on duty, there were barracks below the palace, as well as training facilities. There would be regular shuttles between the ship and the military airfield, farther out from the city.

For the moment, a normal day at the palace would require sixteen warriors on duty. Zard Win had sat down with him and Orik, as well as Targitai, Ariapithes, and Scyles, to explain how the warriors needed to be organized.

Eighty warriors, sixty male, twenty female, had been chosen to be the first company of the Scoloti Emperor's Guard. That was ten squads of eight. Two squads on duty at all times, with each day and night divided into three periods. That gave two squads several days when they weren't scheduled, giving them some rest, and opportunity to train. It also gave them a chance to have visitors during their downtime.

The barracks had been designed to house several hundred guard at a time, so there was plenty of space. When the Emperor traveled, it would entail more warriors, and Gelon and Orik were already discussing who else they could use that were already awake, and how many more warriors and their dependents they should waken and begin to train. They would also need to be educated about their new world and life.

Gelon and Orik both agreed that the Caitiari would not be needed for this. They could sleep on.

He saw Scyles and Arga, standing over by where she and the two queens would sit, during the ceremony. He could almost feel his chest grow, trying to hold in his pride in his youngest son. Targitai had always told him Scyles had hidden skills that would serve him and the tribe well, but Gelon could never get past comparing him to his older brothers, and seeing the discrepancy.

But he'd been wrong. Scyles was smarter than either he or Myrina. He was brave, stayed calm in a crisis, and the people loved him.

When the time comes, he will easily replace Orik and me, and become the Great King in everything but name, Gelon thought. He and Orik had talked about this last night. They both thought that, in time, they should consider merging the two tribes. They got along well, and this new life raised new problems. Having two kings, and a very competent prince, all capable of leading both tribes, as needed, was both a luxury, and, from the look of it, a necessity, in the future. They both agreed that Scyles and Arga should succeed them, and that Scyles and Serlotta would work well together.

But all that could be worked out later. They had enough to deal with at the moment.

He looked at Myrina, and grinned. And Scyles would have a little sister to spoil, and cause him to age faster.

His wife seemed to feel his gaze, because she turned her head to look at him, and smiled, making his blood race faster through his veins. She pointed with a nod, and Gelon turned.

Zard Win and Shae Apon had arrived. He looked at them, wondering why they looked different. They were dressed in fine Egelv clothing, but that wasn't it.

Orik said something to them, and they stopped to talk with him for a moment. Gelon turned back to his wife and shrugged his shoulders.

She laughed and said something to Opis. Arga heard her, and they all looked past Gelon and nodded, then began to laugh. Puzzled, he turned back and gave the couple a closer look.

Oh.

The couple.

He quickly turned away to hide his smirk. He looked at Myrina and grinned, nodding. All three women laughed, and he was pretty sure it was at him, for being so slow to see it.

These women need more chores, he decided. They have too much free time to gossip.

He felt someone behind him and turned around, thinking it was them. But it was Orik. His friend tried to be discreet, but it was beyond his skills.

"Well, they crossed that river," he said, and Gelon chuckled at his choice of words.

"Aye, and about time," he responded, and they both nodded.

Scyles kissed Arga and moved towards his father. He was surprised to see the stands were filling fast. He wondered how many Egelv lived in Egelva, because there were a lot of them here. He'd never been to a large city before. He'd been to Olbia once, when they'd gone to meet Theophilus, his Grecian tutor. It had ten thousand people living there at that point, and that had been almost overwhelming.

It looked like there were already that many people here, just in the stands. In fact, it looked like there were many more than that.

Scyles saw Arga was now sitting with their mothers. She waved, and he nodded back to her. She seemed to find that funny, and made a comment to her mother, who laughed. Then all three women looked at him, and he felt flustered.

He sighed and looked around at the men milling aimlessly, nervous themselves. They were no more used to this than he was, he realized. He needed to rally them, settle them down and get them in ranks.

Ranks, he thought. All these new words with meanings they'd never needed before. Ranks, companies, planets, stars, stunners, ships, stasis, the list went on. His eyes ran across the staging area the Scoloti were to stand in, and he saw Zard Win and Shae Apon.

He was glad they were staying with the ship. He liked them both very much, and they seemed to really care about helping the People learn to live and thrive in this new world they lived in. He cocked his head curiously as he watched them walk in the general direction of where Arga was. They kept getting stopped by Egelv and engaged in conversation.

They must know a lot of other Egelv, he decided.

Arga caught his eye, and she grinned at him, deliberately looked at their two Egelv friends, then back at him. Confused, he looked at the two closer. Oh.

Scyles shook his head, frowning at her, but chuckling inside.

It was about time. He wondered if he'd hear Zard Win call her Shae in front of him. Probably not, he decided. They were a private kind of people, very reserved.

Scyles looked around and decided they needed to get into position. The stands were almost full, and he knew the Emperor was about to arrive. He would be riding a small floating raft to the stage, where he would speak to the crowd.

I hope he has a strong voice, Scyles thought. This is a big area, and it doesn't look like these packed temporary stands will provide the best sound conditions.

He called out to the warriors nearest him.

"Let's go. Everyone get lined up in the order we showed you. Move yourselves."

His father and King Orik appeared on either side of him, and Orik nodded to him approvingly.

"Good thinking, getting them started. Standing in a straight line isn't one of their better skills," he said, and Scyles' father laughed.

"Not one of ours, either."

Targitai's voice sounded in Scyles' ear.

"Scyles, I need you to come to the west entrance, now. The Emperor wishes you here."

"On my way," Scyles said, and wondered what the Emperor wanted. This show was about to begin, and he should be in position himself.

He set off at a trot and when he got there, the doors of the west entrance opened wide. He slowed to a walk as he entered, and saw Targitai and three other warriors, one of them a Warrior Woman, already on the raft, spread in a line across the back of the raft.

"What is it?" Scyles asked, and Targitai nodded towards the raft.

Emperor Balco Deh stepped forward, and it obediently lowered to the ground. He looked at Scyles with amusement.

"I can't very well go out in front of that big a crowd without my best warriors around me, now can I?"

"You honor me, Emperor," Scyles said, bowing his head, embarrassed. He'd thought he'd blend into the mass of the Scoloti warriors during the ceremony, and nothing would be required of him, other than not dozing off.

The Emperor stepped onto the raft, and Scyles dutifully followed him. One of his attendants followed, and whispered to him.

"You will stand to the right of the Emperor, one step back."

Scyles nodded, a little rankled at being told where to stand by some palace official.

"You needn't whisper, Tran Orb," the Emperor said cheerfully. "It's just us and the Scoloti here." He laughed. "Oh, that reminds me. Please set your new hand weapons on stun. I know you haven't had all that much time to train with them yet, and if we have an incident, I would much rather any bystanders only be stunned, not dead. If we have some sort of threat, please use your arrows to kill them instead."

"Yes, Emperor," Scyles said, and forced his lips to stay together as he heard Targitai begrudgingly say the same, almost in unison with him.

The raft raised, and they floated slowly down the walkway, between gorgeous blooming plants and trees, until they reached the stage. The raft came up flush to the back of the stage. Sycles saw there were already two pairs of Scoloti warriors in the front corners, facing the crowd, at attention, their eyes searching for anything that seemed out of place.

The Emperor walked forward, Tran Orb just behind him, to the left. He began to whisper instructions to Scyles, and the Emperor cleared his throat. "I think he has it."

Scyles dutifully followed, staying one step back, keeping the grin off his face. They reached the middle of the stage and the Emperor faced the crowd.

Scyles could feel more than hear, Targitai and the other warriors get into position in the back corners of the stage, watching off to the side and behind.

The Emperor raised his hands.

Somehow, none of the Scoloti jumped, and hardly any flinched, when his voice carried, strong and loud, across the open space, to everyone in the stands and beyond.

He has some sort of machine that makes his voice loud, Scyles realized, and wondered how it worked. Add that to the list of things he'd seen recently that he didn't understand, he thought ruefully.

"Citizens of Egelva, of the Empire, I greet you with news of change."

Scyles decided that Egelv audiences were no different than Scoloti audiences. Many of them clapped and cheered for a moment, then died down.

"As most of you know, we all were almost the victims of traitors," he said, and his voice showed both anger and sadness. "With a complete disregard for Egelv life, the Quo Family attempted a coup, and tried to assassinate me, and my family and court."

There were low rumblings of anger in the crowd, and Scyles decided they were genuine. Everything he'd seen so far, showed the Emperor to be very popular with his subjects.

"They very nearly succeeded. They would have succeeded, if not for the heroic efforts of a mere handful of these fine people, the Scoloti." He paused, and swept his hand around, pointing at the mass of warriors, lined up in neat rows, looking so impressive in their new armor.

"The plan of the traitors was to use these fine people as scapegoats for the rebellion. The Scoloti would be blamed for my death, as well as my family's, and so many loyal Guards and palace staff. Even though they had only just been introduced to the court, when the revolt broke out, they didn't hesitate. At great risk to themselves, they sprang into action, attacking the traitors, surrounding my person to protect me, and immediately rushed to the palace to rescue Empress Lasa Sheen, and our three children. The same brave acts also saved countless lives both here in the palace, as well as in the fleet. We were able to warn loyal forces, and all Quo Family members were either killed or captured."

The Emperor didn't speak for a moment, and his anger was easy for all to see. Scyles noticed there were many screens spread around the stands and the stage, like the ones on the ship, only much larger. These screens showed the Emperor up close, and everyone could see the pain and anger in his face. Scyles thought some of it might even be sincere.

"Anyone proven to have taken part in the plot to overthrow the throne was executed. All other family members have been exiled to a very distant planet on the outskirts of the Empire. The family name Quo has been stricken from the List, and will never be mentioned in court again. It is harsh, but a better fate than death. I wish them well, but will not risk more

Egelv lives hoping there will be no further attempts by this family to usurp the throne."

The crowd roared its approval, and Scyles was impressed. They seemed sincere as well.

"We have already honored and rewarded with promotion, the Egelv that fought in the defeat of the traitors, but I feel it important to acknowledge the actions of the Scoloti that came to my aid that day."

The Emperor smiled and pointed down at the front of the ranks of the People.

"King Gelon, of the Auchatae Tribe, and King Orik, of the Paralatae Tribe, led their meager forces and defeated a superior number of the Emperor's Guard that were from the family of traitors."

Loud applause broke out in the stands, and the two kings stepped forward, drew their long swords, and slapped them twice against their shield, then sheathed them again, stepping back into formation. That seemed to spark the crowd into cheering even louder.

The Emperor raised a hand and the cheering calmed.

"Their wifes, Queen Myrina, and Queen Opis, both also fought bravely, first here in the garden, and then to free my family within the palace."

Scyles watched them look at each other, uncertain what to do. He saw Arga's mother say something quickly, and they both stood, drawing their short swords, which they rapped together, then sheathed them, bowed their heads to the crowd, and sat back down.

He almost started laughing at the variety of responses that got. Most of the crowd was galvanized by their actions, and there was another surge in applause. But some of the Eglev sitting nearby were clearly startled to find their neighbors had weapons, and were comfortable drawing them.

Scyles brought his attention back to the stage and saw that the Emperor had been amused by the actions of the women.

"I learned a new word that day," Emperor Balco Deh said, smiling. "And I saw the true meaning of the word, when 'Swordmaster' Targitai personally decimated the ranks of some of the finest Egelv warriors we've ever known."

Scyles turned his head far enough to watch Targitai step forward and mimic the action of the kings with his sword and shield.

The Emperor smiled.

"Along with Queens Myrina and Opis, another woman rushed to help save my wife and children. And she helped calm the fears of my children, until I was able to join them. Daughter of King Orik and Queen Opis, I thank Princess Arga."

Scyles smiled, despite himself, as Arga put her hands over her mouth in embarrassment. She stood, looked up at the crowds in the stands, and finally pulled out her short swords, clapped them together several times. Her face was flushed with excitement, and it was very visible on the screens. Scyles was happy to see the crowd showing their appreciation. She put her swords away and quickly sat down, then popped up again and waved, and finally sat back down.

"Is she always like that?" the Emperor asked quietly, and Scyles noticed his voice didn't boom out over the crowd.

"Or worse," Scyles admitted, and saw the corners of the Emperor's mouth lift in smile.

When the applause slowed, Emperor Balco Deh, lowered his head for a moment, in silence. The crowd grew quiet and watched, curiously.

Finally, he raised his head.

"I was intended to die that day. And I would have died, if not for the swift action of a young man, barely a warrior, yet already one of their finest." The Emperor turned to Scyles and beckoned him forward. "I want you to meet Prince Scyles, son of King Gelon and Queen Myrina, husband of Princess Arga. He certainly saved my life, and, I suspect, the lives of at least some of my family, when he helped rescue them."

The screens suddenly changed to show that day in the gardens, as Scyles rose, blades in both hands. When he gutted the first Guard, there was a collected gasp, and then another when he stabbed him in the throat. But when he threw the knife, causing the weapon to miss the Emperor, the crowd went insane with excitement.

How do I match that? Scyles wondered. He glanced around the area and saw the gazebo they'd walked past, that first day, on their way to meet the Emperor, more than twenty horse lengths distant.

He didn't think about it. He turned slightly, drew his bow and an arrow, and shot, and quickly followed it with four more arrows.

There were shrieks of fear and surprise from the audience, but they quickly turned to roars as the first arrow hit in the white circle above the steps into the gazebo, and the following four bracketed it.

He put the bow back in his gorytos and stepped back into position. The Emperor stared at him, and finally grinned.

"You certainly know how to play the crowd," he said. "Well done."

Scyles nodded, and they waited for the applause to die down. It took longer than Scyles would have thought necessary.

The Emperor raised his hands and spoke to the crowd.

"Citizens of Egelva. Citizens of the Egelv Empire. The rebels decimated our Emperor's Guard, and only a few survived. The rest were murdered in their sleep, in their barracks. I am saddened by their loss. By the loss to their loved ones. But the Empire must carry on, and the Emperor must have a Guard. But," he said, and the crowd watched him intently.

"But, rather than continue a tradition that turned out to have a serious flaw, I have decided it is time to make a change. We have a unique opportunity, and a people in need of purpose and livelihood. And they are a people worthy of such a challenge."

Scyles marveled that as he paused, there wasn't a sound from the crowd.

"The Emperor's Guard are no more." He looked suitably sad. "The few that survived will serve as advisors to my new security force. They have done their duty, for countless years and more. I wish to introduce you to the men and women that will form the force that keeps your Emperor safe. That helps keep the Empire safe. I give you, the Scoloti!"

Scyles was pleased to see the entire mass of the warriors take a step forward, all moving as one, pull out their long sword, and slap it twice against their shields. Of course, having their kings standing right in front of them, leading them through the steps probably helped. He and the eight warriors on the stage did the same.

The Emperor watched and looked satisfied to Scyles. He waited until the thunderous clapping slowed, and stopped.

"If you look to the sky at night, you may be able to see the new home of the Scoloti. It is the generation ship they were forced onto when they were kidnapped from their home world. It belonged to the Hshtahni, but no more. It was called the Muschwain, but no more."

Emperor Balco Deh raised both hands and spread his fingers wide. His long, white braided hair slid off his shoulders and hung down his back.

"The name of my personal guard, and that of their new home, will be one and the same."

The crowd waited, and the view on most of the screens shifted to them. Their faces looked excited, a few looked bored and condescending. Those looks quickly changed as they realized they could be seen by all.

The Emperor smiled, and Scyles wondered if he would follow up on that. He hoped not. He rather liked the man, and wanted him to be a good leader, not a vain one. He concentrated on the Emperor's words.

"May I introduce you to the Hashir, whose home is now the Hashir."

The Emperor smiled with satisfaction.

"The Emperor's Blade."

Epilogue

Now, on a planet, far from everything, except the star it circles.

Lady Telepileya stood as the last student Speaker finished her accounting. She walked over to her, and gave the student a hug. The girl was barely ten, but her poise was already pronounced.

"Thank you, Opiya. Your voice was clear and strong, and your memory sound," she said, and turned to the audience.

The amphitheater was packed with other student Speakers, their families, students studying the history of the People, and more than a few older residents, preferring to spend a beautiful spring day surrounded by people. The acoustics were phenomenal, if the stone seating was a bit uncomfortable. Most listeners brought thick pads, pillows, even folded blankets to sit on.

Lady Telepileya smiled to the audience, and gestured at her protégé.

"I hope everyone has enjoyed our program this year. Young Opiya has come far in the few years since she became a probationary student Speaker. Please let her know you enjoyed her recital, and how much you appreciate her efforts." She kept her smile strong, although the idea of the end of yet another year of teaching the young how to become superior Speakers, and why there was such a need for it, saddened her.

"This concludes our annual program. And please remember, our program is greatly enhanced by the generosity of all of you. Feel free to donate or pledge, before you leave."

There was enthusiastic applause, and she hoped it translated to donations. Although there was public funding every year, it hardly covered minimal basics. She hugged Opiya once more, and watched her start to run, then remember where she was, and slow to a happy walk to her family, who waited politely at the edge of the stage.

Lady Telepileya turned away from the rapidly emptying theater, and began straightening the stage area, securing loose objects in the cabinets at the side of the stage area. Several of her students helped her, while several others walked each level, looking for any trash left by a careless or inconsiderate patron. She was happy to see they weren't finding anything.

"Lady Telepileya, may I ask you a question?" Second year Student Speaker Iphito asked.

"Of course, Child."

"I know that long ago, the People had no writtten language, and the Speakers were all that kept us from not knowing ourselves, where we came from, and by understanding our history, not repeating mistakes of the past." She hesitated, the shyness that made her struggle in her training as a Speaker showing clearly to Telepileya. "Why then, if we now have a written language, and we all learn to use it at a young age, why do we continue the tradition?"

Lady Telepileya smiled and took her hand, sitting them both down on the first row of stone benching. She immediately stood back up, pulling the girl with her, removed her long cloak, and spread it on the cold stone. They sat back down, and the girl smiled, showing her appreciation.

"How does your learning to read and write, progress?" she asked, and the girl made a face.

"It goes slowly, but I am learning," Iphito admitted. "I have trouble making my letters clear enough for others to read."

Telepileya laughed and put her arm around the girl.

"Many of us have that problem," she admitted. "I myself have writing skills so poor that my students insist they can't read anything I write."

"I am sure it is not that bad," the little girl protested, and she nodded.

"Probably not, but that is not my point." She looked at the little girl. "Everything we have recited this last year is in the House of Knowledge, more than a few copies. Other than for your school assignments, how often do you go to read them?"

"Sometimes," Iphito said slowly, hedging her words. "Not often," she finally admitted.

"How often do you go to Speaker programs we offer?

"Oh, I come with my mother almost every week," she blurted out, and paused to consider her words in surprise.

"And why do you come so often, so much more than to the House of Knowledge?" Telepileya asked pointedly.

"Because my mother and I do it together," the little girl admitted. "And there are always at least a few of my friends here. It's something we can do together, and when the Speakers tell the accounting, it is so much more interesting than page after page of just words."

"Oh!" she exclaimed, looking at Telepileya in wonder.

"Exactly, dear girl," she said, and looked up as Iphito's mother hesitantly approached. "Please, join us. I was just telling your daughter why we have Speakers, in addition to books."

"I would always find a reason to not make a trip to the House of Knowledge to read," the woman admitted. "But coming here, and listening to the stories and accounting, and sometimes when there is discussion about the events spoken that evening, is so enjoyable. With my husband a member of the Border Warriors, this is our only outlet for recreation together."

"How did the great storm come just in time to give us a chance to meet the Egelv and fight the Hshtahni?" little Iphito asked. "Does it just appear? Does someone make it go where they want?"

"No one knows, Iphito," Lady Telepileya told her, and instinctively looked upwards. Rarely, in fact, only four times in her own long life, the giant mouth of the storm opened over their world. They knew not why, or if anyone passed through the mouth, either coming to Glas, or leaving their world. "If someone was able to control the storm, they would have to be very powerful."

"Not as powerful as our warriors, though, right, Lady Telepileya?" the little girl asked, and she looked at her mother. "Not as wise and skilled as Great King Scyles, surely."

"It would be hard to imagine such a person," said Lady Telepileya. "But I truly do not know."

"Will it ever return, and sweep us away, back to our own world? Back to the steppes of the stories of our earliest people?"

"It has been over two thousand years since we left our tribal homelands," Iphito's mother said, and gave the sky a worried look. "I am sure it is very different now. Who knows, there might not be Speakers there. Perhaps no one would even remember us."

"Who could forget us?" Iphito said, and the two women exchanged glances.

"Who indeed?" Lady Telepileya said, and the girl's mother told her it was time to let the Lady Speaker finish her work, so she could go home and have a warm dinner.

After a few pleasantries, the mother and daughter were gone, and she put her cloak back on, pulling the hood up over her head. Once darkness fell, there was still quite a chill in the air.

She looked at the black sky, full of gods, both known and unknown, too many to count and recognize, and hoped Ares, and his right arm, Scyles, would prevent them from ever meeting whoever controlled the storms.

Lady Telepileya gathered her things and hurried home, to a warm hearth and bowl of dinner.

Made in the USA
Columbia, SC
21 October 2022